Dear Readers,

Welcome to our annual Historical Christmas Collection. This year, we bring you *Christmas Rogues,* a collection of stories by three favorites of historical romance— Anita Mills, Patricia Potter and Miranda Jarrett.

All three stories take place in America, and although they are set in states as different as Kansas, Georgia and Rhode Island, they all share the common themes of hope and a belief in the power of love. We hope you enjoy them.

The editors at Harlequin Historicals would like to take this time to thank all of you who contribute to the ongoing success of the line: our talented authors; our art and marketing departments, who have worked so hard to get the books the covers and the attention that they deserve; the supportive reviewers and, most important, our very loyal readers. We wish you all a wonderful holiday season and a prosperous and happy New Year.

Sincerely,

*Tracy Farrell*  *Margaret O'Neill Marbury*
*Deborah L. Beaudry*  *[signature]*

The Editors
Harlequin Historicals

Don't miss this
delightful collection
from three
award-winning
historical authors!

# CHRISTMAS ROGUES

## Anita Mills
## Patricia Potter
## Miranda Jarrett

# *Harlequin Books*

TORONTO • NEW YORK • LONDON
AMSTERDAM • PARIS • SYDNEY • HAMBURG
STOCKHOLM • ATHENS • TOKYO • MILAN
MADRID • WARSAW • BUDAPEST • AUCKLAND

CHRISTMAS ROGUES
Copyright © 1995 by Harlequin Books S.A.

ISBN 0-373-83297-4

The publisher acknowledges the copyright holders of the individual works as follows:

THE CHRISTMAS STRANGER
Copyright © 1995 by Anita Mills
THE HOMECOMING
Copyright © 1995 by Patricia Potter
BAYBERRY AND MISTLETOE
Copyright © 1995 by Susan Holloway Scott

**Printed in U.S.A.**

# CONTENTS

*Western Kansas*
*December 20, 1871*

Above them, the wind howled, pounding the round chimney as though it were a tin pan. Inside the close confines of the sod house, Beth Linderman rocked her feverish daughter and prayed. Never in all of her nearly thirty years had she felt so completely helpless, so desperately alone.

*Dear God in Heaven, please don't take my baby. Please don't take my baby.*

The child lying against her was so hot that her red, mottled skin nearly burned Beth's arm. The small amount of willow bark Beth possessed had already been steeped and dribbled into Emily's mouth, and still the fever raged. Beth squeezed her tired eyes shut, wetting them with tears, then looked again to the black iron stove. Steam rose from the kettle, moistening the air, but it wasn't helping.

Before long, they were going to be out of wood, and Beth wasn't even sure she could find the woodpile anymore. Two hours ago the snow had come to her hips. By now the drifts would be deeper. She glanced at the door, seeing where melted snow had turned to ice at the bottom of it, sealing out the cold draft that usually blew across the puncheon floor. Then she looked up at the bowed cottonwood poles, wondering if they would hold, or if the roof would cave in, burying the two of them alive.

Dear God, how she hated Kansas. It was the only place she'd ever heard of where you could stand ankle-deep in mud and have dirt blow in your face. The only place where the wind howled three hundred days a year, carrying thick, choking dust in summer, and drifting snow six feet deep in winter.

When she first came out here, as a mail-order bride eager to escape the dull life of a twenty-five-year-old spinster seamstress, she'd been so stunned by the utter isolation of the place that she wanted to turn around and go back. But she'd made her bed, and she'd lain in it. Besides which, John Linderman hadn't possessed the money to pay her return passage to Missouri.

The letters he'd written her had been a mixture of omissions, distortions, and outright lies. His large farm had turned out to be one hundred and sixty acres of desolate prairie, the rich pastures nothing more than dry grass, the herd of cattle only three rangy cows, and the commodious home this one-room sod house situated in the middle of nowhere. And, of course, he'd never mentioned rattlesnakes, wolves, coyotes or Indians. Or the wind. Before she left St. Joseph, an old bullwhacker had warned her, saying, "I seen womenfolk go crazy from hearin' that wind out there." Now she believed it.

# THE CHRISTMAS STRANGER

## Anita Mills

No, John had written of his dreams, and what he'd provided had shattered hers. Yet it was John himself who'd been her greatest disappointment. Unlike his letters, he'd turned out to be a distant, taciturn, emotionless husband, a man incapable of giving comfort when she lost not one, but two, stillborn sons. But it was the culmination of her third pregnancy that had hurt the worst. After a long, lonely, hard labor, she'd brought forth this baby on Christmas last. And when it was over, John had just stood there staring at his daughter, saying nothing. Beth could remember whispering, "She's beautiful, isn't she? Look—she's got your nose and my hair." When he didn't answer, she'd persisted, asking, "What do you want to name her?" His cold reply still echoed in her mind.

*I've got no use for a girl, Elizabeth. A farmer needs sons to work his land with him. Call her what you want—I don't guess it matters.*

At first, Beth had toyed with Angel and Mary, in deference to the holiday; but in the end, she'd chosen Emily Anne, her own mother's name. And thus Emily had come to be the most important being in her isolated world. Beth looked down at the small body she cradled in her arms and felt a rush of tenderness. Emily was so perfect, so beautiful. God's gift on a Christmas Day.

She could almost feel sorry for John now. The freak wagon accident that took his life had robbed him of seeing his daughter's two-toothed smile and her first tottering steps, of feeling those soft, chubby little arms hugging his neck. Death had cheated him of all those things. And it was such a pity, for she was certain that if he'd lived, he'd have come to love Emmy.

As Beth's hand smoothed the fine, dark ringlets against the small head, her daughter's body suddenly went rigid, her eyes opened vacantly, and then she began jerking violently. Frantic, Beth pulled the shawl from around her shoulders, rolled up a corner of it and pushed it between the little girl's teeth. Dragging the shawl with them across the floor, she found the bucket of melting snow and began scooping handfuls to press against Emily's neck and face.

*Dear God, don't let her die . . . don't let her die . . .* she pleaded silently. *She's all I've got— Dear God, she deserves more than one year of life.*

Carrying her daughter and the bucket, she managed to get the convulsing child onto the table, where she quickly undressed her, then continued smearing the cold, wet snow over the small body. Gradually the awful jerking stopped, and Emily whimpered. Beth sank into a chair and leaned against the table, resting her head as she wept. Small fingers caught in her hair, pulling it.

"Mama," the baby croaked.

Beth sat up and wiped her eyes with the back of her hand. "It's all right, Emmy—it's all right," she whispered, her throat aching. "It's all right—Mama's not going to let anything happen to you." Drawing her daughter close, she held her, feeling the wet, baby-soft skin. "You're going to get well," she promised.

But it wasn't all right, and Beth knew it. Before long she would feel the fever rising again through Emily's skin. No, it wasn't over, and she was powerless to stop it. She bundled the dry part of the shawl around Emily and carried her back to the rocking chair. As she sank down, she folded her arms protectively over her child.

She resumed rocking as Emily's head turned against her breast. "Hush, little baby, don't you cry," she crooned softly. "Mama's going to sing you a lullaby."

The sickness had struck so suddenly, stealing into the sod house in the dead of night, waking Beth to Emily's cries. At first she'd thought it nothing more than a winter cold, but by morning she'd realized the worst, when she saw the telltale gray patches in Emily's raw throat and felt the swollen glands in the baby's neck. *Diphtheria.* She'd seen it once before, when it took her landlady's little grandson in St. Joseph, so she knew what to expect. Convulsions. A choking death.

A family named Cox had stopped by about ten days ago. Because of his father's unexpected death, Mr. Cox was hurrying back to St. Louis to take over his business. Fool that she was, Beth had been so glad to see company that she begged them to stay the night, then stood watching wistfully as they left the next morning. But their little son had been fretful and feverish, complaining that it hurt to swallow. He wouldn't keep his shoes on, his mother had said, blaming that for his cold. Now Beth knew Rebecca Cox had been mistaken, and she wondered if they'd had to dig little Billy's grave before they reached Kansas City. She could still see the frail woman, her arms wrapped protectively around her small son as they'd driven off. Poor Becky. She'd been so happy at the notion of leaving Kansas, of being in St. Louis by Christmas.

Forcing that painful memory from her thoughts, Beth rocked steadily, keeping time with the clock that ticked away time from its place on the little round table she'd brought all the way from St. Joseph. Her eyes strayed to the clock, then to the covered knitting basket, and the lump formed anew in her throat as she thought of the unfinished rag doll it contained. The doll was to have been Emily's birthday present. Now it was unlikely the chubby-cheeked baby would see that first Christmas. Beth closed her eyes and swallowed.

*She couldn't face this alone. God couldn't ask that much of her. He just had to help her.*

There was no sky, no sun, no visible landmark, only snow so thick Matt Wiley could barely see his horse's head as the animal plodded through the chest-high drifts. The biting wind gnawed at the buffalo-hide coat and tore through the woolen muffler that covered his face. His fingers tingled within his heavy hide mitts, while his toes had passed the point of pain. If he didn't stumble onto some sort of shelter, he was going to freeze to death.

No, he couldn't die. He still had to settle the score with Haynes and Cogburn. As long as they lived, as long as they were out there somewhere, he couldn't die. They were the last ones, and once they were dead, the vendetta that had driven and consumed him for more than six years would be over. Then God or the law, whichever struck first, could have him. But not quite yet.

The norther had come up suddenly, catching him out on the open plains alone. A sensible man would have turned around and tried to make it back to Ellis, but he hadn't wanted to do that. Not when he'd seen the poster with his name on it plastered on a wall. He'd even tossed down a drink standing next to the town marshal, who'd failed to recognize him from the artist's picture. Maybe next time he wouldn't be so lucky. Maybe next time he'd encounter someone who knew him. No, he had to keep going.

He'd tracked these men from Missouri to Texas, through New Mexico and Arizona, across the border into old Mexico, then back up into Texas and Oklahoma, and finally halfway across Kansas. Now, according to what they'd told a barkeep in Dodge City, they were headed for the gold mines of Colorado, hoping to lose themselves in the rough mining camps. But if Matt had any say in the matter, they weren't going to get that far. He was just too close to ending it now. Sometime within the next day, he was going to look Elihu Haynes and Tom Cogburn in the face, and then he was going to kill them.

He'd been on his way back from the Confederate loss at Franklin, Tennessee, when his sister Maggie's letter telling of his father's death reached him. The details of the murder were still as clear in his mind as the day he'd learned them. When William Wiley tried to protect his stock, Union soldiers had hanged him in his own front yard, ignoring the frantic pleas of his wife and daughter. Then, while the old man still swung from the big walnut tree, they'd forced the women to prepare a meal. Afraid of being raped, Maggie had fled the house while the men dunked corn bread into beans her mother had liberally dosed with castor oil.

An unfortunate incident, the army had called it, denying Matt's mother compensation or justice. Lieutenant Crawford, who'd led the group of soldiers, had testified that Wiley was a spy, and that he'd died during interrogation, but not before he admitted his guilt. It was an almost laughable lie—the apolitical old man hadn't even wanted his last surviving son to go to war. Yet when the trial was over, despite the testimony of witnesses, all seven men had been acquitted by the carpetbag jury.

The verdict had broken Sarah Wiley's heart and health. Within a year of it, she'd died, leaving Matt to mete out his own brand of justice. By then, the war was over, and Crawford and the others had scattered, making the task difficult, but not impossible, as long as he was willing to sacrifice everything in the cause.

He'd spent years carrying out his vendetta, beginning with the lieutenant. Crawford had died a coward's death on his doorstep in Lima, Ohio. Then there'd been Jack Burton, who'd fled all the way to California, only to discover there was no hiding from a driven man. And after that, Iowan Ben Cashman, who'd thrown up his hands, confident Matt wouldn't shoot an unarmed man. He'd died with a look of surprise frozen on his face. In the Arizona Territory, Big Bill Hixon had been a second late on the draw. Then there was Jacob Hanks, who'd tried to hide behind his Bible, claiming he'd gotten religion after the war. Maybe the Almighty had forgiven him, but Matt hadn't. Ironically, Hanks's last words had been blasphemies.

Now there were only Cogburn and Haynes left, and it would be over. Then Matt would go back to Missouri, probably to hang. The way he looked at it, it really didn't matter a whole lot. In thirty-one years of life, he'd managed to accumulate precious little—no wife, no children, no real ties to much of anything. Only Maggie, married now, with her own life to live, and Rambler, the horse laboring beneath him.

Time was running out now, probably in more ways than one, giving an urgency to his mission. Afraid for their lives, Cogburn and Haynes had gone to the U.S. marshal in the Arizona Territory, and now there were at least three warrants out for Matt Wiley's arrest, including the one he'd seen in Ellis. Five hundred dollars, dead or alive. Enough to make most thirty-dollar-a-month lawmen sit up and take notice.

He had to live at least long enough to finish the business. Hunching lower over his saddle, Matt ducked his head into the bitter wind. The deep snow had slowed the horse to a walk, but stopping now would mean certain death. "Come on, Rambler," he urged, nudging the animal with numb knees. "A few more miles, and we're bound to find something. There's got to be somebody's farm out here somewhere."

His words rang hollow in his own ears, and he'd scarce spoken them when Rambler went down. The horse sank to his knees, done for. Cursing under his breath, Matt managed to get out of his saddle, but when he tried to raise the big bay gelding, he couldn't make the animal budge. Rambler just lay there, legs tucked under him, watching Matt with widened eyes.

"Come on, big boy," Matt coaxed. "If you don't get up, we're both going to die." He tugged on the reins, trying to lead the animal, and for a moment, hope rose as Rambler lunged, attempting a footing in the heavy snow. "Attaboy—that's the way! Come on... you can make it... just a little further..." The exhausted horse stumbled, then collapsed again.

It was no use. If he was to have any chance of surviving, Matt was going to have to walk on alone. He regarded the animal soberly, knowing he ought to go ahead and put a bullet between those eyes. He hesitated, thinking it was a whole lot easier killing a man than putting his horse down. No, he couldn't do it, he decided.

He'd always heard freezing to death was pretty much painless. He hoped so, anyway, because it looked like it was going to end that way for both of them. The irony of it wasn't lost on him—he'd always figured he'd either go out at the end of a rope or die in a hail of gunfire. Now God was stepping in, stopping him before he was done. And for that, he felt an impotent rage—he'd come too far, he was too close to Cogburn and Haynes now. He picked up his Spencer rifle and started walking. No, by God, he wasn't ready to go yet. He was going to beat the odds and survive. The snow was so thick he couldn't see more than five or six feet ahead of him. Hell, he didn't even know what direction he was going. Within a hundred yards, he plunged into a drift and sank all the way to his chest. Digging his way out, he turned back for one last look at his exhausted horse. Already there was a blanket of white over him.

It was then that he smelled smoke. No, he was so far gone, he was hallucinating now. Loosening the muffler with numb fingers, Matt sniffed, taking care not to get too much of the cold air into his lungs. It was smoke, all right. Wood smoke. Somebody had a fire going. And anyone living out here had to have a horse. There was still a chance he could save Rambler.

His hope renewed, Matt struck out again, using the rifle to probe the depth of the snow. His mind worked feverishly, urging his body on. The howling, squalling wind was now heavy with the smell, as he climbed and sank, climbed and sank, pressing on blindly. He had to be getting close to that fire.

Then he saw it. Rising out of a drift within a hand's reach, a soot-blackened chimney pipe puffed out a dark, acrid curl that disappeared into swirling white clouds. He was on the roof of a sod house. He moved cautiously, trying to find the edge, then plunged over it. He began shouting.

"Open up! Open up! For God's sake, will somebody let me in? Open up!" It was as though the wind caught his words, carrying them the other way.

Inside, Beth rocked, telling herself she had to conquer her fear before Emily felt it. She'd been afraid before, but never like this. Not even when two Cheyenne Indians had come, demanding food, then camped overnight outside her door after she fed them. She'd stayed up all night, holding John's double-barreled shotgun, waiting for an attack, only to discover that they'd left sometime before dawn. For more than a week afterward, she'd slept with the gun beside her, lest they come back, but they never had. She'd been so sure that God had watched over her and Emily then. Surely, if she prayed enough, he would again.

Expect the best, and you'll get it, her mother always used to say. But that was before John Linderman. That was before she'd come to Kansas. That was before the Coxes stopped by. *And if you think the worst, it's bound to happen.* That was the other side of her mother's saw. No, she had to think the best. She couldn't panic. She took a deep breath, clearing her mind of the fear. Emily needed her too much. Unless it became truly hopeless, Beth was determined to think the best. It was all she had to cling to.

She looked down, seeing that Emmy now slept. Brushing her fingertips lightly over the soft cupid curve of her daughter's cheek, she felt an aching tenderness. If it hadn't been for the rattle of the membrane growing in the baby's throat, and the hot, rosy skin, Beth could almost have believed she was better. At least for now. But there was still that corner of her mind that refused to be deluded, that told her this was but a brief respite.

And now the wind was playing tricks. She stopped rocking in midsqueak and strained to listen. There it was, this time louder. As impossible as it seemed, a man's shouts broke through the door, rising above the howling storm.

"For God's sake, you've got to hear me! Open up, or I'm going to freeze!"

His words were punctuated by a desperate pounding that shook the lock bar, rattling its iron supports. Beth didn't know whether to laugh or cry as relief washed over her. Someone had found her, and she wasn't alone. It was as though God had answered at least one of her prayers.

Hastily placing Emily on her pallet by the stove, Beth ran to help him. As she lifted the bar and struggled to pull the door open, the man threw his weight against it, breaking the threshold of ice. It gave way, and a wall of snow caved in, sending him reeling past her. He stumbled as his boot caught on the uneven puncheons, and then he fell heavily, striking his head against a table leg. His battered, snow-laden leather hat skidded across the floor. For a moment, he just sat there, trying to catch his breath.

Using her foot, Beth cleared enough snow away to close the door. As she turned back to the man, she had to admit he didn't look much like a savior. The heavy hide coat he wore was crusted with snow, and ice clung to his eyebrows, mustache and beard, making him look more like a grizzly caught out in winter than a man.

Overwhelmed by emotion, she felt her eyes fill with tears. "You don't know how glad I am to see you, mister," she managed. "My baby's awful sick, and I—" She averted her face and wiped her wet eyes. When she turned back to him, she'd composed herself. "I'm sorry," she said huskily. "I don't usually cry in front of strangers. It's just that I've tried nearly everything, and she keeps getting worse." Her mouth twisted. "I can't think of anything else to do for her."

Too numb to think clearly, Matt tried to collect his wits. He'd done the impossible—he'd made it to safety. Snow-blind, he stared blankly at the woman. Gradually she took shape, standing out from the white spots floating before his eyes. Right then, she looked like an angel of mercy. But she was crying, telling him she had a sick baby, and all he could think of was that he was going to live.

"My horse went down...couldn't go any farther..." Squeezing his eyes shut for a moment, he tried to adjust them to the sod house's dim interior. He took a long, deep breath, savoring the warm air, before letting it out slowly. He felt better already. "Whoo-ee— I was beginning to think I was a goner. Damned lucky to stumble onto your house—snow must be six feet deep in places."

Realizing she had to back off long enough for him to get his bearings, Beth tried to sound more rational. "Yes—yes, I expect it is. When I went out at noon, there were drifts almost to my waist. I'd hoped to milk the cow and feed the animals, but I couldn't get there.'' Her resolve weakened, and she couldn't help blurting out, ''I've been so frightened, mister! I'm afraid Emmy's dying!''

''Whoa, now—'' He rolled to his knees, then struggled to stand. ''I don't know much about young'ns—I never had any, leastwise none that I've heard of, anyway.'' Knowing how that must sound to a woman, he added apologetically, ''I'm real sorry.'' He pulled one hide mitten off with his teeth and held out his hand. ''Name's Wiley, ma'am—Matt Wiley.'' Even as he said it, he could have cursed himself for using his own name.

''Beth Linderman,'' she managed, gulping back tears. His grip was like ice, but the firmness reassured her. ''You don't know how I've prayed for someone to come, Mr. Wiley.''

''Yeah, but I had to leave my horse out there. If I don't try getting him in, I'm on foot when the snow's over.''

Scarce hearing what he'd said, Beth took a gulp of air, then forced herself to speak in even, measured tones. ''It's got to be divine Providence that you stumbled onto the only house in twenty miles.'' Her dark eyes sought his, hoping for affirmation. ''If God hadn't sent you, mister, you'd have never found us.''

''Oh, I don't know as the Almighty cares much about what we do until it's all over,'' Matt said uncomfortably. ''Then I expect He gets even.'' He stomped a foot, dislodging the snow, and winced. ''Damn,'' he muttered. ''There's just enough feeling left to hurt.'' He looked up, meeting her gaze. ''When I smelled your smoke, I was kind of hoping you had a man here to help me out.''

"My husband died last July."

"I'm sorry—real sorry. I guess it's pretty hard on a woman, trying to make it alone." Matt felt awkward, not having any real words of comfort to give her. "No kinfolk around here?"

"No." Beth pushed an errant strand of hair back from her face. "Believe me, if I'd had anywhere to go, we'd be gone," she said bitterly. "As it is, if Emmy survives, I'm going back to St. Joseph and start over. If not..." Her voice trailed off, and then she looked away. "Then I guess I'll just go mad."

Matt's gaze swept the single room, taking in the stove, the homemade table and benches, the bedstead, and a scarred chesser she must have hauled out here from back east. If she held a sale, she couldn't get fifty dollars for the lot. His eyes strayed to the lace curtains hanging over two small windows, then to the rag rug covering much of the floor. "I'd say you've made it real homey here."

"Yes, well, I didn't have much choice. I wanted it to be as decent as possible for Emmy." Beth looked toward the pallet. "She's all I have, mister," she said simply. "She's everything in this world to me."

As pressed for time as he was, Matt was loath to leave the warmth of the sod house. He guessed he could spare his tired body a few minutes before he went back out. Pulling off the other mitten, he reached for the woolen muffler. It was frozen to his beard in places, forcing him to jerk it loose. His wind-chapped face burned as the warm air hit it.

Now that his eyes were better adjusted to the dingy coal-oil light, he turned his attention to the woman before him, thinking she seemed about as out of place as those lace curtains. The West was hard on females, wearing them down, making them old before their times. He'd seen a lot of them—stooped, toothless, and shapeless in mended flour-sack smocks, exhausted by too much work and too many babies. Most who survived looked sixty at forty.

Yet, despite the anxiety in this one's dark eyes and the tired set of her shoulders, she looked as if she could still be in her twenties, and her figure was slender rather than thin beneath the neat, well-made cotton dress. And with that knot of chestnut hair atop her head, she looked almost pretty. Given the shortage of decent women, and the practical nature of folks on the frontier, it was hard to imagine she was still a widow. If she'd gotten herself into Hays, or even Ellis, she'd have had herself a respectable offer by sundown. Instead, here she was alone, mourning a dead husband and tending a sick child.

Beth returned his gaze, thinking he looked miserably cold and exhausted. She realized guiltily that she'd been so glad to see him, so occupied with her own needs, that she hadn't even invited him to warm himself at the fire. No wonder he was staring at her. She'd completely forgotten her manners.

"Here...let me take that," she said quickly, reaching for his muffler. "While I've been screaming and squalling, you could have been over there by the stove. Go on—sit down, and take off those boots, Mr. Wiley, and I'll get some cold water for your feet. I'd warm it up, but if you don't thaw them out slowly, you'll lose your toes."

"I'll be all right. I just wanted to catch my breath, then I've got to—" Realizing she was already halfway across the room, and he was facing her back, he stopped. She was too absorbed in getting the water to hear him.

"Once you get to soaking your feet, I'll try to find you some dry clothes. John was about your size, so they ought to fit," she said over her shoulder. Leaning over a bucket, she began ladling out melting snow into a pan. "The kettle's hot, and I think there's some whiskey and enough honey to make a toddy—John always believed his toddies warded off pneumonia. I don't know about that, but I expect the hot water at least warmed him up from the inside out." She straightened, lifting the washpan, then saw he hadn't followed her. "You'd better get to thawing out your toes before you lose them, Mr. Wiley. Last winter Mr. Hansen lost his foot, and even then it wasn't enough."

"I thought you said there wasn't anybody else out here."

"There isn't. Once the gangrene went up his leg, he died."

"Oh."

"His wife passed on from a fever the year before, and he sent his kids back to Illinois. So the Hansen soddie's empty, and so far nobody's wanted to move into it—at least none that I know of. Even when they were alive, they were more than ten miles from here, and we almost never saw them. I don't suppose we'd have known anything about what happened, but John went over there to see about asking for help with spring planting, and found the poor man half out of his mind from the fever."

"A bad way to go," Matt murmured.

"Very." Beth set the pan down in front of the stove, then pulled the rocking chair over by it. This time, when she straightened up, she turned to face him. "So you'd better get started soaking, because if Emmy wakes up, I'm going to have my hands full. When I laid her down, her fever was coming back up, and I'm just praying she doesn't have convulsions again.''

Matt was so tired he could scarce stand, and as he looked over her shoulder, the warmth from the stove beckoned him. But no matter how bad his hands and feet hurt, no matter how much his body ached, he knew he couldn't wait any longer. He might not have much chance of saving Rambler, but without the horse, he'd be in one hell of a fix. As jittery as Haynes and Cogburn were, they might not stop in Colorado. They might change their minds and run for Wyoming. Or worse yet, Montana. And with a price on his own head, if Matt made one mistake, he'd be swinging at the end of the hangman's noose before he found them.

"Would you rather have the toddy now, or after you get into dry clothes?" Beth asked, betraying her impatience.

"Much obliged to you, ma'am, but if you've got a horse I can ride, I'd better get back to Rambler." As her eyes widened in disbelief, Matt murmured apologetically, "I've raised him from a colt, and we've been together for eight years now. Maybe if I had a rope, and your horse to pull the load, I could get him up before he freezes."

"You're going out again?" Beth asked, her voice rising incredulously. "Have you lost your mind, mister? You're more than half-frozen yourself!"

"Yeah, I know, but if there's a chance, I've got to take it. If it doesn't work, then I guess I'll have to shoot him. Maybe I should have done that when he went down, but I didn't. Either way, I'll be back," he promised.

"But what if you can't find your way back? Then where will you be?" Beth demanded.

"Probably hell." He shifted his weight uncomfortably. "Look, I can't just leave him out there."

"But you already have! And I don't want to be alone—no, I *can't* be alone," Beth pleaded. Her lower lip trembled until she bit it. "Please..." she whispered. "I think my baby's got diphtheria." Her chin came up. "No, that's not true—I *know* that's what it is."

*Diphtheria.* The word just hung there before it really sank in. If she knew what she was talking about, he'd be scraping off three or four feet of snow, then digging a grave in frozen ground. Not to mention that diphtheria was as contagious as it was deadly.

"You might be wrong, you know," he said when he found his voice. "My ma used to say babies run high fevers no matter what ails them. When I was growing up, my sister got real sick every winter. But she made it—she just turned twenty-seven last month.

"Mister, I once watched a two-year-old boy die of diphtheria. It was a long time ago, but you don't ever forget something like that. I still remember that gray membrane choking the life from him. That, and the awful convulsions."

"My God." Matt ran his fingers through his hair, combing the melting snow from it. "Yeah, I guess that'd stay with you, all right...." was all he could think to say.

"Forever." Beth took a quick gulp of air to fortify herself, then went on, "There were some folks that came through, and their little boy was coming down

with something while they were here. He was about
two or three, and he said his throat was sore. They had
to leave before we knew what was wrong with him.
Now I know it was diphtheria, because there's been no
one else stopping by, no other way Emmy could have
caught it.''

Beth's mouth twisted, but she didn't cry. ''The last
company I had before them was way back in September, when a circuit rider lost his direction, and I never
let him in the house. All I did was point him toward
the South Solomon so he could follow the river. He
might have been a man of the cloth, but I didn't like
his looks, and Emmy and I were alone by then.''

The irony wasn't lost on Matt—she'd turned away
a preacher, but she was welcoming a wanted man.
''You never know what you'll meet out here—I expect a lot of desperadoes pass through Kansas,'' he
murmured wryly.

''I could count on my fingers everyone who's
stopped here, Mr. Wiley, and most of them didn't bear
knowing. But with the Coxes, it was different. They
were a family, the sort of people I knew in Missouri.
And it's my fault,'' she said, her voice dropping
huskily. ''All they wanted was fresh water, but nobody else had stopped in months, and I was so glad to
see them. I begged them to stay overnight—that was
when the little one took sick. I even asked them to wait
until he was well, but Mr. Cox wanted to go on—he
said they had to get out of Kansas before the weather
worsened.''

''He was probably right about that.''

''Now Emmy's got it bad—her throat's gray, and
she's already convulsed from the fever. But I've got to

hope, mister—as long as she's got breath in her body,
I can't give up.''

"Yeah.'' Matt's gaze returned to her troubled face.
''I'm not much of a hand around sickness, but once
I've taken care of Rambler, I'll do what I can to help
out. I guess I can pitch hay to your animals. Maybe
that'd make things a little easier for you.''

He'd said he was coming back, but Beth still felt
uneasy. ''How long will it take?'' she wanted to know.
''If I let you take Old Peter, how long will it take?''

''Not long, I hope. If it wasn't for the storm, I'd
have seen your house when he went down. And if I
can't get him right up, believe me, I'm not going to
linger out there. Either way, I expect I'll be needing
that toddy.''

There was nothing for Beth to do but let him go.
''All right. I guess that's fair enough.''

''Where do you keep your horses?''

''Horse—there's just one. You'll find Old Peter in
with the cows and chickens. Just follow the rope I tied
over the door. It's the one that goes to the right.''

''To the barn?''

''There's not enough wood out here to make much
of a barn, so we called it a cow shed, and even that
flatters it,'' she responded dryly. ''It's more or less just
two hay mounds, with a roof piled on a cottonwood
frame. The side of the house is the back of it, and
John built another sod wall in front. You have to
watch the door—it's just some boards nailed together, and it doesn't hang very straight. Even in good
weather, it scrapes the ground, so you'll have to work
to get it open.''

''Is there a saddle and bridle?''

''On the other side of the feed trough.''

"Thanks."

"You may not thank me when you see Old Peter. He's a plow horse, and he doesn't much like being ridden." Moving between Matt and the door, Beth picked up another water bucket. "If it's not too much trouble, could you water the animals while you're out there? There's just two heifers, besides the cow, the horse and the chickens. I fed the chickens this morning."

"Sure." He rewound the damp wool scarf around his neck, then pulled it up to make a mask to his eyes. Thrusting his hands into the mittens, he awkwardly took the bucket. "I'll be back," he promised again.

Beth waited until he lifted the bar before cautioning him, "Be careful. He'll try throwing you if he can, then he'll run back to the shed before you can say, 'Johnny Jack.'"

Matt turned back briefly, his smile grim. "I've ridden some mean cayuses in my time, ma'am."

With that, he dragged the door across the shards of broken ice. A blast of cold air hit Beth's face as she caught the door and pushed it closed after him. For a moment, she leaned against it, and then she dropped the bar, shutting out the snow. Later, she was going to have to mop the floor, but not now, she decided wearily.

As she returned to warm her hands at the stove, an almost eerie emptiness descended over the room. The only sounds came from sap popping in the fire, the ticking clock, and the throaty rattle of Emily's breathing. The baby was on her stomach, her face turned against the shawl. Beth leaned over, lifting her limp, unresponsive body. Sitting in the chair and leaning back, she held her daughter close and began to rock.

The rungs of the rocker squeaked rhythmically, keeping time with the clock, while her fingers stroked Emily's hair. "Please, dear God," she prayed, "don't let him get lost. Now that he's found us, please don't let him lose his way back."

Matt couldn't see much of anything in the swirling snow, and he stumbled blindly, guided only by the rope, until he collided with the bank of hay. Scraping the drifts away with his hands, he managed to find the front wall, then the makeshift door. Beth had been right—it didn't want to open. But at least the wind had swept a hollow in front of it, giving him room to maneuver between drifts. He threw his shoulder against the door, pushing it inward. The smells of animals, musty hay, damp sod, cow chips and wet chicken feathers enveloped him.

He pulled the scarf down and peered into the dimness, trying to make out the horse. Even inside, out of the wind, it was so cold that his breath clouded in front of him. The new ice in his mustache cracked as he pursed his lips and whistled softly. At the sound, a cow sidestepped, slapping him with its tail, while a squawking hen flew up in his face.

Wishing he'd asked for a lantern, he sloshed most of the water into the trough. If the animals didn't drink it up quickly, it was just going to add another layer of ice. As he set the bucket down, he whistled again, this time loudly. The horse snorted, drawing him to the other side of the cows.

"Easy, boy...easy, boy..." he murmured soothingly as his hand caught his muzzle. The animal's head
jerked back, teeth bared.

He was a plow horse all right, heavy-boned and tall.
If he'd had to guess, he'd have said he was more than
eighteen hands at the shoulder, with a back broad
enough to flatten a saddle. He ran a mitten down the
well-padded ribs. It wasn't hard to tell that it had been
a while since anybody'd worked Old Peter.

The horse moved sideways as he tried to take a bite
out of Matt's shoulder. As he backed away, Matt got
a good look at his eyes. Yeah, he had a mean streak a
mile wide. Matt grasped his mane and forced his head
almost to the ground.

"Next time you try that, I'll punch you right between those eyes—you hear?" he growled. "Now, if
you've got that straight, we'll get along," he added,
releasing the mane. The animal answered him by
moving away.

Pulling off the mittens, Matt groped behind the
trough, finding the bridle and a coiled rope looped
over the horn of the saddle. Not taking any chances,
he made a noose, then slipped the rope around Old
Peter's neck, jerking out the slack before he tried the
bridle. The big animal planted his feet and flared his
nostrils. Matt gave another jerk, bringing his head
down again.

"They ought to have called you Old Nick, after the
devil," he muttered under his breath. This time, when
he eased the rope, the big horse just stood there, regarding him warily. "Now, let's get this straight right
off—we do this my way, or you're going to regret it,"
Matt warned. "I don't want to hurt you, but if you act
up, I'm going to be the only one standing."

He slipped the bridle over the horse's nose, forcing him to take the bit. After that, it was easy enough to throw on the saddle. He pulled the cinch tight, then tested the stirrups. Holding the reins in his teeth, he grasped the saddle horn, braced a boot against the sod wall, then stepped into the stirrup. With an effort, he threw his leg over the broad back.

"If you were mine, I'd cut down on that hay," he grumbled, settling into the saddle. Old Peter tensed beneath him. "Hey—right now, I've got a worse temper than you do, fella."

Matt flicked the reins against the heavy shoulder, and the big horse moved toward the open door. He leaned forward, ducking his head beneath the cottonwood frame, and then they were clear of the shed. Old Peter sank to his flanks in the snow, then began plodding toward where the wind had cut a path between drifts. Matt looked back, fixing in his mind the location of the sod house.

Skirting around it, he nudged the big draft horse in the direction he'd come, hoping to find what was left of his tracks. They were there, but just barely. He urged the big plow horse into them.

They didn't have far to go before he found what he was looking for. They'd been so close to making it— Rambler had gone down about five hundred yards from the soddie. But as he approached the bay, Matt could feel his chest tighten. The horse was on his side, his head resting against the ground, his body blanketed with snow.

Gripping Old Peter's reins, Matt swung down, dropping waist-deep into a drift. As he barreled his way through it, he realized he hadn't brought his rifle, and that his old army Colt was probably too wet to fire, if he had to put Rambler down. He reached his horse and bent down to brush the glistening powder from his head. Rambler's eyes were open, unfixed, and his ribs were still rising and falling. He was conscious. Matt jerked on the reins, pulling Old Peter closer.

He took off his mittens, and with stiff, awkward fingers he managed to loop one end of the rope to the plow horse's saddle horn, the other around Rambler's neck. It was a long shot, but he didn't have anything more to lose. Reaching for Old Pete's bridle, he drew the bigger horse forward. As though Rambler somehow understood, he rolled over onto his knees. The rope went taut. Feeling the weight of the bay, Old Peter took over. Pulling a load was what he'd been bred for, and he knew his business. His head thrown back, his shoulder muscles rippling, he strained against the rope. Rambler's eyes bulged as the rope cut off his breath, and he lurched, but he couldn't quite get up.

Matt removed the noose from his horse's neck and worked it under his front legs at the shoulders. This time, when Old Peter pulled, Rambler lunged, coming forward on his knees. Matt went to work again, widening the noose, bringing it up over the neck and around the shoulders, hooking it over Rambler's saddle horn. Now it was saddle to saddle, and he had to hope both cinches held.

"Come on, boy," he urged. "You're not done yet— you've got to give it another try." He returned to Old Peter's head and tugged, shouting back at the bay, "Now, Rambler—*now!*"

Old Peter took one step, then another, and another. Behind him, Rambler staggered, then stumbled, then came up. The snow blanket slid from the animal's flanks, disintegrating into wind-whipped powder. In his exhilaration, Matt forgot his stinging eyes, his raw face, his frostbitten feet.

"By God, Old Pete, we've done it!" he shouted gleefully, slapping the plow animal's rump. "I take it all back—you're one hell of a horse, Pete! Come on, Rambler, it's not far now!"

Matt was in a hurry now, eager to get out of the bitter storm. There was a fire in a stove, dry clothes and a whiskey toddy waiting for him. And a frightened woman with a dying baby. He looked up into snow so thick it was hard to tell where sky and earth met. It was going to be days before he could leave, and he knew it. His only consolation was that Cogburn and Haynes were going to have to stop and wait it out as well. Nobody was going anywhere in this.

Raising a hand, he shaded his eyes against the blinding brightness. "If you're really up there, God," he murmured, "you've got one hell of a way of showing it."

Once he got the horses into the cow shed, Matt grabbed a handful of hay and rubbed Rambler's legs and flanks roughly, trying to increase the bay's circulation. Then, before he fed the animals, he wiped Old Peter down. While he wielded the pitchfork, piling hay into the wide iron trough, one of the cows bawled, drawing his attention. As the animal moved into the light from the open door, he could see that her udder was painfully full.

*I haven't even milked today, but somehow that doesn't seem very important right now.*

As cold as he was, he hesitated, looking at the empty water bucket, then reluctantly made up his mind.

Taking the hide mittens off again, he cupped his hands over his nose, trying to warm them. Hell, he could hardly flex his fingers. He worked them vigorously, rubbing and blowing. Then, as the feeling came back, he picked up the bucket.

"Come on, Bossy," he muttered, dropping down beside the cow. "It's been a while, but I'm going to give this a try. Let's both hope that milk isn't frozen in there."

His hands grasped the cold teats, massaging them, squeezing gently, tugging downward. As the first stream of liquid hit the pail, the cow lowered its head and went to work on the hay. It took a few tries to keep the milk coming, but finally Matt established a rhythm. As miserable and bone-weary as he was, he felt a certain satisfaction. After nearly half a lifetime away from the old Wiley place, this Cass County farm boy had kept the touch.

Carrying the steaming pail, he followed his own footsteps back to the front of the soddie. This time, when he pounded on the door, Beth Linderman was waiting for him. When he heard her throw the lock bar, he pushed on the door, and milk sloshed from the bucket, spilling over onto the stoop. She stepped back, and warmth from the room embraced him.

Shifting the shawl-wrapped child onto her other shoulder, Beth ducked behind him and forced the door shut. She turned around and saw the milk. "Oh, but—"

One corner of his mouth turned downward, twisting in a self-conscious smile. "Yeah—well, I figured you might want some for the kid. Besides, it wouldn't do for your cow to go dry."

She looked down at Emily's curly dark hair, then to the floor. "I don't think she'll swallow," she managed. "All she seems to do now is sleep." Composing herself, she lifted her eyes to his face. "Thank you, Mr. Wiley. I hope your horse was alive."

He nodded. "When it came right down to it, Old Pete did the job. They're both in with the cows now."

"I'm glad—real glad." Moving away, she jostled Emily in her arms, but there was no response. Only those closed eyes, that labored breathing. "I guess you'll be wanting that toddy, won't you?"

Matt's feet felt as though a thousand cold pins were poking the soles, while his toes had no feeling at all. "Yeah—but I'd better have that pan of water first." As she started to lay the little girl down, he said over her shoulder. "I don't reckon you need to get me another one. It kinda looks like there's still some ice left in this."

"I'll fix the toddy, then."

Matt could see now that the baby was in a bad way, that Beth Linderman probably only had hours, not days, left with her daughter. "Later," he told her. "You take the rocking chair, and I'll drag a bench over."

"You'll need dry clothes."

"Right now all I need is that stove," he declared flatly. "Later, if you'll tell me where to find the whiskey, I can make my own toddy. I'll probably make it a whole lot stronger than you would, anyway." His gaze strayed to the feverish little girl in her arms. "I expect we'll both need one before nightfall."

"I never drink spirits, Mr. Wiley." Then, realizing how inhospitable she must sound, Beth forced a tired smile. "Thank you, sir," she murmured, sinking into the rocking chair. "For everything."

"Anybody can milk, ma'am."

"Just for being here."

Afraid she was going to weep again, Matt busied himself taking off his muffler, coat and mittens, draping them over the wood box by the stove. Scarce able to walk now, he retrieved the bench from beside the table and carried it back, placing it on the other side of the pan of water.

Sitting down, he leaned forward and grasped one of his boots. It didn't want to come off—he had to force it—and the second one was even worse. As his burning fingers rolled down his socks, he got a good look at the skin underneath. His toes were bluish, mottled, the foot above flushed, almost red. Thawing them out was going to be painful. He almost wished he'd asked for the whiskey bottle. Right now, he could swig the liquor down straight; then, maybe, pretty soon he wouldn't feel anything. Sucking in his breath, he thrust his bare feet into the cold water. They were so frozen it felt almost warm where he could feel it. Because there was no back to the bench, he bent forward, resting his elbows on his knees, his head in his hands. He closed his eyes, thinking he was too tired to live.

Emily's skin was hot and dry, and her closed eyes were like bruises, sunken within her small face. It was hard to imagine that yesterday the chubby-cheeked little girl had played with pan lids, clanging them together gleefully, keeping up a steady stream of babyish chatter, while Beth painstakingly embroidered the pretty face on pink cloth. Now the Christmas doll still lay in separate pieces—the round head, arms, legs, cotton-stuffed body and unfinished dress—all waiting in Beth's sewing basket for something that might never come. And Emmy lay against her breast, her whole being enveloped in a feverish stupor.

Beth stared at the ticking clock. It said a quarter to four, and yet she felt as though she'd been struggling with this unseen killer for days, rather than a mere thirteen hours. She racked her brain, trying to remember every detail of how little Ben Wilson had died. It had taken him almost two days, and when the doctor arrived the morning of the second one, he'd said he'd been summoned too late. As though he could have done something. As though there'd been a chance. And yet, as he tried to console the grieving grandmother, he'd shaken his head, telling her, "When they're little like this, they don't have much to fight with. I'd say not two in a hundred below the age of four survive." Two in a hundred. Nearly impossible odds.

It had been the convulsions, and the choking that ended it—most of all the choking. As though some phantom were gripping the little boy's throat, cutting off his wind. That thick gray membrane. And one just like it was going to choke Emmy.

Forcing her thoughts from the inevitable, Beth looked to Matt Wiley. His shoulders shook with chills as he huddled miserably over the pan of water. It was obvious that he was utterly, completely exhausted. He needed dry clothes, that toddy, and a bed. He needed to be sleeping now, if he was going to be any help to her later.

As loath as she was to part with Emmy even for a minute, Beth gently laid the little girl on the pallet, then rose and went to the cupboard. Rummaging on the shelf below, she found John's whiskey. The bottle was still more than half-full. Straightening up, she searched for a cup. No, her grandmother's German china wouldn't do—the cups were too small, too dainty. It would have to be the crockery John's mother had brought from Sweden. The cups were substantial, albeit chipped, veined and worn. Moving to the other door, she found the crock of wild honey behind the bean sack.

She uncorked the whiskey and poured a generous amount, then dribbled honey from its wooden paddle over it. Not knowing how sweet he'd like it, she decided to err on the side of the honey. As far as she was concerned, anything that obscured the taste of spirits had to be an improvement. She stirred, then dipped a finger into the sticky mixture to taste it, bringing back memories of her mother's cough syrup. Strong enough to put hair on a man's chest, her father used to say. But maybe it'd improve if it was thinned down enough. For good measure, she sprinkled it with a little of her precious cinnamon. Carrying the cup back to the stove, she finished filling it with steaming water. Then she approached Matt Wiley.

"How are the feet?"

He sat up and flexed his tired shoulders. "I think I liked 'em better when I couldn't feel 'em," he muttered. He glanced down, seeing that his toes were red now. "If they don't turn black, I expect they'll make it." He reached for a piece of rough cloth and started to dry them.

"I made your toddy. I thought you could drink it while I got you some clothes."

"Thanks," he murmured, taking it. "How's the baby?"

"No better."

"Bad time for something like this to happen." As the words escaped him, they sounded ludicrous. "But then, I don't guess there's a good time for sickness," he added.

"No."

Sipping, he smelled the cinnamon. "Pretty good stuff," he remarked, "but it could use more whiskey."

"Mr. Wiley, there's at least a quarter of a cup of the stuff in there," she protested weakly. "Surely—"

"It's all right." He took another drink, then observed, "It tastes like candy."

"Yes...well, I might have used too much honey."

The warmth was spreading from his stomach, mellowing him already. "You ought to fix yourself some of this—it'd probably do you some good."

"I need my faculties," she reminded him grimly. "Besides, once when I had a toothache, my mother made me drink some."

"And it helped, didn't it?"

"No. If you want the truth, it made me sick."

"You probably didn't like the taste, so you got it down in one swallow."

"Something like that. I held my nose and kept drinking until it was gone, anyway."

He took another good gulp, then nodded. "Goes to your head too fast that way."

"I should rather say it hit my stomach like Vesuvius."

"Came back up, eh?"

"All day. It certainly disabused me of the notion I could drink whiskey," she recalled, shuddering. "I have never been so sick in my life. I don't see how men can drink the stuff.''

"A little of it makes a man feel good, and a lot of it makes him forget his troubles.''

"Well, I don't think it did either for John. In fact—'' She caught herself. "Well, it doesn't matter now, anyway. I expect you'd rather have something dry to wear than listen to me rattle on,'' she murmured, starting toward the bedstead. "It seemed a shame to burn John's clothes, so I've been making Emily's dresses out of his shirts. Every time I turn around, it's as though she's doubled in size.'' Beth's face clouded momentarily. "Yes, well—there ought to be one or two left, and there's no shortage of his pants. I was going to make myself a walking suit from them, then thought better of it. It isn't as though anybody'd ever see me in my finery out here, and I've been rather busy,'' she added in understatement.

"You've managed this place by yourself since July?''

"I'd say it's more like I've survived.'' She bent down, drawing what appeared to be a wooden box from beneath the bed. Taking out a folded shirt, she shook the wrinkles from it vigorously. Then she laid a pair of trousers over her arm. Standing up again, she went on, "I'm not exactly the city girl I was when I came out here five years ago, Mr. Wiley.''

"It's hard out here for a woman—living, I mean,'' he murmured.

"Yes—yes, it is. I've learned to milk the cow, deliver a calf, clean the shed, keep house, cook, can vegetables, butcher game, and salt meat for winter. And since John died, I've become a fair shot, which comes in handy when the wolves and coyotes attack.''

She carried the clothes over and held them out. "Next year's another problem, though—the ground's too hard for the plow, even when I stand on it and make Old Peter pull my weight with it."

"Maybe you could look for a hired hand, ma'am—or for another husband."

"I wouldn't know where to find a hired hand. I certainly wouldn't try to mislead anybody by advertising back east—I'd have to lie to get anyone out here. I can assure you that if I'd had any idea what it was like, I'd never have come here."

"Hays looks like a prosperous place. Go over there and get yourself a husband," he told her practically. "It'd be easy enough—you're a good-looking woman."

Beth fixed him with a baleful eye. "Thank you for your advice, Mr. Wiley—but no, I don't think so. One husband was quite enough."

"You can't mourn a man forever. Leastwise not out here."

"I told you—if Emmy lives, I'm not staying. I want to go somewhere where rattlesnakes aren't under my feet, where wolves don't dig at my door, where Indians don't show up looking for food or worse, and where the wind doesn't howl nearly every day of the year. And," she added tiredly, "I'm not exactly mourning John. Here—you'd better get out of those wet things before you catch your death of pneumonia."

"Yeah." He looked around the one-room house, taking in every cranny, then returned his gaze to her. "Er. . . where do you want me to do it?"

She followed his gaze, then sobered. "Oh. I guess I've become so used to it, I don't think about the lack of privacy. I suppose I could turn my back—or, if you'd rather, you could do what company does in most soddies."

"Which is?"

"Get under the sheets—they get in bed and undress under the sheets. That way nobody sees anyone."

"Yeah, well, I think I'll just as soon take my chances with your back," he decided. "I'd just get tangled up in the blankets."

For the first time since he'd arrived, Beth felt awkward and self-conscious. "Uh...that'll be fine, Mr. Wiley. Would you rather stay over here by the fire? I mean, I could go over there and find something to do—maybe get another blanket out, or something," she offered lamely.

It was then that his eyes strayed to the wood box he'd scarce noticed before. "Is that all the wood you've got?" he demanded suddenly.

"There's more outside. I just have to go out and get it. I guess I could do that while you change your clothes."

He felt goaded. "No. My mother would roll over in her grave if she knew I let a woman carry wood. But it seems a damned sight more sensible for me to go out now rather than later. There's no use in soaking two sets of clothes," he added, pulling on his boots.

"I said I'd get it."

"The hell you will." He stood up and reached for his coat. "I'll take another one of those toddies when I come back. And if you don't mind, I'd like it a little stronger." His eyes met hers for a moment. "Anything else you want from outside? More water for the cows? A path dug to the outhouse maybe?"

He seemed almost angry, and it made her defensive. "Look," she snapped, "I didn't ask you to go out for wood. And as for the outhouse, it's on the other side of the cowshed, so if you want to dig your way there for yourself, that's fine with me. Usually in weather like this I just use the pot under the bed."

"I'll find the privy," he muttered.

He'd wrapped the wet muffler around his face and was pulling on his mittens as he headed for the door when she thought of something else. "But if you want, you could bring in some eggs, and I'll fry them up for supper," she said to his back. "And the wood's by the outhouse," she added.

"Just watch the kid," he growled, throwing the bar. A gale wind blew past him as he ducked his head and forced his way outside.

It was as though all the warmth the whiskey had given him was sucked from his body in one great howling whoosh. His head cleared, and he felt more than a little ashamed. Beth Linderman was doing her best, offering him hospitality under the worst possible circumstances, and he'd done damned little to show his gratitude. She'd laid down her sick baby to fix him that toddy. She'd even found him some clean clothes. And now she was offering to make his supper. But here he was faulting her for not having enough wood or enough room. Without her, he'd have frozen. Without her horse, he'd have lost Rambler.

Thoroughly chastened by the cold, he groped for the rope leading to the cowshed, then found what the wind and snow had left of his earlier tracks. Retracing them back to the door, he went the other way, stumbling through deep, seemingly virgin snow, reaching out for a reassuring touch of sod wall to tell him he was still by the house.

And people laughed at Seward for buying Alaska, calling it Seward's Icebox. He guessed they'd never been to Kansas. If the snow didn't stop soon, there'd be no crossing the western plains for a week, maybe more. Somebody should have called Kansas Jefferson's Icebox, since it was old Tom who'd made the Louisiana Purchase. But then they'd have had to call it Jefferson's Oven come summer.

Matt squinted up into the blinding snow, seeing the curve of the sod roof. Damn, but it was bowing under too much weight. Pretty soon the whole damned thing was going to come crashing down, burying everything in the house.

He found the woodpile by tripping over it. As his hands dug at the split logs, he could see there was quite a pile of it, and he had to wonder if she'd done that, also. Recalling her list of accomplishments, he knew Beth Linderman was pretty close to what his mother would have called a saint. She had a right to be a mad woman by now, but so far she'd managed to survive.

He couldn't carry enough in his arms to keep them warm through the night, so he'd have to make several trips, stacking what he could by the door. Resigned, he gathered a load in his arms and started back.

He finally trekked back and forth five or six times, until he was sure there was enough to last until the snow stopped. Then he turned his attention to the outhouse. Taking off his scarf, he tied it around a bark-covered log, then dragged the log over the path he'd already made, smoothing the way out, making it wider.

The outhouse was a mound of snow when he located it. Again he scraped and cleared until he found the door. Dragging it open, he let himself in. Everything was so frozen that it smelled more of old newspaper than of human waste. There was a bag of quicklime on the narrow dirt floor. He'd give Beth Linderman one thing—she was a good housekeeper, all the way down to her privy. He dropped his pants and his drawers and, hoping his buttocks didn't freeze, he eased them down onto the cold wood seat. At least he had privacy.

His teeth were chattering when he came out, and he still had to gather the damned eggs. But this time, at least, he had a path as far as the front door. As he passed the wood he'd left there, it was tempting to just go inside. Instead, he dragged the log on around to the cow shed.

Rambler was standing against the back wall, but he looked downright good, given what he'd been through. He snorted as Matt came in, then went back to munching on a pile of hay. Old Peter eyed him appraisingly, as if to say, "Just because you rode me once, don't think you can do it again." It wasn't until Matt went the other way that the horse dropped his head down and ate again.

There weren't many chickens, and it was so dark back there it was hard to tell what was a nest. Finally, Matt took off his mittens and just thrust his hands under one of the birds, feeling the warm straw, then closed his fingers over an egg. There were three there. Another hen, situated a couple of feet away, attacked, beating her wings at him. She had two more. Stuffing the eggs in his pockets, he let himself out and secured the rickety door.

Beth was back in the rocker when he carried in the first armful of wood. He dropped it in the box, then dug the eggs out. "I only found five," he murmured apologetically.

"That's pretty good."

"Not too many chickens out there."

"No. Between us and the coyotes, most have been eaten. Come spring, I was planning to hatch out several dozen." She took the eggs, then turned away. "You go ahead and get out of those clothes, and I'll dig some salt pork out of the keeper."

"I'm not done yet." Matt looked up at the cottonwood lattice, noticing where it bowed the most. "I'm going to need a shovel or something—if I don't get some of the snow off up there, it's going to be sitting on our heads come morning."

"You didn't see the shovel in the cow shed?"

"No, but I suppose you're going to tell me it's out there," he decided wearily.

"In the back corner."

"Damn." As she winced, he mumbled, "Sorry—I don't guess it's your fault you didn't tell me. Maybe I should have asked."

"No, I should have said something, but I didn't think you'd want to be digging snow, as cold as you were."

"It would have been a damned sight easier than dragging a log back and forth. I guess I should have taken a closer look. Damn," he said again, taking no satisfaction from it.

"Tell me, Mr. Wiley, do you always cuss so much?" Beth wondered aloud.

"Cuss?"

"All those *damns*."

"Never thought about it much." A faint, rueful smile lifted the corners of his mouth. "Actually, I was probably being on my best behavior. We all learned to say a lot we wouldn't want our mas to hear when we were in the army. A lot of profane things get said when men are afraid of dying."

"I'd think they'd be praying."

"No. Oh, I guess some did," he allowed, "but after you've seen half your battalion fall in places like Cold Harbor, you begin to wonder if anybody up there's listening." He slapped his mittens together, dislodging the snow, then started back toward the door. "This may take a while," he muttered grimly.

"Surely you could warm up for a few minutes. I already made your toddy, and it's on the table. I was thinking you were coming back sooner."

He stopped, turning back momentarily. "I was making a path between the cow shed and the outhouse. At least that way, if you don't mind bundling yourself up, you won't have to—well, you won't— Hell, you know what I mean. I just sort of thought, with me being here, you might not want to use the pot," he added.

"I wouldn't want to go out and leave Emmy." Her dark eyes met his soberly. "If you're any kind of gentleman, you won't look when I drop down behind the bed."

"No. I'll take that toddy with my eggs, I guess. But don't start cooking until I get back. I don't know how much snow's up there and how much has been blown off. All I know is there's a hell of a lot of weight on that roof."

"John said the whole place, without the floor, weighed ninety tons, but I expect he was exaggerating."

Matt considered the information a moment, then nodded. "I expect that's about right. That'd make the roof about twenty-two and a half— Yeah, he probably wasn't missing it by a whole lot." Seeing that she was regarding him skeptically, he explained, "I was an engineer in the army. Me and Bobby Lee. Only he had a lot more authority than I did. He went to West Point. Me, I just enlisted before I got out of college." He laid a hand on the lock bar. "Like I said, this may take a while."

As the door closed behind him, Beth rubbed her arms and turned back toward the stove. Emily lay still, her small body curled up on the pallet. Beth bent down, picked her up, and sat down to rock by the fire. As hopeless as everything seemed, she nonetheless felt a small measure of comfort, knowing Matt Wiley was out there. Now if only he wouldn't have to use that shovel for something far worse.

It was the most physical labor Matt had done since he'd been a farm boy, and yet he actually felt good about it. At least he would until he woke up in the morning. Then he'd probably be so sore he wouldn't want to get out of bed. But for almost an hour, he'd been up on that roof, pitching that snow like it was hay.

He leaned forward over the table, warming his hands on the reheated toddy, watching Beth Linderman fry four small pieces of salt pork. Either John Linderman hadn't been one to eat much, or she didn't have much left to feed anyone. Matt took a deep breath, smelling that pork, and his stomach almost cried for it. But he'd survive—in his six years of hunting, he'd been hungry before. A lot.

Beth drained the fried meat, then whipped all five eggs with a little of the milk he'd brought in earlier. Pouring salt into her hand, she measured it in her palm, then shook it into the egg mixture. The grease sizzled as she dumped the contents of the bowl over it. Leaving the eggs to thicken, she cut two thick slabs of bread, spread extra grease over them, then placed them in what looked to be a cake pan. She moved that to the other side of the stove, then returned to the skillet, scrambling the eggs.

Matt sat there, thinking John Linderman had been a lucky man, at least for a little while. He'd had a fine wife, and that pretty, dark-haired baby. Damn, but it had to have been hard to leave that. If it had been him, he'd have been arguing with Saint Peter, begging to be sent back from those pearly gates. Providing there was a Saint Peter waiting up there. Not that it was going to make much difference. He had, by rough calculation, killed more than a hundred men in the war, and five more after, so if he'd been a believing man, he'd have had to expect the hotter place. Yeah, if there was a heaven, then there'd have to be a hell.

He kind of wondered about Linderman. Beth talked a lot about John, but when he told her she'd have to quit mourning the man and find herself another husband, she'd said she wasn't. And then there'd been that comment about advertising back East, when she'd seemed almost bitter. It was like she was telling him she'd been lied to.

John had been a fairly tall man. Matt stretched out his arm, noting that the clean, bleached shirtsleeve came exactly to his own wrist. The collarless neck was a little big, the body a little loose, but otherwise it wasn't a bad fit. The pants came down past his ankles, touching the top of his foot in just about the right place, but the waist had to be cinched in with his belt. The small oval photograph by the bed must be Linderman, for the man peering out from the gilt-washed frame looked like a burly blond Swede. Sober, without a hint of humor in those pale eyes.

They must have made a strange pair—the big, rough farmer and the slender, pretty woman who'd left the comparative civility of St. Joseph, Missouri, for this. Matt studied her again, taking in that rich chestnut hair, imagining a glint of fire in those brown eyes. Yeah, John Linderman had been a lucky man, all right.

But old John was gone, leaving his widow to struggle for survival alone. And now she was facing the worst thing Matt could envision—the loss of her only child. He could still remember the depth of his mother's grief when she learned his brother Billy had been killed early in the war. Nothing that came after, not even the death of his father, had been as devastating. And when Billy died, there'd at least been the comfort of a husband and family. Things Beth Linderman didn't have. All she had was a stranger, a wanted man, a killer. A stranger who knew nothing about diphtheria, who couldn't help much, even if he wanted to.

As she turned the bread in the pan, Beth looked over, seeing that he was watching her. Any other time, she'd probably have been offended, but not now. As he sat in shirtsleeves, his elbows on her table, he looked almost as though he somehow belonged. It was an illusion, but nonetheless a comforting one. The day after tomorrow, or possibly the day after that, he'd be moving on, continuing his journey to wherever. Like nearly everybody else she'd met out here, he was just passing through.

Despite that sandy beard and drooping mustache, he was a nice-looking man—big, muscular, well proportioned. Unlike John, who'd been built a little like the bull they'd sold after they bred the cow last spring, hoping to raise a replacement. They'd used the money for seed corn, then watched half the crop die from too little water. The rest had been stunted, but she'd managed to parch some for meal and she'd canned what she could out of what was left. As for the calf, it had been a male, all right, but the wolves had gotten it. And the two unbred heifers were useless without a bull.

She had to get away from blaming John for everything. In his own way, he'd done the best he could with what he had. She'd just never forgiven him for not being honest with her, for not caring enough, for not loving his daughter. Resolutely she again turned her attention to Matt Wiley.

She couldn't help wondering how he'd come to be caught out alone on the prairie. Surely if he'd known the norther was coming he could have stopped somewhere and waited it out. He'd mentioned Hays and Ellis, so he must've been through them. Why hadn't he stayed there? What would make any man, at least an apparently sane one, tempt fate in this weather?

"I don't like my eggs too hard," Matt murmured, breaking into her thoughts.

"What? Oh—yes, of course. Neither do I," she said quickly, returning her attention to the food. Dividing the eggs with a wooden paddle, she slid them off onto the two cracked plates, giving him most of them. Then, using her fingers, she deftly retrieved the fried bread, dropping one atop each plate of eggs. "Well, I don't know how good this is," she told him, placing his meal on the table. "But I expect if you're hungry enough, you'll eat it."

"Right now I could eat damned near everything."

"There you go again," she murmured, setting her own food down across from him.

"What?"

"Those *damn*s."

"Sorry. I guess it's been a while since I was around a lady."

A lady. Beth looked down at her callused palms, thinking the word didn't much fit her anymore. A lady wore nice dresses and busied herself with good works, while she simply worked. Still, it was nice to hear the word again.

"Thank you."

"For apologizing? Isn't that what you wanted?"

"I didn't mean that."

He was too tired to follow her reasoning. Changing the subject, he asked, "Did the baby take any of the milk?"

"She wouldn't swallow. I tried dribbling a little of it into her mouth, but she wouldn't swallow." Her voice dropped. "I don't think she can," she said painfully. "All she does now is sleep. I—I don't even know if she knows when I hold her." She pushed her plate across the table toward him. "Here—you eat this. I'm not very hungry."

"You've got to eat, Beth. You can't afford to let yourself get down."

"It's not going to make much difference what I do," she said wearily. "It's—it's like I'm just sitting there, watching her slip away."

Afraid she was going to start crying and wouldn't be able to stop, Matt leaned across the table and took her hands between his. "I don't know much about diphtheria, Beth. I've never seen it before. Maybe if I knew what to expect—well, maybe it would help just to know," he finished awkwardly.

"I don't think it's going to make any difference. All day, I've prayed, and I've hoped, but she just keeps getting worse," she said low. She looked at his hands covering hers, then dropped her gaze. "I'm losing her, Mr. Wiley."

"You've seen it once, Beth. I want you to tell me everything you remember about it."

"I—I can't. I just can't."

"I can't help if I don't know what's happening."

"Mr. Wiley— I—" She felt his fingers tighten around hers. Swallowing, she nodded. "All right."

"Were you there when the little boy died?"

"Yes," she whispered. "I sat up with Mrs. Wilson all night—we just watched and waited until the doctor came the next morning." She looked up, her eyes burning with hot tears. "Please—"

"Go on."

"I don't see how this—how this will make any difference."

"It may not."

"The doctor said only about two in a hundred children survive this awful thing."

"I never heard of *any,* so that's something. Go on. I want to hear everything about that happened that night. I want to hear every word that doctor said."

"It's painful to remember. I'm not sure I want to relive it," she said uncomfortably. "Not now."

"Humor me, will you?"

She sucked in her breath, then let it out slowly before nodding again. "From the beginning? From how it started—all the way to the end?"

"Yeah."

"Oh." She fell silent for a long moment, then sighed. "It wasn't much different from what's happened with Emily. Ben awoke with a fever—it was actually a pretty mild one when it began—and he complained his throat hurt when he tried to swallow. We all thought it was just a cold—not even important enough to send for the parents, who were out of town. Mrs. Wilson made a plaster for his chest and boiled water for steam. I think she made up some slippery willow-bark tea and added some honey to soothe his throat. I don't know if he drank all of it or not, but I know she said he wouldn't eat."

"When was that?"

"All day—from when he first got up. Then, a little after noon, his fever shot up—just like Emmy's—and it wouldn't go down, even when she soaked him in water. But we still thought it was just a cold," she recalled. "Until about midnight. That's when the convulsions began. I heard Mrs. Wilson scream, and I ran downstairs. His head was thrown back, and he was jerking all over, and then suddenly he got rigid. He was so stiff that she couldn't open his hands.

"Mrs. Wilson begged her husband to go for the doctor, but he didn't want to—he said it was a waste of money, that the boy'd be all right if she'd just get the fever down. Then he went back to bed, so I stayed downstairs with her. She was crying, saying her daughter-in-law would never forgive her if anything happened to Ben, and she was never going to forgive herself for not wiring Iris and Jack to come home—they were Ben's parents, you see—and they weren't even there to hold him," she whispered, her voice breaking. "His mama wasn't even there."

Matt looked across the room to where Emily lay, just as Beth had placed her, making no sound beyond the harsh, labored breathing. "Go on. I want to hear the rest."

Beth wiped her wet eyes with the back of her hand, then continued, "We tried everything, Mr. Wiley. Everything both of us knew. Cold-water baths, vinegar baths, bundling to stifle the fever . . . lemon juice to clear his throat. Nothing worked. Absolutely nothing we did had any effect." She blinked back more tears. "About four in the morning, she woke Mr. Wilson again, and this time even he could see something was terribly wrong. He threw on his clothes and went for the doctor. It was less than an hour before they came, but to us it was an eternity. Ben got real quiet—like Emmy is now. Then, just before Dr. Stephens arrived, he began to choke real bad. He couldn't get any air . . . he couldn't breathe . . . and . . ." Tears were streaming down her cheeks now, and she couldn't stop them. "Dear God in Heaven, I—"

Matt cut in, trying to get her back to her story. "What did you do then?"

"Nothing—there was nothing to do. Don't you see, Mr. Wiley? There was nothing to do! He was turning blue! And Mrs. Wilson was hysterical, so I grabbed him and pounded on him, trying to make him breathe, but he couldn't! Finally, I carried him to the washbasin and pried his mouth open. The whole inside was covered with this thick white stuff—it was like a skin. Not knowing anything else to do, I tried to run my finger down his throat, but there was too much of it." She caught her breath, then looked at him through swimming eyes.

"When she heard the men at the door, Mrs. Wilson pulled the little boy from me and ran to thrust him into Dr. Stephens's arms. He just stood there, holding Ben, looking at her. Finally, he turned to Mr. Wilson and said, 'He's gone.' Just 'He's gone.' That was it. And Mrs. Wilson fainted."

"But it was the choking that killed him?"

"Yes. I think so, anyway. That's when he quit breathing."

"Because the white stuff inside was choking him?"

"Yes."

"Hmm..."

"What's that supposed to mean?" she demanded.

"I don't know—I guess it was something to say. This Dr. Stephens—you said he told Mrs. Wilson that he'd been called too late."

"Yes. That's when he also said that only two out of a hundred survive, so I don't know what good it would have done for him to have been there. But I guess then Mrs. Wilson would have known they'd done all they could. Now they probably wonder if he could've made any difference, if Ben would have been one of those two. I don't know." She pulled her hands from his and stood up. "I've got to get back to Emmy, Mr. Wiley. Whether she's too sick to know it or not, I want to hold her."

"You didn't touch your food."

"I can't eat. Go ahead and help yourself to it, if you're still hungry."

"I will."

Matt took a sip of the now tepid toddy and watched as she lifted the limp child and sat down to rock her. The clock seemed to tick louder, in rhythm with the squeaking rocking chair. Later, when he wasn't too tired to think, he'd try to grease those rungs for her. Then he realized why every noise within the sod house carried across the small room now—the wind outside had died down. The storm had passed. It was about time, anyway. Another few hours of snow, and only the stove chimney would have marked the soddie.

As he drained the cup absently, he thought Beth Linderman looked like one of those Christmas pictures of Madonna and child. Her arms enveloped her little daughter so protectively, and her hand stroked the dark head resting against her breast. It was enough to make a man ache, watching her try to come to terms with impending loss.

He'd seen so much suffering and death that he thought pity beyond him, but he felt it now. It wasn't right that a man like him lived while a child died. It wasn't right that a woman like Beth Linderman, who'd borne so much, had this added to an already unbearable burden. The world was upside down, and he was powerless to right it. The God of his mother's teaching didn't exist, else his father would be alive and men like Crawford, Cogburn, Haynes and the others would have died in the war.

It was a man's world, but it was the women who had the courage. They bore the babies, and they were the givers throughout life. It was odd—he'd never thought much about it before. Now he wondered what it would have been like if things had been different. If Billy hadn't died young, if the Yanks hadn't murdered their father. If he hadn't gone off to fight in a hopeless cause. If he'd made use of his engineering studies, he could have been a maker and a builder, instead of a killer.

He probably would have married pretty Caroline Shepherd and had four or five children by now. That was what he'd thought he'd do, anyway, before he went off and enlisted. Instead, she'd wed Tom Murphy sometime during Crawford's trial, then gone off to Kentucky with him. The odd thing was that it hadn't hurt at all.

But right now, as he looked at Beth Linderman, Matt felt a real regret. He wished he could have met her in St. Joseph. He could have made a home with someone like her. He could have amounted to something. Now things like a wife and kids weren't in the cards for him. Instead of loving a woman, instead of building a future with a wife, he'd become a saddle tramp without so much as a roof to call his own. And when the law caught up with him, he was going to hang, leaving only a sister to mourn him.

With that sobering thought, he pushed away from the table and stood up. "Guess I'd better check on the animals before I bed down," he announced. "It's about time I brought in my bedroll and warmed it up."

"You can have the bed. I'm not going to sleep any, anyway, and one of us might as well be comfortable."

"Yeah, I guess so." Matt was so weary he couldn't think straight, and the toddy hadn't made it any easier. He shrugged on his coat and tied the wool scarf over his face. "Need anything while I'm out?"

"You make it sound as though you were going into town."

"No, but I thought you might want extra wood or something," he offered lamely. "Hell, I don't know what I was thinking. It was just something to say, I suppose."

"You'd better take your gun and a lantern. The wolves come out at night."

"Not this close to the house."

"If they get hungry enough, and if there are enough of them in the pack, they aren't afraid of anything. When you go out, turn around and look at the door frame, Mr. Wiley, and you can see where they tried to dig inside. Last February, John shot one as it crashed through the window. You're standing just about where it fell. We stayed up all night, nailing boards over the windows, and even then I was as afraid as I've ever been. Until tonight," she added quietly.

Matt looked down, seeing the dark stain on the irregular wood puncheons. "I'll take my rifle," he decided. "It repeats."

"And the lantern."

"And the lantern." He reached out and unhooked the tin-hooded lamp from the wall, then picked up the rifle. "I'll try not to be gone long," he promised.

He let himself out, then stood there, staring up at the night sky. It was clear, clean, and filled with stars. The snow beneath it was crystalline, sparkling as though it had been sprinkled with silver. It was so still that the flame in the lantern didn't even flicker. He started for the cow shed, his boots crunching the packed snow, making the only sound to break the silence. Then, as he turned the corner, his blood almost ran cold. In the distance, the faint baying of wolves echoed. And coming from another direction, coyotes struck up a chorus of those mournful howls that made a man glad for a fire. Matt's grip tightened on the icy barrel of his Spencer.

It was still damned cold out, probably close to zero, even without the wind. Pulling his coat close to his neck, he hurried along the path he'd made earlier. The wolves were chasing something, barking excitedly as they closed in on it. A high-pitched squeal cut through the air like a knife, followed by growling snarls. They'd brought something down, and they were fighting over the kill.

Matt made quick work of feeding the animals, then secured the shed. Coming back, he was tempted to just go inside, to turn his back and use the chamber pot. But, for all the sympathy he felt for her, Beth Linderman was still a stranger. And a woman. He went on around to the outhouse, pried the frozen door open. Before he could unbutton his pants, he heard her scream.

He ran, slipping and sliding along the house, cursing under his breath. When he got inside the house, she was standing in the middle of the floor, white-faced and shaking. Tears streamed down her face. In her arms, Emily was bucking, her head back, body arching, limbs twitching.

"She's—she's having a fit! Dear God, but she's having a fit! Mr. Wiley, I can't stop it!"

"My God!" In an instant, he was at her side, prying the baby from her. His mind was working feverishly, telling him to try anything. "Get some hot water!" he shouted.

"Give me my baby!" she cried. "Emmy! Emmy!"

"The hot water—get the damned hot water!"

As he yelled over his shoulder, he pulled open the door and carried the violently convulsing child outside. Laying her down, he began scooping handfuls from the drifts over her. Beth came after him like a wild woman.

"You're burying my baby!" she screamed. "Give me my baby!"

"Put a pan of hot water on the table, and I'll bring her back inside!"

The jerking was subsiding, but little Emily was having trouble getting her breath. He could hear the thick membrane in her throat vibrating as she tried to suck air. Holding her chilled body against his, he ducked back inside. Beth was filling the pan with water. Her hysteria seemed to have passed, but tears were streaming from her eyes.

"How hot—? I put some cold from the water bucket in first." She barely choked the words out. "I don't want to scald her."

Instead of answering, Matt thrust his hand into the pan. It was hot, but not enough to burn. He began pulling the baby's clothes off. "I need a knife," he ordered tersely. As the last stitch gave way, he plunged the small body into the hot water. Emily's eyes flew open, but did not focus.

"What are you doing?" Beth demanded anxiously.

"I don't know for sure," he muttered. "Where's the knife?" When she didn't move, he spied her unused fork on the dinner table. Reaching across the baby, he got it. "Open her mouth," he ordered. When Beth didn't move, he shouted again, "For God's sake, pry open her mouth!"

"She can't breathe!" But she moved her arms to Emily's head, and forced open Emily's jaws. The thick white membrane covered everything from the tongue back. She looked up, pleading, "Please...try anything... I don't want her to die."

He was beginning to feel almost calm now. "Just keep her head back enough for me to see inside." Telling himself there wasn't anything to lose, that the baby was going to choke to death, he turned the fork, tines down, and tried to rake the tissue back. It was like cutting cold gravy. Under his hands, the baby went rigid, then started jerking again. "Hold her down— Don't let her roll off the table."

"I'm trying to— I've got her, but—" She leaned over, pushing Emily flat, pressing the small arms against the flat wood. The baby fought back with surprising strength.

He pushed the fork back farther, until he felt resistance. He'd hit the back of her mouth. He pulled back carefully, hand shaking, then tried again. Her face was darkening, and her eyes were rolling.

"If you're up there, God, now's the time to let me know," he muttered between clenched teeth.

"She can't die...she can't die..." Beth whispered frantically. "Emmy, can you hear me? Oh, please, Emmy— Mama loves you so much— Dear God—"

Matt plunged the fork in again, pushing down on the little girl's tongue, probing for the throat. He felt something tear, and he gave it a twist, pulling backward. With his free hand, he pushed down on the small chest, straining to hear the air expelled. It was like a sigh.

"Give her air. You've got to get her lungs full," he told Beth.

She braced herself on her elbows and blew into the baby's mouth. The baby's chest rose. When she lifted her lips, Beth looked up at him. "She's getting air," she whispered huskily. "Dear God, she's getting air."

"For a while, anyway." He pushed down on Emily's rib cage and heard the *swoosh*. "Let's see if she can do it on her own." Picking up the little girl, he lifted her arms. There was no mistaking the breath she took. Relief washed over him as he watched her color come back and heard her wail. He'd never been one to notice babies, but right now this one looked downright beautiful to him. He held her out to Beth. "Let's just wrap her up and wait to see if we have to do it again."

As she took the wet child, Beth's swimming eyes met his. There were no words for the gratitude she felt. Her mouth twisted into a quivering smile, then she nodded. Retrieving her shawl, she wrapped it around the crying baby, murmuring soothingly over and over, "It's all right, Emmy... it's all right... everything's going to be all right... Mama's here, Emmy." Holding her close, Beth rocked her daughter in her arms until the baby's frightened wails subsided. "Yes, Emmy—it's all right."

"I poked the back of her mouth some with that fork, so she's going to be sore. You might want to put a little whiskey on some sugar and try to get it down her. My ma always said whiskey cut down on infection."

Matt washed his hands in the pan of water, then wiped them on his borrowed pants. He was still shaking, and when he looked down, his shirt was soaked with his sweat. He still couldn't believe he'd somehow done it, that Emily Linderman was breathing. When he turned around, Beth had gotten hold of herself, and this time, when she smiled, it lit her whole face.

"Thank you, Mr. Wiley," she said softly. "Whether you believe it or not, you are the instrument of God's miracle."

"It may not be over yet."

"I'm sure it isn't, but I think maybe the crisis has passed. And at least we have a notion of what to do." Her throat aching with emotion, she added huskily, "I really believe Emmy's going to be one of those two in a hundred."

"Maybe." Embarrassed by the gratitude in her eyes, Matt looked away. "Look, can I have a favor?" he heard himself ask her.

"Anything, Mr. Wiley— I don't have much, but all I have is yours. I owe you everything, Mr. Wiley. There's nothing I wouldn't give to repay you. I— Well, there just isn't."

"It's this 'Mr. Wiley' business. It may not be exactly proper, but do you think you could call me Matt?"

In her euphoria, Beth would have gladly offered to cook his meals, mend his clothes and wait on him for the rest of her life. Not trusting herself to speak, she nodded.

"Good. I haven't been a mister since I came back from the war." He fixed his gaze on a broken place in one of the puncheons. "My mother had a lot of hope when she named me Matthew—it was her favorite Gospel."

"Matthew," she repeated softly.

"Matt," he said. "Yeah . . . well, I guess I'd better get on back outside and finish my business." He smiled sheepishly. "I sort of left the lantern and my gun out by the privy."

It wasn't until the cold air hit him that he realized the enormity of what had happened. A miracle, she'd called it. Yeah, he sort of felt that way, too. His eyes strayed upward, taking in the clear sky, the stars, the man's face in the moon.

"Well, I guess you let me know, didn't you?" he said softly. "Thanks."

There was no answer, but now he didn't need one.

Fatigue and exhilaration vied within him as Matt lay there, staring up at the latticed cottonwood ceiling. As strange as it seemed now, he'd never much thought of a sod house as a home. He could remember being camped out, hunched over a little fire, drinking bitter coffee. There he'd been, without so much as a bed to lie on, and he'd been almost contemptuous of farmers holed up inside big blocks of dirt. Yet as he looked around the Linderman house, he could see he'd missed a lot of things in his first assessment of the place.

Maybe nothing Beth had was worth much. Maybe life was cramped in one sixteen-by-sixteen room. But none of that took into account those handmade lace curtains, that big, round rag rug, the lacy shawl draped over the old rocker, the warm handmade quilt he was lying under. His gaze swept the room, discovering the pretty clock, the painted china stacked beside the veined crockery dishes. Yeah, she'd done a pretty good job of making a home out of this little soddie.

He rolled over on his side and looked across the room to the stove. She was pouring water from the kettle into one of those big cups. As he watched, she took out a small tin from the cupboard and sprinkled a handful of something over the water. He swung his feet over the edge of the feather bed and sat up.

"You ought to make yourself a toddy. You'd probably sleep better."

Startled, Beth looked up. "I thought you were asleep. I was making tea. I've been hoarding this for a long time, but I was just sitting there, thinking if ever there was an occasion to use it, that must surely be now."

"How's the baby?"

"She's still got a fever, but it's not going up. I tried the whiskey and sugar, and it seemed to help. She drank a little milk afterward, and I find that encouraging. Maybe tomorrow I can get her to eat something." She hesitated, then offered, "Would you care for some tea, Mr.—Matt?"

"Never drink the stuff."

"Maybe another toddy?"

"Yeah—I guess that'd be all right." His feet touched the cold floor, and he suppressed a shiver. "Yeah, I wouldn't mind something hot right now." He found his boots and stuck his bare feet into them. Standing up, he stretched his aching muscles, hearing his tired bones pop. "Damn, but I'm sore." She didn't say anything, but he could almost see her back tense. "Sorry—I'll try to watch it," he mumbled.

She turned around at that. "After what you did for me and Emmy tonight, you could turn the air blue with curses, if you wanted to. And I mean that— Matt."

"There now—that wasn't hard to say, was it?"

"That I don't care if you swear?"

"No. 'Matt.'"

"No. No, actually it wasn't." Picking up both steaming cups, she carried them to the table. "I probably didn't put as much whiskey in as you'd like, but I figured, as tired as you look, you don't need it."

"You sound like a wife." He saw her wince, and he wished he could take the words back. "I just meant that seems to be the role of women—to rein in the men and civilize them," he explained.

"Somehow I never thought of it like that," she murmured, taking one of the benches. "The way John put it, I was supposed to be the other ox in the yoke."

Matt sat down and leaned his elbows on the table, holding his cup with both hands. "You talk a lot about him—you know that?"

She considered her tea for a moment, and then her eyes met his. "He was the only company I had for five years—until Emmy. And Emmy's just now talking."

"I guess you miss him."

Her gaze didn't waver. "Yes, but not for the reasons you think. I came out here as a mail-order bride," she admitted baldly. "I was a twenty-five-year-old spinster, making a small living sewing other people's clothing, and I was tired of it. I wanted to do something more exciting than pin patterns on rich women. One day I saw John Linderman's advertisement in the newspaper, and he sounded so sincere that I wrote him. I must have been the only fool who answered."

"You sound bitter about it," he prodded, taking a sip of his toddy.

"Disappointed. I felt deceived—just plain deceived. In his letters, he painted a picture of this big ranch, a nice house, tall, waving grass—he even wrote that I should find the climate quite healthy, if you can imagine that. The only thing that wasn't a lie was the grass. When I saw this house, I wanted to cry, but it was too late.''

''You were already married to him.''

''No, but I had no money, and the woman I worked for in St. Joseph was a spiteful witch who was furious when I left her. I knew she wouldn't take me back, even if I could get there. And since I had neither the money nor the clientele to start my own business, I didn't have much choice. Besides, John made it quite clear that he wasn't going to spend a dime for a return passage.'' She stirred honey into her tea, then sighed. ''The simple truth was that the thirty dollars he paid to bring me out here was all he had.'' She looked up again. ''Look around outside, Mr. Wiley, then tell me where I could have gone. There's nothing out here.''

''Matt.''

''I'm sorry. Matt. John slept on the floor, and I took the bed, until the Methodist preacher stopped in to marry us. By then I'd decided to make the best of it.'' She paused, sipping her tea pensively, staring across the room as though she could see the past. ''John wasn't a bad man—he was a dreamer. He was filled with plans, some practical and some just plain fanciful. And what he wanted from me was somebody who'd keep his house, cook his meals, sew his clothes, tend the stock and work in the field beside him. He wanted big, strapping sons to help him build his dreams.''

''You don't have to tell me this, Beth.''

''I haven't had anybody to tell it to. You don't understand—I never had *anybody* to tell anything to. For five years, I sat across this table from him, and we never talked about anything but his dreams. The sons he wanted me to have for him. Well, when the first boy was born, it was dead. He tried to console me, saying there'd be others. The second time it happened, he accused me of causing it—I hadn't eaten enough meat, he said. Matt, we didn't have any meat!''

"Beth—"

"No. When I was carrying Emmy, he didn't pay much attention. I think he was steeling himself for another stillbirth. When my time came, he went hunting and didn't come back for four days. It was Christmas, and he wasn't even home. There was no-body here—nobody. It was a long labor, one I didn't think I'd survive. After nearly two days of lying in bed, I got up and walked and walked and walked. I must've circled this room two hundred times, hoping that somehow gravity would do it. By the time John came home, I'd had Emmy. She was the prettiest baby I'd ever seen, but he didn't want her. She wasn't the son he'd planned for. Because he didn't care anything about her, I named her for my mother. She has dark hair like Mama did.''

There was so much pain in her story that Matt wished John Linderman were alive, just so he could thrash him. No, so he could kill him. He was silent for a moment. Then he shook his head.

"Linderman was a fool, Beth. A damned fool. And he was dead wrong. If I had my life to live over, I'd give almost anything to have a little girl like Emily. A boy grows up, and there comes a time when he feels like he's got to struggle with his father, when he thinks he has to be his own man. A girl grows up thinking her papa's this wonderful man who can mend her dollies and make swings and do all sorts of things. If he does half the job he's supposed to, she wants to find a husband just like him. Hell, why wouldn't a man want a daughter?"

Beth found herself smiling. "You make girls sound like treasures."

"Well, I hadn't thought much about it before, but I guess they are. My sister idolized my father. And when it came right down to it, she married a man a lot like him. If Linderman had lived, and if he hadn't learned to love her, Emily probably would be looking for someone the opposite of him, don't you suppose?"

"I'd hope so, anyway. I hope she gets to marry someone she can love. But I know one thing for sure—she's not going to find him in Kansas. Not unless a lot more people move out here."

"I thought you wanted to go back to Missouri," Matt reminded her.

"I do, but I'm going to have to get enough money together to make the trip. Right now, there's forty-five cents in the coffee tin, and that's all." Afraid he'd laugh at how little she had, she lifted her chin proudly. "But I'll do it—I know I will. I'll take the heifers over to Ellis and sell them."

The thought of her driving two cows alone was nothing short of ludicrous to him. Apparently it showed in his face, because she looked him in the eye and said, "You don't think I can do it, do you? Well, I rode Old Peter over there in September and dragged a travois back with supplies tied to it. I made a sling and carried Emmy against my chest, but we got there and back."

"You're a resourceful woman, Beth—no doubt about it."

She eyed him suspiciously. "Are you laughing at me, Mr. Wiley?"

"No, I'm admiring you," he admitted. "And it's Matt—remember?"

"I don't know why I do that. I guess it's because you just came here today, and it doesn't seem right to be so familiar with a stranger."

"Even with what happened to Emily?" he asked.

"Well, no, but I don't want to appear forward, or anything like that. I mean, I want you to be comfortable here, and I'll never forget what you did, but I don't want you to think I'm so lonely I'm throwing myself at you." She was botching what she really wanted to say, and she knew it. "After what you did for Emmy and me, you can stay here forever, Matt, but I don't want you to feel like—"

"But you don't want to prey on my sympathy," he finished for her.

"Yes. That—and I know you'll be leaving in a day or two, going on to finish whatever you were doing before you found us."

"Yeah." Seeing that her cup was empty, Matt poured the rest of his toddy into it. "Here. You need this more than I do, Beth. You've been through hell today."

"I thought I told you I'm not much for spirits."

"You did, but there's not enough in there to disgrace either of us."

"No, I suppose not." She lifted the cup and sipped gingerly, making a face over the rim. "Well, I can't say it's improved much since the last time I tasted it."

"After a while it'll make you feel better. It's when you drink too much that you pay the piper." He stood up and looked toward the cupboard. "Where's the bottle?"

"Over there. Why?"

"I thought I might make myself a fresh one."

"There's not much left."

He found the whiskey and held it up, measuring the contents by eye. "There's enough."

Beth took another small taste, then said, "The honey pot's behind the doors at the top."

"I found it." He carried the bottle and pot back to the table, then went to fetch the kettle off the stove. Returning, he poured hot water into his cup. "Here— pass that over, and I'll show you how to make a real toddy." Before she could demur, he took hers and added to it. Then he opened the whiskey bottle. "Now, watch carefully, and I'm going to divide this. Some for me and some for you."

What had seemed like very little suddenly became too much. "I'll be drunk if I swallow all that," Beth protested.

"Now for the honey—twice as much for you as for me," he went on. "How's that?" he asked when he was done.

She managed a dainty sip, and nearly choked. As tears came to her eyes, she mouthed the word "Strong."

"It'll grow on you," he promised her.

"Yes, but what's it going to grow?" she countered archly. "I don't have much need for hair on my chest." Then, realizing what she'd said, her face went hot. "I'm sorry—I must be too tired to know what I'm doing, let alone saying."

"Probably." He lifted his cup, touching it to hers. "Here's to Emily."

"Emily," she repeated, taking another swallow. The warmth was beginning to diffuse through her body. "God was in your hands tonight," she said huskily. "You know that, don't you?"

He started to deny it, but couldn't. "The Lord works in mysterious ways," he murmured, hoping he'd gotten the quote right. He couldn't even remember who'd said it, but it somehow seemed appropriate right now.

"See, you *are* a believer." She sipped again, this time savoring the wonderful warmth. Leaning forward, she smiled almost dreamily. "What made you think to do what you did?"

"I don't know," he answered honestly. "I don't know."

"You could have wandered in a hundred different directions over this prairie and not found this house," she pointed out. "I can recall half a dozen times when John got lost, and it was his place."

"Sometimes a man just gets lucky."

"I'll never believe that. I *prayed* for you to come."

"That doesn't explain why I was out there in the first place, Beth." Almost as soon as he heard himself say it, he wished he hadn't. Tonight he didn't even want to think of Haynes or Cogburn. He just wanted to sleep in a soft bed and forget everything until he had to leave. "Well, it doesn't matter, anyway," he muttered.

Beth propped her chin up on an elbow and studied him, then finally dared to ask, "All right—why *were* you out alone in a norther?"

"Damned stupid, I guess. It had been so warm yesterday that I thought the storm wouldn't amount to much. I thought maybe it would snow a little bit, then melt. I didn't know that wind was going to come up, and the temperature was going to drop to zero after I left Ellis.''

"You could have gone back."

"No. You see some grand scheme in this, some great purpose, but there wasn't one." His mouth twisted wryly. "Maybe I'm not what you think, Beth."

The whiskey was making her giddy. She blinked, focusing on his eyes, thinking they were blue gray, almost like slate. "I don't care what you are, Matt Wiley," she decided solemnly. "Because of you, Emily's got a chance to see Christmas, to have her first birthday. Now I can finish that doll, and I can hope she'll get to play with it. Maybe she'll cherish it, and keep it, and pass it on to her little girl someday. Don't you see, Matt? You've given her a chance to grow up. You could be a horse thief—or a murderer, even—and it wouldn't make any difference. Emily Anne Linderman is alive this morning because of you."

"Stop it," Matt said harshly. "You don't know what you're talking about. If you want to give the Almighty credit, that's fine with me. Just don't try to paint me as a saint. I could be a real hard case for all you know about me." He dropped his head into his hands and began combing his hair with his fingers, trying to clear the cobwebs from his brain. "Hell, I'm so damned tired, I can't even think."

Reluctantly, Beth drew back, and straightened her tired shoulders. "You'd probably better go back to bed."

"And what about you?" he demanded.

"I'm going to stay up with Emmy. She's sleeping like she ought to, but I want to be watching her just in case the fever goes higher. If I get tired, I'll wrap up in a blanket and sleep in the rocker."

"I can take the chair."

"No. I've got something I need to do before I go to sleep, anyway."

"Look—I'm sorry if I bit your head off. I just can't take too much gratitude. It's just another way to tie a person down."

"I can assure you I meant no such thing, Mr. Wiley," she said wearily. "I guess I haven't met anyone before who didn't want to be thanked."

Matt felt almost ashamed. "I know. I don't know why I said it," he murmured ruefully. "Maybe because I've been alone a long time."

"Don't you ever get lonely? Don't you ever wish for someone to listen to you?"

"I can't afford to think about it." He stood up unsteadily, and the room spun around him. "I'm turning in," he told her gruffly. "If you change your mind about wanting the bed, wake me up and I'll switch places."

"I'll be all right."

Matt woke up once and looked across the room. She was sitting there, her head bent low as she sewed. The light from the kerosene lamp cast a yellow halo over her chestnut hair. He sat up groggily and yawned.

"What time is it?"

"Three o'clock. You can go back to sleep."

"What the hell are you doing? If it's three o'clock, you ought to be in bed yourself."

"I wanted to finish this doll, so I can put the hair on tomorrow night. Then maybe I can get the dress done by Christmas. There's only three more nights left, and I don't want her to see it until Christmas morning.''

"She won't know Christmas from any other day. She's not old enough."

"But I will. Maybe I'm doing this as much for me," she murmured. "I want to see her eyes get big when she unwraps this."

"You'll weaken *your* eyes, working in that light," he muttered, lying down again.

Matt turned over, facing the sod wall, and tried to go back to sleep. Funny how he hadn't thought about Christmas, not at all. Here it was December the twenty-first, and it'd just sort of crept up on him. Not that it made any difference. He hadn't bothered celebrating it since the last time he'd visited his sister. Four years ago. In some ways it didn't seem so very long ago, and in others it was as if an eternity had passed.

He'd killed three men in those four years. He'd ridden thousands of miles on horseback since that Christmas. Twice he'd spent the holiday alone, camped out in deserts. Once he'd been in a sleepy Mexican town, drinking tequila to the sound of the church bells, waiting for a cantina girl to come back from mass. Yeah, he'd sort of celebrated Christmas that year—it had been one of the all-too-few occasions in the past seven years when he'd slept with a woman.

He tried to remember what the girl had looked like, but as he drifted off to sleep, she took the form of Beth Linderman. And his last waking thought was that he had to get away while he could. Right now, he couldn't afford to care about anyone.

It was a restless sleep, one filled with turbulent dreams. *His mother in her widow's weeds, weeping*

*over the closed cedar casket... His sister standing
there, each hand holding a child... Crawford answering his door...his look of bewilderment as he
died... A Mexican town that could have been anywhere... His father coming in, leaning over his own
casket as the undertaker opened it for viewing... The
chill in his own bones. He was there, also, at his
mother's shoulder, looking down, staring into his own
alabaster face.*

Matt came awake, shivering not from fear, but from
cold. The place was cold, as though the fire had gone
out. Throwing back the quilt and blanket, he padded
across the floor to the stove. He wrenched open the
iron door, and the blast of heat almost burned his
face. There was nothing wrong with the fire—it looked
as though a fresh log had just been added. He half
turned to the rocker. It was empty.

The room was too dark for him to see much. He
groped for the kerosene lamp, found it, and carried it
to the stove. Using a piece of tinder, he lit the wick,
and trimmed it down. He turned around slowly, following the yellow light as it flickered along the walls.
There was no sign of Beth. He backed up, and stumbled, sending the small pile of wood tumbling.

"Ahhhhh... Ahhhh... Akaaaaaa..."

Damn. He'd woke the baby. "Sorry," he mumbled.

"Ahhhhh... Aaaaah... Aaaaaah..." Her cries rose
as she sat up. "Aahhhhhhh... Aaaahhhhhh..."

"Shh..."

It did no good. As the little girl's eyes searched
frantically for her mother, she went into a full howl.
"Mama...Mama...*Mamaaaaaaa!*"

Matt could have cursed. "Yeah, I can't find her, either," he muttered under his breath. "Look, it's all right—she's not going anywhere very far."

The child grasped the seat of the rocking chair and pulled herself up. Teetering unsteadily, she leaned toward the stove. Afraid she was going to fall into it, Matt caught her from behind, then swung her up to his shoulder. The squalls grew louder.

"Hey, Emmy..." He began jiggling her up and down with no effect. "Shh...shh..."

"Mama! Mama!"

"Look, I don't know where she is—probably the privy. Shh..." Her chubby hands grasped his hair, twisting it as she continued wailing. "Ouch! You little she-demon! Let's see...there's got to be something..." What he knew about a year-old baby wouldn't have filled a thimble. The only time he'd ever held one, it had been his nephew, and his sister had hovered over him, acting like he was going to break the boy. Balancing Emily's back with his hand, he sort of danced across to the cupboard, looking for something, anything, to shut her up. "Hungry?" he asked her.

"Mamaaaaaa!"

"I'll say one thing," he muttered as he rummaged through the shelves. "You're damned sure getting air." Sugar. Yeah, his mother used to use that to shut his sister up. All he needed now was a piece of cloth. "Hold on a minute," he told the baby. He was in luck. Picking up a towel, he poured some of the sugar into it. "Don't know if you've tasted this before, but Maggie always liked it." Holding the baby in the crook of his arm, he managed to roll the sugar into a corner and tie the towel around it. "Okay—let's give this a go."

At first she turned her head from side to side, trying to avoid the cloth he was pushing into her mouth. Then she tasted the sugar, and the tears subsided as she began to suck loudly. "Yeah. That's a whole lot better, Emmy," he said softly.

He carried her back to the rocker and sat down. Laying her against the crook of his arm, he began to rock. Either he was damned cold, or she was damned hot. She wiggled restlessly, as though she couldn't find a comfortable place. He finally let her go, and she climbed to a stand, then leaned against his shoulder, her hot face against his cheek, her free arm around his neck. She stayed there, her head resting on his shoulder, sucking on the sugar towel.

"I don't know, Emmy—it looks like there's a way to go before you're well," he whispered against her baby-soft hair. "I'd say you're not over this yet." He rocked, listening to the squeaking rungs, wondering where the hell Beth was. Finally the little girl gave a deep sigh and slid down into his arms. Her eyes closed, and she dozed off. He looked down on the small face, and felt an unexpected bond between them. There was something about struggling for a kid's life that made it seem more precious than any gold.

He was jarred from his thoughts by a gunshot. He came down hard, his pulse racing. A second shot. Grabbing the shawl, he wrapped it around the baby and headed for the door. Just as he got his hand on it, it opened inward, nearly hitting him. Her face flushed from the cold, her hair hanging loose over her shoulders, Beth faced him, his rifle in her hand.

"What the hell—?"

"They were trying to get into the cow shed," she said simply.

"What?"

"Wolves. I think I got two of them."

"Are you crazy?" he demanded angrily.

"I don't have enough livestock to lose any, Matt. I've got to try to keep what I've got."

"Well, you should have woke me up," he snapped. "Here—" He thrust the little girl into her arms, then took his gun. Setting it down, he rounded on her, his anger rising. "Dammit, woman! What if I hadn't been here? What if they got you? Then what would happen to the kid? Huh? Did you ever think about that?"

White-faced, she just stared at him as he vented his fury. "Are you quite done?" she asked finally.

"Hell, I don't know." He ran his hand over his tired eyes, then sighed. "I don't guess it's really my business," he said more calmly. "When I'm gone, you're going to do what you damn well please, anyway."

"Yes." She turned away and started toward the fire. "I have to survive."

It wasn't until she'd laid the child on her pallet and straightened up that he noticed how her shoulders shook. She turned around as he came up behind her.

"Hey, are you crying?"

"Of course not!" But even as she said it, the tears streaked her cold-reddened cheeks. "All right, so I am! What difference does it make to you?"

Later, he wouldn't be able to say why he did it, but at that moment, he caught her, enveloping her in his arms, holding her against him. "Go on...cry," he whispered. "You've got it coming."

"No, I don't have any right to cry!" she wailed into his shoulder. "Emmy's alive, and that's all that matters. But—but I c-can't h-help it! I just can't!"

"It's all right...it's all right..." he murmured soothingly, stroking her back. It had been a long time since he'd held a woman close, and as her sobs subsided, he was acutely aware of the soft curves of her body. He smoothed her silky hair with his palm, then rubbed her spine between her shoulder blades. It was almost more than he could stand. His imagination was already running wild, tempting him with his own thoughts. His mouth went dry with desire. "Sweet Beth..." he said thickly.

"I'm sorry," she whispered, raising her head to look at him. What she saw sent a shiver down her spine. "Matt, I—"

She got no further. His face swam before her eyes, and his breath caressed her cheek as he bent his head to hers. Her breath caught at the touch of his lips, and it was as though her heart paused as his arms tightened around her. She stood very still within his embrace, as though if she responded she'd shatter into a hundred pieces. Until his tongue probed, daring her. A low sob began deep within, then rose, tearing at her breast as she threw her arms around him and returned his kiss.

There was nothing else in the world for Matt at that moment. His hands moved over her eagerly, smoothing her dress over her hips, pressing the small of her back, molding her body to his. And every fiber of his being was urging him on. He was hot, almost feverish with desire.

Suddenly, she stiffened in his arms, then began to struggle. "They're out there again!" she cried. "I hear them—they've come back!"

It took a moment for his mind to master his body. "What in the devil are you talking about?"

"The wolves—they're out there again."

"Damn."

She was out of his arms and halfway to the door before he caught her. "You don't understand—I've got to stop them!"

He swung her around and set her aside. "You stay here with the baby, and I'll go. I've got a horse out there, too." Turning her loose, he reached for the rifle. "How many shots did you fire?"

"Two."

He took down his coat from a peg by the door, and reached into a pocket, checking for his box cartridge loader. Satisfied, he shrugged on the coat, and lifted the bar. Turning back, he said tersely, "You'd better see what you can do for the baby—I think her fever's up again."

As she nodded, he went out the door. The cold air hit him, taking his breath away. By the time he got halfway to the cowshed, he could see the wolves outlined in moonlight along the horizon. One of them loped down the hill, seemingly unafraid, and a couple of others followed more cautiously. Matt held his breath, waiting.

He lifted the rifle, taking aim, hooking the trigger with his finger. The metal was so cold it numbed his skin. The big wolf came closer, trotting at an angle, moving away, then circling back. Just as he squeezed off a shot, it broke into a run, charging the cow shed. He missed it. He had to be more patient. He lifted the rifle to his shoulder again, and held his breath as the animal came into his sight. This time, when he pulled the trigger, it yelped, ran a few feet, and dropped dead.

Undeterred, the pack charged. Matt fired four more shots, taking three down. Crouching against the sod house's wall, he opened the rifle's butt trap, pulled out the magazine spring and dropped in seven rounds from his loader. It didn't take him ten seconds, but by the time he was done, the three remaining wolves circled him, snarling, emboldened by the silence. In the moonlight, their eyes seemed almost red.

Matt closed the lever just as a female jumped him. When he pulled the trigger, she spun around in midair and fell less than six feet from him. A gaunt, rangy male backed away, turned tail, then retreated. The last one seemed to hesitate, then dodged at the last second and ran. Matt fired after them, but apparently didn't get either one.

For a moment, he remained in position, waiting for them to come back. But the mournful howls of the two survivors grew more distant. As hungry as they were, they'd apparently decided to try for something easier.

He checked the cow shed door, and found it still secure. Coming back, he visited the outhouse. Then, thoroughly cold, he let himself back inside the soddie. As he hung up his coat, he glanced toward the stove. Beth was holding the baby, wiping her body with a wet cloth.

His desire gone, he muttered, "I got four, anyway."

"That's six that won't come back."

"Do you have to do this often?"

"Only in drought and bad winters. They come after livestock because there's not much out there to eat. Except coyotes. And they're in pretty much the same predicament. I can't let the chickens out to peck without going with them, or the coyotes will be right there. That's why there aren't many layers. So," she added, "the chickens eat parched corn."

"I guess I should have watered everything while I was out there."

"I already did it. Your horse seems to have survived pretty well."

"He's a tough horse." He moved closer, looking over her shoulder at the little girl. "How's the fever?"

Beth laid a hand on Emily's forehead, then on her chest. "It seems about the same to me."

"Maybe I was just cold."

"Probably. I had the door open twice."

"You still should have got me up to do it."

She looked up. "You were dead to this world. You didn't even hear Emmy cry earlier. I thought about it, but it seemed a shame to wake you."

"She was crying when I got up."

"She's been a little fussy. I think that's a good sign, don't you? Last night, she was too sick to fuss."

"Yeah." He felt like he ought to apologize for kissing her like that, but he just didn't know what to say. "She was crying when I got up, so she must be getting plenty of air."

"Yes. I looked down her throat with a spoon earlier, and the only white stuff you didn't get is on the sides." She stroked the baby's hair absently, then smiled. "You were quite a sight when I got back in, you know. If you hadn't been so mad, I'd have burst out laughing. John would *never* have picked her up, much less thought to fix the sugar.''

''Yeah, well, it was an old family recipe.''

''Yours and a thousand others,'' she murmured mildly.

''It worked, didn't it?''

''It usually does.''

He felt an almost uncontrollable urge to touch her. Instead, he walked around and looked at the little girl. ''She's a pretty little thing. If Linderman had lived, he'd have been beating off the suitors by the time she turned sixteen.'' He sobered abruptly. ''He was a fool, Beth.''

The way he said it, she wasn't quite sure if he was still speaking of Emily. She took a deep breath, then studied the iron door on the stove. ''Yes. I think so, anyway.''

''Beth, about—''

She could feel the blood rise in her face. ''He never kissed me like that, you know,'' she whispered. ''Never.''

''Yeah, I sort of figured that. And if it hadn't been for those wolves, I'd probably have taken advantage of you,'' he admitted. ''But the cold air cleared my head, so you don't have to worry about it. You're not that sort of woman, and I know it.''

Beth sat very still. There was something within her that wanted to cry out that she *was* that sort of woman, that her body would have gladly betrayed her. That she would do nearly anything to be held like that again. Instead, she took a deep breath and let it out slowly.

''You'd move on, anyway'' was all she said.

"Yeah. I'm not the kind of man you want, and I'm sure as hell not the kind of man you deserve."

"Sometimes, Matt, we are harder on ourselves than on anyone else," she said carefully. "Sometimes we think we are beyond redemption, but we aren't."

"And sometimes we are worse than anybody knows."

"My mother used to say that there's very little that cannot be forgiven. She always held that only suicide kept one out of heaven, and that was because the person killed himself before he could repent of it."

"A man has to be sorry, Beth, and I'm not. Given half a chance, I'd do it all over again."

Beth wanted to ask what he'd done, but didn't. She was probably better off not knowing, she told herself. That way she could remember only the kindness of the man. But she couldn't help feeling a great deal of pity for him.

"Didn't you ever want to settle down?" she asked softly.

"A long time ago, but she had sense enough to marry someone else."

"I'm sorry. I shouldn't have asked."

"Don't be. I came home a different man than when I left. Nothing was the same—damned near everything I fought for was gone. My pa was dead, and his farm was sold for taxes before I could even get there. And I got a firsthand look at carpetbagger justice," he added bitterly. "There wasn't much left in Missouri for me."

"A lot of men came west because of that."

"Linderman?"

"No. He was the youngest of six, and he just wanted to come somewhere where he could own his own piece of land."

"Ever meet any of 'em?"

"No. And I can't say I ever wanted to. So if you are thinking I ought to take Emmy and go live off them, you're wrong. For one thing, they never wrote John once after he left. For another, the weather's even worse in Minnesota. He told me everything up there stays frozen all winter."

"So I've heard." He felt awkward, just standing there making small talk. "Yeah, well, I guess I'd better turn in again." He started toward the bed, telling her over his shoulder, "It's not long until morning, and I figure I'll be milking the cow come sunrise."

"You don't have to."

"Maybe I want to do it. You might as well let me take over the chores tomorrow, because I'll probably be leaving the day after. By then, we'll know for certain the baby's going to survive."

"Yes."

Matt sat down on the side of the bed and removed his boots. He might have gotten some sleep, but he was feeling as tired as ever. As he lifted the covers and rolled under them, he faced the back of her chair. She wasn't even rocking. He felt goaded.

"Look, I said you could have the bed."

"I'm all right."

"The hell you are. How long have you been up, anyway?"

Beth was so weary that every muscle ached, and her eyes felt like cinders, burned out and red. "I don't know—twenty-six hours, maybe more."

"Pretty soon you won't be any use to that little girl, Beth. You need the rest more than I do." When she didn't answer that, he turned to lay on his back, and stared at the ceiling. "You ever hear of bundling?" he asked finally.

The suddenness of the question startled her. "What?"

"Bundling. It makes a lot of sense, you know."

She could feel the heat creep into her face. "You're offering to share the bed?"

"Look, I don't have any ideas now. If you want, you can put the baby between us."

Her limbs were cramped from too many hours spent in the chair, and her head ached, probably from the toddy. The lure of the feather bed and a good over-stuffed pillow was almost too much to resist.

He could tell she was hesitant. "I've got all my clothes on except for my boots, and I don't aim to take any of them off, if that's what's worrying you."

"No, of course not."

"Then bring the kid and that blanket, and let's try to get some sleep." With that, he turned onto his other side, faced the wall and pulled the covers up over his shoulder.

"All right," she decided. "I'll put a double diaper on Emmy. She probably hasn't had enough to drink, anyway."

His breathing was even as she laid Emily in the middle of the bed. The child curled up against Matt's back and went almost immediately to sleep. For a long moment, Beth stood there, just looking at them, the big man and the small girl, and she felt an aching tenderness for both of them.

He lay still, feigning sleep, as Beth sat down on the other side and unbuttoned her shoes. Very gingerly, hoping not to waken him, she eased under the covers and lay down. For a time, she was very quiet, listening to the night sounds of settling logs in the stove, the ticking clock, and Matt Wiley's measured breathing. And she was filled with an intense longing.

Matt could feel the heat of the little body touching his. And he remembered those chubby little arms clasping his neck, the softness of her hair against his cheek. His thoughts turned to Beth, and he relived the pent-up passion of her kiss. God, but John Linderman had been a fool not to appreciate what he had. Any other man would have been proud to claim both of them.

But there was nothing Matt could do about it. He'd discovered them too late. And the sooner he could leave, the better it would be for all of them. Come spring, Beth would sell out and take Emily back to St. Joseph, where she'd be sure to find a husband for herself and a father for her daughter. It was better that way. The lucky fellow would be respectable, able to provide them with a better life.

Somehow that didn't console him. Not much, any-way. If he lived to be a hundred, which wasn't likely, he'd always remember the innocent power of Beth Linderman's kiss.

*He never kissed me like that, you know.*

Well, you never knew what you missed, John, and the loss was yours, Matt thought silently. If I thought there was any chance for me, I'd probably try to stay. But there isn't. She's got enough grief without falling for a murderer. No, I've got to move on, maybe even tomorrow.

Beth closed her eyes and waited for sleep to come, but it didn't. Instead, her thoughts rolled endlessly, carrying her back to that day John had lifted her bags from the platform at Hays. She'd been too shy herself to notice the matter-of-fact way he did everything back then. It was a warning she had been too green to heed. Little had she known then that his chaste kiss was the best he had to offer. She'd thought him a man in control of himself, that was all.

Not once during the month they waited for the preacher to come had he so much as tried to touch her. He was a gentleman, she'd told herself. A liar, but nonetheless a gentleman. It wasn't until after he slipped that little silver ring on her finger that she'd learned he had a cold, distant nature.

She'd never ever forget the shock of that wedding night. He'd just crawled into bed, lifted her night-gown, thrust her legs apart with his knee and flung himself over her. When it was over, he'd rolled away, turned his back and gone to sleep. He'd never heard her weep that night, or if he had, he'd ignored it. The next morning, he'd seen something was wrong, but instead of trying to make it right, he'd just told her she'd get better with practice.

Not once had he ever said he loved her, not even when she got the courage to ask him. She could still hear his answer. *Elizabeth, you read too many books. It might be fine on paper, but folks don't live that way. You've got a roof over your head and food on your table, don't you? It ought to mean something that I provide for you.* As if that was all that a woman ought to wish for.

There had been more fire in a stranger's single kiss than there'd been in all five years of her marriage. And now, as she lay in the same bed with Matt Wiley, she dared to wonder what it would be like to be held by him, to be touched like that. It would never happen, but she knew in her heart that he would be nothing like John Linderman.

It was December 24, and Matt still lingered, milking, gathering eggs, and doing as many of the chores as he could. He'd even stayed over that extra day to make sure that little Emily would survive. And this morning, she'd rewarded his patience by eating a coddled egg, while he and Beth washed down an egg apiece with weak coffee. Yeah, he could leave now, knowing that baby was going to be all right.

Leading the big bay from the cow shed, he stopped just outside the soddie door. He hesitated, knowing it wasn't going to be easy to say goodbye. But he had to do it. Cogburn and Haynes were still ahead, out there somewhere, and he wouldn't be done until they were dead.

He didn't have to go inside. Holding her arms across her breast, Beth came out. Her face was still pale and drawn, but she was trying to smile. She held out a small package wrapped in a yellowed newspaper.

"What's this?"

"I knitted you some socks."

"When?"

"After you went to bed last night. I'd finished Emmy's Christmas doll, and I had a little time left over. I know they're not the best color for a man, but I figured you'd be wearing your boots, anyway."

He tore a corner of the newspaper and looked inside. They were the brightest blue he'd ever seen.

"Thanks. If I had anything fit for a lady, I'd give it to you."

"You already have." She shaded her eyes against the brightness of the snow. "All I ever asked God for was Emmy's life, and you gave that to me." Her smile twisted, and she looked at him through a mist of tears. "God bless you and keep you safe, Matthew Wiley," she whispered.

"You'll be all right now, won't you?"

"Yes. Since Emmy's better, I'm not afraid anymore—not even of the wolves."

"Good. You be sure to keep that loaded gun out of her reach."

"I will."

It was even harder leaving than he'd thought. "Here..." he said gruffly, handing her a folded paper. "Look at this when I've gone, then maybe you'll understand." Putting his hand on the saddle horn, he swung his leg up and over, then adjusted his body in the saddle. "Well, I guess it's goodbye, Beth." Reaching into his coat pocket, he found a silver dollar. "Looks like I was wrong," he said, leaning down to press it into her hand. "It's not much, but maybe you can save this for Emily. That is, unless you need it for yourself." Before she could refuse it, he tugged the reins, turning Rambler. "You take care, you hear?"

It was all she could do to nod. It wasn't until the horse cleared the path he'd made and sank into snow almost as deep as his withers that she remembered something else.

"Wait!" she called out. "I forgot something!"

He reined in as she ran up. Taking another small package from the pocket of her apron, she reached up to give it to him. "It's not much, but you're bound to get hungry on the trail. I just put some fried pork between bread."

"Thanks. I reckon it'll be a while before I find a place to camp, so this will come in pretty handy." With that, he nudged his horse forward.

"Merry Christmas!" she shouted after him.

He couldn't look back. She might be reading that flier he'd given her, and after that, she wouldn't be wanting to see him again. "Well, Rambler," he told the horse, "we'd better get a move on, in case that wind comes up. Without it, the sun makes the air seem downright warm."

Almost. Apart from a few icicles hanging from the house, nothing was melting yet, and the snow was still pretty deep, but if he followed the ridges, there was a path swept clear by the wind. At the top of a gentle hill, he headed westward again, wondering how far he'd have to go before he caught up to Haynes and Cogburn. They'd probably had to take shelter themselves, maybe even as close as the next town, whatever it was. But they knew he was after them, so he'd bet they hadn't stayed around once the snow stopped. That'd make them one and a half to two days ahead of him at the least.

Certain that Beth had gone inside by now, he turned in his saddle to take one last look at the half-buried sod house standing alone on the open plain. No, she was still out, and she'd unfolded the bill. He had to get the hell out of there before she looked up.

Beth stood there, staring at the creased picture of a man she didn't know. The artist had given him a glowering look, and enough beard to satisfy the likes of old John Brown. But there was no mistaking the printing underneath. It leapt out at her, sending her heart plummeting within her breast.

Wanted Dead or Alive: Matthew Wiley, age 30

Below, in smaller print, it gave the particulars, saying he was a murderer, giving a description of him:

About six feet two, 180-190 lbs, blue eyes, brown hair and beard

There was a five hundred dollar reward for his capture.

She reread the flier in disbelief, letting it sink in slowly. Suddenly it all made sense, everything he'd told her. He couldn't stay, because the law was after him. Nearly numb, as much from the poster as from the cold, she turned around and slowly went inside. Emily was in the middle of the rug, playing with a small wooden box, pushing it across the floor as if it were a cart. It was Matt Wiley's cartridge box. And it had probably fallen out when he took his coat from the peg.

"See, Mama?" her daughter chortled, banging it on the floor. "See?"

There was an ache beneath Beth's breastbone as she nodded. Matt Wiley might be a murderer, but as she looked at Emily, she knew nothing bad he'd ever done could take away from the good he'd done for her baby. She walked over to where he'd set out the half-full milk pail. It was ready to be skimmed for the cream, but right now she didn't feel like doing much of anything. Here it was Christmas Eve, and Matt Wiley was gone, making the tiny house seem almost as empty as his half of her heart.

But she couldn't cry, not in front of Emily. Instead, she added a couple of pieces of wood to the fire. Then she sat in the old rocking chair and pulled the shawl around her shoulders. Sighing, she looked up at the cottonwood lattice above her head, and remembered how long he'd worked in that bitter wind to make sure the roof held. Yes, sometimes God did work in mysterious ways, after all. In her time of greatest need, He'd sent Matt Wiley to her door. Closing her eyes, she said a prayer for him.

As he came to a shallow ravine, Matt could see what was left of a small animal—not much beyond a few bits of fur and blood staining the snow. There were enough tracks around it for a dozen wolves, and by the looks of things, they'd all gotten about three bites apiece. Tonight they'd be back at Beth Linderman's soddie, trying to get what little livestock she had left.

A startled jackrabbit popped out of the other end of the little draw, breaking for open ground. Almost without thinking, Matt grabbed the rifle and fired. There was a squeal, a couple of jerks, and the animal was still. Dismounting, Matt went after it on foot. Come nightfall, it was going to look real good on a spit. He was already hungry. An egg and fried bread weren't enough for a full-grown man, and in the three and a half days he'd spent at Beth's, she'd only fed him four pieces of fatty salt pork. The rest had been cornmeal mush, eggs and flour biscuits, but he hadn't complained. He'd been pretty sure she was sharing all she had.

He carried the rabbit back to his horse, and was fixing to tie it to the saddle horn when he saw the corner of yellow newspaper sticking out of his bag. It was either those bright blue socks or the salt pork sandwich she'd made him. He secured his kill and swung up into the saddle, ready to press on.

Tomorrow morning, Emily was going to celebrate Christmas and her first birthday. He could almost imagine her chubby little hands tearing the newspaper wrapping off her rag doll. If that didn't make her eyes light up, nothing would, for Beth had poured a lot of love and effort into making it. In his mind's eye, he could still see her sitting in that rocker, leaning forward toward the yellow light of that kerosene lamp, stitching so carefully on the little calico dress. And he could hear her satisfied sigh as the last piece of red yarn hair went into place.

In contrast, by tomorrow morning he was going to be somewhere in the middle of nowhere, cold and lonely, with no company but Rambler. He hadn't been gone an hour, and already he missed that little sod house, the cast-iron stove, the warm feather bed. No, it was more than that. He was missing Beth and the kid almost enough to go back, to let Cogburn and Haynes disappear into Colorado.

No, he hadn't spent six years of his life chasing after them and the others for nothing, he decided. Setting his shoulders, he straightened in the saddle and slapped the reins against the big bay's rump. Maybe if he was real lucky, he'd stumble onto a town come night, and maybe someone there could tell him if Haynes and Cogburn had passed that way. If it was a big enough place, he might even look for a woman.

Hell, who was he kidding? If he was even halfway honest with himself, he'd admit the last thing he wanted was to find himself drunk and in bed with some nameless tart come Christmas morning. What he really wanted was to see a little bitty girl giggle as she unwrapped that first doll. What he really wanted to do was tell a pretty chestnut-haired woman that he'd fallen hard for her.

But he'd pretty much burned that bridge behind him when he gave her the wanted poster. Now she probably wouldn't want a man like him around her little girl. Now that she knew he was a murderer, she'd be justified in barring her door. No matter how grateful she was for her daughter's life, she wouldn't want him to stay. And even if, by some miracle, she did, he couldn't. He didn't have any right to bring the law down on anybody but himself.

More tracks, either wolf or coyote. Damn, but there were a lot of them out on the prairie this winter. And if they were already attacking houses, it was going to get a whole lot worse before spring came. A man would've thought that the drought had killed them off, along with the other animals, but apparently not.

*I'm not afraid anymore—not even of the wolves.*

But if they caught her outside some night, with only that old single-shot Sharps for protection, she'd be in one hell of a fix, maybe even dead. And that little girl would be left to starve in that sod house, all alone.

No, he'd been a fool to think he could leave them like that. He had to go back. Haynes and Cogburn would have to wait for that final reckoning. He'd followed cold leads before, and he could do it again. Sooner or later, they'd surface, and he'd get them. But there was a little girl celebrating her first Christmas

tomorrow, and if Beth Linderman would let him in the
door, he was going to be there to see it.

Turning back, he saw the tracks of another rabbit
going into that same ravine. Taking the Spencer from
its saddle sheath, he fired into the dried brush, scar-
ing it up. As it came out, it flew, taking to the air in
one long leap. He fired again, and it plummeted,
staining the bright white snow with red. Yeah, tonight he was going to watch her feed Emily rabbit
stew. And tomorrow—well, maybe she'd fry up the
other one. As he got down to get his kill, his eyes were
drawn across the ravine to the scraggly branches of a
stunted tree.

She couldn't believe her eyes when she saw him
standing there, two dead rabbits in one hand, a funny-
looking little tree in the other. Her heart was in her
throat as she looked up at him, and her eyes burned
with unshed tears. She couldn't even find words to say
what she felt.

Matt grinned crookedly. "I brought you some meat
for Christmas dinner." When she didn't move, he took
a deep breath and let it out slowly. "I, uh...I was
kinda hoping to see Emmy get that doll, but if you
don't want me here—"

"I was afraid I'd never see you again," she managed to say, her voice choked. "I was afraid you'd go
someplace and get yourself killed, Matt. And I
couldn't bear to hear of it."

"I guess I could stick around and help you out with
things, until you get ready to leave in the spring. Then
I'd be moving on."

"That picture doesn't look anything like you," she said foolishly. "You could come back to Missouri with us, and—"

"Too many folks know me there. Besides, you wouldn't want to be looking over your shoulder for the sheriff," he said soberly. "And it isn't like I'm innocent, Beth. I deserve everything they're going to give me when I get caught. I've killed five men, and I hope to get two more. Then the law can do with me whatever it wants. All I ask you to believe is that every one of them had it coming."

Beth stepped back, giving him room to come inside. "At least you're here for Christmas. It'll be almost like having a family, Matt, and none of us will be alone. I'll fix those rabbits, and we'll eat until we're full..." She wiped her wet eyes with a corner of her apron. "I'll even get to see if those stockings I made fit you."

Matt stepped past her to lay the rabbits in her washpan, telling her over his shoulder, "I'll clean these up after a while." He turned around and stood the tree in front of her. "I don't know how your folks celebrated, but mine always had one of these," he said, giving her a lopsided smile. "It's kinda small, and there's no green to it, but maybe Emmy won't know the difference after it's dressed up a bit." He looked up. "Hey, you aren't crying, are you?"

"No, of course not," Beth lied.

He turned loose of the tree and moved closer. And as he looked into those brimming black eyes, any resolve he had ever had was lost. "Beth... don't... Hey..." He lifted her chin with his hand. "God, how I wish you'd have come into my life a long time ago," he whispered.

Her chin quivered against his fingers. "It isn't too late, Matt—it can't be too late."

"You don't want a wanted man."

She closed her eyes and nodded mutely.

"They'll hunt me down. You don't want that for yourself, or for Emmy."

"No, but God's given me one miracle—is it too much to think He could give us two?"

He dropped his hand and stepped back. "Yeah. That was your miracle, not mine. Things like that don't come my way."

"You don't know that, Matt."

Rather than dispute it, he looked around the room. "Where's Emmy?" he asked, seeking safer ground.

"Asleep. I put her in the bed about an hour ago. I don't think she's even running much of a fever now. She's barely warmer than I am."

"Good." He hesitated, then turned back to the sink. "I guess I'd better take care of the meat so we can have supper. They're probably pretty tough—you may want to stew them."

"While you're outside, I'll put the water on the stove," she offered. "What do you want me to put with them?"

"What have you got?"

"Potatoes and onions. And dried beans, but they take too long to cook."

"Then I guess it's going to be potatoes and onions. Maybe you could save one rabbit to fry for tomorrow. Beans might go pretty good with that."

"Yes. I think so."

He felt awkward, clumsy. "Yeah, well...do you want to stew the first one whole, or do you want it in pieces?"

"It doesn't matter."

As he took the rabbits out, she picked up the water bucket and carried it to the cupboard, where she found her stockpot down below. She filled the pot about half-full, added a palmful of salt, then put it on the stove. Returning to the sink, she retrieved the sack of potatoes and set out enough for supper. As she peeled them, she hummed softly. She didn't know how she was going to do it, but somehow she was going to convince him to stay.

By the time Matt came back inside, she was sitting at the table, cutting narrow strips of newspaper with her sewing scissors. She looked up, smiling. "I fixed flour paste so we could make a chain for the tree."

"Pump's not frozen up, so I washed my hands outside." He carried the rabbits in a tin pan, and dumped about half of the pieces into the steaming water. "Where do you want the rest?" he asked her. "In the keeping hole?"

"Yes. I think it's cold enough, don't you? They won't spoil by tomorrow."

"Yeah."

In the corner farthest from the fire, he lifted the straw, then drew out the old crock and took off the lid. It was empty. When she made his sandwich that morning, she'd given him the last meat she had. He placed the rest of the rabbit pieces into it, then put it away. Tamping down the straw, he felt a certain satisfaction.

"Want to help with this?" Beth asked from the table.

"Sure." He sat down opposite and reached for the saucer of paste. Rolling a strip of paper, he pasted the ends together. "We used to do this when I was a kid," he remembered. "My ma would make taffy, and Pa would crack walnuts for us. And I could smell those sweet-potato pies baking. One year my sister baked flour ornaments and sugared them so they'd sparkle. She put strings in before they went into the oven so they'd hang up when they were done. You should have seen the light on that sugar. When Ma brought down her glass balls from Germany and hung them with the homemade ones, we thought it was about as pretty a tree as anybody could have."

"Maybe I could just cut some bells out of plain paper and use a little sugar on them—sort of like they were covered with snow," she suggested. "And I can probably make some for cookies. My mother used to sprinkle hers with cinnamon. If I made a pie, it'd have to be custard."

"I always like cookies myself."

"Before Papa died, Mama used to ice some of them, then add currants or raisins to make faces," she recalled wistfully. "But I don't have anything like that."

"Got any candles?"

"None to spare. I guess we could cut some paraffin up and make some."

"No. They'd probably just catch the paper chain on fire, anyway," he decided. "We always used candles because Ma's family was from Germany, and that's the way they did it over there."

"Tell me about your family, Matt," she said quietly. "About the way it was before everything went so terribly wrong."

"Not much to tell. We were pretty ordinary folks—Ma, Pa, Billy, me, then Maggie. We farmed a nice place down in Cass County. I was born there, and I never left until I went away to school.''

''Your brother didn't go to school?''

''No. All Billy ever wanted was to marry Annie Burkett and get his own farm. I wanted to build roads and bridges and help take the railroad all the way to California, so I talked Pa into helping me go back to Indiana to study engineering. When I came home, the war was on, and Billy'd been killed. Pa took it hard—said there wasn't a cause worth dying like that for.''

''And he didn't want his last son to go,'' she said softly.

''He didn't want either of us to go. He said he needed help on the farm. At the time, I didn't want to be a farmer anymore. I wanted the damned war to get over so I could go with the railroad.''

''If...if this hadn't happened...the killing, I mean...'' She chose her words cautiously, haltingly, wanting to know what he thought now. ''Tell me,'' she asked finally, ''if you weren't wanted, if you had a chance to start over, what would you want to do? If you could, I mean.''

He looked across the table at her, seeing the delicate wisps of chestnut hair framing her face, those pretty dark eyes, that almost porcelain-perfect skin, and he knew she could do a whole lot better than him. ''I don't know,'' he lied. ''Maybe go on west to California.''

Disappointed, she dropped her gaze to the paper ornaments. ''Yes, I suppose that would satisfy a man's need for adventure.'' When she looked up again, she smiled, a bit too brightly. ''Well, let's see how these look once they are up. I'd like to surprise Emily when she wakes up.''

By the time they were finished decorating the odd little tree, the sun had gone down, and the stew was almost ready. Beth woke Emily up and washed her, then dressed her in a clean smock before presenting her to Matt. Squealing happily, the little girl tried to climb onto his knee.

"Whoa now," he said, lifting her up. "You don't want to fall now, do you?"

While he played horsey with the toddler on his leg, Beth finished up supper. When she turned around, he had Emmy on his lap, and was whittling something over the wood box. As she watched, fascinated by the sight of the big man with her daughter, he put what looked like a stick to his mouth and tooted, showing Emmy how to get sound out of the whistle. She hated to break into their play.

"Dinner's ready," she announced.

The meal was good, and soon over. As Beth cleared the table, Matt asked suddenly, "I don't suppose you kept John's razor, did you?"

"Well, I didn't throw it out. Why?"

"I thought maybe I'd shave off the beard."

"I'll get it for you, but you'll have to strop it."

"Thanks. I can get the water and soap."

While he leaned over the table, straining to see his reflection in the cracked mirror, the little girl stood holding his knee, watching him with wide eyes. Lye soap never made much lather, but it was enough that once he'd sharpened the edge of the razor he was able to shave without nicking himself. He stared a moment at the man looking out at him. If it weren't for the mustache, he'd have taken off seven years.

"What do you think?" he asked the tiny girl. "Should it go?"

"Go," she repeated knowingly.

"Yeah. I kind of agree with you." Picking her up, he sat her on the table beside the washbasin. "Watch this," he murmured, "and you'll be glad you're a girl."

Beth came back from doing the dishes and watched over his shoulder. "You look a lot different, Matt," she told him.

"Better or worse?"

"Younger."

"Younger better? Or younger worse?"

"Downright handsome, Matthew Wiley."

Her voice was soft, with a husky quality that spoke more than words could have. A quality that gave a man thoughts he had no right to have. He could feel his pulse quicken.

"I'll take that to mean better," he decided.

"Do you want the cookies now, or do you want to wait until afterward?"

The hair on his neck prickled, and his pulse pounded. Even though he knew she wasn't suggesting anything improper with the baby sitting there, he dared to ask, "After what?"

"It's Christmas Eve, Matt. At home, Mama always read the story out of the Bible. You don't mind, do you?"

"No." He took a deep breath and exhaled fully. "No, I guess not. In our house, Pa did it."

"Which Gospel?"

"Matthew. He didn't much like reading aloud, and it was shorter."

"We always heard Luke, but then, if we'd have sat still for it, Mama would have read us the whole Bible."

"I always liked shepherds and angels more than wise men, anyway," he murmured.

"Then go sit by the fire, and I'll get everything ready," she said, reaching for the washbasin. "Here— take Emmy."

Matt wound up sitting in the rocker, the little girl on his lap. For effect, Beth had moved the coal-oil lantern across the room, putting it beneath the tree, where it cast its yellow glow upward, picking up the sugar sparkles on her paper bells. He sat there, rocking the child, feeling a warmth and security he hadn't know for a long time. It was enough to make him wish he could stay there forever. But he wasn't a fool.

She came up behind him and handed the baby a cookie, then moved to sit cross-legged on the floor by the tree. She opened the worn, leather-covered book, leaned close to the light, and began to read.

And it came to pass in those days that there went out a decree from Caesar Augustus, that all the world should be taxed. And this taxation was first made when Cyrenius was governor of Syria. And all went to be taxed, everyone into his own city. And Joseph also went up from Galilee, out of the city of Nazareth into Judea, unto the city of David, which is called Bethlehem, because he was of the house and lineage of David, to be taxed with Mary, his espoused wife, who was great with child. And so it was, that while they were there, the days were accomplished that she would be delivered. And she brought forth her first-born

son and wrapped him in swaddling clothes because there was no room for them in the inn . . .

Matt closed his eyes, and his arms tightened around
the little girl who lay against him, sucking on her
cookie. The sound of Beth's voice was soothing, the
message an ancient one, and yet in his mind he could
see Mary hovering over that manger, Joseph watching as she tended the child.

Beth kept reading, and it sank in slowly that she'd
finished the Christmas story, and now she was finding all the places where Christ spoke of forgiveness—
to Peter, to the two criminals crucified with him . . .
Matt wanted to tell her to stop, that he was beyond
that. Instead, he kept rocking, knowing in his heart
that she was putting her faith in the wrong place. The
law had no place for forgiveness or redemption. It
hanged murderers and left forgiveness to God.

When she was finished, she turned up the wick, then
returned the lamp to the small table by the rocking
chair. "You weren't listening, were you?" she asked
softly.

"I quit about the place where Mary went to the
temple to be purified."

"You don't have much faith, do you?"

"Not like that."

"Christmas began with a miracle, Matt."

"A man can't ask to be forgiven when he still plans
to kill again, Beth. That's like going to church and
saying, 'Lord, I'm sorry for what I've done, but I'm
going to keep doing it.' "

"You don't have to—you could let them live."

"No."

"But why? Who appointed you executioner? Who said you had to do this?"

"They hanged my father, Beth, and then they lied about it. They hanged him in front of my mother and my little sister, then they concocted a story to cover it up."

"Then let the courts decide. It isn't up to you, Matt!"

"The courts decided six years ago. A carpetbag jury believed the lie. Seven Union soldiers said my father was a Confederate spy, and they hanged him for it. Well, he wasn't. He didn't care about Jeff Davis, Bobby Lee, *or* Abe Lincoln. All he wanted to do was farm his place in peace. He didn't even want me going—that's the irony of it. He didn't even want me to fight."

"Then why—?"

"They hanged him because he had a son on the other side, Beth. *Because he had a son on the other side.* It was *me* they should have hanged, instead of him.

"Then they were wrong—terribly wrong."

"They said it was war, Beth, but for me the war's not over until this is done. It's taken me a long time, but I'm just about even with them."

"You don't have to do this. You could forgive them," she countered. "They'll still pay someday. The Bible says you should forgive your enemies seventy times seven. Let God punish them."

"And in another place, it says to take an eye for an eye, a tooth for a tooth."

"You could start over—you could go somewhere and start over."

"That poster's going to follow me until I'm dead, Beth." He eased Emmy off his lap and stood up. "There's no sense talking about this. Wishing won't change anything. Maybe if I'd met you back then..." He caught himself. "But I didn't. Look, it's Christmas and the kid's birthday, and I don't want to ruin either one of them."

"No, of course not. Neither do I." She turned away. "I wish I'd met you back then, also," she said, her voice so low he could scarce hear it. "Maybe we could have found love with each other. Maybe we wouldn't have lost so much of our lives."

Rather than respond, Matt headed for the door. Taking his coat from the peg on the wall, he let himself out. "I'll be back," he muttered. "Right now, I'd better feed the animals."

Yet that night, as they lay abed with the little girl snuggled between them, he couldn't help thinking of what Beth had said. He wished he had met her in another time, before he had blood on his hands and a price on his head.

By the time Matt woke, Beth was already up, and the smell of cinnamon vied with that of coffee. He sat up, and his hand went instinctively to his beard, drawing back with the discovery that it was gone. He'd had it so long, it felt like he was touching somebody else's face. "What time is it?"

Beth turned around, smiling. "Ten o'clock. I've been up since six, and Emmy's already been fed. You were sleeping so soundly that it would have been a shame to wake you."

"I don't think I've slept past seven in my life," he murmured ruefully. Then he recalled the occasion. "I suppose you gave her the doll?"

"Not yet. We were sort of waiting on you." Moving purposefully, she carried the steaming kettle to the washbasin and poured his hot water. "While you wash up, I'll fix your eggs."

His feet had just touched the cold floor when someone pounded on the door. "Mrs. Linderman! Are you all right in there?" a man's voice called out.

"Who is it?" Beth asked, hesitating to draw the bar.

"Sheriff King!" he yelled back. "I need to talk to you!"

Beth's heart sank. A painful knot formed in her stomach, making her feel utterly sick. "Just a minute!" she managed, looking to Matt, panic written in every line of her face. "I've got to get dressed!" Even as she said it, she knew how ludicrous it must sound at ten o'clock. "Dear God, what do I do?" she whispered. "He'll find you."

It had been bound to happen sooner or later, but Matt bitterly regretted that it had come now. He'd wanted these few days with Beth and the baby, days when he could pretend he had a family. Still, he didn't want to make things any harder on her.

"Open the door," he said quietly. "You don't know me—you just offered a stranger a bed in exchange for a few days' work. That's all you tell him, you hear?"

"But what will you do?"

"If he recognizes me, I'm going to give myself up. You don't need any more trouble, Beth. Now, get ahold of yourself before you open that door."

"I can't."

"Go on. You're a strong woman, Beth. You've survived hell on earth, and you'll be all right."

"No."

"Mrs. Linderman!" the sheriff called out. "I'm asking you again—is everything all right in there?"

"Yes—yes, it is!" Turning back for one last look at Matt, she whispered, "Maybe you could hide under the bed."

"No. Just open the door."

He stood up, watching her for what seemed an eternity as she slid back the bar and stepped aside. As the sheriff came inside, Matt went almost numb. It was Tom King—Major Thomas King, as he remembered him. They'd both been at Franklin under General Hood, only King had been an aide, while Matt had been just one of the army engineers. As the older man faced him now, Matt felt empty, strangely devoid of emotion.

Oddly enough, the sheriff just glanced his way, then turned to Beth. "I'd have been out here sooner, but the weather was mighty bad for traveling," he said apologetically in his soft Southern drawl. "Today's the first day we've been able to get out looking."

"Looking for what?" Beth dared to ask him.

"Got word over from Hays that a fellow named Wiley might be coming through. Man's wanted for murder. Tall fellow with a beard, according to the poster."

"I see."

The lawman took another quick look Matt's way, then went on. "They say he's a real hard case, ma'am, so I thought we'd better check in on you to make sure you were all right. Tough enough on a woman alone out here, anyway. Saw tracks coming up to the house," he added significantly.

"But I'm not alone, Sheriff." Moving to Matt's side, Beth laid a hand on his arm, feeling him tense beneath her touch. "I don't guess many people know it yet, but I got married last month." Her fingers tightened their grip. "We just got back from our wedding trip before the storm hit. I wanted to show Emmy off back in St. Joseph while she was still little."

This time, the older man studied Matt appraisingly, as though he knew she was lying. "Married, huh?"

"Yeah."

"Hard to find a preacher out here."

"It was in St. Joseph."

"Wiley's from Cass County. Don't suppose you've been there, have you?"

Matt could see that King was toying with him, watching his eyes. Damn the man. *He knew.* He was just incriminating Beth. But now she'd gotten herself in too far. "Never," he lied. "Somewhere over by St. Louis, isn't it?"

"Kansas City." The sheriff sighed. "Well, I guess maybe I've been looking for a dead man."

"A dead man?" Beth asked cautiously.

"Found two fellows caught out about ten miles from here. One was maybe a mile ahead of the other. Froze to death, by what we could tell. Wolves pretty much tore up the carcasses, so there's not much left of them except bones and hair." Seeing that Beth flinched, he said hastily, "Sorry, ma'am, didn't mean to upset you." He paused for a moment and then started up again, as if he'd come to a decision. "Way I got it figured out, the second one must have been

Wiley. He was trailing somebody, according to the marshal over at Hays.''

"Oh," Beth commented, struggling to control the tremor in her voice.

"Looks like neither of them made it." This time, when his eyes met Matt's, King added, "I guess Wiley had an old score to settle—something from the war."

"Maybe," Matt replied, meeting the older man's gaze.

"The war's over, son."

"Yeah. Yeah, it looks that way." Actually, it looked as if God had taken care of the matter for him. Matt took a deep breath, then straightened his shoulders. "Thanks, Sheriff."

King turned back to Beth. "The boys out there are getting cold, so I'd better get going. Any papers those two had on them are long since blown away, but I'm sure enough going to report that Matthew Wiley died in that blizzard." He jammed his worn felt hat back onto his head. "Glad you found somebody to help take care of that young'n, ma'am. Merry Christmas."

Beth let the sheriff out the door and closed it behind him. As soon as she heard them mount up and leave, she threw the bar. She stood there, her back pressed against the iron supports, her whole body shaking.

"I thought for sure he had you." Then, as she realized the enormity of what had happened, something odd occurred to her. "He didn't even ask your name."

"He didn't have to."

"You don't think he knew?"

"Yeah. I think he did. I expect those two bodies were Cogburn and Haynes. But, like he said, the war's over now." He walked toward her, closing the gap between them. "Looks like all I've got left to do is make an honest woman out of you."

"Please—you don't have to," she whispered, looking away.

Matt lifted her chin and turned her head with his knuckle. "I'm not going anywhere, Beth. More than anything in this world, I want to make a home with you and Emmy. We can't go back to Missouri, but there's a whole world out here for us."

"Oh, Matt! I—" She got no further before his arms closed around her and he kissed her thoroughly. It wasn't until Emily cried out that he released her. She stood there a moment, looking up at him through a mist of tears. "Don't ever tell me again that you don't believe in miracles, Matt Wiley. I'll never believe it."

It came to Matt then just how blessed he was. He'd come a stranger, stumbling into Beth Linderman's sod house in a blizzard, and he was staying to be a husband and father. And he was downright eager to see Emmy's face when she opened that doll. As he looked at her and Beth, he was overwhelmed by the love he felt for them.

\* \* \* \* \*

## Anita Mills

Since the publication of her first book in 1987, Anita Mills has written titles that have been making the bestseller lists. Her writing has been greeted with outstanding reviews in such diverse publications as *Romantic Times, Publishers Weekly, Affaire de Coeur* and *Library Journal.* In that brief time she has won eight writing awards, sixteen nominations for Best Medieval Historical, Best Sensual Regency and Best Medieval Adventure, among others.

# THE HOMECOMING

Patricia Potter

# Chapter One

*Hope's Way, Georgia*
*December 1865*

Ryan Baxter was home!

Cherise Saunders didn't know how she was going to tell her brother, Jeremy. She was still having trouble digesting the news herself.

As she carefully hung up her last good coat on the hook inside the door, she debated on ways to tell her older sibling that his one time closest friend had returned after a seven-year absence.

She knew the news would not be met with any pleasure by Jere, even though she felt a prickling of anticipation. More than a prickling. More like waves of anticipation, flashes of pure joy. Ryan Baxter had returned home.

Some of that joy seeped away as she glanced around the cold room. Only ashes remained in the fireplace. Jere had not even bothered to do that small chore. Cherise stifled her impatience. It was going to take time, she kept telling herself. Jere was inherently strong; he would revert to being the man he'd once been—decisive, fair. That mischievous sense of humor would return. She had to believe that.

It was just that he had lost everything, including part of himself: his left arm. At least, he believed he had lost everything. They still had this land, though, a roof over their heads, even if it wasn't the grand Georgian manor in which they'd been raised. They had more than a lot of people did after the war.

But Jeremy had lost his limb in one of the last battles of the war, and he'd reached Oak Bend to find the main house burned to the ground and Cherise living in the overseer's cottage. The once fine cotton fields were overgrown with weeds, and new taxes had made it necessary to sell off portions of land that had been in the family for seventy years. The prospect of meeting next year's taxes loomed terrifyingly uncertain.

They'd also lost a brother during the war, just as Ryan Baxter had lost one. They were lucky though—many families in the county had lost more.

Ryan and Jeremy. The two had been inseparable as children and young men. But when George had seceded from the Union, Ryan Baxter had shocked everyone by deciding to stay with the Union army, in which he'd been an officer for nearly three years. Cherise had been as startled as anyone at the news when it had come. Jere, however, had been less surprised, and his reaction surprisingly mild. "He's a maverick," he'd told Cherise privately. "Always has been. Just like you," he'd added, with an affectionate pull on one of her wayward curls. "But he'll change his mind. When it comes down to war, he'll come home."

But he hadn't, and his name had been banned in the Saunders home as the war grew more and more bitter, and the toll grew steeper. On Jeremy's last leave before he was wounded, the laughter had been gone. He'd heard that Ryan, a colonel then, had been at the Battle of the Wilderness, in which tens of thousands of men were killed, and every mention of his name now brought curses. No one had expected Ryan to return, particularly now that it had been eight months since the war's end.

Cherise sighed. Jeremy would find out one way or another, most likely when Calvin Sooner appeared with more of the homemade whiskey Jere was using for escape. Better that it should be she, before Calvin fired him up with his hatred. She detested Calvin, a man Jeremy wouldn't have associated with years ago, but who now provided Jere with something he thought he needed desperately.

She went to his room and knocked. "Jere?"

She received a mumbled reply that she decided to take for consent and went inside.

Her brother was sitting in a cane chair, one of the few pieces of furniture that had survived Sherman's assault, his right hand clutching a glass of whiskey. He had not shaved this morning, and his dark hair was uncombed.

"The fire's out," she said.

His eyes, green like hers but slightly glazed now, settled on her. "Sorry," he said.

"The eggs brought a good price." She hesitated, desperate to lighten his mood. "Enough to buy coffee and sugar. And we can buy a ham for Christmas."

"Christmas?" His eyes drifted away from her.

"It's only two weeks away," she said. "Maybe you can help decorate a little."

"Why?" he said flatly.

"It's your first Christmas home...."

"This isn't home," he said bleakly. "And I don't give a damn about Christmas."

"I do." She hated the small break in her voice. Patience, she reminded herself. He needed patience. He'd lost so much, including his belief in himself.

Perhaps something in her voice struck a chord, because his eyes seemed to focus then, and he smiled. It was a small smile, so very small, but one nonetheless. "You always did like Christmas better than anyone I've ever known," he said.

But the hope that leapt in her heart died quickly as he lifted the glass and took another drink from it. Suddenly, she wanted to startle him out of that cocoon he'd wrapped around himself.

"Ryan Baxter's home," she said, and the glass dropped from his fingers, the liquid staining the wood floor.

"He wouldn't dare," Jere said through clenched teeth.

"Everyone in town is talking about it," she persisted. "He's apparently been at Baxter Trace the last week or so. Rode into town yesterday. He told Stan Fisher he intended to stay."

"Hell he will. Damn traitor."

"He's your friend."

Jeremy exploded. "Not a damn bluebelly, he isn't. I don't want him here, and he's a damn fool if he tries to stay in Hope's Way. He'll be asking for a bullet." He stared angrily at Cherise. "And I don't want you to go to Baxter Trace as long as he's there."

Anger suddenly eclipsed any sympathy she had for him. "Mrs. Baxter is my friend, and so is Ryan," she added defiantly.

"I forbid it."

"You have no right to forbid anything. I'm the one that's been keeping this place going. You won't even keep a fire burning," she said, hating the tears welling up behind her eyes. She whirled around before he could see them begin to drop. She had tried to be strong, for both of them, but she was infuriated.

There was a deadly silence behind her. She thought about doing what she had for the past five months, turning around and apologizing. But this time she couldn't.

She left the room without another word.

Ryan Baxter eyed the spindly pine tree judiciously, trying his damnedest to summon some enthusiasm for the Christmas-tree-to-be. The tree was for his mother, a hopeful symbol of normality, something that had been gone from his life so long he scarcely could recall it.

His mind flipped through past Christmases. He tried to remember the good ones, and not the last bitter years before the war, when his father had kept calling him a changeling, a disappointment. He tried to recall, instead, trees with candles and strings of popcorn and the merry little handmade figures his mother had worked so hard to produce. She deserved this Christmas, not one haunted by his ghosts.

This pine tree, small and thin and forlorn, seem to fit his life. Ryan was alone, as alone as he had been the past four years, fighting his countrymen for his country. A paradox. Certainly a damnation.

He sighed, forcing himself to count his blessings. He was alive. His mother was alive. The house at Baxter Trace still stood—stripped and made ugly by an occupying army that had also been *his* army, but standing. Which was more than could be said of eighty percent of the other homes in the county.

It was also another reason for his neighbors to hate him. Not that they needed one. His decision to fight for the Union had made him a pariah. He'd known when he decided to return home that it would be difficult. He just hadn't known how difficult.

Peace had not come to Hope's Way, only defeat. The cruelest kind of defeat. Nearly every material possession had been stripped from the South, and so had the pride of its people. Bitterness abounded in Hope's Way, and the town that had once borne its name proudly now seemed to revel in despair.

He wondered whether Jeremy Saunders felt the same way. He hadn't had the courage, or energy, yet to find out. He knew Oak Bend had been burned by Sherman's men, just like nearly every other plantation in the county.

Christmas should mean friends and laughter. But he had no friends here now. Even though his mother never said anything, and had welcomed him home, he knew she must wonder why he had lived when her older son had died in the Battle of the Wilderness. Had one of his bullets killed his own brother? The question was always there between them.

He tried to tamp down the emptiness, that great painful void he slipped deeper into each day. He thought about going away again, but then what of his mother? She wouldn't leave this land, and the graves of her husband and two of her three children.

When he suggested moving west, she'd just looked at him with those blue eyes so like his own. "This is our land. I won't leave it. You can go—I'll not keep you." The words had stabbed him deep in the soul. Because she was his mother, she had been ostracized by much of the community. Only her lifelong friend Doc Colburn and Cherise Saunders, Jeremy's sister, had visited.

God, but the loneliness was crushing him, squeezing out what heart he had left. He had been alone for so damn long; no one had ever understood the pain of his choice, the mental anguish of being neither fish nor fowl. Even the Union army, which he'd served, hadn't altogether trusted him. Everyone, including every commanding officer he served under, had asked him why. There had been his oath, given freely when he graduated from West Point, though many fellow officers from the South contended that the acts of the North negated that oath.

That oath had played a part in Ryan's decision. But the deeper reason had been his abhorrence of slavery. He couldn't fight to protect a system he believed inherently evil. Even though to fight against it was to fight against friends and family. He had agonized over the decision for weeks, then decided to stay with the Union. He'd thought he understood what the consequences would be, but even he hadn't realized how extensive his isolation would become during those years—much of it self-imposed, some imposed upon him.

He stared at the tree again, and then at the ax in his hand. After four years of carnage, he didn't want to do harm to another single living thing, and yet he hoped this tree would bring some measure of comfort

to a woman who had precious little of it. He felt a
burning behind his eyes, and part of him wished he
could cry, rage, swear. But he'd mastered control long
ago, so much so that his face had become stone, and
so had his emotions.

He stepped closer to the tree, envisioning it lit and
gay, like the one had been fifteen years ago, when the
Christmas tree had become fashionable along the
Eastern Seaboard. Every family in the county had
tried to outdo the others in producing the most beautiful tree. Neighbors had visited one home and then
another, each time tasting the Christmas punch, until
they were fairly reeling. With each stop the trees had
grown taller and brighter and the arguments louder.

But no one would come this year, and there were
few other homes to visit, even if he were welcome.

He swung the ax. No time for self-pity. He'd chosen his path, and he would do the same again. He
could live with the consequences; he just wished with
all his heart that his mother didn't have to do the
same.

Depressed by her argument with Jeremy, Cherise sat
in the main room of what had been the overseer's
house at Oak Bend and stared at the empty fireplace.
Wind crept in through the cracks of the shuttered
windows; glass was a luxury long gone.

She and Jeremy, though, were luckier than most.
They had sturdy walls around them. The home where
she was born had been burned in 1864 by Sherman's
troops, and only the fireplace still stood. Sherman's
sentinels, they were called, reminders of the once gra-
cious homes along his path.

She sighed, feeling closed in. Just two weeks until Christmas, and she should feel the familiar stirrings of gladness. Christmas had always been magical to her, a time of sharing, of love, of hospitality. But now she couldn't get Jeremy out of the house, and they were hard-pressed to set a table with anything but vegetables she'd harvested and canned, and an occasional chicken.

Every penny they had went for taxes or seed. They'd already had to sell off much of Oak Bend for next to nothing. By doing that, they'd gotten enough to seed and harvest a small cotton crop. If only they could survive the next year, their prospects would be better. Cherise promised herself that.

If only Jeremy believed.

If only she believed . . .

"Dash it," she whispered to the empty room. She blinked back tears, knowing they would do little good. The war was over, and at least one of her brothers was still alive.

*And Ryan.* She tried his name on her lips. He'd been back ten days, and she hadn't even known. She had tried not to show any interest in town when she heard the news, although her heart had stopped. Stopped, then beat rapidly, so rapidly she feared the whole town could hear it, and guess at the cause.

She hadn't been surprised at Jeremy's reaction. He had descended deeper and deeper into bitterness. The same bitterness that had affected most of Hope's Way. Dear Mother in heaven, she understood. Less than half of the men had come back from war, and a half of those who had were marred or wounded in some way. All had returned to burned homes and poverty. Some had adjusted as she had tried to, farming a portion of the land, but many just slipped into helplessness as they dreamed of life before the war. Despite the surrender, they still considered the Union the enemy, and Ryan would become a focal point for their rage.

But while Cherise had no intention of obeying Jeremy's edict about not visiting Baxter Trace, she knew she would be careful about it. In his present state, Jeremy was fully capable of taking a gun to Ryan.

She couldn't stand the darkness in the house any longer. She went out to the makeshift stable. It was nothing like the old one, which had held up to twenty horses. This one had two stalls and some space for hay, and nothing more. But then, that was all they had now: Jeremy's gelding, and the mare she'd managed to hide from the Yanks.

Cherise quickly saddled the mare. She needed freedom. Her blue dress was faded and worn, but that was of little matter. She had stopped caring about dresses years ago; they had seemed so unimportant, when friends were dying daily. She ran her hand across Cinnamon's neck for a moment. Poor old girl. Life had changed for her, too, and not for the better. Oats now were a special and rare treat, and Cinnamon had to suffer the indignity of the plow.

She would have an apple after the ride. Cherise went to a stump, which always made mounting the sidesaddle easier. She wished she could ride astride, as she had as a child, but there was little left now but her dignity. She would have scorned even that six years ago, but Jeremy had enough problems without hearing complaints about his sister. And she would do anything to save him pain—anything except stay away from Baxter Trace.

As if drawn by an invisible cord, she headed in that direction. She had loved Ryan Baxter from the time she was six years old, and he was fourteen and knocked down a friend of Jeremy's who was rough with her new puppy. He'd always been her knight, the one among her brothers' friends who'd smiled at her and teased in a kind way. She'd quietly adored him when he came home from West Point in his handsome uniform. She'd been fifteen then, still all arms and legs and thin body, her dark hair wild and unmanageable...

He had been looking for Jeremy, and he'd found her at a stream, her head bent down, reading the inevitable book. He had suddenly appeared on a fine black horse, and she had scurried to hide the volume. But he would have none of it. He'd dismounted and reached for the book, picking it up before she could grab it back.

"Hmmm..." he'd said, looking at the title and grinning. The look he'd given her was understanding, conspiratorial. "*The Scarlet Letter*. I take it your mother isn't aware of your reading preferences."

She shrugged, her gaze fixed on his blue eyes. They were so very blue, and they twinkled. Really, really twinkled. She had decided long ago that he had the nicest eyes she'd ever seen. "I like everything," she said, her heart beating so fast she could scarcely bear it. She wished she wasn't wearing her oldest dress, that her hair wasn't just tied back with a plain blue ribbon. She wished she looked like Mary Elizabeth, who everyone thought would marry Ryan Baxter when he came home from West Point.

Was that why he'd come home?

He gave her back the book and stooped down next to her. "You're growing up, little one," he said.

Any answer she might have given caught in her throat. She could only gaze at him, thinking how wonderful he looked with his sandy hair glinting like gold in the sun, his mouth in a crooked smile, and the blue uniform molded to his lean body. Candy, her dog, who had been stretched lazily next to her, raised her head and wagged her tail.

"Some guard dog you are," Ryan said, reaching over to run a hand down Candy's back.

"She remembers you," Cherise said finally, fighting to keep a waver from her voice.

His grin grew wider. "I didn't think I was that memorable."

"Oh, yes," she blurted out. "I've been—" She stopped suddenly. How could she tell him she had been waiting for him, waiting for him to come home, waiting for him to notice she was becoming a woman? Even if she didn't much look like one now.

"Been what?" he asked curiously.

"Wondering when you'd come home," she said awkwardly, wishing she knew better how to flirt, like Mary Elizabeth. "Are you going to stay long?"

He shook his head. "I've been assigned out west. California. I have only a month's leave."

"California," she whispered. "I would like to go there some day."

"Then you will," he said, his eyes warm and friendly. Affectionate. She didn't want affectionate. She was old enough to want something more. She wanted his eyes to light when he saw her, as Jeremy's lit when he saw Susan Ferguson.

Instead, he stood. "I'm looking for Jeremy."

"He's in the south fields with Papa," she said.

He touched his hat with his hand, dipping it in salute. "I thank you, Miss Saunders," he said formally, and rose, standing there for a moment. "And might I say you're growing into a very attractive young lady."

And then he was gone.

She saw him often during the next month, and though he no longer teased her as he had when she was a child, he often winked at her, sharing the secret of her forbidden book. He and Jeremy would go racing through the woods or disappear at night, Jeremy returning much in his cups. A month later, Ryan left for the west. By then, she'd decided she was going to marry him. And she prayed every night that he wouldn't meet anyone until he returned home again.

Three years later, Georgia joined her sister states in seceding from the Union, and Ryan decided to fight with the North. She was eighteen by then, and didn't share the war fever that so many others had. She'd read too many books about the horrors of war to believe it was a glorious adventure. Jeremy and David, her second oldest brother, had already enlisted in the Confederate army.

Ryan Baxter's name became a curse word in Hope's Way—to everyone but Cherise. She didn't understand his decision, but she couldn't eject him from her heart. He was always there when another young man came courting, and he never left it, not even when David was killed, not even when Sherman's troops ravaged the countryside. Those events had nothing to do with Ryan; in her heart, he was still tall and glorious, with the warmest smile she'd ever seen.

Her father died of a heart attack, then her mother of a broken heart, and all the young men were gone—

killed, wounded, or, it seemed, about to be. Several had asked her to marry; marriage abounded in Hope's Way, as if it could somehow ward off death. But it didn't, and Cherise wouldn't compromise, even knowing, as she did, that her Ryan would probably never return to Hope's Way, even if he did survive.

At twenty, Cherise became the mistress of Oak Bend and, with Cecil Turner, the overseer, tried desperately to keep what she could for Jeremy. There was no accessible market for cotton, and the food crops and animals had been confiscated by the Confederate forces. In 1864, General Sherman and his men took what little food and goods remained and burned what they couldn't carry off, including her home. She saved Cinnamon by hiding her in a swampy woods five miles from her home, a place left uncleared to soak up overflow from Snake Creek. She'd become almost numb to disaster; at least she thought she had, until Jeremy straggled home a month after Appomattox, his left arm gone, along with all his gentleness and laughter...

Cinnamon was obviously happy to be out of the stall this afternoon, her hooves seemed to dance across the hard ground. Cherise's mood lightened with each step. She relaxed her hold on the reins, and the horse shuddered with delight and stretched into a canter.

She saw the wagon from a distance, and her pulse raced. She recognized the faded green trim that had once decorated all the vehicles belonging to Baxter Trace. She recognized the vehicle before she recognized the stiff figure on the seat. The wagon was moving toward her, and she stopped her horse, waiting for it, watching the man on the seat grow larger.

Her heart quickened, even though she knew it shouldn't. He had fought for the enemy, for those who had burned her home, who had destroyed Hope's Way and nearly every family who lived here. Yet she knew she could never consider him an enemy, not her knight protector of old, not the man she'd held in a special place in her heart all these years. She'd tried to think of him as an enemy, tried to dismiss him from her thoughts, tried to interest herself in the courtship of other men. But nothing had worked. He had remained in her heart.

Just as she'd been too stubborn to give up Oak Bend, she was too stubborn to give up Ryan Baxter. Not that she'd ever had him, she thought wryly, or was even likely to. She was on the shelf now, like so many other Southern ladies, and she'd never been beautiful, or even pretty.

She and Cinnamon remained in the center of the road, forcing Ryan Baxter to slow. She saw the straight figure tense, saw the wariness creep into his face. His hair was the same sun-glazed gold she remembered, and the eyes were still as blue as a clear fall sky but the mischief was gone from them. His frame, once lean and muscular, was now thin, his brown denim work clothes hanging on him. He looked a decade older than his years, but then, most men did today. War had aged an entire generation. They had seen hell, and they would never be the same. *She* wasn't the same.

"Ryan," she said softly. "I heard you'd come home."

Weariness deepened the crevices in his face. He met her eyes directly, though, and his mouth attempted a smile. "Miss Saunders." He acknowledged her with the easy courtesy she remembered. But the wariness didn't leave his gaze, and she had the impression that he was bracing himself for a blow. Cinnamon danced nervously under her, as if she sensed the disquiet in her. His reply, as courteous as it was, was a very careful question. She bit her lip, knowing the kind of reaction he must have received here.

"How long have you been back?"

"Long enough to enrage the entire town," he said. "I seem to be a talking, walking insult."

"They're just surprised," she said. "Give them time."

"And Jeremy? Has he heard?"

She nodded.

"He's also... surprised?" His voice was wry, accepting. And vulnerable. His face didn't show any emotion, but she saw the tension in his body, and the quick flicker of hope in his eyes. Her heart broke for him.

"Yes," she said quietly.

"And you?"

"I don't think the word *surprise* exactly fits."

"What does fit, Miss Saunders, since you're so... good with words? Or should I say careful with them."

She smiled suddenly, but his expression didn't change. It was just as watchful and wary as before. "I'm glad you're home."

"Why?" The question was as blunt as a hundred-pound stone being dropped.

"Because of Miss Sarah." Because Milly, Sarah Baxter's maid, called Mrs. Baxter "Miss Sarah," everyone else did too. At least the few who bothered to visit her.

"I don't think I made my mother's life any easier."

"I think your being here does."

His expression disagreed. She wished those wonderful blue eyes would glint roguishly at her. But they didn't. The silence lengthened between them, but then he shifted his weight slightly, as if impatient to leave. "I'm sorry... about your parents and David," he finally said. "And Jeremy. I heard about his arm."

Cherise's eyes started to mist. They always did when she thought about her family, especially David and Jeremy. Her parents, at least, had had love and a family. David would have none, and Jeremy... he didn't believe he could have one now, not as a cripple. She hated that word. Especially when Jeremy used it to describe himself. She nodded, unable for a moment to say anything, and then she rattled out the first thing in her mind. "Are you going to stay?"

He hesitated and shrugged. "My mother wants to stay, and I can't leave her now. I hadn't realized how fragile she'd become. It's been ... difficult having a ... turncoat as a son."

The blankness in his eyes lifted a moment, and she saw the bleakness beneath it, the raw, stark loneliness. It deepened the lines in his face, lines that had transformed the classic handsomeness of his features to sharp angles.

But the pride was still there, despite his words. He had been making an observation, not an apology.

"I should have come by earlier and welcomed you," she said slowly. "I didn't know..." Her voice trailed off.

Surprise flickered across his face. He raised an eyebrow. "Welcome?"

She smiled at his reaction. "Is that the first?"

"Yep," he said, "and, I expect, the last. General Sherman sure as hell didn't make my return any easier."

The smile left her face. "No," she said simply. "He didn't have to... burn every house."

"Except Baxter Trace," Ryan said wryly. "I almost wish he'd burned it along with the others."

"That wouldn't have helped anything."

"No," he agreed. He stared down at the ground. "I thought perhaps Jeremy..."

"Jeremy least of all," she said honestly. He had to know, to be prepared. "He feels the most betrayed."

"And you, Miss Saunders?"

"I didn't approve of either side. They were all thieves, as far as I was concerned." And it was true. The Confederates had robbed as much as the Union, though they hadn't burned so ruthlessly. She had stood and watched them take her best horses, her milk cow, the mules.

He grinned suddenly. His smile wasn't as wide or as natural as it once had been, but she still felt as if stormy skies had opened and a ray of sunlight had struck her.

"Not a popular viewpoint around here," he observed wryly.

"No," she agreed. She moved Cinnamon a few feet and looked at the back of the wagon. "A tree?"

He grimaced. "Not a very fine one, but I'm... still regaining strength."

"Your mother said you were wounded and sent to—"

"Libby Prison," he said shortly, abruptly cutting off the conversation. "You'd better move on, Miss Saunders, before anyone sees you talking to me."

"I don't care," she said stubbornly.

"And Jeremy?" he asked.

She couldn't miss the regret in his voice, even pain, despite the fact he tried to disguise it.

"Jeremy doesn't like a lot of things I do, and I don't like a lot of things he does," she replied tautly.

He looked at her then, his blue eyes darkening as they studied her. "I heard you ran Oak Bend by yourself after your father died."

"With Cecil's help," she said. "He's gone now, though. We couldn't pay him, and he has a family."

"And Jeremy?"

He kept coming back to Jeremy. She wondered whether he knew how much he was revealing by doing that. Her hands clenched into fists. "He's trying."

His hands tightened on the reins. "I'd better go, Miss Saunders."

"You used to call me Cherise."

"You used to wear pigtails and pinafores."

"It isn't gallant to remember." She offered the rebuke with a smile.

"Gallantry disappeared a long time ago," he said wearily.

She felt her smile disappear. "Yes."

His face darkened. "Nothing...happened?"

"Other than pillaging and robbery and burning?" she asked. "And a few killings here and there?" But she knew exactly what he meant, what he was asking. "No."

He closed his eyes for a moment, and she knew it was relief he felt, and she felt her heart knock against her rib cage.

But when his eyes opened again, they were distant. "Thank you for visiting my mother. She needed friends."

"I like her," Cherise said simply. And she did. She always had.

He tried to smile, but the result was only a bitter grimace. "A lot of people liked her, but not enough, it seems, to forget her rogue son."

"A lot of people don't have time for visiting these days," she pointed out.

"And that's the reason they don't come to Baxter Trace?"

"One of them."

The smile suddenly turned real, nearly blinding her with its force. "You're a liar, Miss Saunders, but I thank you for it, and I thank you for your welcome, especially as it's the only one I believe I'll get."

"I *am* glad you're home," she said, her hands clenching together nervously, her heart fluttering like some wounded butterfly.

The smile dropped from his lips. "I wish—"

But she never discovered what he wished, for he interrupted the partial sentence with a nod. He clicked the reins, and the horses started moving, forcing her backward. She watched him move away, his back still stiff, shoulders still straight. There was a quiet desperation in that lone figure that came close to breaking her heart.

# Chapter Two

As he drove away from Cherise Saunders, Ryan's back was so stiff he thought it might well break. And God knew he didn't need any additional injuries to his body.

Her heart had been in her eyes, just as it had been when she was fifteen.

Her fierce streak of independence hadn't dimmed, either, or she wouldn't have welcomed him when everyone else had turned their backs, both literally and figuratively. He cursed under his breath. There was something else. The appealing child had turned into a very attractive woman.

He had always been enchanted by her. She'd never had the look of a classic beauty, but she'd had a zest for living that delighted him. As a child, she'd been a free spirit, and he'd always had a soft spot for her, ever since that day she lit into a boy twice her size who was tormenting her dog. He'd thought of her often in Libby, in the isolation cell where he spent so much time, mainly because he was a Southerner in a Yank's uniform. He'd pictured, over and over again, the sheepish "I'm caught" look that last time he'd seen her, her face buried in a forbidden book.

He'd chosen to remember Cherise because she represented the good things about his former life. She had been so impossibly young, full of curious innocence and well-being, a quiet mischief lighting the gamine face as she suffered his inspection of her book. She had been far too young for him, and yet those wide, admiring eyes had remained in his mind during years of war, when more beautiful faces had not.

He caught himself smiling slightly. She had the greenest eyes he'd ever seen, even more spectacular since they dominated a thin, pixieish face. He had thought his preoccupation with her during his time in prison was only because she represented something fresh and untouched. He was stunned now to realize that it had evidently run deeper than that; sheer want had rampaged through him minutes ago. She was no longer a child, that much was obvious. She had been tempered, forged by grief and tragedy and obviously made strong by it. He'd heard from his mother the way she'd somehow kept at least a part of Oak Bend alive through sheer determination.

But those memorable eyes were the same, and they still shone with mischief and determination and, hell, just plain life. He'd wanted to reach out and grab some of it.

He knew better, though. He had practically destroyed his mother. He wasn't going to destroy Cherise, too, by linking her with the pariah he'd become. And he knew, deep down to his soul he knew, that he was no longer the man he'd once been. Four years of war and imprisonment had destroyed all the good things in him: laughter and hope and faith. He was a walking shell, nothing more.

And so he'd been rude, cutting off her questions and driving away. He couldn't explore that slight invitation in her eyes, the surprising friendliness he had not expected, especially after his trip to town to see Doc Colburn. People he'd known his entire life had turned their backs to him; those who hadn't had cursed him. One had even spit on him, while others applauded. He'd known then that coming back had probably been a mistake, but he couldn't give up. Not now.

He reached the road that forked off into Baxter's Trace, still thinking of Cherise Saunders and that astounding welcome home. Some of the suffocating heaviness lifted from around his heart. Perhaps there was a small shaft of hope after all. He didn't want to leave, didn't want to admit defeat, not after everything he'd gone through these past years. Baxter Trace was his, by God, and he owed it to himself, and to others, to change it from the hell he remembered into something fine.

As he stopped the wagon in front of the sprawling Georgian house, Milly, the one remaining servant, came running out, panic written all over her face. "Mister Ryan, Miss Sarah, she done fell down the steps, and I can't wake her."

Ryan stepped quickly down and held out a hand to her. "Can you take the wagon into town for the doctor?"

"Yes, suh. I've been doing a lot of things I ain't never expected to do, Mister Ryan."

He nodded. He'd seen as much in the time he'd been home. "Where is she?"

"Bottom of the stairs. I was scared to move her."

"You were right," Ryan said. "You drive as fast as you can."

She chucked the reins with some expertise. Once Sarah's personal maid, she'd taken on more and more duties as the Baxter slaves slipped off, one by one. She'd been Sarah's nanny before Sarah's marriage to James Baxter, and her full loyalty had always been to her mistress. Seemingly ageless, Milly was the only former slave who remained at Baxter Trace.

He hurried up the steps and through the door, his steps quickening to a run when he saw the still form at the bottom of the stairs.

He knelt down. "Mother," he said. Then again. Louder. "Mother!" He heard the edge of panic in his voice, and forced calm into it.

He felt her pulse. It was slow but steady. His hands ran quickly over the now frail body, finding little but a large bump on the back of her head. He leaned down and picked her up. God, she was so light.

Ryan carried her up to the bedroom his parents had once shared and laid her down on the bed. It was not their marriage bed, nor was it the one he'd been born in. The house had been used as an Union hospital during Sherman's march to the sea, and every piece of furniture had been destroyed. Its usefulness was the reason Baxter Trace had survived when other homes hadn't.

She moaned slightly as her body met the hard mattress. "Radburn," she whispered, and he felt a stabbing pain at the mention of his brother.

"No," he said gently. "It's Ryan."

Her eyes opened, and she tried a smile, but it was faint at best.

"Ryan," she whispered. Her eyes closed again, and he could only guess as to what she was thinking.

He felt the familiar ache. Rad had been the oldest, and the favorite. Ryan had been the odd one, always questioning, always doubting. He'd never been comfortable with slavery, and he'd been happy that he was the second son and not expected to take over. His father had been proud, probably for the first time, when he decided to attend West Point, and prouder still when he received his commission. All that had ended, though, when Ryan elected to stay with the Union army, and he'd received a short, curt letter in which his father disowned him.

James Baxter had died in a horse fall three months later, and Radburn had inherited everything. Ryan's brother could have claimed an exemption from service because of his responsibilities; instead, he had promptly joined the Confederate army, in part, Ryan suspected, to compensate for Ryan's defection. Ryan felt responsible for that, too.

Damn, but he wished the doctor would arrive, even though he knew from a brief encounter in town that Dr. Thaddeus Colburn felt the same way about him as the rest of the town.

He paced the room, going frequently to the window and staring out at the bare branches of the huge oaks that lined the driveway. The front lawn, which had always been meticulously groomed, was now overgrown, weeds overtaking the flower beds his mother once loved so. Trampled, he supposed, by army horses and wagons full of wounded. The wind outside was rising; he heard it brush against the window, and he felt the chill in his bones.

And then he saw the horses, the staid black carriage, the black-dressed form of the doctor. He had gone to the doctor's office when he first arrived back here; he'd had a recurring fever since his wound and imprisonment. The doctor had examined him without the usual pleasantries, then merely nodded. "You seem fit enough," he said. "Fitter than most around here."

But then, Ryan had spent three months in a hospital, and another four in a Washington office, to recuperate from Libby Prison. He hadn't even been able to leave the prison on his own two feet. That hellhole would always be alive in his mind—and, damn it, his nightmares.

None of that mattered now, though, as Ryan went down the steps at a run.

The doctor barely looked at him when he stepped down from the seat. "Sarah?"

"She's upstairs. She regained consciousness for a moment, then..."

But Doc Colburn was already going up the stairs, faster than Ryan would have thought possible.

When they reached her room, Doc Colburn turned to him. "You stay out here. Milly, you come in with me."

Ryan shook his head. "She's my mother, damn it."

Colburn turned on him, his mouth grim. "Haven't you done enough? She's been alone these past years, except for Milly here, and a few of us trying to look in on her."

Ryan clenched his hands into fists. "I'm home now, and the war's over."

"Tell that to your military. They just took young Corey Reynolds to Athens for trial."

"Corey?"

"He's sixteen, and he objected to a soldier propositioning his sister," Colburn said bitterly. "It's against the law now to argue with a soldier of the Union army, even to protect one's own kin."

"I'm not—"

"But you were," Doc Colburn said. "Now wait outside until I'm finished, damn it, or..."

Ryan stepped outside. He didn't want to test the doctor. His mother couldn't lose one of the last friends she had. He leaned against the hall wall, waiting. He thought about Cherise Saunders, about young Corey, who'd been seven the last time Ryan saw him. He slammed his fist against the wall.

Cherise shed her jacket and went into the small main room of the house. Jeremy still hadn't started a fire. She sighed and went outside to bring in some firewood.

It was growing dark outside, and she stopped a moment to look at the first star of the night. As a child, she used to wish on it. She found herself doing it again.

"It's nearly Christmas," she whispered. "A time of peace. Please let there be some. It's time." She bit her lip, remembering her brother's angry face, Ryan's lined, tired one. Her heart hurt for them both. It also hurt for her.

One look at Ryan Baxter, and all those old feelings had flooded back. Only they weren't a child's fancies anymore. They were a woman's feelings. Her heart had thumped so loud, she was afraid he would hear it, and the core of her had seemed to melt at the sight of him. He'd looked so world-weary, yet that pride she'd always so admired still shone in his eyes, daring anyone to try and tamp it down. There'd been no apologies, no explanations, for his decision years ago—not to her, probably not to anyone.

Dear Mary in heaven, but she still cared. Cared to the bottom of her soul.

She went back in with her load, just as Jeremy emerged from his bedroom, his face still unshaven. "Where have you been?"

"I went for a ride," she said, setting the wood down next to the fireplace.

"It's cold."

"Cold didn't used to bother you." She looked at the fireplace. "Apparently it still doesn't. And a ride would do you good."

"Ever saddle a horse with one arm?" he asked bitterly.

"Have you even tried?" she retorted, and watched surprise flash across his face. Since he'd come home in April, she'd done nearly everything for him. His wound had been raw and bleeding, his mind even more so. She'd let him escape from pain in homemade whiskey, and now she wondered whether she'd done him a kindness.

His jaw set stubbornly as he purposely ignored her challenge. "Where did you go?"

"I saw Ryan," she said flatly.

"I told you . . ."

"I know what you told me. But he was my friend, as well as yours." It was a direct challenge.

"He's a damn traitor."

She studied him. His hair was dark brown, almost black, just as hers was, and his eyes as green. But now they were dull, and his hair was unwashed, and longer than he used to wear it. He just no longer seemed to care about anything but burying himself in the small room he'd made into his private cave.

"You need to shave," she said, changing the subject.

"Why?" he said bleakly. "To go dancing? To go to town to get fence posts I can't even put in the ground?"

"You can't if you don't try."

He glared at her for a moment, but then he fell into a chair and seemed to crumple in front of her eyes. "Why?" he asked. "We're going to lose everything anyway. Damn Yanks have seen to that. There's no way we can pay the taxes next year. Why work for some carpetbagger?"

"They might get some of Oak Bend," she said, "but not all of it. More and more of the workers are coming back, asking if they can work shares. But they need help, and you know more about planting than anyone around here."

"And where will we get seed money?"

"We can borrow some from the bank."

"No one's getting any loans now," he said. "I already asked."

That surprised her. "When?"

"Three weeks ago."

Three weeks ago. That initiative pleased her enough that she didn't get irritated that he hadn't mentioned it to her. At least he'd tried. Three weeks. That had been when he started drinking heavily again.

"Why didn't you tell me?"

His eyes finally met hers. "I wanted to wait until after Christmas."

She thought back. He had gone into town with Sooner. She had thought he'd just gone to a tavern; he'd been almost passed-out drunk when he'd returned. She remembered the tongue-lashing she'd given him.

"We'll try again."

He shrugged. "It's no use. There's no money. The bank's dependent on the government, and the newcomers, and they don't give a damn if we keep our land." He rose from the chair and went over to the pile of wood near the fireplace, awkwardly picking up several pieces with his one arm and letting them fall between the andirons. "I'm sorry about the fire," he said as he placed some kindling between them, then picked up a match from the container on the mantel and struck it on a stone, watching as the fire struggled to catch.

He looked so thin to her, so vulnerable, but Cherise felt her first hope in months; there was something left of the brother she remembered from before the war. He had tried. He just had to try again.

The flame was creeping up now, hugging the logs, and his eyes seemed fastened on it. She barely heard him when he started to speak again. "How...is Ryan?"

"He looks... older. Tired. He was in Libby, you know."

"At least he has both his arms," Jeremy said, the bitterness back.

"And *you* have friends," she said quietly.

"I don't have many of them left, thanks to him and his fellow Yanks," he said in a voice as full of pain as Ryan's had been. "He made his choice. He might have been the one who took our brother's life, or whose bullet took my arm. He was with the army that burned our home. He made war against his own."

"He did what he thought was right, just as you did."

"He just had to go against his father. That's all it was. And I would never have fought against my neighbors."

Cherise didn't agree with his first assumption, but she didn't have a ready answer for the latter argument. She, too, struggled with that. "It had to have been hard...."

He sneered. "Being on the winning side?"

"I don't think he believes he's won anything," she said.

Her brother shrugged. "I obviously can't tie you up to keep you from him," he said in a ragged voice. "But, so help me God, if he sets foot on Oak Bend..."

His mouth slammed shut, but the words echoed in the room as the fire finally started to blaze and some warmth crawled slowly into the room.

Cherise watched the flames dance, casting darting shadows across Jere's gaunt, hard features. Even as she started feeling the heat from the fire, a chill clamped around her heart. She thought of her wish. Of how many she had made in the past five years.

But maybe it was time now for one to come true. Just maybe.

She clung to that thought as she started their simple meal.

Dr. Thaddeus Colburn took off his coat as he entered his office. He was getting too old for this, but there wasn't another doctor within fifty miles, except for the Union army doctor, who attended only the occupying troops.

He had hoped to retire, leaving his practice to a young colleague. But his young partner had joined the Confederate army, had survived, and then, like so many others after the war, decided to go west, to get away from the killing ground.

He unlocked the door to his house. Locks were necessary now. The occupying army had brought camp followers and all sorts of other riffraff, and he had a few drugs in his office. Not nearly enough, but most of his patients couldn't pay him these days, and his supply was depleted. He'd given little more than a pinch of laudanum to Milly for Sarah Baxter. Sarah would be all right, but she would be bruised and hurting for the next several days.

He sighed. He'd told Milly to use it sparingly, since he had so little. At least Ryan Baxter had paid him, so he could purchase another small quantity. But, dear God, his quinine, acetated tincture and morphia were gone, his stores as empty now as they had been during the war. Only now it wasn't the blockade, it was lack of money.

Thaddeus hung the coat on a hook next to the door, noticing a bulge in one of his pockets. He didn't remember one being there, but then, he seldom paid attention to what he wore. He had taken off his coat at Baxter Trace, given it to Milly, and taken it from young Baxter—though Sarah's son didn't seem so young any more. Thaddeus felt a little ashamed of his attitude toward the boy. Ryan Baxter was a patient, after all, and he'd obviously had a hard time during the war. He had several slash wounds, a bullet hole, and some other scars. Thaddeus hadn't asked about them, and Ryan hadn't volunteered any information, except that he'd had a recurring fever since an infection he'd acquired at Libby.

But Thaddeus had lost too many friends to the Yanks, and he considered the withholding of medicine from the South nothing less than criminal. He also blamed the boy for his father's death. James Baxter had been beside himself after he heard Ryan was staying with the Yank army; he had taken to riding wildly through the woods and fields, jumping fences he had no business jumping at his age. And it was one such jump that had killed him.

He sighed heavily and investigated the pocket. Inside was an envelope loaded with greenbacks. He counted them slowly. Over two hundred dollars. He frowned. Young Baxter? Couldn't be. As far as he knew, the young man had only Army pay, and he certainly hadn't displayed any sign of wealth. When was the last time he'd investigated his pockets? A week? Longer?

He straightened up. He wasn't going to question this kind of gift. With a sudden lightness to his feet, he headed for his study to make out an order for supplies.

# Chapter Three

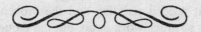

Ryan spent the morning cleaning out the horse barn. Only two horses remained, including the one he'd bought in Washington after being released from the hospital. They were getting used to each other now, but he missed his old mount, who had carried him through three years of war, only to be lost when he was wounded and captured.

The only other horse was an old mare, left by both the Confederate and Union armies because she was too old to be of any value to them.

All the good horses were gone, horses bred for speed and endurance by his father and his father's father. That was the one thing they'd agreed upon: the horses.

The barn evidently hadn't been cleaned since its use by the Union cavalry. There had been so damn much to do around the house that Ryan had made only superficial efforts with the barn. He was paying for the neglect now. Every muscle in his body complained. But, given the past year, the pain felt good. His strength was returning, slowly but steadily. If only the damn fever was gone for good, too.

He stopped raking out the last of the stalls and made his way to the open door. He never wanted to be closed in again, and the brush of cold air felt good to his skin. The sky was a pure blue today, so pure it hurt. A ray of sun hit his face, and he reveled in its warm, sensual feel.

He looked around at the overgrown grounds, the house that needed painting and the broken fences. There was so much work to do, but the thought challenged rather than daunted him. He needed work—hard, physical work—to take his mind away from the last four years. He needed to build, instead of destroying.

Ryan squinted when he saw a movement in the distance. His eyes darted to the rifle in the corner. Though he wanted peace, he knew his presence here had stirred anger, even raw hatred.

He forced his body into a relaxed position against the door as he watched the figure near, and then he stiffened when he identified the rider as Cherise Saunders. His eyes feasted on the faded but still attractive green riding costume, and the long, streaming hair pulled back by a ribbon. He had forgotten how well she rode, had ridden as a child, taking fences easily as she flew recklessly across pastures.

She had been making for the house, but then she saw him and turned the horse toward the barn, stopping just feet from him. "Dr. Colburn was over earlier to see Jere and said your mother had been injured," she said, looking down at him. "I wanted to see if she was all right."

He walked over and offered her his right hand. He felt it burn as her smaller gloved hand clasped it tightly and she slipped easily down. His other hand caught her waist, and her hand remained in his as she stood and looked up at him, while his own arm stayed around her longer than was proper. He knew he should release her, but he couldn't.

Her vivid green eyes met his, and he had to struggle to catch his breath. For a moment, it seemed the fever had returned, for he felt a strange kind of numbing warmth.

She felt good, soft but not fragile, and he found himself hungering to pull her close, to touch that curling, windblown hair that looked like silk. He closed his eyes, fighting himself, fighting the reactions she so unexpectedly created in him. He felt a pull in his lower regions, and, just as strong, an aching need for something tender in his life.

But he was poison to her now.

He opened his eyes and moved away. "She'll be glad to see you," he said, keeping his voice impersonal. "Thank you for coming. She gets lonely." He turned away. "You said Doc Colburn saw Jere. Anything wrong?"

"Not more than usual. He still has a lot of pain. The wound hasn't healed well, not well enough to...use anything artificial, and he feels so helpless."

Damn, but he knew exactly how Jere felt. They both used to think themselves invulnerable. They had courted the same girls, had raced each other, had even fought each other, except when someone else attacked one of them. Then they had fought together.

Until the war.

"I'll take care of your horse," he said.

She smiled at him. It was a breathtaking smile. No, heartbreaking, because he wanted to grab her and kiss her, and while it might be right for him, it would only be trouble for her.

"Thank you," she said, and walked quickly to the house.

He led the mare into one of the newly cleaned stalls and took the bit from its mouth. He then gave her fresh water and some oats he'd bought for his own mount. She whinnied her pleasure, and he realized they were probably a rare treat these days. The Saunderses were in as much financial trouble as nearly every family left in the county.

He wished he could do something about it. He had money. He'd used damn little of his pay in the past five years, instead sending nearly all of it to his West Point roommate's brother in New York to bank and invest. He had felt from the beginning that this was not going to be a short war. Ryan knew the South, knew its sons would fight to the bitter end, and he'd realized there would be precious little left. He hadn't known exactly how little until he came home, traveling past hundreds of burned houses and thousands of acres of ravaged fields.

Ryan could use the money to rebuild Baxter Trace, while watching his neighbors go under, one by one. He could say it was their own fault for putting everything they had into Confederate bonds and script. But he wouldn't do that. He wanted to rebuild Baxter Trace, but he also wanted to help rebuild Hope's Way. Still, no one was going to take one dime from him; he knew that as well as he knew anything.

His stallion nickered softly, wanting some attention of his own, and he thought about saddling the horse and taking a ride, delaying his return until he knew Cherise was gone. She was too much of a temptation.

He could ride through the fields, trying not to remember what they once had been. He could go to town, where he'd probably wind up in a fight; it had taken every bit of his willpower not to do exactly that days ago. Or, he thought suddenly, he could visit Jere. Maybe...just maybe, there would be a remnant of friendship remaining. If Cherise...

He had not visited Oak Bend since he'd returned, partly because he'd been so busy trying to restore some dignity to Baxter Trace, and therefore to his mother. But he also remembered the hatred on the faces of the townspeople, even those of women he'd once courted. He hadn't wanted to see that on Jere's face.

Ryan looked down at his clothes. He was wearing work clothes now, cotton shirt and denim trousers stained by sweat and smelling of horses. He'd discarded his uniform the day his resignation became final, but he was still wearing blue as far as everyone here was concerned.

Still, he wanted to see Jere, his friend for so many years. Maybe, just maybe, he would understand. Ryan quickly saddled his horse and left the barn in a canter.

Sarah Baxter looked even more fragile than usual in the bed. But she was stronger than she appeared, though it had taken Cherise years to realize that. Cherise hadn't liked Sarah's husband, Ryan's father.

He had always reminded her of a bully, and Baxter Trace had had the reputation of being harsh with its people.

But once James Baxter died, Sarah had seemed to blossom, coming into her own, and, like Cherise, had managed the plantation in the absence of any male family members. The two of them had become good friends during the past few years, especially as Sarah Baxter became more and more isolated from her neighbors after her Confederate son died, leaving only the Union one.

Her oldest son's death had hit Sarah hard, and probably only Cherise knew how she had worried about Ryan during the years when there was little or no news from the North. His father had destroyed the tintypes of him, all except one Sarah had managed to save. Cherise had found her looking at it often, although she said little. Sarah Baxter seldom showed emotion, probably, because it had been locked within during her married life with a man who despised any kind of weakness, or what he perceived as weakness.

Milly had answered the door and given Cherise a big smile, "She be mighty glad to see you, Miss Cherise."

"How is she?"

"Stiff and sore. Her eyesight isn't so good, and she stumbled on the steps." Milly had looked worried. "She won't tell Doc Colburn or Mr. Ryan and won't let me tell them. She didn't say nothing about you, though," she added slyly.

Cherise nodded. "I'll tell them."

Milly nodded with satisfaction.

Cherise had followed her to the bedroom, and Sarah looked at her intently from the bed. "Did you see Ryan?"

Cherise nodded.

Sarah's mouth worked as her eyes asked the question that she apparently couldn't put into words.

"He's as handsome as ever," Cherise said, and Sarah's anxious look eased. "I saw him yesterday. Didn't he mention it?"

Sarah shook her head. The anxious look was back in her eyes.

"I told him I was glad to see him."

Sarah smiled then. "Come sit next to me and tell me all about it."

Ryan felt sick as he rode up the driveway to Oak Bend. The main house had once been the most graceful structure in the county, and now only crumbling fireplaces gave any evidence of where it had once stood. He ached for both Cherise and Jere as he remembered the house, the picnics held under the sweet-smelling magnolia trees. Those, too, were gone, probably cut for firewood.

Smoke was coming from the chimney of the overseer's house, and he guided his horse in that direction. The slave cabins were gone, and so was the big barn. He was surprised that the one structure still stood, but his mother had told him that Cherise had stood at the door, refusing to move, and finally the officer had relented. It sounded like her, he thought, and he felt a gentling inside, a flicker of warmth in a space grown cold.

And Jere? He'd lost so much. Most of his family. His arm. His home.

Ryan dismounted and went to the door, his hand rapping against it. There was a shuffling inside, then footsteps, and the door opened. Ryan came face-to-face with Jeremy Saunders.

His boyhood friend stared at him, stunned at first. Then anger suffused a face that was much too pale. He had shaved, but his hair was long and uncut and his clothes hung on him. One sleeve was empty, pinned up. Jere's eyes, lifeless when he'd first opened the door, turned a vivid green with fury. "What in the hell are you doing here?"

God, it was good to see him alive. Even angry as he was at the moment.

"I wanted to see you."

"Now you've seen. Or did you just come to look at what your army did? Well, it did a damned thorough job. Now get off my land."

Ryan's hand reached out. It was an automatic movement, an entreaty he couldn't stop. "Jeremy—?"

Jere stepped back as if the hand were a snake. "You've won. Take your damn victory and go," he said bitterly.

"No one won," Ryan said. "God knows I didn't."

"You're trespassing," Jere said coldly. "Of course, we're damn used to Yanks trespassing and taking what they want. What do *you* want?"

Ryan wanted what he couldn't have. He swallowed, nearly choking on words that had to remain buried within him. *A friend. The best parts of the past. Memories untouched by death.*

He dropped his arm. It wasn't pride. He didn't have much pride anymore. It was uselessness. Hopelessness. The futility of trying to find something lost forever. "Nothing," he said slowly. His eyes raked over his friend, remembering so many things, everything but the hatred in his eyes.

"I'll go," he said wearily. "If you need . . ."

"I won't," Jeremy said. "I won't need anything from a traitor. We'll make it just fine." He backed away from the door and slammed it, leaving Ryan alone on the step.

He took a step backward, leaned on a wood post. At least there was some fight left in Jeremy. It was more than he'd seen in a lot of faces here. But it hurt. That hatred hurt. Dear God, how it hurt.

Cherise looked for Ryan when she left Sarah Baxter. He was gone, and so was the horse that had been in the barn when he'd taken Cinnamon.

She didn't know why she felt such a crushing disappointment. He'd made it clear he didn't want her. This morning was the second time he'd left abruptly, obviously avoiding her.

Because she was a part of a community that rejected him? Or because he still looked on her as a child? Or was it because he didn't want any reminders of the past?

He'd looked so handsome this morning, his hair blowing in the wind, those blue eyes so steady and intense. He'd looked spectacular in his blue uniform years ago, but the work clothes he wore now also suited him. His body, so lean and rangy, had an elemental grace to it that she hadn't remembered. She recalled the sudden heat that had surged through her when he helped her down, and now her body reacted to it again.

She led Cinnamon out to the block that was outside the barn, and used it to mount, wishing once more that she could ride astride and fly over the fields. There were so many disadvantages to growing up, to being at least a reasonably proper young lady. No, she thought, correcting herself. An old maid. At twenty-two, nearly twenty-three, she certainly qualified.

Cherise patted the pouch on the side of her saddle. She'd brought a book with her, one of her few remaining luxuries. They were scarce now, and her time to read even scarcer. There was always so much to do. Clothes to wash and mend, food to cook, vegetables and fruits to can. Fences to patch, chickens to feed and eggs to gather, and trips to town to sell them. She had even mended the roof. She could do all that now, and more. She'd learned that necessity was a good teacher, and she took pride in every newly acquired skill. If only Jere...

If only Jeremy felt the same. But he would. She knew he would. Something just had to jerk him out of the shock caused by all his losses. Hers were minor compared to his. She hadn't seen friends die next to her, hadn't suffered the excruciating pain of amputation. But she couldn't force herself to return quite yet, to see those blank eyes and feel that pervasive bitterness. Instead, she turned Cinnamon toward the creek, toward her secret place, where she'd always gone to read and be alone, where she had seen Ryan Baxter that day so many years ago.

* * *

Ryan wasn't sure why he'd ridden to the small glade just inside the Saunders's property. Perhaps because of its peace. Perhaps because its quiet beauty reminded him of Cherise, of the days before the war.

He dismounted and stood by the quiet, bubbling creek, understanding why Cherise had made this her place. He hadn't had time for peace before West Point. He'd been so damned rebellious, too busy gobbling up life without understanding what was important. He'd been the rogue of the county—drinking, fighting, racing, whoring. He was still that rogue, he supposed, but in a far different way. The word was whispered now in far different terms, certainly not with the smiling indulgence of prewar days.

The day he made his decision to stay with the North had, in fact, been the day he grew up. The day he'd realized the consequences of a conscience that had, until then, been fairly dormant.

Ryan leaned against a tree, listening to the bright, cheery calls of the winter birds, and the scurrying of squirrels through the trees. He'd heard damn little of that during the war. Constant troop movement, the pounding of guns and the tramping of feet quieted all those sounds, stilled all normal living things. Dear God, but the thought deepened the aching in him, the loneliness that had been with him for so long. He'd thought he had prepared himself for Jere's reaction, but still it had been like a fist in the gut.

But then the chattering quieted, and an instinct honed by war made him stiffen. He heard hoofbeats on the soft ground, the neigh of a horse and the answering whinny of his own mount.

He knew it was Cherise, and now he wondered whether he'd conjured her out of sheer need. But she was no dream as she came into sight. Her eyes widened with recognition, and her mouth smiled with something like delight.

How long had it been since anyone had smiled at him like that? If he received no other Christmas present, this would be enough, he thought, even if he couldn't take any more than the memory of it.

He kept his face empty, his eyes shuttered—at least he hoped to hell he did—as she approached and slid easily down from her mare. "I missed you at Baxter Trace," she said softly.

"I went to see Jeremy," he said, his voice harsher than he'd intended.

The smile left her face, and she tipped her head. Waiting for him to continue.

He shrugged, trying to feign indifference. "I wasn't welcome. But then, I didn't expect to be."

But he'd hoped. Hoped against hope that some small piece of friendship remained.

Cherise was silent, watching him. He'd never met a woman before who was good at silence. It wasn't awkward or demanding. More like giving him time to sort out his thoughts. No cheery words, or false optimism. Just supportive understanding.

"He's still hurting," she said finally.

"I know," he said. "I can't even imagine what it might be like to lose a part of yourself."

She turned away from him and stared at the creek. "I think you do," she said, surprising him again. She *had* grown up.

He looked at her, standing under the naked limbs of a giant oak whose gnarled roots seem to twist in a kind of agony. Her green dress was the only spot of bright color among the brown and gray of weathered leaves and ancient trunks. Her body seemed to radiate a kind of energy, the tilt of her head a pride that couldn't be trampled.

"Why did you come back?" she asked finally.

Why had he? It was a damn good question. His mother? That was the reason he'd said aloud, but it wasn't entirely the truth. Because he wanted to prove something? Partly that, too, he supposed. He wasn't going to run from a decision he'd made.

But neither was the real reason. "This is home," he said simply.

"You're going to stay, then?" She turned back to face him.

"Yes."

"There's already been talk of a lynching," she said.

"I'm not surprised," he replied. "I didn't expect a parade."

"Why did you stay with the Union?" she said suddenly. "Jere always thought..."

"I would change my mind?" Suddenly weary, he leaned against a tree again. "That I was just spiting my father?"

She nodded.

He hesitated, but then he felt an overwhelming need to talk. He hadn't discussed his reasons with anyone. They had been too intensely personal, too connected to pain he'd disguised as indifference. "When I was eight, and you, young lady, were still in swaddling clothes..." He stopped for a moment, juggling that image with what he wanted to say. Another defense, he thought, to protect what meant most to him. A pleasing memory, to cover an unbearable one.

But her face was looking earnestly up to his, urging him to continue. "I had a friend . . . the son of one of the slaves," Ryan said slowly. "We used to play together, went fishing on warm afternoons, and I taught him my lessons. My father caught me doing that, and two days later, Cal was sold. Away from Baxter Trace, away from his mother. Away from me. I had to learn, my father said, that slaves were simply property. Damn it, Cal *wasn't* property. He was my friend, and he suffered from something I did. I never forgave my father for that. All my hell-raising was pure defiance, and I went to West Point because I couldn't even pretend to respect him or what he stood for. I couldn't stay on Baxter Trace and condone what he was doing. And I couldn't fight for it, either."

Cherise was standing still, so very still he wasn't sure whether she'd heard what he said, whether she understood. Her green eyes were intent on his, full of emotion he couldn't decipher.

"I killed him, Cherise. I killed my father, just as surely as if I'd put a gun to his head," he said. "Maybe even my brother. Maybe he wouldn't have joined if I hadn't—"

"Your father was always racing all over the county," she said softly. "You know that." Her hand went up to his face, her fingers so gentle on his skin. His arms went around her, holding her closely, even desperately. He was searching for a foothold, grabbing a piece of whatever solid he could find.

His lips touched her hair, and then her face turned upward and his lips touched her cheek. He tasted something salty, and realized they were tears. Tears for him. Tears he hadn't realized existed for him. That foothold disappeared again, and he felt himself swept up by a force he couldn't control as his lips met hers and his world exploded.

# *Chapter Four*

Cherise had thought her heart might break as she listened to him. She could see them all: the bewildered boy, the young, defiant hellion, the soldier caught between two loyalties, and now the weary, soul-wounded man his friends called renegade.

She hadn't really understood his decision years ago, not until now, but he had never left her thoughts or her heart. And now she wanted to heal, to soothe, the hurts she guessed he had never revealed to anyone else.

She lifted his face and saw the clefts worn into his face, the starkness of it, the torment in eyes usually so disciplined and then his lips came down on hers, and she had the dream she'd dreamed for so long.

It was even more spectacular than she'd ever imagined.

The kiss was angry. Hungry. Desperate. So powerful that, had he not been holding her, her legs would probably have folded under her. Her heart beat so hard she could scarcely believe it remained inside her. And then another sensation started, a brand-new one, wrapping its way up and down her spine and lodging in a suddenly writhing place inside her.

She was drowning in a whirlpool of sensation and emotion and need. The sky was no longer clear, the air no longer fresh. There was barely contained raw, sensual energy, instead—emotional thunder and lightning that slashed and roared between them. Her lips responded readily to his, readily and naturally, and the storm gained strength and violence.

His tongue probed the entrance of her mouth with an intimacy she'd never known before, creating another wave of sensation to wash over the first. She opened her lips and felt him explore hungrily, spreading a honeyed, teasing warmth throughout her body. The warmth became heat and then fever, as her body moved instinctively into his and she felt the hard leanness of his frame. He groaned suddenly—it was a stifled sound from deep within his throat—and his kiss deepened, became even more insistent. She felt him tremble, and something about that unexpected vulnerability slammed through her, and her body pressed deeper into his. She wanted more of these marvelous, tumultuous, achingly exquisite sensations. She wanted more of him, of his heart, of his touch, more of . . . everything.

She'd waited a lifetime for them, for him.

His mouth left hers, and she felt his lips against her cheek, then at the curve of her neck, and the yearning inside her grew so great she felt propelled by some great tidal wave of wanting.

"Cherise," he whispered in a hoarse voice. "Dear God, but this shouldn't happen."

She looked up at him and smiled. "Of course it should," she said. "I've been waiting forever."

Surprise, then something else, something preciously close to amusement, darted through his eyes. She wanted him to smile. She would have sold her soul for one of those old smiles. For any smile at all.

He didn't move his body, but he leaned back to look at her closer. "You're a forward young lady," he said solemnly, but she thought, she hoped, she detected just the tiniest humor in it.

"I'm on the shelf," she said primly, unable to hold back a glint of mischief as she said the words. "An old maiden lady, and, as such, can indulge myself."

"An old maiden lady? Hmm..." he said, obviously considering the statement, as his eyes studied her with something like a real smile in them now, and her heart jumped crazily. It was all she could do to stay still, to keep her face from showing exactly how he affected her, how much she cared. Part of her body still clung against his in a way that was most improper. But propriety, as far as she was concerned, had disappeared a long time ago. "I think I like old maiden ladies."

"Do you now, sir?" she said teasingly. Her hand went up to his face, touching his mouth, trying to coax it, too, into a smile—to match that all-too-fleeting one in his eyes. It twitched slightly. "You used to have a wonderful smile," she said wistfully.

"I'm surprised you remembered," he said. "You were just..."

"Old enough to be madly in love with you," she confessed. She had never thought she would do that, but somehow her confessions seem to lighten some of that darkness around him. "You didn't think I was terrible for reading *The Scarlet Letter*."

"I wasn't your parent."

She chuckled. "No, you certainly weren't."

He did smile then, his mouth bending at both sides. It wasn't wide and careless and full of deviltry like the old one, but infinitely more precious for its rarity. He caught her fingers. "How did you remain so untouched?"

She felt her own smile fade. "I'm not untouched. I've just learned to bend with the wind, instead of allowing it to break me."

His smile changed, one side of his lips pulling down, giving him a quizzical look. "I think you challenged that wind a few times."

"But you took on the whole hurricane."

"And got broken for it."

"No," she said softly. "I don't think so." She leaned her head against his heart, just resting there, letting the warmth settle comfortably between them, even though the heat was building again. His arms went around her once more, holding her lightly.

Cherise heard the whisper of his breath, the steady beat of his heart. She was comforted by the quiet strength that was even more appealing than the reckless verve of the youthful rogue. She knew now how much courage it had taken for him to come back, how much his decision and its consequences had hurt him.

"I'm glad you came home," she said.

"You're the only one."

"Your mother..."

"I've made things worse for her. Now the few friends she had won't come."

"Then they aren't friends."

"That doesn't make her less lonely."

"She's more worried about you than herself," she said.

He looked at her in surprise.

"She asked me if I'd been nice to you... or that's what she meant. I think she would have thrown me out if I'd said no. She's stronger than anyone thinks she is."

A kind of wistfulness passed across his face. "I know... she misses my brother."

She stretched up on tiptoe and kissed him again, wanting to bring back the fierceness, the fire that had flamed between them. She wanted that fire, not only for herself, but for him, as well. But his lips, when they touched hers, had gentled. They caressed, like the gentle drops of a spring rain or the first rays of sun after a storm. And there was nothing else in the world for her, nothing but Ryan Baxter.

Ryan knew he should stop now, before he couldn't. He felt like a too tightly strung wire, so taut he might snap at any moment. It had been years since he'd touched a woman like this, and he needed that acceptance in her eyes as dearly as he needed her touch. And he needed that as he needed air to breathe.

She smelled so fresh, so clean. The scent of roses and soap melded together in a bewitching combination that was like nectar after so many years in camp and battle and prison. It was life!

But he knew, too well, the price of divided loyalties. He could never make her choose between her brother and him, and if he didn't stop this, now, that would happen. And she would live with the same hell he had.

He couldn't let go, though. The need was too compelling, the touch too sweet. So he absorbed, memorized, treasured, and then, using all the willpower he could, he pulled away.

"Don't go," she whispered. "Don't run away again."

"I'm not running away, little one," he said, using the affectionate name he used to call her, hoping it would instill some sense in him. She was younger than he... and innocent...

She was also a woman, he argued with himself. Everything about her was womanly.

And she was the sister of a man who hated him. He couldn't get past that. He couldn't, for her sake, for Jeremy's.

He stepped back. "You're too much a temptation, little one," he said. "I won't be a wedge between you and Jeremy, you and this whole blasted town."

"Jeremy..."

"I just saw Jeremy. He's not going to change his mind about me, and he needs you." He walked over to her mare and held out his hand to her. She hesitated, her eyes dominating that pixie face that had always so appealed to him. There was so much else now that drew him to her: a strength and courage that humbled him. He'd discovered long ago that the people the soldiers left behind were often the true heroes. They kept the farms going, their families together. They persevered. Soldiering represented a few moments of terror and an eternity of boredom. It wasn't difficult being brave in the midst of an army, where everyone else had the same fears. It must take incredible bravery to survive alone.

She moved suddenly, as if she'd made up her mind to something. She gave him a hand and allowed him to lift her up into the saddle. Then she looked down at him. "I won't give up, you know," she said, with a cocky little smile.

He found himself smiling back. Foolishly. He shook his head. "Don't do what I did. Don't cut yourself in half."

"But I already have," she said, and lightly touched her mare's withers, sending it into a canter before he could answer.

Calvin Sooner handed Jere the bottle of home-made whiskey and watched as Jere poured each of them a glass.

"Where's your sister?" he asked.

Jere shrugged.

"I thought I might ask her to go riding."

Jere straightened in his chair, surprised. Cherise disliked Calvin Sooner. His family had had a small unkept farm with two or three slaves. Jere had never paid much attention to him prior to the war—they'd been in separate worlds—but now Calvin had something he wanted.

Calvin and Cherise? Never! He took another look at Calvin, a closer one. Calvin had been conscripted the second year of the war and, as far as Jere knew, had served honorably, although his fortunes appeared to improve. He never seemed to work, and he always had plenty of liquor, which he shared with Jere.

"I don't think Cherise is interested in courting now," Jere said cautiously.

Calvin plopped himself down on a chair. "Every woman wants to be married, and there ain't too many choices anymore."

Anger started to flare inside Jere. Calvin had just dismissed Jere's lifelong friends, both dead and alive. The ones alive were like him, trying desperately to hold on to what little they still had. They had no time for courting, no futures to offer.

"And I have money," Calvin said. "Enough to pay taxes on this place next year." It was an offer, plain and simple, to buy his sister.

"How do you know what the taxes are?" Jere asked, feeling suddenly sick. Where had Calvin gotten that kind of money?

"Oh, I made it a point to know. That new clerk likes my brew as much as you do."

The glass in Jere's hand started to shake. He looked down. His hand was trembling. He hoped like hell Sooner didn't notice. Sweet Jesus, the man was comparing him to that sniveling little clerk from Washington. He put the glass down.

But apparently Sooner didn't realize it. "I can help you rebuild here," he said, oblivious of the fury building in Jere's eyes. "There's new times coming, for them that's smart enough to grab opportunity."

"How did you grab opportunity?" Jere asked quietly.

Calvin shrugged, proud of his own initiative. "There were ways. Yank prisoners, mostly. They were real grateful for favors at Andersonville." He changed the conversation. "You used to be friendly with Baxter, didn't you?"

"Before the war," Jere said in a strained voice.

"Well, there's talk he's gonna be burned out." Calvin's voice turned sly. "Thought you might like to join the party."

The sickness fermenting in Jere settled in his stomach, and he thought he might empty it then and there. He had no use for Ryan Baxter, but he had even less for this . . . scavenger. Why hadn't he seen it before?

He hadn't wanted to.

"No," he said. "I wouldn't be any use, with one arm."

"But you would," Calvin argued. "Just having you there would mean you're with us."

Jere shuddered inwardly at the prospect of joining Calvin and some of the other men he'd seen with him. "I don't feel up to it."

"Well, we'll be going Christmas Eve, if you change your mind." He stood up. "You'll ask Miss Cherise about my calling on her?"

Jere nodded, not standing. Self-disgust swamped him. What had he come to, if a man like Calvin Sooner thought he'd sell his own sister and burn out a former friend?

He rose from the chair where he'd spent so much time while Cherise worked. Hell, he himself had practically made his sister a slave. No wonder Sooner thought what he did. Because he'd craved the cheap whiskey to dull the pain, he'd encouraged Sooner. He hadn't known Sooner had been a guard at Andersonville, and he'd heard all the horror stories, even the trial of its commandant. The Northern prison camps hadn't been much better, but to trade off a man's misery . . .

His hand brushed the glass from the table where he'd put it. And then he took the damn jar outside and poured out the contents, watching it seep into the hard winter ground. The doc had said he could find him some kind of contraption to help him use what remained of his left arm. He had refused to listen, refused to admit it was gone forever.

And Ryan Baxter? He would have to fight his own battles. Jere had all he could manage with his own.

Jeff McDonald had been the town banker for forty years, and when Ryan left for California, he'd been robust and jolly.

Now he was weed-thin and tired-looking as Ryan entered his office. "You've received the money?" Ryan said.

McDonald nodded, his mouth pursed in a small frown. He wasn't sure whether he approved of this or not. "You know it's a risk?"

Ryan shrugged. "They can't get loans any other way."

"But at least you should have notes."

"If I got notes, they would know where the money was coming from."

"I don't like lying to them.... They're my neighbors...."

"Who need you and me to survive. I thought we went over all this the other day," Ryan said impatiently.

McDonald looked at him unhappily. He had been cold, even nasty, when Ryan Baxter entered the bank a week ago. And he'd been dumbfounded by Baxter's proposal to deposit a large amount of money to be used as collateral for loans to remaining families. The agreement was to be between McDonald and Baxter; no one else would know.

They had discussed, McDonald reluctantly, the needs of the families trying to survive, and their capabilities to do so. All of them were land-rich but no longer had cash or labor. They would have to turn to less labor-intensive crops and offer tenant farming. They needed cash to do that, cash for crops and taxes, and cash in the Hope's Way bank was scarce indeed. The only funds being deposited were from the Yanks occupying the town, and some of the speculators who had already started buying land.

McDonald had distrusted him, believing he was one of the vultures circling above, until he insisted that the loans have very liberal repayment terms and that his part not be mentioned at all.

"You could rebuild Baxter Trace with this," McDonald said speculatively.

Ryan shrugged. "We'll do as the others are doing," he said. "We'll build slow. We have good land."

McDonald stood, reaching out his hand to Ryan. "I wasn't sure you meant it, Ryan. But I'm grateful, not only for the bank, but for the town. If you need anything..."

Ryan took his hand. "Just make sure no one knows." He released the hand and started for the door, then turned back. "Thank you."

McDonald grinned. "Thank *you*. And merry Christmas. I'll let these folks know their loans are approved. That will be the best present they've had in a long time."

\* \* \*

*Merry Christmas.* Those could be lonely words. They *were* lonely words, yet Ryan felt a lift in his heart, a thread of optimism running through his mind. He was so damn tired of death and destruction. It was good to be a part of building.

But he wasn't a part of it, another voice said. He was as alone as he'd ever been. Those moments with Cherise had only served to show how alone.

If only...

If only pigs could fly, or the moon were really cheese. If only night were day, and dawns were always beautiful. If only there had been no war.

He thought of Cherise as she'd looked this morning, her cheeks flushed from the cool wind, her dark hair tumbling around her face, her eyes so... full of fresh, unawakened passion. They had sparkled with the new magic of it, and he'd... wanted her more than he'd wanted anything.

But he'd hurt enough people in his life.

He stepped quickly away from the door of the bank and down to the general store. He needed to buy some presents for his mother and Milly, some oats for his horse, and some sugar and coffee. He tried not to care as people moved away from him, even going down into the street to keep from sharing the common walk in front of the stores. There were men in blue uniforms, and people he didn't recognize. Newcomers. Carpetbaggers. But the people he'd known all his life moved to the street to avoid only him.

Ryan reached the store, knowing he would receive no welcome here, either. The only reason Sam Bascomb even served him, Ryan knew, was because he needed his greenbacks. There were several other people in the store, and Ryan looked around, trying to find a pretty shawl for his mother, a more practical one for Milly. Hostile eyes followed him around the room, and he knew that if thoughts were daggers he'd be dead. His gaze found a stack of books, and he couldn't resist them, even though he knew he had to watch his money—or what was left of it. He carefully chose two, finding himself smiling slightly as he added the second to his pile of goods. But the smile disappeared as he went over to the counter.

Sam Bascomb didn't acknowledge his presence, except to tally his purchases.

"How's Lisa?" Ryan tried gingerly. Lisa was Sam's daughter. She'd be about fourteen now.

No answer. Ryan shrugged, took his change. "Good day," he said, forcing sarcastic cheer into his voice.

"Why don't you just leave town, Ryan Baxter?" said a voice behind him and he turned to see Mary Bascomb.

"This is my home, Mrs. Bascomb," he said politely.

"We don't want you here."

Ryan fought to control his temper, his words. At least Mary Bascomb said what she thought.

"I know," he said gently. "But I'm staying."

He turned around and walked out.

## Chapter Five

Cherise knew better. She knew it to the tips of her toes. She knew she should stay away from Ryan Baxter—at least for a while.

But she couldn't.

It had been three days since last she had seen him. She had tried, for her sake and Jeremy's, not to seek Ryan out. Despite her brave words that afternoon, she wasn't sure she could survive too many similar encounters with Ryan. And he had enough problems, without her tagging behind him like some lovelorn child. Yet she couldn't forget that kiss, and every time she reviewed, minute by minute, their meeting, the tingling started again, that exquisitely curious tingling that both excited and troubled her.

Her excuse this time was camelias. Beautiful camelias, with a smell to delight the senses and petals like fine velvet. Somehow, two of her camelia bushes had survived the Union invasion, and now she tended them like babies. She had always loved flowers, loved gardening, as she loved the woods and the brook. Most of her garden had been destroyed with the house, but these two ladies—she always thought of them that way, as ladies—had been off the main path, and they had become a symbol of survival and the beginning of a new garden.

They were still in bloom now, the rose and white blooms lovely against the glossy thick leaves. She picked a bouquet and carefully bundled them in an old newspaper. Sarah Baxter loved flowers, too, and her garden had been totally destroyed during the occupation.

She took them to the stable and set them down, then went inside the house to tell Jeremy she would be gone for several hours. Jeremy had changed in the past three days. He still had his black moods, but he didn't seem to be drinking. When she returned after meeting Ryan, she guiltily had expected the usual interrogation over her whereabouts. Instead, he had been cleaning up, on his own, the remnants of a broken glass.

She had stared at him in amazement while he grinned crookedly. It had been a shadow of his old smile, but at least it had been something. "I threw it," he'd said. "I guess it's only fair I clean it up." And he had. Awkwardly, and with obvious frustration, but he had.

Later, over a dinner of beans mixed with a few precious pieces of bacon, he'd fumbled with a fork, then laid it down. His eyes didn't quite meet hers. "Calvin Sooner said he wanted to court you."

She'd sat there, shocked. Shocked not only at the comment but that Jere would even consider it.

But Jere continued, watching her. "He has money, he said. Enough to pay our taxes."

"You didn't—"

"Encourage him? Hell, no," he said, the shadow of a smile back again. "But I thought you should know, before I tossed him off the place..."

"I wouldn't marry him if he were the last man living."

He chuckled at her vehemence. It was the first time she'd heard that sound in a very long time, and she found herself smiling back companionably.

"I'm going to try the bank again," he said suddenly. "Put up more of the land, if we have to." He hesitated. "If that's all right with you?"

It was the first time he'd asked her opinion since he'd been back, the first sign he'd shown any interest in fighting back, in not simply surrendering to what had happened.

"Of course," she said. Maybe his attitude was changing about Ryan Baxter, too, but she didn't want to ask, didn't want to do anything to spoil this mood.

During the next few days, she wanted to broach the subject of Ryan Baxter, even suggest a visit, but there never seemed to be a good time. Jere appeared to have purpose for the first time, and even rode into town to see the banker again. He returned with a smile on his face. "We got the loan, Cher," he said. "Just on our signature. Mr. McDonald said he knew we were good for it, said he just got in an infusion of new capital. Those new Yanks, I guess, but at least the money's coming from our bank."

He was happier than she had seen him since he'd returned from the war. "We'll have enough to have a grand Christmas...and I'll talk to some of our people, see if they want to grow crops on our land."

They would, Cherise knew. A lot of them would. They had already come to her and asked for any kind of job. Most of their slaves had left after the Yankee occupation, and the remaining ones after the surrender. But many had come back, finding freedom had its own disadvantages. There weren't any jobs for the huge numbers of unskilled workers; no one had money, and Cherise had had to turn them away.

Cherise's family had always tried to treat their people fairly. No families had ever been separated, and there had never been physical punishment. She knew it had been far different at Baxter Trace, while Mr. Baxter lived. It was one of the reasons she'd so disliked him. And now she knew it was why Ryan Baxter had made the decision he had.

But a number of Oak Bend's former field hands would be happy to have a piece of land where they could grow their own crops, as well as some for Oak Bend.

The loan was an answer to a prayer. They could build some cabins, buy seed, pay the taxes. Best of all was the hope in Jere's face...

Jere was busy at the table, his eyes intent on a column of numbers. She smiled as he looked up.

"I'm taking some flowers to Mrs. Baxter."

Jeremy frowned.

"I'm not going to stop seeing her," she said.

He sighed.

"I want to invite her and Ryan over for Christmas," she told him, daring what she wouldn't have dared a week ago.

"No," he said flatly. "She's welcome anytime. She can't help what Ryan did. But I don't want him on Oak Bend."

"He's so alone."

"It's his doing."

"It's my house, too."

"What there is," Jeremy said, "which isn't much, thanks to his army. But I damn well won't make him feel welcome. He won't stay long. If he's still in the county."

There was something ominous about that last comment. Something shaded and dark. "What do you mean?"

"I mean there's people who want him gone, so stay away from him." He didn't have to elaborate. The implication of violence was only too clear.

"You're not one of them?" she asked, horror in her voice.

He face hardened into the old, bitter lines. "No, I'm done fighting."

She felt only the smallest bit of relief. "Who?" she insisted.

His mouth set stubbornly, and Cherise frowned in frustration. He could have heard it from anyone while in town. And she obviously wasn't going to pry any additional information from him. She bit her lip. "If anything happens to the Baxters...I'll never forgive you." She whirled around and went through the door.

Ryan finished repairing the fence outside the barn. It was the first step before getting more horses. Baxter Trace had always been known for its fine horseflesh. It was the one interest he had had in common with his father, albeit for different reasons. James Baxter had liked winning, pure and simple. Ryan just loved horses.

During the war, he had dreamed of breeding fine horses. The north Georgia grasses were rich, the climate was ideal.

His goal would take longer, now that he'd committed so much of his capital to the bank, but he still had enough for a good stud and a couple of mares. He would go up to Tennessee after Christmas. There was still good horseflesh to be found there. So much of that in the deeper South had been decimated during the war....

Now he looked out and he envisioned what could be. Not slave cabins, not cotton fields, but green pastures and frolicking colts and fillies with their more sedate dams. Stallions pawing the ground with impatience. It all represented a freedom he'd never really known. He'd escaped his father and a Baxter Trace he'd despised, only to find another kind of hell in uniform. Now, though, he could start building something fine.

But first there was the matter of young Corey Reynolds, who was being held in Athens by the military. He hadn't forgotten what Doc Colburn had said days earlier, but he hadn't had a chance to do anything. He'd wanted to stay close to the house while his mother recuperated from her fall. But she'd come down for lunch, and now he'd finished the fence.

It was a hard two-hour ride to Athens. If he left now, he should be back by nightfall. Just as he finished saddling his horse and leading him outside, he saw Cherise riding toward the house, a package in her arms.

He tried to tamp down the pure joy that spurted so unexpectedly in him. He'd tried not to think of her during the past few days, had driven himself with hard physical labor to keep from doing so. It hadn't worked.

Then or now.

He strode up to her, and she held out her package to him, a bouquet of camelias. "I thought your mother would enjoy them." She glanced at his horse. "Are you going somewhere?"

"Athens," he said. "I hoped I might be able to help with Corey Reynolds."

Her face lit, the green in her eyes becoming emerald fire. "You might, at that. It wasn't right, what happened. He was just protecting Beth Anne. I was even there. I saw what happened, but no one listened. The soldier just said we all stuck up for each other, but you—" She stopped, realizing what she'd been about to say.

"I'm not one of you," he finished grimly for her, "which is constantly being made obvious."

"That's not what I was going to say," she insisted, then looked repentant at his dubious expression. "Not exactly," she added, her mouth suddenly twitching at the lie she was telling.

"Don't worry," he said. "I'm under damn few illusions."

"Perhaps I should go with you. I was a witness."

He started at that. "It would hardly be proper," he said wryly.

"I do a lot of highly improper things," she said. She leaned down and whispered conspiratorially to him. "I even wore pants in the field. I thought I was safe, that no one would come, but old Mrs. Fosnick did. I was the talk of Hope's Way for weeks."

"You'll be the talk of Hope's Way for years if you're seen with me."

He knew he should say no, but the thought of her cheerful company was too great to resist. And she *would* make a good witness.

"Jeremy?" he said with a raised eyebrow.

"Jeremy knows I was coming to Baxter Trace. I used to spend afternoons here. He won't worry."

"All right," he said, against his better judgment. He looked at the bundle of flowers in his arms. "I'll take these in."

She nodded solemnly, but her eyes were twinkling with victory. His legs felt light. So damn light. There was an eagerness to them.

He practically thrust the blooms in Milly's arms, and told her he would be home for supper. Trying to keep his steps even, he headed back toward his horse. He thrust aside his misgivings, the warning signs he usually heeded. It was a beautiful day. He had a feeling that, in fact, it was going to be splendid. And it had been a very long time since he'd had a splendid day.

Cherise's heart just plain sang. It was a lovely December day, not biting cold, but just chilly enough to bring every sense alive. Or was it Ryan who did that?

She wasn't sure, as they took the road south. Hope's Way was north, and so they didn't have to go through it, a fact for which she was profoundly grateful, not for herself, but for Ryan. She didn't care who saw them together. But she knew that, despite his outward stoic indifference to what people thought, Ryan did. He cared very much. It was evident in the wistful, wry way he mentioned his...his too-obvious status as outcast, in that bleak look that sometimes haunted his eyes.

She didn't need words. There was a companionable silence that couldn't be forced, an ease between them that couldn't be feigned. It was enough for her that she was with him. Before long, she was humming, her voice catching up the words of the "Cherry Tree Carol." Ryan suddenly turned to her, obviously listening intently, his face a puzzle of emotions, and then he smiled slowly. It was a real, honest-to-heaven smile, one so sweet and sad she thought she might not be able to bear it.

"Don't stop," he said. "It's been years since I heard that song, or, for that matter, any song sung... happily."

Cherise's heart thudded, turned flip-flops, strained against her rib cage. She had to fight back tears for him at the overwhelming implication of his words. He had been in prison last Christmas, and before that, he had been fighting friends. How terrible it had to have been.

"They didn't observe Christmas...in Libby?"

"They might have," he said offhandedly, but she noticed his hands tightening on the reins. "I was in the hole."

"The hole?"

"Punishment cells in the cellar. You didn't have to do much to get there, and me less than most. They didn't like my Georgia accent, not in a blue uniform," he said flatly.

Her gaze rested on his face. It was slightly sunbronzed now, even in winter, because he seldom wore a hat, but there were still too many sharp angles, so many more than she remembered, and too many lines. Even the cleft in his chin seemed carved in stone, rather than moving devilishly with that old smile.

They were walking their horses, and she leaned over and put her hand briefly on his. "Then I shall make sure you make up for that loss this Christmas."

He raised an eyebrow quizzically.

"I'm not certain how, altogether," she said, answering his unspoken question, "but I know how to start." She started humming again—"God Rest Ye Merry Gentleman"—then grinned at him. "Come on. I know how well you sing. You were ever so much better than Jeremy."

Ryan felt swept up by a force too strong to resist. He hesitated for a moment. He was out of practice. Damn, it had been a long time since he and Jeremy used to sing together, usually some pretty bawdy songs. He hadn't known anyone was listening, least of all little Cherise. He grinned at the thought of her hiding someplace, listening, just as she had had her secret place to read. *Little ears* . . .

Lovely ears now, he noticed, as he tried the first few words of the carol. They sounded strange to him, as if they were coming from some other place. It was even stranger, he thought, the way his voice sounded out on this valley road. But it felt good. So good.

Normal. Happy. And it had been so long since he'd felt any... happiness.

He glanced over at her. She looked like a very self-satisfied cat, one who'd just lapped up a bowl of cream meant for someone else. Her own voice was melding with his, picking up when he faltered, then waiting for him. Her eyes met his, and a quiet understanding flowed between them, a glow that warmed him down to his toes.

*It's impossible. I can't do this to her.* But the afternoon was glorious. It was one of those wonderful Georgia December days where the sun blessed even as the cool temperature made the blood tingle. He would take these minutes, this afternoon, and treasure them.

His voice grew a little louder.

Ryan was not particularly welcome at the military headquarters building, until he showed his discharge papers.

Then the rude sergeant who had tried to dismiss him straightened. "I'll see if the captain will see you," he said.

Ryan didn't look at Cherise's face. As much as she seemed to accept him, he was not unaware of the few times she'd hesitated at the mention of his army affiliation, or the way she'd looked several days ago when she asked him why.

They were ushered into an office where an older man in a blue uniform stood to greet them. "Colonel Baxter," he said. "I'm Captain John Talbot. I'd heard you'd returned home. Not having any problems, are you? If you are..."

Ryan shrugged. "No more than was to be expected." He turned to Cherise. "This is Cherise Saunders, my neighbor, and a witness to an incident concerning a young man . . . Corey Reynolds . . ."

"Your servant, ma'am," the captain said, but his eyes were cool as they moved from Ryan to Cherise and back again. "What can I do for you, Colonel?"

Ryan tried to size up Captain Talbot. He was physically fit, and he had the cautious eyes of an experienced officer, not just a deskman, and that was promising. "I hear he was arrested for protecting his sister from a drunk soldier."

"That's not the way my men told it," Talbot said. "They said the woman insulted them, and when they took exception, the boy drew a knife. I won't allow my men to be insulted."

"He's sixteen," Ryan said, "and the town is mad as hell about it. They all saw what happened, and tell it differently."

The captain moved his gaze to Cherise. "You said you were a witness?"

She nodded. "I'd gone into a store to sell some eggs. When I came out, a . . . soldier had Beth Ann in his grasp. She was trying to pull away, and he . . . made an indecent . . . proposal. She tried again to pull away, and that's when Corey came along. He had a hunting knife with him, and he did threaten the soldier, but only to make him let go of Beth Ann. Then some other soldiers showed up . . . and the first one accused Beth Ann of insulting him."

The captain sighed. "You're willing to sign a statement?"

"Yes. And so are a number of others," Cherise said.

The captain looked at Ryan. "You'll vouch for Miss . . . Saunders's veracity?"

"I've known her and her family all my life." Ryan said. "Of course I will. And I think the soldier in question should be reprimanded, at least. There are enough problems, without this kind of thing."

Captain Talbot nodded, and Ryan secretly blessed the fact he was a reasonable man. He'd seen a hell of a lot of unreasonable men, zealots who wanted to continue to punish the South.

"I'll see that he's released this afternoon. He can return with you."

Ryan shook his head. "I'd rather not be connected with this. He might resent it."

Both the captain and Cherise stared at him incredulously.

Ryan shrugged. "I'll wait outside while Miss Saunders makes her statement," he said, and headed toward the door. Damn it, he didn't want to explain that he wasn't trying to buy acceptance.

He went out to the porch of the house that had been requisitioned as Union headquarters. It felt strange being among blue uniforms and not wearing one. Counting West Point, he had been in uniform more than a third of his life. Perhaps if the past four years hadn't been so terrible, so bloodred, he might have missed it. Then again, he might not. It had taken him years to realize he'd used the army as a shield against his father, who'd wanted a planter son and tried to instill his values, or lack of them, in Ryan.

No, he didn't regret not wearing the uniform. It just felt ... odd, unnatural. He felt out of place, but then, he'd always felt out of place.

He heard the door open behind him, and he turned. Cherise stood there, a pensive smile on her face. "You did it," she said softly.

"It wasn't that difficult. Captain Talbot is a reasonable man."

"He wasn't reasonable before."

Ryan suddenly grinned. "I imagine you've been giving him and his men a bad time. He probably had no ... motivation to be ... reasonable."

"Thank you," she said.

"There's no need for that. It was simple justice."

"There doesn't seem to be a lot of that around these days," she said sadly.

"Would you like to get something to eat?" he asked, changing the subject, "or is it too late?"

"It *is* getting late," she said regretfully. "Jere will worry."

He nodded. "Especially if anyone saw us together."

She shrugged her shoulders in a wry imitation of him, a slight grin on her face. But then it disappeared as she remembered what Jere had said. She'd forgotten about it, distracted by Ryan's presence, by the sheer joy of the ride, of being with him when he wasn't so completely guarded. "Jere said there were some ... people who want you gone."

His expression didn't change. "I'm very aware of that," he said.

"He hinted at something," she said slowly, trying to remember his exact words. "It was a warning of some sort."

"For you or me?"

"Both of us, I think."

"Is he involved?"

"No," she said slowly. "He said he was through fighting."

"God, I hope I am, too," Ryan said. "But I won't be run off."

"If they knew about Corey..."

"No," he said. "There's nothing worse than having to feel gratitude to someone you consider an enemy, especially if they think I used my uniform to do it. Believe me, it won't help anything. The resentment will just get worse."

Cherise gave him a dubious look.

"Promise me, Cherise," he demanded. "Promise you won't say anything."

She saw the plea in his expression, and though she felt instinctively that he was wrong, she had to agree. She nodded her head.

He took her arm and led her to her mare. He helped her mount, and she watched as he swung into the saddle with a cavalryman's grace. He turned his horse north, his face inscrutable again, and she knew he was turning away from the easy camaraderie they'd shared this afternoon.

Another hour, two, and she would lose him again. He'd retreat back into the myth that he didn't need anyone.

But not if she could help it.

## Chapter Six

Ryan stopped at the road leading into Oak Bend. He had set a hard pace, rejecting Cherise's suggestion that they stop once to rest. He'd wanted to get her home before dark.

They'd just made it. Dusk was settling over the hills; shadows from empty branches were casting ever-changing patterns across the road.

"I'll see you to the door," he said tensely, knowing there might be another confrontation with Jere. But safety, as they had once known it, was gone now. Too many men were jobless, desperate.

She turned wide eyes toward him, that chin set stubbornly. "If Jere objects, we can tell him why we went."

"No," he said flatly. "We just met on the road."

"I won't lie to him."

"You made a promise."

"A bad one," she retorted.

"It may be, but you're stuck with it."

She grimaced, and he had to smile. Cherise Saunders's face showed every emotion. Lying wouldn't come easily to her. But he was willing her to keep her promise with his eyes.

"I'll go in alone, then," she said reluctantly. "I don't want to lie to him. If he doesn't see you, there won't be questions. I ride all the time by myself."

He didn't want her to go alone. He wanted her safe. Dear God, he wanted to keep someone safe. He finally compromised, reluctantly. "I'll stay back and watch."

She leaned over and took his hand, squeezing it ever so slightly, but her touch burned all the way through him, soothed the raw places. The gesture was spontaneous, natural. He hadn't realized how much he wanted, needed, that kind of unqualified... affection. He couldn't think it was anything more. It would be much too painful for both of them. Three of them, if Jere was included. And Jere *was* included. To be seen with Cherise, to even appear to court her, would be like waving a red flag in front of a bull. One of them would get killed, or, at the least, badly wounded.

"Thank you for letting me go with you," she said.

"It was a pleasure, Miss Cherise," he said formally, as he had often done teasingly her as a child. He saw the quick realization in her eyes, and then she grinned. "I'm not fourteen any longer."

He had to answer that smile with one of his own. A slow, unwilling one. "No, you certainly aren't, Miss Cherise."

"I'll ride over to see Sarah in the morning."

He didn't know what devil was pricking him, but one certainly was when he replied, "We...I thought we might put up the Christmas tree tomorrow..."

"Good, I'll help," she said delightedly, before using the small quirt to urge her horse into a canter before he could say nay.

Jeremy asked no questions, perhaps because he was too eager to impart his own news. He had ridden out to the camp where a number of the former slaves had gathered, many of them dependent on Freeman's Society food. Ten had agreed to farm shares with them. They would come over after Christmas to start building houses for their families.

He was finally caught up in purpose, and Cherise blessed McDonald, and whatever Yankees had brought money to his bank.

A smile flitted across his face. "Let's buy a ham and invite some neighbors in for Christmas." He looked reluctantly around at the plain, bare room. But then, everyone else was in the same straits. "Maybe we can find you a husband."

She grinned at the teasing note in his voice. It had been too long since last she'd heard it. "Not Calvin Sooner," she said, wrinkling her nose.

"Not Calvin," he agreed. "I told him today that you're much too busy to entertain suitors."

"He'll expect to be invited."

Jeremy's face hardened. "It'll be just a few close friends."

Cherise knew she shouldn't say anything, but it was her house, too, every bit as much as Jeremy's. "I want to invite Sarah and Ryan."

Jeremy's green eyes grew glacial. "Then no one else would come."

"That will be up to them," she said stubbornly.

The glacial eyes narrowed. "You said you were going to see Miss Sarah. Did you see Ryan?"

"Of course," she said.

"I won't have him in our house, and that's final," he said.

"Then I'll spend Christmas at Baxter Trace," she retorted defiantly. "Last year...I was all alone. I didn't know if you were dead or alive, and Sarah...she invited me to share what little she had."

She thought of that bare and lonely Christmas, when both of them had been alone. It had been the worst Christmas of her life. Her father and mother had died. She'd just received news of David's death, and Jeremy was engaged in battle in Virginia. Sherman had virtually destroyed Georgia. So many other neighbors and friends had gone to relatives in other states or areas untouched by Sherman's army. Then Sarah sent Milly to invite her for Christmas dinner, and the three of them had consumed a scrawny chicken and "coffee" made of hickory nuts.

A gamut of emotions crossed Jere's face. A stricken realization. Sorrow. And stubbornness. Always that stubbornness. "I'm sorry, Kitten. Sometimes I forget that not all the injuries occurred on the battlefield. But I still can't stomach Baxter in my home."

There was pain in his voice, so much that she knew she wouldn't pursue it. Forcing him to accept the Baxters would only make him more resentful, would ruin everyone's Christmas, this first one in four years when Jere would be home. He already had too many battles left to face with that arm, and with their financial problems.

She nodded, though she felt tears press against her eyes, and she tried to blink them back. She hadn't cried in a very long time. Grief was sometimes too great for tears.

Cherise felt her brother's eyes on her, searching, and then he moved toward her and put his good arm around her shoulders, hugging her. "Maybe later," he said quietly. "But not now. It's too soon."

"The hate has to stop sometime," she said, hearing the choking sound of her own words.

"I know," he said.

"He had a terrible time, too," she said. "And it's not over for him."

"It's not over for any of us," Jere said, "not as long as Union troops stay here and make us pay for their presence."

He didn't add that it would never be over for him, because of his missing arm, but she knew the words were in him, buried in his heart.

He suddenly tweaked one of her curls, as he used to do, and stepped back, as if embarrassed by his show of emotion. "What about that ham? And some friends?"

One of her hands went up and wiped the corner of her left eye, where an errant tear had escaped. She nodded and forced a note of lightness in her voice. "I'll get some evergreen branches and decorate them with red bows."

He grinned. "Sounds fine."

"No Calvin," she warned.

His smile disappeared. "No Calvin."

* * *

Dr. Colburn, banker Jeff McDonald, Sam Bascomb and Sheriff Tate Evans were having their weekly poker game. The stakes had declined drastically over the past few years. They now used useless Confederate notes; at least they served some purpose.

"I'll see that and raise you two thousand," the banker said, pushing a pile of worthless notes in the middle of the pot.

Sam Bascomb concentrated on his cards, squinching his brows together. He eyed his dwindling pile of bills. "Ah, hell, Jeff, that ain't sporting."

Jeff gave him a glare he usually reserved for delinquent customers. "Put up or shut up, Sam."

"Hell, I fold," Sam said, watching balefully as Jeff swept the wrinkled notes to the corner of the table. He pushed his chair back. "Guess you heard the Yanks released my nephew, Corey."

"Yep," Doc Colburn said. "I was out to see his mother when he came riding in."

The banker raised an eyebrow. "Why did they change their mind?"

"Damn if I know," Doc Colburn said. "Something else, though. Found two hundred dollars in my pocket a few days ago. Don't know whose it was, but it sure as hell was a godsend. I finally was able to get some medicine I needed."

Jeff McDonald raised an eyebrow. "Been anyplace lately?"

"Hell, my usual rounds."

Jeff leaned forward. "Where specifically?"

"Johnsons, Mrs. Reynolds, Careys, old Mr. Simpson, the Baxter place."

"Baxter," Sam Bascomb said in disgust. "There's going to be trouble with Ryan Baxter coming back. I already heard rumors some hotheads want to burn him out."

McDonald's head snapped around. "I don't like that."

"Hell, Jeff, you were as angry as anyone when he turned traitor."

Doc Colburn took a long pull at his glass of whiskey. "So was I, but I don't want Sarah hurt, and she sure as hell will be."

"Maybe one of us should tell him to leave," Bascomb suggested.

Jeff McDonald sighed. He lit a cigar and dangled it between his fingers, watching the smoke drift upward. It was a familiar practice to the others. Jeff always used it to gain time when he wanted to say something. "We may be wrong about Ryan Baxter," he said slowly. "About treating him like a leper. He followed his conscience, like we all did. Ain't nothing evil about that."

The other three stared at him. Jeff McDonald never relapsed into improper language unless he wished to make a point.

"Maybe you can forget and forgive," Sam said, "but I lost a brother and two sons. Baxter may be the one who shot them."

"We all lost people," Jeff said. "But we all were real proud when Ryan went to West Point, and he took an oath when he did that. Who's to say he's wrong in keeping his word?"

The other three were silent, obviously not convinced, but not willing to argue, either. Soon, they broke up.

Cherise found herself humming a Christmas carol as she approached Baxter Trace, the same one Ryan had sung with her yesterday.

He hadn't wanted to ask her to come today, she knew that. The words had slipped out before he could stop them, and she planned to take advantage.

She'd started early this morning, wanting to finish all her chores before leaving. She'd made two pies, one to take to Baxter Trace and one for Jeremy. She used the last of her dried apples and sugar, but now, with a loan, they would have enough for a few small luxuries. Not a lot, but some. She had learned to be careful, to hoard every little bit of food.

Her heart was singing this morning, too, every bit as fulsomely as those winter birds she'd heard when she first woke up. Jeremy was improving, both in body and in spirit, and they had the loan they needed to keep Oak Bend.

And she was going to see Ryan Baxter!

It was just a few days until Christmas, and for the first time in years, she felt a surge of hope. No, not a surge of hope, great waves of hope. She found herself smiling to no one in particular.

When she reached Baxter Trace, she dismounted, sliding easily from her mare and hitching the reins to a post in front of the house. She skipped up the stairs, holding the pie carefully.

Milly opened the door before she could knock. "Miss Cherise, don't you look pretty!"

Cherise found herself blushing. The Christmas mood was obviously affecting Milly. But Cherise *had* tried hard. The Yanks had allowed her to take some clothes before they burned the main house, and this was one of the few she'd selected. It was one of two she considered her Christmas dresses, a day dress of fine green cotton. The other, still protected in sheets of paper, was a red velvet. Both had been bought the Christmas of 1860, the last Christmas before the war, and neither had been worn since. They had always reminded her of that Christmas, when last her family was together: her father, her mother, her two brothers and herself.

"Thank you," she said. "Is Miss Sarah home?"

"She and Mr. Ryan are in the drawing room," Milly said. "I'll bring some hot tea." At Cherise's lifted eyebrows, Milly giggled. "Mr. Ryan bought some real fine tea from the store. Been a long time since we had tea." Milly leaned over. "I don't think he likes it much, but Miss Sarah, she's happy as a pig in a mud puddle."

Cherise couldn't help but giggle at the image of the reserved, dignified Miss Sarah in a mud puddle. "I will be, too," she confided to Milly as she took off her coat and gloves and laid them down carefully on a chair in the hall. Then she moved toward the drawing room, pausing in the doorway to watch Ryan and his mother.

He was teasing her as she strung popcorn and bright red holly berries on a string. Sarah looked up, and there was laughter in her eyes, the first Cherise had seen in years. Cherise looked over at Ryan as he followed his mother's gaze and saw her. He stood and smiled. It was such a handsome smile, like the ones she remembered. Open and fine, without the wariness she'd seen so much recently.

"We need another pair of hands, especially for this tree," he added wryly. "In fact, what we really need is magic."

Her gaze went to the scrawny pine in the corner. She'd paid it little notice several days earlier, when he was bringing it home, but it did look...a little forlorn, its branches sparse and its top far below the high ceiling.

"It seemed to need a home," Ryan said, a touch of amusement lighting his eyes.

"I think it needs more than that," she said.

"Ah," he said, "a few red berries, popcorn and some candles and it will be..."

"Beautiful," she finished.

"Don't overdo it," he said, chuckling.

She was delighted with him, with the smile that played around his lips, with his blue eyes, which seemed to twinkle as they had years ago. Christmas. It was wonderful what it could do to the heart.

Cherise started humming, as she had yesterday, and soon he and Sarah both joined in. Milly came to the door with a tray filled with tea and cups and cookies. She stood there for a moment, listening, a faint smile on her lips as she looked at Sarah and nodded her head.

Then Ryan noticed her and was up swiftly, taking the heavy tray from her hands. "Join us," he offered, but she just shook her head.

"I'll just watch," she said. "Sure is good to see a smile on Miss Sarah's face. Good to have you home, too, Mr. Ryan. Does my old soul a heap of good to see you two together. And you, too, Miss Cherise.'' And then she ducked her head slightly, as if embarrassed by her own words.

Ryan just smiled that lazy, wondrous smile Cherise had missed so much.

The afternoon seemed to speed by. The tree looked more respectable, though still scraggly. Yet it was glorious in the hope it signified, Cherise thought. A beginning.

It was time to go. Past time. She had things she had to do at home, one of which was to make their own small house ready for Christmas. Jeremy needed it as much as the Baxters had. She needed it.

''I'll accompany you home,'' Ryan said, and though she often rode alone, she gratefully accepted. More time with him. More time to coax that too-rare twinkle from his eyes, the smile from his lips.

The wind was turning cold. This was more like Christmas weather than the relatively mild days they'd been having. The sky overhead was gray, and the clouds were plump with moisture. The barn, though, was snug and smelling of fresh hay from Ryan's recent cleaning. She paused at Cinnamon's stall, reluctant to leave. She turned and looked up at Ryan, who was staring down at her, a hungry yearning in his eyes before he could check it, hide it behind that usual curtain of reserve.

''Ryan...'' she said, knowing that her whisper was throaty, her own longing as obvious as that which blazed across his face.

He closed his eyes, as if that alone could restore a balance dangerously awry, as if he could check the electricity that ran so strongly between them. But when he opened them, there was defeat there, and he pulled her to him.

His hand touched her face, a finger tracing her right cheekbone, so gently it felt like a down feather. It went up to her forehead and then down to her chin and hesitated at the nape of her neck before moving to the back of her hair, burying itself in her curls. "You're so beautiful," he said. "You gave my mother a wonderful present today, just by being here."

She heard the sadness in his voice, a wistfulness. "It was you," she said. "She was smiling when I came in. She has her son back."

"One of them," he said. "The black sheep. The prodigal. I wish . . ."

*I wish I could give her Rad.* The thought assaulted her consciousness as if he had spoken out loud. She knew him so well, or at least she sensed those things she didn't know. He was still so filled with guilt that he believed Sarah wished he were Radburn. She wished she could take away that guilt, just as she wanted to banish that frown marring his fine, strong face.

She buried her head against his chest, listening to the steady beating of his heart. Such a strong, sad heart. Her arms went around his neck, and he pulled her against him, his arms circling her waist. She felt his breath against her face, his lips touching her forehead as gently as his finger had a few seconds earlier, and she lifted her mouth to meet his.

The first touch was gentle, searching, seeking. Then his tongue teased her lips open and her breath caught in her throat as the kiss deepened and his tongue played lovely, exotic games inside her mouth. That odd, warm rush flooded through her again, pushing her body against his as she sought something utterly compelling. She felt his hardness, heard his own breath catch, and his heartbeat seemed to stop for a moment, or was she simply deaf to anything and everything, her whole world centered on the feel of his lips against her lips, his body against hers?

The world seemed to dip and sway and whirl. The ground was no longer solid, as his hands moved over her hips, along her waist. Every part of her, physically and emotionally, was responding to every part of him. She burned with his touch, ached with the need for more.

"Damn it," he whispered achingly as he released her lips and pulled away. Not much, just a small step, as if every move away from her required supreme effort. "I'm poison, pure poison."

She swallowed at the note of pure desperation in his voice. "I've waited for you all my life," she said, meeting his pain-filled eyes. Hurting for him.

"You've waited for a mirage," he said.

"I don't think so." As if to prove the truth of her words, she stretched upward and kissed him. She tried to give him the world with that kiss, her hands touching his face, loving his face, loving him.

And then his arms went around her again, and she knew he wasn't going to let go this time. He'd lost the battle—or won it. She didn't care, as long as he continued to hold her.

She felt his hands along the back of her neck and then downward. Even through her coat, she felt the intimacy of his fingers, and her senses started whirling again, the warmth pooling deep inside her.

He picked her up and carried her to fresh hay and knelt there, setting her down gently and pulling the coat from her. It could have been freezing outside, even inside, but all she felt was the heat radiating between the two of them. He sat down next to her, his hand releasing the top buttons of her riding costume. Ryan bent his head, a lock of his thick sandy hair falling over his forehead, and his tongue found her throat and caressed it lingeringly.

A tremor shook her body. He hesitated. Then drew back. "Dear God, how I want you. You are so...alive. You can't know..." His voice trailed off, and he sat there looking at her helplessly.

Cherise swallowed hard. She knew what they were doing was wrong. Yet it seemed so right. So natural. She had waited for this moment too long. She leaned into his arms, her back settling against his chest, her hand holding one of his as the other trailed fingers across it.

"I don't want to go."

"If anyone sees you... with me..."

"I'd be proud," she said softly. "It took courage to do what you did."

"It's going to take a long time to knit this country back together," he said tiredly. "There's going to be a lot of pain, particularly in the South."

"I know." She looked up at him. "Have you... thought of going somewhere else?"

"Every day I've been back," he said. "But this is my home, too. I'm not going to run off like a whipped dog."

She brought his hand up to her mouth and nuzzled it. "Me, either," she said.

His arms went around her, pulling her closer again. "You feel so good."

"So do you."

"Too good."

"So do you."

"But the hay doesn't," he said wryly.

"Yes, it does," she disagreed, amusement making her words like small chimes.

"That's because you're mostly on me."

"True."

He chuckled, the sound coming from deep in his throat, and Cherise felt it vibrate throughout her. That, too, felt good. Wonderful, in all truth.

"Doesn't anything bother you?" he whispered.

"Not when I'm with you," she replied blissfully.

His arms tightened again, and he groaned. That also felt fine. He was groaning because of her. It was, she thought, a good groan. A wanting groan.

She wriggled inside his arms and felt the changes in his body again, a sudden hardness, a tensing of his muscles. It did wonderful things to her, too. Just like before. She looked up at him. A mistake.

His face didn't look fine. It was almost contorted, with a pain she didn't entirely understand, but from her own reactions she guessed it had something to do with the friction of their bodies. And his own sense of honor. She'd learned, since he'd been back, exactly how strong that sense was. And she didn't want to make it any more painful for him.

She put her head to his cheek, feeling its smoothness, its remaining gauntness. So many lines, so much age in eyes that should still be young. "I love you, Ryan Baxter," she said, feeling so full of it she could no longer keep it to herself.

The lines didn't ease. They grew deeper. She saw, and heard, the deep sigh that made his body shudder. She thought she saw an answer in his eyes, a yearning there, but then it disappeared under that shield he'd perfected. "You can't," he said simply.

He didn't wait for her to answer, but lifted her to her feet and stood himself, brushing the hay from his clothes with a studied deliberateness, as if it were the most important task of his life. He was shutting her out again, as effectively as slamming a door in her face. When the very last speck was gone he walked to Cinnamon's stall and led her out. He then leaned down and picked up Cherise's coat, assisting her with the coolness of a man who stood across the room—or even across the country. She had no choice but to shrug the coat on, then take his hand to mount.

He then saddled his own horse and led both horses out the door, closing it after him before mounting himself. Without looking at her again, he guided the stallion into a canter, precluding further conversation.

She followed slightly behind, watching the straight, proud back. Too proud, she thought. Too proud to be loved.

But she would change that. And Christmas, she sensed, would be her ally.

# *Chapter Seven*

Impatiently Jeremy waited for Cherise. Calvin Sooner had dropped over again with some of his whiskey. Sober for several days now, Jeremy had looked at him, wondering why he'd ever thought the man his friend.

The answer, after painful self-examination, was even more agonizing. After he lost his arm, he'd felt himself worthless, and had needed Sooner's deference, no matter that it came from a white-trash rascal. He'd used Sooner's false comfort to mask both the physical pain and that overwhelming feeling of being half a man. He'd used it to run and hide.

Ryan Baxter had the guts to come back and face derision. He, Jeremy, had no guts at all.

*Christmas Eve.* Sooner had mentioned it again, had asked him once more to participate in the raid on Baxter Trace. Jeremy thought of Sarah Baxter, of all the good times he'd shared with Ryan, and felt sick to his stomach.

Christmas Eve was in two days. He'd thought it was Ryan's problem: the community's outrage, even Calvin Sooner's plan. Ryan Baxter shouldn't have returned; he deserved what he got. But Jeremy was

slowly realizing how much courage it had taken for
Ryan to return, and how much it must have taken to
remain with the Union. He didn't want to realize it,
but those thoughts were snaking insidiously through
him just the same.

*He didn't owe Ryan a damn thing.*

But his sister? He didn't even want to think of the
hell he'd put her through since he'd returned home,
with his drinking and self-pity, not to mention the
years she'd been alone, fighting to keep at least a part
of their family's heritage.

And now...

He didn't like the amount of time she was spending
at Baxter Trace. He didn't want her involved with
Ryan Baxter, although once, when she was still in pigtails, he had thought it would be nice—his sister and
his best friend.

Suddenly he remembered all the good times with
Ryan, times he'd tried to block away. He felt an overwhelming sense of nostalgia, accompanied by a sad
emptiness. He'd never had a friend like Ryan, before
or after the beginning of war. Ryan had been closer to
Jeremy than his own brother, which was why Ryan's
defection had hurt so damned much. He'd always
thought they would ride into battle together, not face
each other at the opposite ends of rifles. Now he
wondered if that wasn't why he was so bitter. Not because Ryan had followed his conscience, but because
Jeremy had felt deserted, personally betrayed.

He closed his eyes. Dear God, he wanted a drink.
He wanted to forget. Damn, he wanted his friend
back. His head went back, and he heard his own roar
of raw pain. Pride. Pride had lost him everything, but

it was still there, an inherent part of him. He could no more go to Ryan now, after the words that had been said, than he could jump over the moon.

Why then, did he feel so desolate?

Christmas. Perhaps that would brighten his mood. He'd bought Cherise a new coat, a scarf and matching gloves. It had been more than they could afford, but she had so little. He anticipated the look on her face when she saw them, and he felt better. Cherise had always loved Christmas, and if nothing else, he would try to make it a good one.

He heard the whinny of a horse eager to get home to its stable, and he walked outside. The wind was bracing. It was getting colder with every hour. It had been unseasonably warm until now, and that had kept Christmas at bay for him—or had it been simply the rough emptiness of this house, the loss of Oak Bend and all the happy days it represented?

But Cherise brightened all that with her smile, a smile that said how glad she was to see him, no matter that he'd been such a bear these past months.

She glowed now, as she hadn't since he'd first stumbled home and she'd known he was alive. Her cheeks were flushed, and her eyes were alive with light. She looked like a woman in love.

He walked out to her and held out his good arm, catching her with it as she slid down. "You were gone a long time," he said, trying to keep his voice neutral.

"I helped Sarah and Ryan decorate a tree," she replied, watching him carefully. "She's so happy he's home."

"And you?"

She nodded. "I've always been in love with him," she said frankly.

"Even if he's a traitor." Damn, he hadn't been able to resist the comment. He hated to watch the light fade from her eyes.

"One man's traitor is another's patriot," she snapped back.

"Is that what you think he is?" *Why couldn't he stop?*

"I don't know. I just know he did what he had to do."

"Hell, let's not argue about Baxter anymore," he said. "He won't last here."

"Yes, he will. I told him . . . there might be trouble."

"You didn't tell him from where?"

"Protecting Calvin Sooner?" she taunted. "Your boon companion?"

"Christ, I'm protecting you. If he knew . . ."

"When did you become a coward?" The words left her mouth before she could call them back. She watched his face drain of color, watched him step back as if he'd been hit. She felt her own stomach drop. She'd never purposely been cruel. She hadn't been now, but she knew the result was the same.

That reckless charge was a body blow. "I'm sorry, Jere," she said contritely. "I didn't mean it."

"Yes, you did," he said, "and maybe you're right." He turned and walked away, almost stumbling as he did so, as if blinded by something. She wanted to call him back, but the hurt ran too deep. Words would do little to recall it.

She went inside. Flames blazed in the fireplace, and wood was stacked next to it. A lot of wood. The room was neat, neater than when she'd left. Jere had made a conscious effort to please her, to make this place he hated into some kind of home. She felt now as if she'd kicked an already wounded puppy.

Except Jere was no puppy, and she had to remember that. He was a man, a man who had to learn to live with both his memories and his physical loss. He would never survive if he didn't.

She sighed and hung up her coat, trembling slightly as she remembered that warm, tingly feeling when Ryan had taken it from her earlier. She went over to the cookstove and started a fire. She would make biscuits, roast two potatoes, and fry the last of their bacon, making gravy from its drippings. And she had that pie. Maybe she and Jeremy could make peace tonight.

*Coward!* The word echoed in Jere's mind, over and over. It had been easy to be brave in battle, when everyone had the same enemy and the same fears. It was a great deal harder in private, this battling with his conscience.

He had meant for this to be a good evening for Cherise. He'd had found some holly branches with berries for above the rough fireplace, and he'd purchased some bright red ribbons for bows. He'd hoped to hear her sing tonight; it had been so long since he'd even thought of music, thought of anything happy.

Why had he destroyed the mood by attacking Ryan Baxter again?

Because hoarding his hatred made it easier for him to do nothing about Calvin Sooner. *Coward.* Cherise was right, ever so right.

He had time to change, though. He stopped fighting the growing conviction within that he could never live with himself if he allowed a group of masked bullies to attack two lone women and a man who had once been his friend. He would stop it. He didn't know how. But he would.

Christmas Eve dawned gray and cold. Cherise shivered as she slipped from the bed, replenished the wood in the fireplace and lit the kindling. Then she stepped back and viewed the now decorated hearth.

Hope danced lightly in her heart. Jere had returned last night and revealed his pile of holly. She knew he had gathered it for her, and there had been something new in his eyes, a combative spark that had been missing since he'd returned home. They hadn't mention Ryan Baxter, but she sensed something in him had changed.

Together they'd wrapped the holly with bright red bows, Jere holding the bunches, and she tying the knots. He'd even started a carol on his own, and they'd ended up laughing while singing "The Twelve Days of Christmas" and getting thoroughly confused between the setting hens and the geese a-laying. It had been so good to hear Jere laugh again, to watch him eat with something close to enjoyment, not as if it were a chore he was enduring.

If only she could get them together again—Jere and Ryan. But she wouldn't try now, not and ruin that closeness beginning to forge itself between her and her brother.

But she caught herself humming as she started to fix breakfast. It was so nice having someone here to do for, especially with the lightening of Jere's spirits. She hoped it came from deep within, and was not just surface smiles to please her. She wanted him happy.

She pulled on her coat and went to the small chicken house for some eggs. Christmas Eve. Magical things happened at Christmas. Already Jere had smiled. And Ryan had kissed her, had admitted he wanted her. Happiness rose within her as she thought of both.

But as she collected the last of the eggs and left the coop, she saw Jere. His face was grim again, and he was wearing a hat, meaning that he planned to ride into town. She met him as he headed for the stable.

"Breakfast?" she questioned warily, the joy draining from her as she saw the harsh, icy look in his eyes.

He shook his head. "I have some errands."

"It's Christmas Eve," she said, hearing the disappointment in her own voice.

He smiled slightly, a mollifying smile that hid what he was really thinking. She didn't like it, especially when his eyes refused to meet hers. Apprehension snaked through her, and her eyes questioned him.

"Just Christmas things." He was trying to reassure her, reminding her of times when every member of the family used to sneak off to deal with individual secrets.

But instinct told her something else. She hated the suspicion building inside her. Calvin Sooner came readily to mind, and Calvin was trouble, pure and simple.

Jere didn't wait to give further explanations, though. He strode to the barn and, faster than she would have thought possible, he had saddled his horse and was riding away.

"Why don't you invite Cherise and Jeremy tonight?" Sarah asked her son. "I'll ask Milly to make some of that eggnog Jeremy used to like so much. It will be nice to have young people around again." She'd asked few questions these days Ryan had been home, especially about Ryan's former friends. Evidently she thought Cherise's presence meant more than it did.

He hesitated, wondering what to say. He didn't want to hurt her more than she had been. "I don't think..."

"Jeremy will come around," she said softly, understanding in her eyes. "Christmas is the time to make it happen. Just ask him."

"He's already made it clear he doesn't want anything to do with a...traitor." The word still came hard to him.

"Ask him," she insisted.

He shook his head. His pride wouldn't, couldn't, go that far. He had swallowed too much already. It was Jeremy's decision now. Still, he wished it didn't hurt so damn much. "We'll have a good Christmas," he said. "The three of us. It's just good to be home."

She looked at him sadly, but didn't say any more.

Cherise couldn't stop the nervousness that ate away at her. She hadn't liked Jere's face this morning, and fear had been gnawing at her ever since.

She kept remembering his words a few days earlier. There were people who didn't want Ryan Baxter in the community. She knew one of those people was Calvin Sooner. Jere had said he wasn't a part of whatever mischief was brewing, and Cherise wished she believed him. But Jere had changed so much, and his dislike of Ryan Baxter was open and raw.

And there was something in the air. Something dangerous, when there should just be happiness and hope and faith and charity. There seemed to be precious little charity around, where the Baxters were concerned.

How was Ryan this day?

Her heart hurt every time she thought of him and Sarah, so alone and isolated, particularly after the four years of horror she knew he'd experienced. This should be a good Christmas for him and Jere alike.

She found herself pacing, needing desperately to do something, to go someplace. To go to him.

His words had made it clear he didn't want her to come to Baxter Trace. He had practically chased her off yesterday. But his eyes had said something else when she so wantonly confessed her feelings. *I love you.* The words had meant something to him. She'd seen it in the warm glow in his eyes before he walled them off again.

*Where's your pride?*

I have none where he's concerned.

*A reason?*

She mulled that over in her mind for a few moments. There were presents, of course, but she had nothing for Ryan, although she'd crocheted a handkerchief for Sarah. If she'd known Ryan was coming home, she could have knit something for him, as well. But it was too late for that now. She reviewed her own possessions. She'd been allowed so little time before the Yanks had burned the house. Dresses, underclothing, and a few precious, much-loved books. She had buried some family keepsakes—silver and jewelry—but they had been sold earlier this year.

But the books... ah, yes, the books. She had managed to save twelve, including a book of Shakespeare's sonnets, and the Hawthorne novel she'd been reading years ago, when she last saw Ryan. She'd clung to that as a talisman. There was a book by Dickens, and *The Last of the Mohicans* by James Fenimore Cooper. That was a possibility. But she suspected Ryan was tired of war, of death and blood and vengeance.

There were several more novels, and two volumes of poetry. One included works by John Keats, and the other by William Wordsworth. She went to the shelf in her room where she kept them and picked up the latter, leafing through it. She felt the books were hers, at least half of them. Jere had never much cared for books, while she... lived much of her life in them. This one, this volume by William Wordsworth, was her favorite, and its pages were well worn. It had saved her from loneliness many nights. One passage, in particular, had called to her:

I wandered lonely as a cloud
That floats on high o'er vales and hills,
When all at once I saw a crowd,
A host, of golden daffodils.

The words had so often caught her mood, the knowledge that beauty could heal. A sun-filled day could brighten the darkest of spirits, and a field of flowers could bring joy to the loneliest of moods.

That was it! She would wrap the book and the handkerchief for Sarah in cloth from a dress that was no longer redeemable. She smiled, feeling the undeniable pull of Christmas, the joy of giving something that meant so much to her. She would mark her favorite passages in the book and hope it had the same meaning to him as it did to her.

She wrapped her gifts, along with two shirts she'd purchased for Jeremy. She wanted to wait for Jeremy, give him one more chance to go to Baxter Trace, even beg if she had to. She made some cookies as she waited for him to return. One hour, two, three, passed. Then she had a better idea. She would ride on to Baxter Trace and leave a note for Jeremy to meet her there and ride home with her. Jeremy didn't like her out at night. He would be forced to come to Baxter Trace this Christmas Eve.

Ryan took a long ride on Christmas Eve, away from town, away from the censorious faces, away from his mother's hopeful one. She still believed friends would come, even though they hadn't for the past three or four years. He didn't share that hope.

Another thought plagued him. Could he give up Cherise?

She had been the one bright, shining light in his homecoming. He still felt the tenderness of her touch, remembered the loving longing in her eyes. He wanted her more than he'd wanted anything in his life, and the greatest gift he could give her was to keep her away from him.

Still, he found himself riding in the direction of Oak Bend, looking down from a hill at the winding road below, which led to a place where once he'd spent so much of his youth, which now held so much of his heart.

He watched the smoke trail from the chimney of the overseer's house. He wanted to gallop down to the door and pull Cherise to his chest. He wanted to seize Jeremy in a bear hug. He wanted, needed, both of them. But he had no right to either of them. He'd surrendered that right when he stayed in a blue uniform. For the first time, he thought seriously of leaving Hope's Way. Reluctantly he turned away from the house, from futile dreams, and rode back home. There would be eggnog tonight with his mother, and forced gaiety to chase away the ghosts. He would pretend, for her sake, that all was normal and that he was glad to be home.

But home was a strange, hostile land. It had been even before the war, and it was even more so now.

Jeremy had still not arrived by late afternoon. Cherise saddled her horse, packed her presents in saddlebags and left a note for Jeremy.

She didn't understand why Jeremy wasn't home yet. They had planned the small gathering tomorrow with a few of Jeremy's friends. She'd stopped insisting on Ryan's presence. Neither man would have been happy, under the circumstances, and she felt it was important to give Jeremy this day. He needed it, and planning the gathering had been the first sign that Jeremy, usually so garrulous in the past, was ready to get out among people again.

She shrugged away her apprehensions, focusing on Ryan and Sarah, hoping they would take pleasure in her offerings. A cold wind was sweeping the hills, and she urged Cinnamon into a gallop. Billows of clouds raged overhead. A storm?

Or was it just the storm in her heart that seemed to put the cold, raw chill in the air?

Ryan was chopping wood when she rode up. He apparently didn't see her, and she watched from a distance. Even though it was cold, he was in shirtsleeves. He still looked gaunt to her, yet there was power in his movements. Another stroke, and the wood split, then he rested against the handle of his ax, with his head bowed. He looked so defeated. So alone. Then he turned his head and saw her, and his shoulders straightened, and a brief, welcoming smile spread across his face.

He laid the ax down and walked toward her. "You're out riding alone again," he said, glancing around her. "And on Christmas Eve. Where's Jeremy?"

"He's been gone most of the day," she said. "I left a note saying where he could find me."

The smile disappeared from his face. "You can't force him to accept me."

He was too intuitive. She held out her hand, and he had to approach her and help her down. She thought about the gifts in the saddlebags, but suddenly felt shy. Perhaps later.

"Sarah will be delighted to see you. She was hoping someone would drop by. Like they used to," he added, not entirely keeping the bitterness from his voice.

*And you?* she wanted to ask. *Are you delighted to see me? At least a little bit pleased?*

But he was guiding her toward the house, his face empty of emotion. Milly was standing by the door, as if she'd expected Cherise, and then Sarah was descending from the stairs, her mouth wide with welcome.

"Merry Christmas," she said, holding her hands out to Cherise.

Cherise put her cheek to the older woman's. She felt the warmth of welcome in Sarah's hands. "Merry Christmas, Mrs. Baxter."

"You'll have some eggnog with us." It was more an order than a request, and Cherise nodded, ignoring Ryan's wary look.

"I have the most wonderful story," Sarah said. "*A Christmas Carol,* by Charles Dickens." She glanced sideways at her son. "It's all about a man named Scrooge."

There was something mischievous in her voice that made Cherise turned to Ryan. He shrugged his shoulders helplessly as they went into the nearly bare room, made colorful by greenery and bows and the Christmas tree.

Milly appeared again, this time with a tray laden with a bowl full of eggnog and individual cakes. A huge smile wreathed her face. "Stay with us," Ryan said as he took over the pouring duties, giving one of the three glasses to her. "And Miss Cherise, will you pleasure us with a song?"

She nodded happily, until she saw his face. She knew suddenly that the welcome was for Sarah's sake, not his own. Worry creased the area around his eyes, and she knew he was thinking of Jeremy, of what Jeremy would think when he found her note. She knew he would give her the one song, maybe two, and then offer to take her home.

She wouldn't go. Maybe she couldn't force Jeremy to accept Ryan, but she could try to make him see reason, and tonight—Christmas Eve—was the time to do it.

She wished there was a piano, but the piano had been chopped up for firewood, Sarah had said, along with much of the other furniture, so Cherise started softly, finding her own key. The sweet strains of "Silent Night" wafted through the room, and soon the others picked up the words. "Silent night, peaceful night..." How she yearned for it. Her eyes met Ryan's. She wanted a smile, but there was none. He didn't believe.

Not yet.


Jeremy rode home as if the devil were after him. He had tried to convince Calvin Sooner not to go through with the raid. He hadn't succeeded. It had done nothing for his ego when Calvin laughed at Jeremy when he said he'd stop him.

"You and who else? A cripple and a turncoat. Ain't no one in this town gonna help you."

And they wouldn't. Jeremy had been to every home with an able-bodied man—which weren't many these days. All had said either that they would be on the raid, or that it wasn't their business. They wouldn't lift a hand, much less a firearm, to defend a traitor. Miss Sarah? Too bad about her. She should have moved north with her son. And it being Christmas? Hell, there was damn little Christmas this year.

It had made Jeremy sick.

His last stop had been to see Dr. Colburn, a long-time friend of Ryan's mother and father.

The man had been closing his office. He sighed heavily as he heard Jeremy out. "I've been expecting this," he said. "Just didn't think it would happen this soon."

"Can you do anything?"

"You want to do anything, boy? Thought you didn't have any use for Ryan Baxter. That's what you told folks."

Jeremy went rigid. Was he partially responsible for what was going to happen? "I don't want Miss Sarah hurt," he said harshly.

"And Ryan Baxter?"

Jeremy hesitated, then said slowly, "The war's over."

"For most of those who fought in it," the doctor said slowly. "Not for those who want to make a profit from it."

Jeremy stared at him.

"Baxter Trace is prime land. If the Baxters are killed, it would be sold for taxes. Who has money to buy?"

Jeremy closed his eyes. Why hadn't he seen it? Calvin Sooner and his cronies. He had offered to pay the taxes for Oak Bend. How had he been so blind? "I've got to go, warn them," he said. "I don't know how much good I'll be, but I have to try."

The doctor nodded and showed Jeremy out.

Now the urgency sped Jeremy on. He would stop at his home, get his rifle and sidearm, and hope like hell he could use them. He would make sure Cherise was safe.

The house was dark, though, as was the falling night. Clouds curtained the moon, and only a few stars were visible. He found the note and cursed. Grabbing his guns, he tucked the handgun into the waist of his trousers and cradled the rifle in his good arm. He put the rifle in the scabbard on the saddle and mounted, spurring his already tired animal into a gallop.

# *Chapter Eight*

Cherise had just finished a song when she heard a pounding at the door. There was an urgency to it that drew all four of them to the front hall. Ryan opened the door.

Jeremy stood there in the darkness, but the light from the oil lamp in the hall revealed a face creased with anxiety.

"Jere?" Ryan's voice was tentative, a welcome hovering at the edge of it.

Jeremy looked past him, to his sister, then back to Ryan. His mouth turned down at the corners in a frown, and the green in his eyes deepened. He swallowed hard as Cherise moved closer to Ryan protectively.

Jeremy wasted no words. "You're going to be attacked tonight. Probably fifteen to twenty night riders. They intend to burn you out."

"Tonight?" Cherise said, a sickness gnawing at her stomach. "Christmas Eve?"

He nodded. He turned to Ryan. "We've got to get her out of here. You'd be wise to leave, as well."

Ryan turned toward his mother. Her back stiffened. "No," she said. "The Yanks couldn't push me out. My neighbors certainly won't." She turned to Ryan. "Your father taught me to shoot, and I've been keeping in practice with all the ... deserters and white trash around."

"I'm staying," Cherise said firmly. "I know how to shoot, too, and—"

"No," Ryan and Jeremy roared in unplanned unison.

Then Ryan looked at Jeremy. "Will you take them to your place?"

Jeremy hesitated. "You can't fight them off alone." Ryan's gaze met Jeremy's. Cherise saw something pass between them.

Something dangerous flickered in Ryan's eyes, a hint of the old recklessness Cherise used to see there. "Hell, I can't. Now take them and get out of here."

Sarah Baxter's shoulders squared—a profoundly determined gesture for such a slight woman. She suddenly looked inches taller. "No," she said, "unless you want to drag me."

"And me," Cherise said.

"That's possible," Jeremy said through tight lips.

"We'll just come back," Sarah said, as the two men looked at them with astonished frustration."

"There will be four of us," Cherise said, "and we have the house for protection."

"Five," Milly put in, and four faces turned toward her. "Miss Sarah taught me how to shoot, what with all the rabble 'round lately."

They all looked at Jeremy. Cherise had said "the four of us" so easily, with so much assurance.

"I don't like it," Jeremy muttered. "I'll stay if the women go. Though I don't know how good I'll be."

Cherise smiled at him. Despite the danger, she realized Jeremy hadn't come just for her. Otherwise, he wouldn't have told them about the raid, but would just have demanded she leave. And Ryan would have supported him. Instead, Jeremy had warned them, and was offering his own help, as poor as he thought it was. "We won't leave," she said, and Sarah Baxter nodded. "Even if you do," Cherise threw in as a challenge.

Jeremy and Ryan exchanged looks again.

"Nothing you can do or say will change our minds," Cherise added. "We'd better get prepared. What about the sheriff?"

"I went to see him," Jeremy said. "He won't help. Says it's the army's business. I didn't have time to go to Athens for troops."

Cherise's heart bounced against her rib cage. Jeremy must have sought help before returning home and finding the note. Pride in him swelled within her, even as she saw a similar realization in Ryan's eyes. His mouth moved slightly, but he didn't say anything.

"They won't be expecting much resistance," Jeremy said finally, breaking the uncomfortable silence. "They think it's just you and your mother. Five people shooting at them . . . maybe they'll turn and run."

"And maybe they won't," Ryan replied, looking first at his mother, then at Cherise. "I wish you would go, the three of you," he said, clearly including Milly.

"This is my home," Sarah said. "No one is going to run me off." There was a strength in her voice that Cherise had never heard before.

"If they burn you out," Cherise said quietly, "then they'll think they can burn anyone out. We could be next."

Jeremy suddenly grinned. "I think we'd better get ready. Do you have enough guns? I brought two with me. Don't know how good I'll be with a rifle, but I can shoot a pistol just fine."

"I'm good with a rifle," Cherise said.

Ryan looked at his mother. "I have the two I brought home."

Sarah had a gleam in her eyes. She looked better than anytime Cherise had seen her. "I have a shotgun and three of your father's hunting guns I hid from the Yanks." She ignored the wince on Ryan's face, but Jeremy's smile grew even wider.

Both Ryan and Jeremy had been officers. They didn't waste time, now that the decision had been made to stay. Guns were found and loaded. Lights were quenched. Each person was assigned a room. They would move from window to window in that room. Fire and move. Fire and move. Hopefully the raiders would believe there were more than five defenders, three of them women.

Ryan opened a window so that they could hear horses approach. Cherise came to stand by him as Sarah, Milly and Jeremy went to their posts. Cherise would go to the next room when the riders appeared.

"It's never going to end," he said, regret and despair tugging at each word.

"Jeremy's here," she replied. "One at a time."

"I don't read too much into that," he said. "He's here because of you."

"No," she said slowly. "I don't think so. Or he would have been more insistent on taking me home. He came here for you. It just so happened I was here."

"I don't want you hurt."

"Calvin Sooner is a coward. A few rifle shots, and he and his band of misfits will disappear."

He couldn't see her face, not in the darkness. He saw it, though, in his mind's eye. He saw the small smile, the trust, and above all the gallantry. He'd often thought women, the survivors who picked up the pieces of men's recklessness, were the more gallant of the sexes.

He felt her hand on his, and his fingers interwove with hers.

Time went by. Minutes that seemed like hours. Maybe they wouldn't come. But Ryan knew they would. His instincts were working now. They would probably wait until midnight, when most good citizens were in bed.

Suddenly the sound of hoofbeats broke the silence. A lot of them. Ryan heard a whistle coming from the stairwell. Jeremy was in one of the upstairs rooms. Milly and Sarah were in a second upstairs room. Ryan, the best shot of any of them, had the library overlooking the front lawn. One more squeeze on his hand, and Cherise left for her own post in the parlor across the hall.

Ryan broke out the glass of the window. He heard the tinkling of other glass breaking. And then he saw the lights, torches. And by the torchlight, he saw the riders, perhaps twenty or more. They were masked, with white hoods over their heads, and were yelling.

Rebel yells. He remembered them. They would echo in his mind forever.

He watched the hooded figures approach, and waited until the riders came into range. He aimed his rifle at one of the intruders, hesitating to shoot. Damn it, he had hoped, after the war, never to fire a gun again. He moved his rifle up toward the rider's shoulder, hesitated once more, until a shot shattered a window. Finally, reluctantly, he pulled the trigger. The rider went down. Other shots rang out from the house. Ryan lowered the gun, hoping that the shots would scare off the riders, but they kept coming.

As Ryan started to aim again, more riders appeared. More raiders. Ryan felt his hope dim. Five people, three of them women, could never defend themselves against so many, nor frighten them off. He was the one they wanted. He wouldn't allow the others to be hurt on his account. He was alone now. There was no one to stop him. He left the room and went to the front door, opening it and standing in the doorway.

The yard was bright with torches and all attention was suddenly riveted on him. He leaned down and placed his rifle on the floor and raised his hands in surrender.

Ryan watched one of the hooded men take aim at him, but then a shot rang out, and the man tumbled from his horse. The masked riders tried to control their horses as the newly arrived group of horsemen galloped among them, encircling them. It was only then that Ryan noticed the newcomers weren't masked. Two of the them rode up to the porch.

There were several shots and curses as the masked men quieted their horses. Ryan recognized the two newcomers who approached the porch: Doc Colburn and Sam Bascomb. They dismounted and came to stand next to him, rifles in their hands, rifles that were pointed, strangely enough, at the raiders rather than at Ryan.

Sam Bascomb looked at the rifle on the floor. "What's that doing down there?"

Ryan wasn't sure what was happening. He tried a small smile that he knew wasn't much more than an awkward, unsure movement of his lips.

"Tilting at windmills again, are you?" Colburn said. "Figure you're indestructible? Well, young man, I'm here to tell you different."

Ryan was spared an answer. The man who had aimed at him was rising to his feet. Ryan didn't recognize the voice as he yelled out curses, but the doctor apparently did.

"Take off that silly hood, Calvin. You aren't fooling anyone."

The man did so, and took several feet toward the porch as he held a hand to his bleeding shoulder. "Turning traitor yourself, Colburn?" he asked angrily. "Taking up with a damned turncoat?"

"Better a turncoat than a thief and coward," Colburn retorted irritably. "You been grabbing good folks' land, and we've been sitting back, watching it happen. No more. We're putting you on notice. No more lawlessness, or we'll take care of you ourselves." He paused, allowing his contemptuous gaze to travel over the other riders. "And you...men who hide your faces. Are you going to make Sooner rich by doing his dirty work?''

"Baxter's a dirty Yank," one yelled.

Bascomb moved closer to Ryan. "I lost as much as anyone," he said. "I lost two sons, but by God, the war's over, and I intend it to stay over. I don't agree with what Baxter did, but he went with his conscience, and I gotta respect that. Any of you men have a conscience?" This last was a taunt. "Or do you just do what Sooner tells you to do? Do you know he's been working with the federal tax man to levy taxes on our families, so he can buy the property real cheap? Now he's trying to take Baxter Trace by terrorizing Miz Baxter, who's never been anything but good to everyone in this county."

He hesitated a moment. "We're a community. We should have stepped in to help each other months ago. Instead, we just turned our heads. Everyone but Baxter here."

"What do you mean?" The question came from one of the masked men.

"Baxter helped free my nephew. And he guaranteed his own money for the loans you-all are getting from the bank. But he didn't want anyone to know. He was afraid you wouldn't accept his help. But we sure as hell didn't help each other."

Even in the firelight, Calvin's face seemed to pale. He turned toward the others in his band. "Shoot them!" he ordered.

One of the riders pulled off his hood. "Shoot Doc Colburn? He saved my little girl. I'm going home, where I should be," he added, as if he'd just remembered it was Christmas Eve and he had a family at home. He turned and rode off, without any more words. One man followed him, then another.

"Goddamm you!" Calvin yelled helplessly, as more and more of his followers started to leave. "Tom, you owe me money. Pete..." But one by one they turned and left, until Calvin was the only one left. He turned toward the front porch again. "I'll kill all of you."

"No, you won't," Ryan said as he stepped forward. "You're through in this county. I'll make sure of that."

"So will I," Doc Colburn said. "I'm sure Mr. Baxter here will be glad to prefer charges against you. Attempted murder. I think the... Yanks will believe him, and if he needs our testimony, we'll give it. If I was you, I would get out. And fast."

Calvin stared at them with undisguised hatred, but then his shoulders slumped and he turned toward his horse.

Still stunned by the unexpected help, Ryan turned toward Doc Colburn and saw that the others had come out of the house. His throat was choked with emotion, and he couldn't say what he wanted to say. Cherise slid next to him and took his hand, holding it so tightly, his fingers went numb.

"This young man of yours was going to sacrifice himself," Doc Colburn said, shaking his head. "I don't think he's ever going to get a full head of sense."

Ryan thought he should be insulted. In fact, he didn't know what he was. He was too overwhelmed by emotion, still too stunned by what had just happened. He wanted to say thank you. But he didn't know how. The shock, the disbelief, was too great.

"It's time we got along home to our families," Doc Colburn said. "I don't think you'll have any more unwanted visitors tonight."

Ryan could only nod.

Jeremy stepped up and stood between Ryan and Doc Colburn, turning his attention to the latter. "You said..."

"I don't think I said much of anything, boy," Doc Colburn said. "I just listened. I didn't know how much response I would get. I got a hell of a lot more than I thought. There's good people here." Then his eyes found Miss Sarah, and he grimaced. "Beggin' your pardon, Miss Sarah."

Jeff McDonald, the banker, joined them on the porch, and Ryan turned on him. "You promised not to tell..."

"I lied," the banker said with a small smile.

"It's my fault, Baxter," Doc Colburn said. "He told me in confidence, and I told Sam. I thought it was time people here came to their senses. Including me."

Ryan's frown faded when he saw the pleasure in Cherise's eyes. Her hand squeezed his. His mother was beaming, too.

There was an awkward silence, until Jeremy broke it as he addressed their rescuers. "I'm having a small party tomorrow," he said. "To welcome my friend back home. I hope you-all will come and bring your families."

Dr. Colburn hesitated, then nodded. "If there's no emergency."

Sam Bascomb also hesitated. "I'll have to ask my wife."

Cherise's fingers pressed even tighter against Ryan's, but he understood. You couldn't erase hate in a day, especially when it had festered for years. He didn't offer his hand, because he was afraid no one would take it. "Thank you," he said stiffly. "For my mother and Cherise and ... myself, I ... thank you."

Sarah stepped up. "There's eggnog inside. Won't you come in?"

Bascomb shook his head. "It's Christmas Eve, Miz Baxter. My wife will plain kill me if I don't get home soon."

One by one, the others made similar excuses.

"Tomorrow then," she said hopefully. The five of them—Ryan and Cherise, Milly, Sarah and Jeremy—watched the men ride off, and Cherise moved closer to Ryan.

Sarah led the small procession inside and lit the oil lamp, and Ryan looked toward Jeremy questioningly. "Why? How?"

Jeremy shook his head. "I thought I asked everyone." Then he clamped his mouth shut, as if he'd said too much.

Ryan leaned against a wall. His legs felt weak, unable to hold his weight. At the same time, a seed of warmth started building inside. Cherise was regarding him with an odd smile.

"I don't think you're as alone as you thought," she said softly.

Jeremy hesitated just inside the hall, as if uncertain about his welcome. He looked down at the floor for a moment, then directly at Ryan. "Sam Bascomb said ... you guaranteed money so the bank could make loans. I couldn't get a loan until a few days ago." Understanding spread across his face. Then anger, followed by chagrin. "Why, after the way we all treated you?"

"It's my town, too," Ryan said shortly. A muscle worked in his cheek as he turned toward the front door, opened it and walked outside.

The clouds had disappeared, apparently blown away by the cold wind now rushing through the remaining trees. That same wind seemed to cool the warmth that had been inside. He hadn't wanted to buy friendship.

He walked to the barn, feeling very alone, despite Cherise's assurances in the hall.

"Ryan?" He heard Cherise's voice, soft and worried. He turned toward her.

"What's wrong?" she asked.

"You told them about Corey," he said accusingly.

"No," she said. "They must have found out some other way. It would have been easy enough, if someone checked with the army."

"They came here because they feel they owe me. They don't owe me a damn thing."

"No," she said, her hand seeking his. "If they just felt they owed you, they would have simply resented you more. You said that yourself. They certainly wouldn't have come out on Christmas Eve, away from their families. You made them see what they'd been unable to see before, that you're a good man they want around, a man they would risk themselves for."

"And, Jeremy had no idea how he got that loan. He came here tonight because he...wanted to, because of what you've meant to each other in the past and could again in the future. There will always be some who won't forget, but now you know you have friends and you'll always have a place here in Hope's Way."

He wasn't nearly as sure as as she. His silence said that.

She leaned against him. "Believe." She turned her face up toward his. The moon was out now—not much of it, but between it and the stars, he could see her face, so lovely in its own belief.

It had been so long since he'd believed in anything, in happiness, in peace.

And now he tried. He really tried. He wanted to believe. In the night. In the season. In hope. He wanted to grab her and hold her and ask her to marry him, but he couldn't. Tonight was an aberration. Tomorrow he would be a pariah again. The fact that their rescuers had hesitated at Jeremy's invitation showed that. Rescue and gratitude didn't mean friendship or even acceptance.

He felt her shiver. "We'd better go back," he said, never really answering her.

Jeremy was waiting on the porch, obviously ready to leave. He held out his hand awkwardly. "I wouldn't blame you if you didn't take it."

But Ryan did, and the grip between the two men was strong.

"We have to go," Jeremy said. "Especially if we're having company tomorrow. You and Miss Sarah will be there?"

Ryan released Cherise's hand and held out his arm as if to ward off a blow. "I thank you for the offer, Jeremy, but no one will come."

"They came tonight," Jeremy said. "They'll come tomorrow."

Ryan was dubious, but he didn't want to argue the point.

Jeremy hesitated. "That was a damn-fool thing you did...going out there alone. We could have held them off, even without help."

"I thought Doc and the others were going to join them," Ryan said simply. "My life isn't worth all of yours."

Cherise reclaimed his hand. "Yes, it is," she said softly. "You are my life."

Ryan swallowed hard, a rock choking his throat. She looked so lovely, her green eyes blazing like a defending angel's. He didn't deserve her, nor could he ask her to share an exile's life. But he still gloried in the moment.

He finally forced his eyes from her and turned to Jeremy. "Thanks isn't nearly enough for what you did tonight," he said.

Jeremy shook his head. "I'm...ashamed it was so long in coming. I..." The words stopped, and he looked away. Instead of continuing, he held out his hand to Cherise. "Come on, sis. You'll see him tomorrow."

Cherise hesitated, looking long and hard at Ryan, then stood up on her toes to kiss him. Lightly, tenderly. "Merry Christmas, Ryan Baxter," she said, and then took Jeremy's hand and disappeared out the door.

Ryan watched them leave, still remembering Cherise's words. *Believe.*

Perhaps time would heal wounds. Perhaps someday...

Ryan and Sarah went into the study and just looked at each other for a moment, and then at the thin, homely Christmas tree. It seemed quite splendid, as if some magical Christmas fairies had suddenly added growth to it. Or maybe, Ryan thought whimsically, it had sensed the sudden change in the air. Its very branches appeared to lift upward, instead of drooping toward the ground.

Ryan didn't sleep well that night. He wasn't sure that the night before hadn't been a dream. And he still couldn't believe that the brief goodwill would last.

He and Sarah and Milly exchanged gifts in the morning, and then they prepared to go to Jeremy's. Ryan winced at the ill-fitting nature of his best suit of clothes. He'd not worn them since the beginning of war, and he'd not regained his old weight. They hung on him. But that didn't matter. Preserving something of Christmas did. He desperately wanted Sarah and Cherise to enjoy this day, to regain something they'd lost. He'd known fear during four years of war. He'd known too much of it, in fact. But he'd never known this kind of fear. Ryan knew both his mother and Cherise would be expecting so much today, and he didn't want them shattered on his account, not today. No one would come. He knew that. He wished Sarah and Cherise also understood.

Still, he had promised to go. He put Cherise's present in the buggy. His mother came up to him with a small wrapped package of her own. "You might want to give this to Cherise," she said.

He looked at her questioningly.

She smiled secretly. "You'll know if the time is right."

The sky was clear, the day cold. He helped his mother, who was wearing her new shawl under a cloak, into the dilapidated buggy. He sat still for a moment, then looked at Sarah Baxter. "I'm sorry." he said, "I should have bought a new buggy."

She shook her head. "We don't need a fancy buggy. I'm more pleased you helped the others. I wish you'd told me."

Ryan hesitated, uncertain. He'd trained himself to hold his thoughts and feelings within himself; it had been the only way to survive, both in his father's house and later, in the army. He'd never really talked to his mother since he'd been home, never talked to anyone but Cherise about the pain he felt. But now, this morning, it seemed important. "I'm sorry about so much. I know how much you miss Rad. It should have been—"

"Don't say it," his mother chided, her eyes suddenly filling. She covered one of his hands. "I am so thankful to have you."

"But—"

She stopped him. "I loved both of my boys," she said. "But you were the one that was special. From the beginning, you were special. I'm . . . so sorry that I allowed your father to . . . ever make you think otherwise."

He stared at her. It was the first time she had ever said anything against his father. "I was afraid of him," she said, "and I'll always regret not standing up to him for you. He made Radburn into his own image, selfish and cruel, but you never allowed it to happen to you. Maybe I spent more time with him because I felt he needed me more. I foolishly hoped I could soften his father's influence.'' She swallowed hard. "I was always so proud of you.''

Ryan was stunned. All these years, he'd thought . . . believed . . . he was the unwanted one, the rebel not worthy of love.

His mother's head was down. "I . . . didn't know . . . how cruel your father was until it was too late. When he courted me, he'd been so courteous, so handsome. My family desperately wanted the marriage, and then . . . Rad came. Every time I . . . tried to challenge his cruelty, he would threaten to sell Milly south.'' She put her hand on his arm. "You were my joy, Ryan. And when you came home . . . that was the only thing that mattered.''

Her eyes were swimming in tears. Ryan stopped the horse and put his arm around her. "It's over now,'' he said softly. "I think we're finally going to have some peace.'' He had to believe that. For her sake.

She smiled through the tears—a small, secret smile. "And Cherise . . . I knew she was right for you. All these years . . . I hoped . . .''

His arm tightened around her. "Wise lady,'' he said with love.

"No,'' she said wistfully. "If I had been, you never would have felt that I preferred . . .'' She looked up at him through pleading eyes. "But I knew you were strong where Rad wasn't.''

He put his arm around her and leaned down and kissed her forehead. His heart swelled with the knowledge that he had been truly wanted. Loved. He should have known, should have felt her love, but in his hurt he had looked only for rejection. He was still doing that, he realized. The hope that had started seeding last night grew, crawling into every crevice of his heart.

He and his mother were obviously the first to arrive. No other horses were tethered outside the plain house. He thought of the former great house at Oak Bend, and hurt for Cherise and Jeremy. But Jeremy would rebuild, just as they all would.

Cherise met them at the door, as if she'd been sitting at the window waiting for them. He just stared at her for a moment. She was wearing a lovely red velvet dress, her hair pulled back in a French knot, her green eyes sparkling with pleasure and welcome.

Jeremy's smile was a little stiff, but it was a smile. It bothered Ryan for a moment, until he understood from Jeremy's expression that it was not Ryan's presence, but the house, that shamed him. It was obvious, though, that both Jeremy and Cherise had spent time brightening it. The table was decorated in red, and berry-laden boughs lay on the mantle. Evergreen mixed with red ribbon was everywhere.

A large punch bowl was centered on the table, and cookies and cakes surrounded it.

"I hope," Ryan said, "we don't chase off your other friends."

"If you do," Jeremy replied, a touch of belligerence in his voice, "they're not my friends."

Ryan stood awkwardly for a moment, then handed Cherise her package. She blushed and disappeared, appearing with gifts of her own. There was an unfamiliar shyness about her this morning, and Ryan felt his heart respond in a strange, jerking way. "It...isn't much," she said hesitantly.

He wondered whether she realized she'd already given him the world's most precious gift: her heart. He opened the package almost reverently, touching the frayed edges of the book as if it were made of gold. He turned to a page marked by a small miniature watercolor of daffodils, and he smiled as he read the passage there.

When he looked up, his smile turned into a grin as he offered his own gift. She tore it open eagerly, and stopped, laughter exploding delightedly in the room.

She opened her own volume of Wordsworth's poetry, a newer edition than her own gift, and read what he had written as an inscription.

To Cherise, my phantom of delight.

Her eyes shone as she looked back up at him.

Ryan suspected what was in the package his mother had given him. It was in his pocket, and he fingered it. He wanted to pull it out. He wanted to do that as much as he'd ever wanted anything. But still he hesitated.

His hand came out empty as they heard the sound of buggies and horses from outside. Ryan stood uncertainly, Cherise beside him, as guests came into the house, most of them men who had defended him last night. They had their wives and families, and each greeted Ryan and Cherise, some a little coolly, but most with something close to warmth.

Ryan stood there, his arm around Cherise, thinking about past Christmases: the expansive celebrations, the lines of carriages, heavily laden tables and festively dressed guests. Now the clothes were worn, the food was plain, the house was bare, yet he'd never before felt this wonderful, warm spirit that invaded the room. His hand tightened around Cherise's as the last of the guests, Doc Colburn, came up to him and held out his hand. "I know this is a bit belated, but welcome back to Hope's Way."

The afternoon seemed to rush by. Sarah looked blissful, Jeremy self-satisfied. Ryan found himself watching the merriment, still feeling a bit apart. He had always been apart, a round peg in a square hole. Bewildered and even confused about what was happening, he walked out the door and down to the quiet, iron-fenced cemetery, where one great oak had been spared.

He thought he had left unnoticed, but in a few seconds, Cherise was standing next to him. "I told you to believe," she said.

Ryan looked down at her with a crooked smile. "So you did."

"But you still don't?"

He found his smile turning into a grin. "With you, I believe in anything." His arms went around her. She reached into them, lifted herself on tiptoe and kissed him. A soft promise of a kiss.

"I love you," she whispered as her lips moved away, just enough to say the words. She had said them before; now, for the first time, he could accept them. He saw the figures inside the house. Moving around. Talking. Laughing. Lifting their glasses. They had given him, and what he was, a measure of belonging. It was a wonder to him.

"You make magic," he said softly into her ear.

"No," she replied. "You did it yourself."

He took her hand. "Will you marry me?"

She grinned, her heart contracting madly. "I thought you would never ask."

He reached in his pocket for the tiny package. "My mother said I would know when the time was right."

Cherise held it for a moment, then opened it, finding an antique emerald ring. "It was her mother's wedding ring," Ryan remembered. "She cherished that ring because her mother had been so happy." He slipped it on Cherise's finger.

A tear shone in her eye.

He leaned down and kissed it away. "Let's go tell Jeremy."

They walked together, his arm around her. He felt like dancing all the way. He felt like shouting. He felt like ... a Christmas miracle.

Everyone turned as they entered, as if they had been waiting for them. Ryan looked down at her, and then at Jeremy. He stopped in front of his friend, and former enemy. He still half expected opposition. He hesitated a moment, then asked, "May I have the hand of your sister in marriage?"

Jeremy grinned. "I'd be disowned if I said no." He hugged his sister, then lifted his glass in public acceptance. "To my sister and her future husband."

Another voice, "And to Christmas ... friends ... and peace."

The last word was nearly drowned in the answering refrain. "To peace."

Cherise leaned against him and looked up, her heart in her eyes. "Welcome home, my love."

\* \* \* \* \*

## Patricia Potter

When her impressive first novel, *Swamp Fire*, was released by Harlequin Historicals in 1988, Patricia Potter won the Maggie Award and a Reviewer's Choice Award from *Romantic Times*. Since then, she has written numerous novels and short stories, regularly made the Waldenbooks and *USA Today* Bestseller lists and won another Reviewer's Choice Award. She also received the *Romantic Times* Career Achievement Award for Storyteller of the Year.

**Swamp Fire is currently available from Harlequin's MIRA Books. Don't miss this opportunity to pick up your copy of Patricia Potter's award-winning first novel!**

**On sale now from MIRA Books.**

# BAYBERRY AND MISTLETOE

## Miranda Jarrett

# Chapter One

*Newport, Colony of Rhode Island and Providence Plantations, 1770*

"Mr. Howland has asked me to marry him, Father," said Bethany Sparhawk, her voice trembling just a little, "and I would have you know I've accepted."

For a long moment, her father stared at her, the silence in the chilly parlor growing more ominous with every passing second. Over her father's broad shoulder, Bethany saw them both reflected in the gold-framed bull's-eye mirror over the mantelpiece, his tall, stern figure in dark blue, with his hands clasped behind his waist, herself in pale pink, so small before him as she braced herself for the inevitable blast of his reaction.

At last, too soon, it came. "William Howland has asked you to wed?" thundered Gabriel Sparhawk in disbelief. "Howland has the gilt-edged audacity to ask for one of my daughters?"

"Yes, Father." Though Bethany struggled to meet her father's gaze, she failed miserably as always and instead she stared at the polished silver buckles on his shoes. "We thought we would marry next month, during Christmas week."

"*You* thought! What about what *I* think, Bethany? Why in blazes would you want to shackle yourself to a man old enough to be your grandfather?"

"William's only forty-seven, Father!" protested Bethany, her hands twisting anxiously over her lace-trimmed apron. "I'll be twenty-one myself next October, so that's—"

"I can do the ciphering well enough, miss, and it doesn't please me one bit." Those silver buckles, and the feet beneath them, were widespread now, as if the polished parlor floor were her father's quarterdeck. Whether by his crew or his children, her father was a man accustomed to being obeyed. "Why you'd accept—"

Abruptly he broke off and swore furiously to himself. With his fingers beneath her chin, he lifted Bethany's face toward his, so she had no choice but to look at him.

"Howland hasn't dishonored you, has he, lass?" he demanded, his hard green eyes searching for the truth. "All that time you've spent in his company—has he shamed you so you feel you must wed him? Because if he has, so help me, I'll—"

"Hush, Gabriel, don't be ridiculous," said Bethany's mother, Mariah, drawn to the room by the anger in her husband's voice. Gently she slipped her arm around Bethany's shoulders, leaving her father no choice but to release her chin. "Our Bethany would never do anything to shame the family."

Inwardly Bethany winced at her mother's assurance, in its way as painful as her father's suspicions. Of course Bethany would never shame her family. She was the quiet little wren of a middle daughter that no one ever noticed, overwhelmed on either side by her bold, beautiful sisters.

"William Howland has befriended her, that is all," continued Mariah, her satin-covered arm still resting protectively across Bethany's shoulders, "and though there might be other ways for her to spend her time than with her nose buried in the picture books he lends her, I see no real harm to it, else I never would have allowed her to visit his house in the first place."

"Harm!" repeated her father scornfully. "I'll show you harm! Howland's asked her to wed him, doubtless with his eye on the dowry she'll bring with her!"

"It's not like that, Father, I swear it isn't!" cried Bethany in anguish. "Can't you believe that William might want me for a reason other than your money?"

"Of course he does, lamb," said her mother gently, but Bethany didn't miss the angry look she flashed at her husband. "Your father cares for you, child. We both do—and we don't wish to see you hurt. Marriage is not to be taken lightly, and you are still so young."

"But Jerusa's been promised to Thomas Carberry for nearly two years!"

"Your sister's different from you, Bethany, as different as Thomas Carberry is from William Howland. She knew her own mind, and was more than ready to make a suitable choice for a husband."

Bethany's cheeks flushed with humiliation. Jerusa was the reigning belle of Newport, and even with her marriage to Thomas set for the spring, young men still flocked around her, the same young men that Bethany knew all too well had never noticed her existence.

"I know my own mind, too, Mama," she said with wistful honesty. "I know that I couldn't wish for a finer husband than Mr. Howland."

"But a widower, and so much older, too! Oh, I'll grant you that he's yet a handsome man, but still..." Mariah sighed with concern. "Perhaps we might consider a long betrothal, two years, the same as Jerusa's."

"Oh, no, Mama, no!" cried Bethany, her words tumbling out in a rush. "We wish to marry this Christmas, when Jon and Joshua are home and we'll all be together at Crescent Hill. Dr. Carter can marry us there in the hall, and we can hang holly and bayberry and mistletoe instead of flowers and bring the chairs from the dining room for the guests, and it will all be so *perfect,* Mama, if you and Father will only say yes!"

"Oh, lamb," her mother murmured, and though she smiled, Bethany could have sworn there were tears in her eyes. "You have it all planned, don't you? Do you love your Mr. Howland so very much that six weeks is the most you can bear to wait?"

*Her Mr. Howland.* Bethany had never dared yet think of William like that. Though with his town house on the same street as their own, she'd known him all her life, it was only in these last months that their relationship had so subtly changed, and that his company and his home had become her sanctuary from the noisy Sparhawk household. She pictured William's crooked smile when their eyes met, and how he not only sought her opinions, but listened with genuine interest when she spoke. She remembered how he'd given her the last summer rose from his garden, and then solemnly called her his dearest Bethany as he lifted her fingertips to his lips.

*Her Mr. Howland, soon to be her husband.*

"Yes, Mama," she whispered, almost afraid to confess the truth aloud. "I believe I do."

Another look passed between her parents, a wordless, intimate exchange that had nothing now to do with anger. After twenty-six years of marriage, her mother and father remained almost improperly passionate toward one another, and Bethany felt an unfamiliar anticipation quicken within her. Would she, too, come to feel that kind of bond with William Howland?

"Bethany, child," said Mariah softly, pulling her close into her arms, into the warm, familiar haven of satin and lavender. "Whenever did you grow old enough to fall in love?"

Self-consciously her father cleared his throat. "Howland's trading should have done well enough to support a wife," he said gruffly, "and there's only the single son of his to consider when we arrange the settlement."

"Oh, a pox on your settlements, Gabriel," declared her mother with her customary defiance, and at once Bethany knew she'd won. "We have a wedding to arrange. And my, what a Christmas this shall be!"

# Chapter Two

After two months at sea on the long voyage from England, Robin Howland welcomed the chance to walk again on ground that did not buck and slide beneath his feet, and instead of accepting a ride he had arranged to have his boxes and chests delivered later to his father's house. It was his first return to Newport since he'd left home ten years before, and he walked slowly through the twilight, marveling at all that had changed in that time.

His father had written so proudly of all the new building that reflected Newport's prosperity—fine gentlemen's houses, a new brick market house, warehouses and shops by the dozen along the wharves—and yet to Robin's eyes, long accustomed to the scale of London, the city still seemed hopelessly tiny and provincial.

Yet, above all else, Newport was still Robin's hometown, the place he'd been born, and with a bittersweet eagerness he looked for the landmarks of his boyhood. There was the Widow McGeery's apple tree, the branches bare now, in the winter, that he and his friends had shinnied up and shaken for fruit every

September; there at the head of Queen Anne Square stood the white clapboard church with his family's pew, and the churchyard where they'd buried his mother the same week he was born; and there, to the west of Bowen's Wharf, his father's countinghouse, the discreet signboard with the gilded letters—William Howland & Son, Newport & London—flapping back and forth over the doorway in the November wind.

Robin pulled his greatcoat closer around his chest against the swirling bit of a snow squall and the chill that echoed the uncertainty in his heart. What, he wondered, would his father's reaction be when his only son reappeared on his doorstep?

Ten years, and yet too clearly Robin could remember the shame and disappointment that his father had made no effort to conceal as he saw him off on the wharf. It had been William Howland's dream that Robin would be the family's first true gentleman. While his father dedicated all his time and energy to increasing the family's fortunes, Robin's task had been to study with the best tutors in the colony. So successful had he been that, at sixteen, Robin had easily been accepted into Harvard College.

But when finally freed of his father's stern admonitions and the loneliness of a home without a mother or siblings, Robin's high spirits had exploded with youthful exuberance. He had become a master of gentlemen's vices rather than genteel scholarship, and after one final night of revelry with his companions in a waterfront brothel that involved wine, women and, unfortunately, the night watch, he had been sent home from the college in disgrace.

His father's punishment had been equally swift. If Robin would not make himself a gentleman, then his father would make him a merchant in his own mold. He had been sent to London to learn trade in his uncle's offices, until, in time, he had been able to assume his father's business affairs there.

In heartbroken exile, Robin had strived desperately to redeem himself in his father's eyes, and in time had both turned the profits that his father expected and become the gentlemen that he hadn't. But in ten years the gulf between them had only widened, their letters confined to business, and while his father had never invited Robin to return to Newport, neither had Robin ventured to make the journey home on his own.

Until now. Robin blew into his cupped hands, wishing he'd worn warmer gloves, and tried to imagine how his father had changed. He would be an old man, nearly fifty, and Robin hoped he'd still be strong enough for the voyage back to London he'd planned for them together.

It was nearly dark when at last he turned down Farewell Street and his father's house, with its gambrel roof, rose before him. Snow iced the edges of the dark gray clapboarding and dusted the brass knocker and doorknob, though a servant had already swept the two marble steps clear. Behind the windows of the front rooms, the shutters had been closed against the cold and the night, but the faint gold outlines from candlelight within proved his father was home. Eagerly Robin turned the knob and pushed open the door, shaking the snow from his black tricorn as he drew it from his head.

A young maidservant he didn't recognize bustled into the hall from the kitchen, wiping her hands on her apron. She gasped and froze, startled by the sight of the stranger who'd let himself into her master's house. Quickly Robin lay his gloved forefinger across his lips to beg her silence.

"Did I hear the door, Martha?" called his father's unmistakable voice from behind the closed parlor door. As Martha opened her mouth to answer, Robin shook his head and winked with just the right degree of conspirator's charm both to keep her quiet and make her blush. "Martha? Where are you, girl?"

Then came the footsteps growing louder, the parlor door thrown open, and there, at last, stood his father, dressed to go out, a little heavier, his face a little more lined, but otherwise exactly as Robin remembered him from the wharf so long ago.

"Robin?" he asked, his voice no more than a hoarse whisper of disbelief. "Is that really you, lad?"

"None other, sir," answered Robin, his breath tight in his chest. "The prodigal returned."

"You've prospered more than that, I trust." The older man scowled and fidgeted with his pocket watch. "There's no trouble with the firm, is there, Robin? Some ill news you couldn't trust to letters?"

"No, Father, nothing's amiss." No welcome, then, no greeting, not even the commonest of courtesies. Though Robin had feared all along that his return would be like this, still he'd dared hope it might be otherwise, and bitterly he realized that his father hadn't changed a bit. "We have, as you say, prospered."

His father grunted. "Then why are you in Newport?"

*For your sake, Father!* Robin wanted to shout, but instead he fell back on the speech he'd rehearsed during the voyage. "It has been ten years, Father, and I beg you to consider that in that time I—"

"No begging, Robin," said his father, interrupting him. "Howlands don't beg, not even for the sake of speechifying."

Robin nodded curtly, struggling now to control his temper and not turn on his heel and walk back out the door. Lord knew it couldn't be any chillier in the snowy street than here in his father's front hall. "I believed that it was time enough for us to set aside our differences. Christmas, the New Year—when better, Father?"

"Christmas." His father sighed and shook his head. "By now I'd credited you with more sense than to come traipsing clear across the sea for some silly notion of a holiday."

"Father, if that is all this means to you, then—"

"Nay, Robin, if you would but listen!" said his father irritably. "Now that you are here, it is perhaps for the best. After all these years, Robin, I've finally decided to remarry, and the lady has done me the honor of accepting my offer. We plan to wed at Christmas, and it will look well to have you here."

Stunned, at first Robin could think of nothing appropriate to say. "Congratulations, Father." He finally managed to choke the words out. "I wish you and the lady every joy."

"Thankee, lad." For the first time, his father smiled. "I'll wager you judged your old father too old to be dazzled by a pretty face, eh?"

Exactly so, thought Robin. But in a town like Newport, where so many men looked to the sea for their living and too often found early deaths instead, there were always handsome, willing widows eager to remarry. The surprise was more that his father had remained alone as long as he had.

"And such a pretty face my little Mistress Sparhawk has, too!" continued his father fondly. "Long as you've been away, Robin, you do remember the family, don't you?"

"The Sparhawks?" Of course Robin remembered the Sparhawks. No one born in Newport could ever forget them, the men all brawling privateersmen scarcely better than pirates, and as for the women— Well, Robin couldn't believe his father would form such an attachment. "For God's sake, Father, not the Sparhawks!"

His father glared at him. "And why not, I ask you? Don't judge them fine enough for your London tastes?"

"No, nor for yours, either, Father," said Robin, too tired now to watch what he said any longer. In London he'd had his share of run-ins with the Sparhawk sons, shipmasters like their father when there was no war to condone their form of piracy, and he knew exactly how many fair markets and cargos that Sparhawk audacity had cost the Howlands. The last thing he wanted was to be connected to them by marriage.

"I don't care if that old rogue captain's finally gone to the devil," he said wearily. "No amount of his gold's worth you marrying his widow. You remember the stories, how she ran off to chase Frenchmen with him when she was scarce more than a girl, bearing God knows how many of his baseborn brats—"

"Six," said the small woman standing in the parlor doorway. "I have it on the best authority, you see, since I'm one of them, just as I can assure you that my father is quite well and has no hasty intentions of leaving my mother a widow."

Speechless, Robin could only stare at the young woman in the black cloak before him and mentally curse whatever impulse had made him speak so unwisely. She was young, far too young—who would have guessed his father would choose a bride that could be his daughter?—and though she might be a Sparhawk, she didn't resemble any of the others he'd met. For one thing, she was small, the top of her head barely clearing his father's shoulder as she stood beside him. Her coloring was different, too, her dark blond hair gleaming like honey in the candlelight and her skin as fair as June roses.

He bowed low over one leg, struggling to correct his blunder. Blast his father for not telling him the girl was here before he made such a fool of himself! "Forgive me, Miss Sparhawk, for my thoughtlessness."

"Thoughtlessness indeed," she said, her voice soft but her words tart. "You've not only questioned my legitimacy, but as much as called my mother a harlot."

"I know I've no right to your forgiveness, miss," he said stiffly, his head still bowed low. "I should never have spoken so."

"You only spoke what you believed, sir, and all your pretty apologies can't change that sorry truth," she answered, the edge still in her voice. "I can only promise you that my family is not so very bad as you would make us out to be."

Oh, aye, she was a Sparhawk after all, decided Robin grimly, with a quick eye for another's disadvantage. But as he rose he saw how his father had curled his arm protectively around her shoulders, drawing her close, and how her little gloved hand had slipped into his. There was an understanding between them that Robin couldn't miss, an unmistakable tenderness in the way that William Howland smiled down at her. With a sharp sense of loss, Robin realized that this girl with the honey-colored hair had somehow found the place in his father's heart that he himself had never had.

"This, Bethany, is my son Robin," said his father. "Though the Lord knows I tried to rear him with better grace and breeding than he's shown you."

"Father, I can assure you—"

"I've bloody well had enough of your assurances tonight, Robin," his father said curtly as he settled his hat on his head. "I'll see Bethany home now. You and I shall speak later."

The girl bowed her head to lift her hood over her hair, and with a little swirl of snow from the street they were gone, the door closing behind them with a finality that echoed through the hall, and Robin's heart with it. He rested his hand on the newel post, his fingers tightening around the carved pineapple on the top. The fruit was the symbol of hospitality; the irony was not lost on him.

Welcome home, he thought bitterly. Welcome home, and a merry Christmas.

# Chapter Three

"Jerusa? Are you still awake?"

In the deep feather bed beside Bethany her older sister shifted. "How can I sleep while you're talking?"

"I'm sorry, Rusa, but this is important," said Bethany urgently. "I did something...something very wrong today, and I don't know what to do about it."

"What could you possibly have done that was wrong, Bethany?" grumbled Jerusa. "Stirred Father's coffee in the wrong direction?"

"Don't make light of me, Rusa, I beg you! After all the times I've listened to you talk about your darling Tom, I should think you'd do the same just once for me."

"Oh, very well. Let me get the candle." The bed shifted again as Jerusa leaned to one side to shove back the bed's curtains and reach for the candlestick and flint on the table. There was a little spray of sparks as she lit the wick and then, very carefully, brought the candle into the cozy, curtained space of the tall bed.

Although their mother had strictly forbidden this—candles in bed were dangerous, as well as an expen-

sive luxury—their bedchamber with the fire banked
for the night was simply too cold in November. Besides, as Bethany and her sister had long ago learned,
there was no other place in the house where they could
be sure they wouldn't be overheard by their three
brothers or younger sister.

Holding the candlestick in one hand, Jerusa pulled
the quilt higher over her shoulders, the candle's glow
making a bright circle of light over her face. Unlike
Bethany, she had inherited the family's characteristic
black hair and green eyes and the supreme self-
confidence—some called it brashness, or worse—that
went with it.

"So tell me, Anny-Beth," she said, not unkindly,
"what grievous thing did you do this day?"

Bethany crossed her legs beneath her night rail and
tugged nervously on the end of her braid. Although
her sister was only two years older, she was infinitely
more experienced with the peculiarities of gentlemen.
"You know that brig from London that made the
harbor today?"

"From London? Faith, no, I didn't!" said Jerusa
excitedly. "Do you know if the captain brought any
dress stuffs? I've set my heart on a plum-colored silk
lutestring for my gown for your wedding, and there's
nothing at all suitable in the shops at present."

"Listen to me, Jerusa, this is far more important
than any silly gown! Among the London passengers
was William's son Robin, come back home without
any warning. And, oh, Rusa, the things he said about
Mama and Father when he learned his father means to
marry me, and then what I said back to him!"

"I didn't even know Mr. Howland had a son," said Jerusa, her dark brows drawn together as she considered the possibilities. "How strange to think that you'll be his stepmama."

"It's not strange, it's horrible!" cried Bethany. "He's twenty-eight—even older than Jon—and such a righteous, fashionable London-bred prig you've never seen. Already he hates me, simply because my name is Sparhawk!"

"Is he handsome?"

"Handsome?" Bethany stopped to think. She'd been so horrified by her meeting with Robin Howland, playing it over and over in her mind, that she'd nearly forgotten her first impression of him. He'd been standing there at the bottom of the stairs, his dark chestnut hair shining beneath the hallway lantern and drops of melted snow glittering on the shoulders of his black greatcoat. He had had an undeniable presence, a certain quiet dignity that had impressed her.

Until, that is, he'd opened his mouth to slander her parents and she'd retaliated with a vehemence that shocked her even more than it did him.

"Yes," she said slowly. "Robin Howland would be considered handsome by the world, but he is so mean-spirited and arrogant that I wouldn't trade a hundred of him for William."

Jerusa curled a lock of her hair between her fingers. "Well, then, he likely deserved whatever you said to him. Or did William take you to task afterward?"

"Oh, no, not at all. He asked if I was upset, and that was that. He said scarcely another word until we reached our house." Bethany paused and looked away, blushing so furiously that Jerusa couldn't help but notice.

"Then what, Anny-Beth?" she asked archly. "Then what did your William say, or was it what he did?"

"He kissed me." Bethany's face felt on fire with embarrassment. To Jerusa this would be nothing, considering all the liberties she'd admitted to allowing Tom Carberry, but to Bethany it was all so new, even a quick kiss stolen in the shadows of the house, her chilly lips barely brushing William's as the snowflakes danced around them.

"Not the first time, either, I'll vow," crowed Jerusa, rocking back with a knowing smile. "No matter that he's so old, Bethany, Mr. Howland will treat you well. I've never seen a gentleman so smitten with a lady as he is by you."

But Bethany's expression remained serious. "Yet that's what bothers me most, Rusa. How can he be so kind to me and then so cruel to his own son? I kept thinking how Mama falls upon our brothers whenever they come home, even if they've only been away for a few weeks. Here poor Robin has been gone ten years—ten years!—yet William didn't so much as ask him to take off his coat."

"So you despise your new son for his arrogance, but you pity him, too," noted Jerusa wryly. "He was vastly ill-mannered to you, but because his father didn't welcome him home with bells and whistles, you feel somehow he can be excused, while you, my poor sister, without any such excuse, believe that you've wronged him."

Miserably Bethany looked down at her lap, twisting the pearl ring that William had given her. Her sister always saw these things so much more clearly than she did herself. "Then I should apologize to Robin, shouldn't I?"

"You should do nothing of the sort, you silly goose!" declared Jerusa. "He's the one who owes you an apology, not the other way around. At least that's what William will believe, and so you must, too. He's the Howland you're going to marry."

"But, Jerusa—"

"No, Bethany, you listen to me." Her face solemn in the candlelight, she reached across and took Bethany's hands in her own. "If you wish to be a good wife to William, you won't let anything, not even his son, stand between the two of you. *Especially* not his son! You can see it's that way with Father and Mama, and that's how it will be between Tom and me, too. You must forget all this nonsense about poor Robin this-and-that now, before you bumble in so deep you won't be able to get out."

Bethany nodded, her eyes round and her fingers cold in her sister's hands. For all that she felt overshadowed by Jerusa, she was going to miss sharing this bed with her, and the confidences that went with it. What, she wondered, was it going to be like with William lying beside her instead?

"No more nonsense about apologies, either," said Jerusa firmly. "If Robin Howland apologizes to you, so much the better. And if you've any sense at all, you'll pray he goes straight back to London on the very next ship that will take him."

"This is fine, Robin, most fine," said his father as he held the large Canton bowl in two hands up to the light of the warehouse window. "You say you brought back a score of these? Don't know how the Chinamen use them, but here they'll serve most admirably for punch. I'll wager they'll all be sold to Newport tables before Christmas."

"I thought they'd sell well. The fancy goods generally do." Robin turned to the next crate, prying open the slats himself as he tried not to think of how oddly unreal the conversation was.

Hoping for a new beginning to his visit and a chance to undo as much of the damage as he could, he'd been determined to wait for his father's return last night so that they could talk. But the exhaustion from the long-drawn voyage, coupled with the warm fire in the parlor, had proved stronger than Robin's resolution, and he'd awakened this morning in an armchair with a stiff neck, no closer to reconciling with his father.

Yet, to his surprise, at breakfast his father had mentioned nothing of Bethany Sparhawk or Robin's response to her. Instead, he'd suggested brusquely that they go to the warehouse and inspect the goods that Robin had brought with him from London. Instantly Robin had agreed, pausing only to shave and change his clothes, and together the two men had walked the short distance along Thames Street.

His father had determinedly kept the conversation on trade, just as his letters always had, without a hint of anything personal, and uncomfortably Robin had followed his cue, the unspoken truce leaving him off-balance and unhappy. How could his father behave as if nothing had happened, either last night or ten years ago?

Carefully William set the ornate porcelain bowl down on the desk and turned to the crate Robin had just opened. Shoving back his coat sleeves, he reached deep into the wood shavings for the next treasure. But when he pulled out the little wooden shepherdess with the strings trailing from her jointed limbs, his brows rose with dismay.

"What's this claptrap, Robin?" he asked, the little woman's painted smile unflagging as she dangled from his hand. "Some sort of child's plaything, eh?"

"More a plaything for the gentry, really, a sort of puppet that the French call a marionette." He took the puppet from his father, untangled her strings, and made her execute a clumsy curtsy on the floor. "They're all the fashion in London, at Vauxhall, Ranleigh, even at court."

William stared dubiously at the little shepherdess dancing before him. "They may be the fashion in London, but I doubt they'll find a place here. Too much like playacting, Robin. We've still laws here in the colony against that sort of tomfoolery, you know."

"On the books from an earlier time, perhaps, but I cannot believe that Newport people worldly enough to purchase Canton bowls for Christmas punch would see sin in a little puppet!"

"Worldly Newport people like the Sparhawks?"

Evenly Robin met his father's gaze. "Aye, like the Sparhawks."

"You don't believe I should marry the girl, do you?"

"I believe you should not be hasty in choosing a wife."

"Hasty, my foot." William dropped heavily into the chair beside the desk. "That's the sort of warning I should be giving you, not the the other way around. Why aren't I, eh? You've turned into a handsome enough gentleman. Isn't there some lass in London that's taken your fancy?"

Robin thought of the merchants' daughters that had simpered before him in their fathers' parlors, and thought, too, more fondly, of the succession of little French milliners and aspiring actresses that he'd kept as his mistresses since he'd arrived in London so long ago. "Not really, no. There's no special lady as yet."

"Then you've never been in love?"

"Not the way the poets describe," he said lightly. How the devil he had ever gotten into a conversation like this with his father? "Someday I suppose I shall."

William grunted. "You can fit what the poets know about it into a thimble and toss it in the sea. A lot of stuff and nonsense, that."

He tugged self-consciously at his shirt cuff. "The truth is, Robin, I don't love Bethany the same way I loved your mother, if that's what's eating at you. Your mother was special, and I could no more love Bethany Sparhawk like that than I could make myself eighteen again and cut a jig on Bannister's Wharf. But that sweet little lass will make me happy, Robin, and I mean to do my best for her. You can't wish to deny me that, can you?"

Slowly Robin nodded. For his father's sake, he would try to accept the Sparhawk girl into their family, though how his father could call that sharp-tongued shrew "sweet" was beyond him.

William cleared his throat. "Well then, at least I can count on you not to stand up and stop the wedding. Did I tell you it was Christmas Day, Robin? Bethany had her heart set on it, when she could be sure her brothers would be home. At Crescent Hill—"

"Hold a moment, Father, I beg you."

William stopped, his expression wary at the interruption, and Robin took a deep breath. This wasn't the way he'd planned to make his proposal, but then, nothing about this visit was turning out the way he'd expected.

"Father, I want you to return to England with me. Close up the house, leave the Newport office to an agent, and manage our affairs with me from London."

"Return to England?" repeated William, dumbfounded. "How can I return, when I've never set foot in the blessed place? Have you lost your wits, boy?"

"Of course, I'll expect you to bring Miss Sparhawk, too," said Robin quickly. "The voyage is hard for ladies, I know, but—"

Impatiently, William swept his hand through the air. "The voyage won't be hard for her, Robin, because she won't be making it, any more than I will. You don't need my help in London, if that's what this is about. I was born on this island, and I've every intention of dying here, too."

"But that's my reason, Father! I don't want you dying at all, at least for a good many years, and if you remain here you may well find yourself in the middle of a civil war!"

"Don't be ridiculous, Robin," snapped William. "You make it sound as if the folk here are no better than Nolly Cromwell's Roundheads!"

"Are they?" demanded Robin, concern for his father filling his voice with urgency. "In Parliament there's talk of little else than how the hotheads in the colonies are making demands that no sane Englishman could condone! The disrespect towards the royal governors, the violence shown the tax officers and any others sympathetic to the crown, won't be tolerated much longer, and I don't want you here when a frigate sails into Newport's harbor."

William scoffed. "It will never come to that. Whatever you've heard in London's but hearsay and tattle."

"What I've heard is that last summer the men of this town captured and burned one of the king's own revenue vessels!"

"Oh, aye, poor Captain Reid, left without a command. A pretty piece of work that was, wasn't it?" The mockery in William's knowing smile shocked Robin. "Perhaps now those fancy lordlings across the water will think twice about forcing their whims on us."

"Father, please." Robin struggled to control both his temper and his suspicions, not wishing to have the conversation degenerate into a shouting match. "I don't wish to see you suffer merely because of where you live."

"God help you, boy, have you lived so long among 'em that you've taken their side?" asked William, with a mixture of disbelief and dismay. "When I sent you there, I never intended that. You're a Newport man first, Robin, then an Englishman."

An English gentleman, Robin wanted to shout. As long as he could remember, that goal had been drummed into his head, and after years of striving toward it to please his father, he now learned he'd been chasing the wrong one. He wasn't a Newport man any longer. He was an Englishman who'd been born in Newport. Why else would it matter so much that his father return to London with him now, back to the world where he'd found success?

His father was peering at him uncertainly. "A Howland and a Newport man, right, lad?"

Robin swallowed. "I shall always be a Howland and your son," he answered at last. If he had come by nothing else in London, he had learned the gentleman's art of the properly worded reply.

"As it should be, Robin, as it should be," said his father, smiling as he visibly relaxed. "Now then, I expect you'll wish to call on Bethany to make your apologies. No, don't say it. You said enough last night, and now you must make amends."

"If I apologize to Miss Sparhawk," said Robin as he reached for his hat, "then will you consider coming to London?"

"I'll consider it." William eyed him shrewdly, and with more than a touch of pride. "Oh, aye, Robin, beneath those dandy's threads you're pure Howland, always with an eye for bargaining."

But Robin wasn't so sure.

# *Chapter Four*

Bethany frowned at the picture before her, chewing on the reeded end of her brush as she considered whether the red gown that she'd painted on the figure of her mother was too dark. It was hard, painting from memory like this, but if she wanted the watercolor to be a surprise for Mariah on Christmas morning she didn't really have a choice. Perhaps a drop more cochineal and the red would be truer. With a sigh, she reached for the little bottle of pigment to deepen the wash in the clam shell before her.

"Miss Sparhawk?"

With a startled gasp, she looked up. Not him, she thought with dismay, not William's odious son.

"I didn't mean to frighten you," Robin said as he lifted his hat with a smile and a slight bow. "Your little sister—Rachel, isn't it?—said I'd find you in the garden."

"And so you did." Swiftly she tried to shield her painting with her arm. She hated for anyone to see her work before she was satisfied with it herself, and the thought of what an ill-tempered critic like Robin Howland might say made her even more protective.

"After the flurries last evening, I wouldn't expect to find you here," he said, ignoring her lack of welcome, "but then, I'd forgotten how changeable Newport weather can be. This morning seems almost balmy, and here in the shelter of that brick wall you have a most pleasant situation for your amusements."

"They're not amusements," she said defensively. "They're paintings. Or do you share my father's view that ladies should have no such serious interests?"

His brows pulled together with exasperation, exactly the way that William's did, and Bethany felt an odd little jolt of recognition, and longing. If William were of her generation, he would look like this, his hair dark chestnut instead of gray and his handsome face unlined, his body still lean beneath the elegant fitted waistcoat.

"If you would be so kind as to let me judge for myself," said Robin, leaning to one side to look past her arm to another painting spread on the table to dry, "then I could offer an opinion."

Bethany hesitated, considering how deeply his criticism might sting.

"I swear that I will judge only the painting, not the painter."

He smiled again, and Bethany remembered Jerusa's question. Oh, yes, there was no denying that Robin Howland was a handsome man, and in the warmth of that smile she felt her face grow hot.

"Please, Miss Sparhawk."

"Oh, very well." She'd show him anything to make him stop looking at her like that. She reached for the printed map of the southern colonies that she'd col-

ored as a Christmas gift for her father, still shielding
the painting of her mother. "Here."

He took the map and tipped it toward the sun, and
the careful way he held the paper, just by the edges,
both surprised and pleased her.

"This is well executed," he said slowly. "The col-
ors are even, and you've managed to stay within the
lines quite nicely."

"That is exactly what my father shall say."

He glanced at her curiously. "What else could he
say? Not that tidiness isn't praiseworthy, but it's not
the same as originality."

"My father doesn't expect me to be original. Genteel ladies color prints, so this is what will please him
most for Christmas."

"And are those Christmas gifts, as well?" He
pointed to several smaller, finished paintings in an
open portfolio on the back of the table.

Bethany nodded as Robin walked around the table
to bend over the pictures. "For my brothers. They're
captains, you see, and I thought they'd like pictures of
their vessels. The sloop belongs to Josh, the schooner
to Nick, and the brig, of course, is Jon's."

They were, as she said, all portraits of sailing ships,
drawn with an attention to detail that astounded
Robin. How had this prim little girl in the fingerless
gloves captured something as masculine as a ship so
vividly? The painted sails billowed and the pennants
snapped in the same sharp breeze that made the bright
blue waves dance about the ships' black hulls.

"They're quite good," he said, and noticed again
how pretty she was when she blushed. "But this ship
here doesn't belong to your family. If I'm not mis-

taken, she's the *Macedonian,* and she belongs to Howland and Son."

"That's for William," she said, and Robin saw how she smiled at the mention of his father's name. "A small gift, but one I hope he'll like."

"I'm sure he will." Robin stared down at the little watercolor. How could his father—or her brothers, for that matter—not be pleased by such a gift? In all his twenty-eight Christmases, he himself had yet to receive any gift made for him alone or with such obvious love. Though he was prosperous enough that he could buy himself nearly anything he wished, nothing would have meant as much to him as a gift like this, made and given from the heart.

"I hope you're right," said Bethany with a sigh, unaware of Robin's thoughts. "I wish I could make something more useful or elegant, like a shirt or embroidered waistcoat, but I'm not very clever with sewing. My little sister Rachel is the seamstress. Lord, she can fashion anything! My fingers could be made of wood, for all that I can do with a needle and thread. Nothing but knots and twisted stitches."

Robin hadn't expected her little self-mocking smile as she described her lack of sewing skills, and he found he couldn't help but smile in return. She wore a wide-brimmed straw hat, tied with green velvet ribbons, and tiny spots of pale winter sunshine filtered delicately through the straw to dapple her face. Beneath her shawl, the line of her back was as straight as the chair she sat upon, her dark blue quilted skirts ruffled around her feet across the dry winter grass, and around her throat she wore a strand of tiny coral beads that she must have had since she was a baby.

Perhaps it was those beads, thought Robin, jewelry more fit for a newly christened infant than for a bride, for if possible the girl seemed even younger than she had last night. But at least now that her face was animated, Robin could better understand why his father was so enchanted. She would never be beautiful in the way the rest of her family was, but she did have her share of the Sparhawk charm.

"If ships and maps for the gentlemen," he asked, hoping she'd keep talking, "then what for the ladies?"

"Oh, for Rachel and Jerusa, I'll color French fashion plates. That's no better than the map, I know, but it's what will please them."

Suddenly aware of how much she was chattering, Bethany fell silent, glancing down at the piece she'd been working on when he arrived. She was proud of it, and even though she hadn't quite finished, she knew it was one of the best she'd ever done. And he did seem truly interested in her paintings, in a way that few other people bothered to be.

Shyly she moved her arm and tipped the picture up for him to see. "This will be for Mama, though you've probably guessed as much. I wanted to show her here in the garden with her roses, so that when it snows she could remember the way it is in summer."

As she saw how Robin frowned, her heart sank. She should have been content with his praise for the ships, and not been greedy for more. And how easy it had been to forget Jerusa's advice!

"It's not quite done, of course," she said hurriedly. "The figure's clumsy, and the gown is too bold a red."

"No, it isn't," he said quietly. "It's perfect."

"You don't have to say so just to save my feelings," she said, flustered by how intensely he was considering the painting in her hands. "I know the truth."

"And the truth is that you're very, very good. I wouldn't lie about that." He didn't have to. With the minimum of brush strokes, Bethany had captured the essence of Mariah Sparhawk and the elusive quality of a summer afternoon. Technically, Bethany was untutored, that was true—the color did lack subtlety, as she'd seen herself—but she had the eye and emotion that came only with real talent. Robin knew the difference; he'd traveled the Continent and viewed the greatest masters, and he knew there were painters in the Royal Academy who'd trade their eyeteeth for this girl's gifts.

But she, of course, could not know that, and he kept back his smile at the anxiety in her eyes. "How did you learn to paint like this, Miss Sparhawk?"

"The usual way, I suppose. Coloring prints was boring, and besides, the subjects were often so silly. I wanted to draw real things. So I did." She gave her shoulders a self-deprecating shrug. "Or at least that's what I try to do."

"No lessons, then?" The beginnings of an idea were forming in Robin's mind. His father might not listen to his son's reasons for moving to London, but if his fiancée could be convinced to add her voice, as well, he might yet agree.

"Lessons? Oh, no, Father would never countenance that!" She smiled wistfully. "There is a young man from Kingston named Gilbert Stuart who paints most beautifully, and he will, I've heard, accept students. But not ladies, and especially not Captain Sparhawk's daughter.''

"Oh, your Mr. Stuart is poor stuff, compared to the painters in London!'' declared Robin expansively, feeling only the slightest twinge of guilt. His motives, after all, were the best. "Joshua Reynolds, Tom Gainsborough, George Romney—they all keep studios there for the gentry to visit, even the finest titled ladies.''

"Mr. Reynolds, you say?'' Bethany leaned forward excitedly, clasping her paint-daubed fingers. "William—I mean your father—has a book with engravings from some of his portraits, and I vow, his ladies look more lively than some of the faces I've seen in the Market House.''

Robin nodded in agreement. He knew the book well enough, since he was the one who'd sent it to his father. At least now he was sure that someone had bothered to slit the pages. "You would adore London, Miss Sparhawk. You could view the paintings in a different studio, gallery or museum every day of the week, and still not see the same works twice.''

He'd meant it only to convince her, yet in his mind he could already picture her delight in the sights of London that he would show her.

"So in London even the finest ladies can go a painter's workshop,'' marveled Bethany, her blue eyes dreamy at the possibilities he was holding out to her. "Tell me, do they ever paint in oils, or must they, too, use only watercolors or chalks?''

"Alas, Miss Sparhawk, I cannot say,'' admitted Robin with some reluctance, "for all the ladies I've ever known have preferred to stay on the far side of the easel.''

''Oh.'' The single word held a world of disappointment that was reflected in her open face. ''Then London's not so very different from Newport after all, is it, Mr. Howland?''

Before Robin could answer, she rose and shoved the now dry painting of her mother into the portfolio, along with those of her brothers' ships, and with a rag busily began wiping out the clam shells that served as her paint dishes.

''Not that any of it matters,'' she said brusquely, as if every hasty gesture didn't betray the depth of her regret and frustration. ''Because I'm a lady, I'll never be free to sail and wander like my brothers, and most likely I'll never leave this island as long as I live, let alone see London. William indulges me in my painting, and I'd do better to be grateful for that, instead of sighing over things that can never be.''

Robin had stood when she did, and now he watched awkwardly as she dropped the square-sided bottles of color—ocher gold, lapis blue, cochineal red—into their wooden case, the bottles clattering against one another with her haste. In another moment, she would be done, and he would have lost his chance to speak.

''Miss Sparhawk,'' he began, sweeping off his hat in an unconscious gesture of sincerity. ''Miss Sparhawk, please, I beg your attention for a moment.''

''Yes?'' she said, suddenly wary of his new formality. She was staring at the black tricorn in his hand as if she expected a weasel to leap from the crown.

''A word, that is all.''

"You wish a word, Mr. Howland," she repeated as she dumped a jar of blue-tinted water onto the grass. "If what we've been sharing this past quarter hour haven't been words, then I vow I can't venture as to what they were instead."

Robin sighed impatiently, wondering what had happened to the easy, pleasant mood between them. "I wish to speak with you of my father."

She froze with the last paintbrush in her hand, her expression oddly stricken. "So all your pretty talk about my paintings and London and Mr. Reynolds was nothing but claptrap and nonsense. Nothing at all. You didn't mean a single word of it."

"I didn't—"

"No, stay!" she cried, her eyes now flashing at him with the same fury she'd shown the night before. "What you mean to say—what you meant to say from the minute you intruded on my peace was that you find my attachment with your father most unsuitable. You as much as said it last night. You believe me to be a dreadful upstart little baggage, unworthy of your father and your grand family that's absolutely not one whit better than mine!"

She was doing the same thing that she had done last night, cutting him off without a word or a leg to stand upon. Damnation, she'd no right to treat him like this. He'd come here to apologize, to make things right between them for his father's sake, and she wouldn't listen to a word of it. What he was trying to do would benefit them all, if she'd just let him speak. "I swear to you by all that's holy, Miss Sparhawk, that I never once—"

"Nay, you never should have opened your mouth, and I'll thank you never to speak to me again out of your father's presence!" She slammed the lid shut on her paintbox and swung it off the table. "I have every intention of honoring William by becoming his wife, and nothing you can say will ever convince me otherwise. Good day, Mr. Howland. If you found your way in, you can just as easily find your way out."

Left speechless once again, Robin watched her stalk to the house, her skirts sweeping indignantly from side to side across the grass and the portfolio jutting out awkwardly from beneath her arm.

Impertinent little chit, he thought crossly, wondering how she'd twisted his best intentions around so that once again he'd insulted her. He wouldn't dream of trying to stop this marriage now. But she was right in one thing: he did think she was a dreadful upstart baggage.

And he'd never met another woman quite like her.

# Chapter Five

"So that's your new son, Anny-Beth," whispered Jerusa behind her fan. "You're to be congratulated. What a vastly handsome gentleman!"

"He's a vastly arrogant cock of the walk," answered Bethany warmly, "with entirely too high an opinion of himself to make for pleasant company."

Twisting the silk cord on her own fan nervously around her fingers, Bethany glanced across the parlor to where William was introducing Robin to her father and the two of her brothers, Jonathan and Joshua, Jerusa's twin, who had just arrived in Newport.

This supper was all her mother's idea, a chance for the Sparhawks to welcome Robin back home and for the two families to know each other better. Her mother was always full of such wonderful ideas, thought Bethany unhappily, as if all the world's problems could be solved around their long mahogany dining table over a big bowl of rum punch.

But Robin Howland wouldn't be one of them, at least as far as Bethany was concerned. Her pride still stung from how she'd so eagerly lapped up his false compliments for her paintings two days ago. As if that alone would have been enough to make her abandon William!

Warily she watched Robin now, amazed by how he seemed to be holding his own among the men in her family, no easy task for any stranger, even when her mother had ordered Jon and Josh to behave themselves. Though Robin wasn't nearly as imposing as her shipmaster brothers, he did have an elegance in his dark green velvet suit that they never would, a gentleman's presence that was probably more of the same London-bred folderol that she herself had swallowed so completely. How had a man as good and honest as William sired a son so given to deceit? No, as far as she was concerned, the sooner Master Robin went back to London, the better.

"'An arrogant cock of the walk'!" repeated Jerusa, her green eyes full of amusement, as she waved her fan languidly through the air. "'Unfit for decent company!'"

Her laugh was low and deep in her throat, the same knowing laugh that had helped make Jerusa so popular. Even though this was only a family supper, her glossy black hair was piled high on her head and laced through with a red satin ribbon and brilliants that sparkled in the candlelight. Beside her, as always, Bethany felt small and insignificant in a gown of blue-gray lutestring, with only her coral beads for decoration.

"Well, he is, Rusa," said Bethany defensively. "You'll see for yourself soon enough."

"What I see, Anny-Beth, is your own most remarkable outrage. I vow, I've never heard you express yourself so strongly about any gentleman, to his credit or not," Jerusa said teasingly. "Perhaps the problem is that you don't truly find Robin Howland odious at all. Whatever happened to feeling sorry for him?"

"You were the one who told me I shouldn't!"

"That was before I saw what a comely gentleman he was," purred Jerusa. "I vow you'll be the lucky one, having *him* living under your roof."

"Jerusa!" exclaimed Bethany, appalled by what her sister was suggesting, even if in jest. "If William ever heard—"

"If William heard what?" asked William himself, his hand slipping familiarly around Bethany's waist.

Mortified, Bethany's cheeks flamed as she tried to think of an explanation.

But Jerusa only smiled archly, closed her fan and gently tapped the ivory blades on William's shoulder. "I was merely telling Bethany how fortunate she was to be marrying into a family with two such handsome gentlemen, and she didn't wish the compliment to turn your head. But there is my own darling Mr. Carberry, come at last, and I must leave you two until later."

With another smile over her shoulder for William, Jerusa sailed across the room to greet her own fiancé, the silk of her skirts rustling behind her.

For a long moment, neither Bethany nor William spoke, while Bethany miserably wondered if in fact he'd heard what Jerusa had said. All her life Jerusa had made mischief for her like this, saying whatever she pleased and leaving Bethany to settle the consequences.

At last William sighed and shook his head, his gaze still lingering on Jerusa, across the parlor, as she warmly—perhaps a shade too warmly for the taste of her father and brothers—welcomed Tom Carberry.

"I know she is your sister, Bethany," said William softly, for her ears only, "but to be frank, Jerusa frightens the daylights out of me."

Bethany laughed, giddy with relief. One of the things she liked best about William was how easily he could make her laugh over the most common things. "She scares me, too. Though sometimes she can be kind and good, I never really know what she'll say or do, and because she's so beautiful, and Father's favorite, she never is blamed."

"Hush now, dearest, I've told you before, I won't listen to another word like that from you." He chided her gently as he chucked her beneath her chin. "Jerusa can keep her whole flock of featherbrained gallants. I'm the lucky man who claimed the fairest Sparhawk daughter, and I challenge any one of 'em to tell me otherwise."

"Oh, William," whispered Bethany. "What did I do to deserve you?"

"Been your own sweet self, lass, no more and no less," he said gruffly. He reached deep into the pocket of his coat and drew out a small bundle of patterned silk that he pressed into Bethany's hand. "I saw this and thought of you. Call it an early Christmas present."

Slowly Bethany unwrapped the silk. In the center lay a lily flower elaborately carved of white jade that was almost translucent.

"It's lovely," breathed Bethany. She traced a curving petal with one fingertip. The polished stone was smooth and cool. She remembered what Jerusa had said, that William would always treat her well. Were costly gifts like this one what she'd meant? "I've never seen another like it."

"Nor are you likely to, considering it came clear from Canton in an Indiaman, and then to Newport with Robin." He lifted it from her hand, shaking free the gold loop at the top. "Here, let me hook it onto your beads. I've a mind to see it on a gold-worked chain around your pretty throat, but there's time enough for that once we're wed."

Obediently Bethany raised her chin so that he could hang the lily from her necklace. It seemed strange to have William's face so close to hers, with her family all around her. She thought of how many times she'd seen her father fasten her mother's pearls. Soon, when William was her husband, such casually intimate gestures would be commonplace between them, too.

Pleased with the effect of his gift, William stepped back and smiled. "There now, I knew it would suit you! Whatever other flaws my son has, he does have an eye for finery."

Lightly Bethany fingered the pendant, the heavy weight of the jade unfamiliar around her neck. "Robin chose it?"

"Aye, though of course he didn't know it would go to you, since he didn't know you existed." William frowned, unable to hide his concern any longer. "Did the boy come apologize to you, Bethany? He swore to me he would, but he's said not a word to prove to me he did."

Bethany hesitated. If she told William the truth, that she and Robin had quarreled again, then the ill feelings between father and son would only multiply, and no matter what Jerusa had advised, she knew that could not be right. As turbulent as relations in her own family could be, her father would never dream of exiling one of her brothers the way that William had. Yet how strange that William should regard her as an equal, with such kindness and respect, and still treat Robin, a man in his prime, like a naughty boy in need of a whipping!

"Robin called on me, yes," she said carefully. "The day after he arrived."

William's expression clouded. "Nay, Bethany, you needn't say more to protect the rogue," he said grimly. "I'll see that he comes to put things right with you."

"Ah, Mr. Howland," said Bethany's mother as she suddenly appeared at William's side. Her round face was flushed and her words a bit breathless, proof that, despite the Venetian lace at her cuffs and the rubies and pearls around her throat, she'd been to the kitchen downstairs to oversee the cooking herself. "Would you be so kind as to take Bethany in to supper? I know so close to your wedding you'd never forgive me if I asked you to lead any other lady, but I promise you, after Christmas, I mean to make my daughter share your company with me, as well."

There were sixteen for supper, far too many for the front parlor, where the family usually ate, so the dining table, plus another, been moved into the house's central hall, with a single long damask cloth to mask the joining. The tall silver candlesticks had been polished until they gleamed by the light of the best smokeless spermaceti candles. Because it was so near to Christmas, Bethany's mother had festooned the twin looking glasses on either wall with boughs of fragrant pine interwoven with branches of bright orange bittersweet, and set the table with her best Canton ware, rarely brought from the depths of the parlor cabinets except for the most special occasions.

With William sitting on one side and Jon on the other, Bethany began to relax and enjoy herself. Gathered around her at the table were all the people she loved best, from her Grandmother Gosnold to the youngest Sparhawk, her two-year-old nephew Jeremiah, solemnly propped up on cushions to reach the table. Best of all, her mother had wisely chosen to seat Robin at the opposite end of the table.

Beneath the cloth, William sought her hand and pressed it fondly, and Bethany smiled happily in return. Tonight whatever doubts she might have about the future seemed foolish, and any misunderstandings between Robin and his father could wait until tomorrow.

Contented as she was, Bethany was scarcely aware of the conversations that flowed around her. Trade and politics, ships and markets and cargoes, were such ordinary topics in her father's house that she only half listened until suddenly Robin's angry voice rose above the others.

"And I say the men who signed that abominable non-importation agreement were no better than traitors," he said heatedly. "They're lucky their impertinence didn't bring the entire wrath of the Crown down upon this town."

All other conversation around the table stopped instantly, every fork stilled. Beside her, Bethany heard William swear softly beneath his breath.

As the silence stretched longer and longer, Robin sat with both his hands flat on the table, his head high as one by one he searched the faces of the other men around the table.

He sighed restlessly, running his finger through the moisture gathered on his wineglass. "It would appear, sirs, that I am left in the grievous position of being in the minority," he said slowly, "and that we Howlands shall be left to drink the king's health alone when this supper is done."

Still no one answered, most instead staring uncomfortably down at the plates of half-eaten food before them. At last Gabriel leaned forward, his face troubled.

"In my home, sir, you're free to drink to whomever and whatever you please," he said, clearly taking no pleasure in this task as host. "But perhaps you've forgotten that your father, too, signed the agreement, on behalf of Howland and Son."

Robin's gaze whipped towards William as his fingers curled and tightened into fists upon the damask. "Is this true, Father?"

William's eyes were flinty as he met his son's without faltering. "Given your beliefs, Robin, it was not something I chose to commit to you by letter," he said, biting into every word, "and since you've returned, you haven't ceased your slavering defense of your precious king long enough for me to tell you in person."

Robin recoiled as if he'd been struck. In a way, he had. With practiced composure, he rose from the table and draped his napkin neatly across the seat of his chair before he bowed to Bethany's mother.

"Pray forgive me, ma'am, for so abusing your hospitality." His voice was hollow and emotionless, and he ignored his father as if William were not in the room. "If you'll excuse me, I believe I've caused enough unpleasantness for your family for one evening. Captain Sparhawk, sir, your servant."

Robin's footsteps echoed on the bare floorboards as he left the hall and walked down the stairs to the back door near the kitchen. With a self-conscious heartiness, the others began to eat and talk again, determined to pretend that nothing had happened.

Bethany seized William's arm. "You must go after him," she said urgently. "You can't let him leave like this!"

But William's face remained implacable. "I'll do no such thing, Bethany. Why should I, when the stubborn fool insists on insulting your family and shaming me?"

"Because you shamed *him!*"

"He was preaching like Lord North himself, spoiling your mother's supper!"

"William, listen to yourself!" Beyond William, she saw her grandmother turn and frown, and with an effort Bethany lowered her voice to a fierce whisper. "Do you believe that Robin's the only Tory who's ever dined at this table? He could wear the wretched crown himself and my father would be civil to him. Which is certainly more than you seem able to do!"

With a deep sigh, William slumped back in his chair, his anger fading. "Ah, Bethany, lass, don't scold me," he said plaintively. "Do you think I wish it this way between the boy and me?"

"Then why won't you go after him?"

"Because I can't," he said heavily, toying with his fork. "Better to let him cool his heels in the garden alone, without me."

"Without you, indeed." Bethany ignored the startled looks on the faces around her as she shoved her chair away from the table. "At least now I know where he got his stubbornness."

She hurried down the back stairs, past the glow and warmth of the kitchen fire, and into the winter night. She stood on the step as her eyes grew accustomed to the dark and rubbed her bare forearms against the chill. She'd been wrong to snap at William like that, especially in front of her entire family, and her heart sank at the memory of his forlorn face as she'd scolded him. What had come over her, anyway?

Anxiously she scanned the shadows of the empty garden for any sign of Robin. If she could coax him into returning, then perhaps everything would be all right. But by now Robin could well have walked home; she wouldn't have blamed him if he had. Somewhere in the distance, a sea gull mewed sleepily, and beyond the wall she could just make out the night-lights of the vessels moored in the harbor.

"Come to gloat, Miss Sparhawk?" said Robin. "Or, since you're to be my new stepmother, did Father send you here so you could chastise me, too?"

"Neither." Even though she'd been looking for him, he'd startled her, half-hidden as he was in the shade of the pear tree. "I came to ask you back."

"What, so I could be humiliated again?"

"No one thought the worse of you."

"No one, that is, except my own father." Though his face was still hidden by the shadows, there was no mistaking his bitterness. "Do you know I returned to Newport actually believing I could reconcile with the man?"

Bethany stepped closer. The frost-covered grass brittle beneath her slippers. "There's no reason why you still can't."

"No?" He swung around to face her. "I came here fearing for my father's safety. Did he tell you that? I wanted to *save* him, like some bloody white knight, rescue him from what was happening here. I'd heard rumors that troops would be sent next to Newport, the same way that they were to Boston, and I wanted to bring Father back to London with me while I still could. Only tonight did I learn that he's in the thick of it, and even then he didn't bother to tell me himself."

"Oh, my," murmured Bethany, her head spinning. "Then that was why you told me about the painters in London. Not because you wished to cozen me into leaving your father, but because you hoped I'd want to go, too."

"That's the gist of it, yes." He ran his fingers through his hair, tugging the waves loose from the black silk ribbon that held his queue. "As far as I'm concerned, you're more than welcome to marry him."

But Bethany remembered what she'd overheard that first night. "Even if I am a Sparhawk?"

"At this point you could be an orangutan and I wouldn't care," he said wearily. "Whatever will make him happy."

"You do care for him, don't you?" she asked softly. "If you didn't, what he did would not have hurt as much."

Robin didn't answer, instead looking past her, up to
the house, as the candlelight from the windows washed
over his upturned face. "Sparhawks or not, after seeing you with your family, I know now how hard it
would be for you to leave them. Having such a min-
uscule family myself, I tend to underestimate the pull
that a houseful like yours can have."

"They would understand. They're wanderers,
though they always come back home to Newport, just
the way you did."

"Oh, aye," he echoed sadly. "Home to Newport."

What would it be like, she wondered, to have no
mother or brothers or sisters? The pain and raw longing on Robin's face as he stared up at the windows told
her so much that she almost reached out to comfort
him.

Almost, but not quite, and it was that same face that
stopped her. With the animosity between them gone,
for the first time she truly saw him for the man that he
was. Jerusa was right, Robin was handsome, especially now, with the single dark lock fallen across his
brow to keep his face from being too perfect.

He smiled at her, and she shivered. Did he, too, see
her differently now, or was she only imagining the way
his gaze seemed to linger on her face with a new interest, a new warmth? In her life before this, there had
been no handsome young men in dark gardens, but
instinctively she sensed both the temptation and the
danger. She was promised to William, and Robin was
William's son, and nothing would change that.

*Nothing*.

"I'm glad he gave you the lily," he said softly. "It
suits you."

The compliment startled Bethany, and her fingers flew to the necklace, self-consciously fanning out to cover the bare skin of her décolletage as well. "William is very generous. He said it was an early Christmas present."

Though it was too dark to know for certain, Robin would wager fifty guineas that he'd made her blush. He hadn't meant to, but he simply wasn't accustomed to women this modest. And the lily did suit her, the pale jade resting above the swell of her breasts. Lucky lily, he thought wryly. Before, he'd seen her only in bulky outdoor clothing, but dressed as she was now, for evening, he could appreciate the full young curves of her body, the narrowness of her waist. He hoped his father wasn't too old to make the most of his good fortune.

"The Chinese believe that jade brings long life and happiness to the wearer," he said, forcing himself to raise his eyes again to her face. The girl was going to be his stepmother, not his mistress, and he'd do well to remember it. "That little blossom's quite a treasure. I didn't trust the piece to a crate in the hold, but carried it wrapped in silk with me for the whole voyage."

The way Robin spoke, it was almost as if the gift had come from him, instead of his father. Bethany wished he hadn't; she'd never think of the lily the same way again. Her fingers curled around it as she caught herself imagining it not in William's pocket, but in Robin's, riding there safely against his thigh . . .

Abruptly she pulled her hand away, once again rubbing her forearms against the cold. "Will you come back in the house now?"

"Lord, how selfish of me! You must be half-frozen. Here," he said as he shrugged out of his coat and draped it over her shoulders before she could protest. "As Father would tell you, I have my temper to keep me warm."

Bethany smiled uncertainly as she held the edges of the coat together. True, she was cold, and even a gentleman's dress coat was warmer than her gown. But the silk lining of the coat still held the warmth and fragrance of Robin's body, and wrapping herself in it seemed too much like feeling herself in his embrace.

"We should return to the others," she said uneasily. "Surely your temper's cooled enough by now."

"But what about Father's?"

"He's not nearly so fierce as you would make him out," she said, remembering how contrite William had been by the time she left the table. "Truly."

"Then it's you that's tamed him. The lamb and the lion." Strange how it didn't sound nearly as blithe as he'd intended. The more time he spent with her, the more he realized that, by being at once oddly shy and outspoken, she could probably tame any man without the poor fellow realizing it. "Once you're wed, you could likely persuade him to come with me. The three of us could sail together."

"But why should we leave Newport?" she said, shaking her head. "You heard your father, and mine, too. The non-importation agreements, the protests, are all related to trade, that's all. There's no real danger to us."

"Then your father and mine are believing what they wish to hear," he said firmly. "Parliament holds a very different view of their activities. Do you think I would have sailed clear across the Atlantic if I didn't believe it?''

Troubled, Bethany didn't answer. William had never confided to her all his political and business activities. Perhaps he was in more danger than she realized.

Robin reached out to pull the coat more evenly onto her shoulders. He'd meant only to convince her, not frighten her, but her eyes were enormous in her little heart-shaped face. How she must love that stubborn old man, to worry so about his safety!

"Come now," he said softly, "it wouldn't all be so dreadful. I promise I'd see to it that you enjoyed London."

She stiffened, both at the familiarity of his gesture and at all his promise seemed to imply. "You are kind to offer, Mr. Howland, but I—"

"Robin," he said, lifting his hand to brush the back of his fingers across her cheek. "No more of this 'Mr. Howland.' Robin. We're almost kin, you know, though I can't swear I'll call you Mama."

Swiftly she shook her head, unaware that she'd backed away from him until she saw how ruefully amused his smile had become.

"As you wish, Miss Sparhawk. Ma'am." He pointedly clasped his hands behind his waist, as if to keep them out of mischief. "If you would but ask Father—"

"Please don't ask *me!*" she cried. "Please—just please don't."

He stopped, surprised by the agitation in her voice, his head cocked to one side. "If you love him, you would."

"It's because I love him that I won't! I know your father, and I know that nothing will make him turn tail and run from Newport now, not you, not me, not even soldiers on his doorstep."

"Yet if you—"

"No ifs, Robin," she said, unconsciously using his given name for the first time. "If I could bring you two together, I would, but to come between you as father and son, to take sides, even with a good reason, would be wrong, and I won't do it. I can't. Not for you, not for your father."

"And not for all the soldiers in His Majesty's army." Robin sighed, tapping the trunk of the pear tree lightly with his fingertips. "You're wise beyond your years, Miss Sparhawk, and here I'd thought Father was marrying you for your beauty alone."

"No," said Bethany. *"No."*

That was all, the single word that denied everything. She turned and fled into the house, and not once did she look back.

# Chapter Six

Though the conversations around the long table didn't stop, Bethany was painfully aware of every eye upon her as she tried to slip back into her chair unnoticed. There was her father's severity at one end of the table and her mother's concern at the other, Jon's open incredulity and Jerusa's knowing grin, and finally the unreadable expression on William's face as he helped slide her chair under the table.

"Well now," he said gruffly, "at least the boy's learned some manners, sharing his coat with you like that."

Bethany gasped, her hands flying to Robin's coat, still across her shoulders. No wonder they'd all stared at her!

"Manners had nothing to do with it," said Robin curtly as he, too, returned to the hall. "Miss Sparhawk was cold, and I saw no reason for her to suffer while on your diplomatic errand."

To Bethany's dismay, William tensed beside her, ready to snap back at Robin.

But before he could, Bethany's mother spoke first. "Your father's been telling us, Robin, of all the wondrous things you've brought with you," she said, with a cheerful directness that dared both men to counter her. "He was just describing a set of puppets. Neapolitan, I believe?"

"Yes, ma'am." Ignoring his father, Robin came around to Bethany's chair to take the coat as she offered it to him. His quick smile was so obviously meant for her alone that she flushed with embarrassment, only making it worse as she looked hastily down at the napkin in her lap.

Pulling on his coat, Robin dropped back into his chair with one final glance at Bethany at the far end of the table. Her cheeks were on fire, and her honey-colored hair was bright in the candlelight as she bowed her head in confusion. Lord only knew what devil was driving him tonight, making that poor lass blush again like that!

"Neapolitan, you say, Robin?" said Mariah, the edge in her voice letting him know she'd spoken before.

"Yes, Madame Sparhawk, and I'll wager you've seen nothing like them here in Rhode Island," Robin answered quickly, praying he hadn't waited too long to reply. "Pretty little creatures fashioned from wood and gesso, with jointed arms and legs that, when their strings are tugged, can make motions most lifelike. Every fashionable diversion in London has featured them this season."

"They do sound vastly amusing," said Mariah eagerly, relieved to have saved the peace of her supper. "But did you also bring some sort of actor or conjurer to show them?"

"Nay, ma'am, but I didn't think it necessary."
Robin plucked the ruffles of his cuffs free of his coat
sleeves and just barely stopped himself from looking
back again at Bethany. What was wrong with him tonight? "After a bit of practice, the strings can be easily manipulated by most anyone."

William cleared his throat. "If it's so blessed easy,
Robin, then why don't you put on a show for us all?
Something edifying, for the season."

"What a marvelous idea!" exclaimed Mariah. "Do
you think you could possibly prepare something for
the night before the wedding? We'll all be out at Crescent Hill by then, and it will be Christmas Eve. The
children especially would love any sort of amusement."

"I'll be delighted to oblige, ma'am," answered
Robin. "Just promise me you won't be disappointed
by my humble efforts."

"Of course not," she said, beaming. "But surely
you won't be able to do it all yourself, Robin? Would
any of us be able to assist you?"

A ripple of laughter circled the table at the idea,
centered among Bethany's brothers. Bethany's head
rose swiftly as she glared at Jon and Josh, both
smirking behind their hands at the very idea. She knew
what they were thinking: that such nonsense was all
well enough for a London macaroni like Robin Howland, but no man worth his salt, no Sparhawk man,
would ever be caught fiddling the strings above some
fancywork dolly. They had no right to make fun of
Robin like that, just because he cared about something that wasn't a sloop or a ship or a—

"Bethany will help you, Robin," said William, covering her hand with his on the cloth. "She's the cleverest lass I've ever seen with painting and such, and if anyone can make your puppets jig, my Bethany can."

Bethany's mouth fell open in dismay. She'd resolved never to be caught alone with Robin again, and here William was proposing *this!*

"Oh, William," she protested feebly, not daring to look at Robin. "Not the night before our wedding! There's still so much to be done—"

"Nonsense, Bethany." Her mother interrupted, an unmistakable note of warning in her voice. "There's scarcely a thing left for you to worry over about the wedding. If William wishes you to do this little trifle, then you can certainly oblige him."

"See now, sweetheart, your mother seems to have all that well in hand," said William, smiling indulgently as he patted Bethany's hand. "And you'd enjoy this, don't say you wouldn't. It's exactly the kind of thing you'd fancy. Maybe you could even paint up a little stage."

With growing desperation, Bethany shook her head. "I can't, William. This is Robin's surprise, and I'm sure he'd rather do it all himself."

"Hang what he wants, Bethany!" declared William. "The boy can damned well do what I say for once, and that's for him to learn what a fine young lady I'm marrying. What better way than this, eh?"

"But, William..."

"Hush now, sweetheart, I know what you're thinking." William sighed deeply and lowered his voice so that only she could hear. "I know my son's a trial, as pompous and stubborn as they come. He always has been. God only knows what he said to you out there in the garden. But can you just give him another chance to prove himself, just this once, for me?''

Left without a choice, Bethany slowly nodded her assent.

"Rusa?"

"I'm awake, Anny-Beth."

"Rusa, you'll tell me, won't you?" In the dark, her voice sounded small and forlorn, even to her own ears. "What did they say about me when I went after William's son?"

"Would you believe me if I said nothing? Oh, Father looked at Mama, Jon looked at Betsy, Rachel looked at her pudding, and baby Jeremiah smeared the chocolate sauce all over the tablecloth, but no one said a word."

"And William?" whispered Bethany. "What did he do?"

"Chattered on about the things that Robin brought back from London. Mostly about those puppets, to amuse Mama. But he didn't appear upset, if that's what you mean."

"I don't know what I mean," said Bethany unhappily.

In the dark, Jerusa sought her hand beneath the coverlet and linked their fingers together. "You're going to have to know, Anny-Beth," she said softly. "You're bound to marry William."

"And I shall marry him, Jerusa! You know I promised I would, and I mean to keep that promise, else I would never have agreed to be his wife!"

"But that was before Robin came home."

"Oh, Jerusa, it's not like that at all! He wants me to wed William and then for us both to return to London with him after we're married. He says it's not safe here in Newport, that all the complaining that Father and William and the others have done will only cause trouble. Robin wanted me to convince William to go, and I refused."

"Well, at least that was wise," said Jerusa. "But you came back to the table wearing Robin's coat, and that wasn't wise at all. I did that once during a dance—I think it was with Joseph Hazzard—and Father dragged me home in disgrace, calling me a hussy the whole way."

Bethany didn't answer. She thought of how Robin had smiled as he slipped his coat onto her shoulders, and how she hadn't come right back into the house, but had lingered there with him in the dark, letting him touch her cheek with his fingers. Did that make her a hussy, too?

"Anny-Beth?" said Jerusa hesitantly. "About what I said before, about you and William and Robin in the same house? I was only jesting, you know. I'd never have said any of it if I'd known."

"If you'd known what?" demanded Bethany defensively. "I intend to marry William, as I promised, and Robin can go back to London alone."

"Then there's nothing amiss at all, is there?" Fondly Jerusa squeezed Bethany's fingers. "Just be sure, Anny-Beth. Be very sure, before it's too late."

Lying in the same narrow bed that had been his as a boy, Robin stared up at the ceiling and wondered what the devil had happened to him last night. His head ached from too much drink, but he couldn't blame it all on Captain Sparhawk's rum and smuggled brandy. This morning it was his conscience that pained him the most.

There was no good reason for him to be attracted to Bethany Sparhawk, and a score for why he should not. She was the daughter of a family he had little use for; she was small and pale and quiet, while he preferred bright, witty women who laughed loudly and easily. She was provincial in both her breeding and her outlook, and she'd be hopelessly lost in any London parlor of note.

And, of course, she was going to marry his father.

So why, then, had he spent the night haunted by her, unable to find any peace from the memory of her in the garden?

She cared. It was as simple, and as complicated, as that. She had risked his father's censure and her family's displeasure to come after him last night, and then she had stayed to listen to him. She hadn't laughed at his wish to save his father, as he'd feared she might. Instead, she'd praised his love and his loyalty, understanding him and his reasons far more than his own father did. He'd come clear from London hoping for that same understanding from his father, and instead he'd found it in a small, wise girl with honey-colored hair.

The rest was easier to explain: the sweetness of her smile, her round, graceful figure, the pleasure he found in seeing her blush, the way her lips had parted with wonder when he told her about the London painters. She was lost in that family, overwhelmed and underappreciated, and he wasn't sure that the same thing wouldn't happen when she was married to his father.

The old man had admitted freely enough that he didn't love Bethany. Oh, he'd buy her trinkets and indulge her whims and amuse himself with the novelty of her youth and innocence, but he'd miss everything that made Bethany special and would make loving her such a rare joy.

*Loving her.*

Robin groaned. God help him, what was he thinking? He had three weeks to survive until Christmas and their wedding, three weeks of being with her while they practiced for this ridiculous puppet performance, three weeks to get it through his own thick head that if he ever hoped to reconcile with his father, he'd best drive every sweet, tempting image of Bethany Sparhawk from his thoughts and dreams.

Three endless weeks of hell.

"Are the puppets in that box?" demanded Rachel excitedly. "Oh, Mr. Howland, I can't wait to see them!"

"Then see them you shall," said Robin as he set the crate on the floor of the Sparhawks' parlor. Immediately Rachel began to help him, plunging both hands deep into the wood shavings that filled the crate.

"Don't crowd Mr. Howland, Rachel," said Bethany. "I said you could help, not hinder."

"Very well." Dejectedly Rachel sat back on her heels. At eleven, she was halfway between being the young lady she so desperately wanted to be and the child she still was in so many ways. Already as tall as her older sister Bethany, Rachel showed all the signs of becoming a beauty like Jerusa, with the family's green eyes and black hair, hers still braided in a single thick plait that hung nearly to her waist.

Over the girl's head, Bethany's gaze briefly met Robin's. "I told Rachel she could help us," she explained, almost apologetically. "She wanted so badly to see the puppets after your father described them. I hope you don't mind."

"Not at all," said Robin, with a heartiness he didn't feel. "Another pair of hands would be most welcome."

The real reason hung unspoken between them. Rachel would be their unwitting chaperone, and though part of Robin wished the girl wasn't here, he grudgingly recognized the wisdom of her presence.

Clearly it wasn't the only precaution Bethany had taken. She and Rachel had been waiting for him here in the front parlor, the door to the hallway propped open to leave them in plain sight of all the craftsmen and sailors from the shipyard on their way to Captain Sparhawk's office, in the back of the house. There was not the slightest chance of their being left alone, with what seemed like half the town parading past.

And Robin had smiled when he saw that this morning Bethany had chosen a demure linsey-woolsey bodice and skirt, with a dimity kerchief tied over the neckline for good measure. What Bethany didn't realize was that to him she'd look lovely in old hopsack. Lovely, and undeniably, unattainably desirable.

Bethany watched Robin as he felt around in the crate for the puppets. She was relieved that he hadn't sent Rachel away, not only because she didn't wish to be alone with him again, but also because his kindness had spared her younger sister's feelings. Being so often in Jerusa's shadow had made her unwilling to doom her younger sister to the same plight, and she was happy that Robin had understood. Most men wouldn't. Strange how William characterized his son as selfish, when to her Robin seemed unusually thoughtful of others' feelings.

Rachel gasped with delight as Robin, with a flourish, pulled out the shepherdess, her little legs flopping and her strings dangling. He handed the puppet to the girl and then reached for a second puppet, a grand lady with a stiff lace headdress and gilt-paper ruffles on her skirts. The last he'd brought was a shepherd with the same painted blond curls that graced the shepherdess.

"That's Chloe you have there, Rachel," explained Robin as he untangled the strings of the puppet in his hands, "and this is her true love, Daphnis. Though you'd never guess it from how they're dressed, they're supposed to be a shepherd and shepherdess from ancient times."

Rachel frowned, concentrating on working the strings the same way Robin was. "I think Chloe's far too pretty to be a mere shepherdess. There's heaps of sheep and shepherds in Portsmouth and Middletown, and I've never seen a single one that looked like this, or had a queer sort of name like Daphnis, either."

"In old Athens they'd probably think the same of Robin." He made the ill-named shepherd amble toward his lady, his little painted arms outstretched in an overblown show of devotion.

"Oh, my darling, darling, dearest Chloe!" He spoke in a high-pitched voice that, to Bethany's ear, seemed to have exactly the inflection of the minister of their church. "Whatever would I do without you?"

Rachel giggled, letting poor Chloe's strings fall so slack that she drooped to her knees. With a jerk, she pulled them up, sending the puppet's feet flying into the air. "Oh, Daphnis, my perfect boy! How barbarously cruel of you to pay more court to your sheep than to me!"

Robin swung the hand with the pan-pipes glued in the palm over Daphnis's chest. "My darling, darling Chloe, I have no choice! Shepherding is my trade, and if I pay no heed to my flock, I shall never have gold enough to keep you happy!"

Bethany gasped, then laughed, her suspicions confirmed. Robin was imitating Dr. Carter, mimicking his mannerisms so outrageously through the shepherd that Bethany couldn't help but laugh.

Swiftly she gathered the strings of the last puppet and swept her grandly between the other two. "Halt this at once!" she said in a haughty voice. "I'll have no such base, shameless displays in my parlor!"

"Then where would you have them, *mia dolce contessa?*" Daphnis leered like the world's most practiced rake. "Your bedchamber, perhaps?"

"Mr. Howland!" exclaimed Bethany, trying helplessly to look stern while Rachel shrieked with laughter at the silliness of her elders. "Mind my sister's age! When my mother agreed to this performance, she didn't intend it to lapse into—into *bawdry!*"

But Daphnis only swaggered more boldly. "'Bawdry,' *mia signorina?* I do not understand!

Please, please, please, I beg of you, you must explain for my tender ignorance!''

"Stop it at once, Robin!" ordered Bethany, her laughter bubbling over in spite of her best intentions. "Stop it *now!*"

"Oh, but, *mia cara, mia signorina,* you must help me to improve myself!" Robin made Daphnis drop to his knees before the countess with a heartfelt sigh. He'd just discovered how much he loved to make Bethany laugh, almost as much as he loved making her blush, and right now he'd managed to do both. He danced his puppet closer to hers, making the little wooden limbs twitch and quiver. *"Mia carissima!"*

"Lord, Robin, I haven't the vaguest idea what you're saying to me, but I'm sure it's vastly wicked," said Bethany as she gasped for breath. Wicked it might well be, but she couldn't remember the last time she had laughed this hard. "Oh, stop it, please!"

Robin tried to lift Daphnis back to his feet before the countess, but as he did, the strings that held the two puppets snarled together. In response, Bethany jerked the countess's strings to free her, but instead all she did was tangle them more, and suddenly, without Bethany quite realizing how it had happened, her hands and Robin's were as tangled together as the two puppets.

Startled, still flushed and breathless from laughing, her gaze locked with Robin's. This close, she could see the gold flecks in his brown eyes, and how his grin was more charmingly lopsided than she'd realized before, with only a single dimple for punctuation. She bit her lower lip, unable to think of anything to say, and as she did she saw how his grin faded, his expression changing from teasing good humor to something darker that she didn't understand.

"Really, Bethany, look at the mess you've made," said Rachel with eleven-year-old severity as she bent between them to separate the puppets. "All you and Mr. Howland have done is make cat's cradle of the strings."

Robin didn't falter a moment. "It's not so very bad, Rachel. At least poor Master Daphnis has made your sister call me 'Robin' instead of this grim 'Mr. Howland.' You, too, now—if we're to be family, then we must have no more stiff-backed names."

Rachel grinned with delight. "Very well, Robin. But we're going to have to invent a better amusement than this for Mama. It's not in the least bit Christmasy."

"True enough." Robin sighed as the separated puppets swung apart. He didn't dare look at Bethany again, and he wondered if she knew how close he'd just come to kissing her. "Perhaps we could make the countess into some sort of angel. You could do that, couldn't you, Bethany? Fashion a pair of painted wings for her?"

"I don't see why not," she murmured, cradling the countess' wooden body in her hand, as if to decide where the wings would be attached. She'd look at anything to hide her confusion, and prayed neither Robin nor her sister could hear the pounding of her heart. How could he do this much to her with so little? "She'll make a quite creditable angel."

"You must give her a halo, as well." Rachel nodded, unaware of the emotional currents swirling around her. "All angels must have halos, as well as wings, to show they're blessed."

"You sound as if you know exactly what to do, Rachel," said Robin. "Why don't you take the angel, and let Bethany have Chloe instead?"

"Oh, could I?" asked Rachel excitedly, and at once Bethany traded puppets with her. "The angel must have the last speech, you know. Then, no matter how foolish Chloe and Daphnis are, the angel can still come down at the end and put it all to rights by wishing everyone a happy Christmas."

"True enough," agreed Robin softly, so softly that Bethany felt her heart twist and tangle like the strings of the puppets. "Too often, love alone isn't enough, is it? Now come, let's see what we can make of this muddle."

# Chapter Seven

Bethany walked quickly through the streets toward the wharfs, the wind off the water swirling her skirts around her and catching in the willow basket slung over her arm. Somehow the weeks until her wedding had dwindled to a handful of days, with only four left now until Christmas itself. She had promised her mother to make another trip out to Crescent Hill this afternoon with more provisions for the wedding supper, and she'd have to be back at the house by noon to meet her brother with the wagon.

But first she wanted to see William. She found him where she'd hoped he'd be, in the offices at his warehouse. His eyes lit as he saw her in the doorway, and he quickly came forward to greet her, waving away the clerk who had been copying letters.

"Bethany, sweetheart, what a fine surprise." He took her hands, pulled off her mittens and gently kissed each palm. "You're cold, lass. You should be home, snug before your fire on a day like this, instead of traipsing down here to see me."

"But I wanted to," said Bethany softly, leaning

forward to brush her lips across his cheek. "You know I'd come farther than this to see you."

He grunted, self-consciously shifting away from her kiss. "Crescent Hill on Thursday will be all the distance I ask."

"And I promise I'll be there." Bethany's cheeks pinked as she realized too late how that tiny kiss had shamed him before the clerk, and sadly she told herself to remember not to be so demonstrative in the future. She slid the basket off the crook of her arm and set it on the desk. "Actually, Josh is driving me out to Crescent Hill this afternoon. Mama's assembled one more wagonful of things that simply must be hauled out there."

"This afternoon?" William frowned. "You and Joshua be careful, mind? There's a snow sky today, if ever I saw one."

"The sky's looked exactly the same every morning this week, with nary a snowflake in sight. Besides, Newport never has any real snow before Twelfth Night. You know that as well as I."

"Just tell that roguish brother of yours to hold back on the whip," cautioned William. "I don't want to risk anything happening to you now."

Bethany smiled, touched by his concern, and reassured, too. William did care for her in his way. "All three of my brothers are rogues, so don't go singling out poor Josh. But you can be sure I'll watch him. I've no wish myself to go headfirst into a meadow full of brambles."

She drew back the checkered napkin on the basket and carefully lifted out a small fruitcake. "And see, William, you do benefit. I feel as if Jerusa and I have been cracking nuts and chopping fruit since summer for all the cakes Mama wanted to bake for Christmas, and the wedding, too, and now that she's finally finished, they'll all be in the wagon this afternoon. Except for this little one for you."

"A fruitcake?" William stared at it dubiously. "Ah, well, you won't have to do any more of that sort of thing after Thursday. I'm not marrying you for your cookery."

Stung by how he'd misinterpreted her gift, Bethany set it carefully down on the desk, her head ducked low. "Why exactly are you marrying me, William?"

"To be my wife, of course," he said gruffly. "And no wife of mine need spend her time in the kitchen. I've a cook for that, and you can discuss the meals for the day with her each morning in your parlor, as is proper."

"Of course," she echoed faintly. William had never been a man for flowery protests of love, and she hadn't really expected them. At least she hadn't before this morning.

*It has nothing to do with this morning,* whispered her treacherous heart, *but everything to do with Robin Howland.*

Bethany closed her eyes, her hands still resting on the plate with the fruitcake, as she struggled with her doubts. Her mother had already told her what she could expect from William on her wedding night, emphasizing the pleasure that would follow the first discomfort. But, though the talk was meant to reassure her, Mariah's frankness had only made Bethany more confused.

She thought she loved William, but she'd never once experienced the sparks of desire and joy that her mother declared she'd felt from the first time she met Gabriel Sparhawk. Even the one time William kissed her, she'd felt nothing more than a certain contentment.

Nothing at all like the way she felt when Robin looked, just looked, at her...

She squeezed her eyes more tightly shut, struggling to think only of William. He was the man who cared for her, the man she was going to marry. Maybe that was the secret: once she was his wife, then maybe her feelings for him would grow deeper and more passionate. Mama had promised that marriage made love better. Maybe that was all that was lacking now between her and William.

Maybe that was all.

*God help her, she had been so sure before Robin Howland returned to Newport!*

Briskly she turned to the basket as she cursed her own weakness. It wasn't as if Robin had done or said anything untoward, or shown any interest in her at all beyond what was to be expected. They hadn't even been alone since that one night in the garden; she'd made sure of that. Yet no matter how many others were in the room with them, still she felt it there between Robin and herself whenever they met, an intangible, unspoken *something* that attracted her even as it terrified her.

William cleared his throat. "I'd no notion the kitchen meant so much to you, Bethany. I thought a lady wouldn't care to be bothered with the heat and the mess, but I want you to be happy, and if it pleases you—"

"Oh, no, William," she said hastily. "Whatever pleases you. I'm sure your cook is more accomplished than I, anyway."

He beamed with relief. "Good lass! I wouldn't want something as foolish as that to come between us."

"Certainly not," she murmured, and, unable to meet his eye, she stared down at the floor. She must never hurt him, she thought miserably. He was far too good a man for that. Better to forget her girlish infatuation with his son than break his heart.

She reached for the last bundle in her basket, a flat package wrapped in a scrap of calico.

"Here, William," she said as she handed it to him, praying that he'd understand this better than he had the fruitcake. "Another early Christmas gift."

"At this rate, Bethany, we'll have nothing left to give on the day except ourselves." He fumbled a little with the ribbon bow, chuckling at his own clumsiness. But as the fabric slipped away from the oval frame inside, he abruptly fell silent.

"I know the likeness isn't as good as it could be," said Bethany, her hands twisting anxiously while she waited for his reaction. "But I thought, since you have no portrait of your son in your house, and with him going back to England after Christmas—"

"Hush, sweetheart," he said quietly, and when he looked up at her she was stunned to see the unshed tears bright in his eyes. "You don't know what you've done. But then, how could you? You've made me see the boy as he truly is, so much like his mother it takes my breath away."

"Like his mother? I've always thought he looks like you."

"Nay, he favors his mother, and has from the first. Like having a blessed ghost in the house, it was, seeing that boy always looking up at me with my poor dead Sarah's eyes."

Bethany curled her arm around his, and this time he didn't pull away. "I think that's the first time I've heard you speak of your first wife."

"Most likely because there isn't much to tell." William's smile was bittersweet. "Sarah was only seventeen when we wed, and I the greenest eighteen you'd ever hope to see. But, oh, didn't we love each other for the eleven months God granted us!"

He looked again at the portrait in his hand. "I lost her when Robin was born. He cried all the time, that baby did. Wailed fit to break your heart, day and night, from missing his mama. Not that I blamed him. I cried, too."

"Oh, William, I'm sorry." Touched by his sorrow, Bethany rested her cheek on his shoulder, wishing there was something she could say to lessen the pain that still seemed so fresh after nearly thirty years. It was easy for her to imagine him then, scarcely more than a boy himself, left to grieve with a baby that was all that remained of his young wife. "You must have loved her very much."

"That I did," confessed William softly, still lost in his memories. "That I did."

Tears stung Bethany's eyes, not only for William and his lost Sarah, but for herself, as well. Could a man who'd loved his first wife so dearly have any of that same love left for his second?

Awkwardly William patted her hand. "Not that I should be telling you all this now, eh?"

"Don't be foolish," she said, swiftly blinking back her tears. He was still a good man and a kind one, and she'd be fortunate to have him for a husband. "I care for you all the more because of it."

William grunted. "It makes for a sorry sort of conversation from a bridegroom."

"Now you hush." Over his shoulder Bethany looked at her painting of Robin. Because she hadn't wanted to ask him to sit for her, she'd done this picture, too, from memory. Instead of the stiff formal pose Robin himself likely would have preferred, she'd tried to show him smiling and happy, the way he was when they rehearsed with the puppets. Perhaps that was what had reminded William so much of his first wife, just as it might well explain so many other things.

"If Sarah had lived," she asked softly, "would you have been so hard on Robin?"

"Hard on Robin?" repeated William, automatically slipping back into the familiar scorn he reserved for his son. "I pampered him like no other lad in town, setting him up to be a little gentleman, the way Sarah would've wanted. There wasn't a thing that boy desired that I wouldn't give to him."

Except for love, thought Bethany sadly, with a new understanding. "Robin told me how he wished you to return to London with him."

"London, for all heaven! Have you ever heard such a featherbrained scheme?" demanded William. "As if King George were going to waste his soldiers or sailors on the likes of us! He can't even be bothered to answer our petitions, let alone send a frigate."

Abruptly he folded the cloth back over Robin's portrait and placed it in his desk, letting the top drop with a finality that didn't escape Bethany. So much for the picture bringing any reconciliation between them, she thought wistfully.

"So then none of us is in any real danger?" she asked uncertainly. "Not you, or my father or brothers?"

"Can you imagine a man like your father being so wrongheaded about something like this?" William shook his head with obvious disgust. "I don't know where Robin got this notion that the king would dare declare war upon his own subjects. It's daft enough to make me wonder if the boy's lost his wits, trying to hector me into sailing away like this."

"I think Robin believed the rumors because he wanted an excuse to come home," said Bethany slowly. "He's not daft, William, just lonely."

William stared at her, incredulous. "How could he possibly be lonely, in the middle of London? Finding company—especially expensive, wanton, female company—has never been a problem for that boy."

"He's not a boy, William," said Bethany firmly. She'd tried to stay clear of the ill feelings between father and son, but after what William had told her about his first wife, she found it impossible to keep quiet any longer. He'd teased her that she'd have no gift left for Christmas, but this one might be the best yet. "Robin's years older than I, and more than old enough for your respect. You trust him with your affairs in London. Why can't you trust him as a man—as your son—as well?"

Glaring, William folded his arms over his chest. "For God's sake, Bethany, has Robin forced you into this? I'd thought you two were getting on well enough, but if he's said or done something to make you speak like this—"

"He didn't have to say anything, William. To me it's plain as day. Can't you understand that he came clear across the sea because you're his father and he loves you?"

"Damnation, Bethany, I don't need you telling me that!"

"No?" she demanded. "Then why don't you tell Robin how you feel, instead?"

With chin tucked low against his chest, he shook his head, holding his breath before letting it out in a long weary sigh. "Damnation, Bethany," he said again. "Blast and damnation."

She linked her arms around his shoulders. "Oh, William," she said gently. "My mother insists my brothers—at least two of them, anyway, for no one can make Nick do anything—come home for Christmas, and no matter how far they've sailed from Newport, they always do. Do you think your Sarah would have waited ten years to welcome her only son home again?"

"Bethany, love, you don't know what you ask," he said, his voice raw with emotion. "Of course Sarah wouldn't want it like this. Neither do I. But you're asking for years to be undone."

"Not undone, William," she said softly. "Just left behind."

She knew what she was asking would take a miracle. But it was almost Christmas, and what better time to ask?

When Bethany turned the last corner, she saw that the wagon was already loaded and waiting before the front door. Although there was no sign of Joshua, Rachel stood in the street before the tethered horses, feeding them bits of dry grass that she'd pulled from the garden.

Pulling her cloak more closely around her, Bethany quickened her steps. She would have been here a quarter of an hour ago, if she hadn't been stopped again and again by friends and neighbors who wanted to wish her well. While there were still people in the colony who refused to celebrate Christmas—both the Friends and the Congregationalists dismissed the day as little more than a pagan feast—everyone loved a wedding, especially one with a bride who blushed as readily as Bethany.

She glanced up at the sky, the clouds a flat slate gray behind the brick chimneys. William was right, it did feel like snow.

"Where's Josh?" she asked Rachel. "We were supposed to leave at noon, and I don't want to be caught on the Middletown road if it snows."

"It never snows before Twelfth Night," said Rachel as she stroked the horse's velvety nose. "Josh's in the house, quarreling with Mama."

As if on cue, the shiny black door swung open and Bethany's youngest brother stepped out, jamming his beaver hat angrily onto his head. Josh was Jerusa's twin, and his volatile temper was a darker version of her unpredictability. Framed in the doorway behind him stood Mariah, her small hands at the waist of her apron and her fury a match for her son's.

"If you'd no intention of doing what I asked, Josh," said Mariah, caring not a whit that the argument had shifted into the street, "then I wish you had told me earlier, before I'd loaded everything into the wagon."

"I did tell you this morning that I'd other plans," he answered testily, "but you chose not to listen. We're going to step the *Tiger*'s new foremast, and as her captain, I must be there."

"I cannot believe that Mr. Henning at the shipyard would dare begin such a project this late in the day," said Mariah. "More likely you're bound for a bench at Whitehorn's, with a pot of rum the only thing to be stepped."

With an exasperated sigh, Josh stopped beside his sisters, and Bethany fought back her smile at the black look on his face. At sea he was master of a sloop and a twenty-man crew and his word was as good as God's, but the minute he came home, their mother still expected him to answer to her. Bethany had seen it with all of her brothers, and every time, regardless of how much the men kicked or squawked, their mother got her way.

"Listen to me, Mother," said Josh, striving to sound reasonable. "There's not a reason in the world why Bethany can't drive herself."

"I could, Mama," said Bethany as she pulled off her mitten to stroke the nearest horse. "I've done it before, you know."

"Only with your father on the seat beside you."
Crossly her mother shoved a loose strand of hair back
under her cap. "It's not decent for you to go alone,
Bethany. You're not some farmer's daughter, to go
wandering about the county, and I'm not about to
answer either to your father or to Mr. Howland if any
harm came to you."

"Then let me take her, Mrs. Sparhawk," said Robin
as he joined them. Clearly he'd hoped for another rehearsal, for under his arm was the box with the puppets. "I wouldn't want you having to answer to my
father for anything. It would be my pleasure."

"And it's mine to accept your kind offer, Mr.
Howland," said Mariah. "Lord knows I shouldn't be
letting this sorry rascal off so easily." Though she
smiled sweetly at Robin, she gave Josh's shoulder an
impatient little shove.

But to Bethany the short journey to the other house
now stretched out interminably before her, with only
Robin for company. By the time they unloaded the
wagon at Crescent Hill and returned, they could be
alone together three hours or more.

"Why don't we wait until Josh can go tomorrow?"
she asked, trying to hide her dismay. "I'm sure that
Mr. Howland has other, better ways to pass his time."

"Not at all," declared Robin, with such warmth
that Bethany didn't dare meet his gaze. "I'll consider
it my small contribution to the celebrations."

Bethany opened her mouth to protest further, then
saw the look on her mother's face that said she was
satisfied that everything was settled. If Josh had been

doomed to lose to their mother's will, then she wouldn't fare any better.

"Then let's bring Rachel, too," she said quickly. "You'd like to come along, wouldn't you, Rachel?"

"Oh, yes!" Her sister's face lit with dreamy anticipation. "I'd go anywhere with Robin!"

Robin smiled and bowed to the girl, wondering why in blazes Bethany didn't share her sister's eagerness. For weeks he'd been trying to be alone with her to talk again, but she'd neatly dodged him at every step.

But, though Bethany always managed to shield herself behind her family or his father, she'd failed miserably at masking her feelings. Without a single spoken word, Robin had sensed the attraction between them, felt the sparks when their fingers brushed, and the longing, so keen it stopped his breath in his chest. He knew she felt it, too; the charmingly bewildered look in her eyes told him that, as did the way she worked so hard to keep her distance.

She was kind, she was clever, she was lovely, with a special beauty that was hers alone, and he craved her company so openly that he wondered why the whole town didn't know it. Yet in four days she would be wed to his father. The whole situation was worthy of the lowest farce, and try as he might, he could see no happy way for it to be resolved. He was frustrated and miserable, because for the first time in his life he was hopelessly in love.

Even now his heart was pounding at the prospect of sitting beside her, and he watched as she pointedly turned away from him to her brother for help climbing up onto the wagon's seat. He added the puppet's box to the others in the back and hoisted himself up next, carefully sitting between Bethany and her sister.

Try as Bethany might to ease away from him, the hard wooden seat was a narrow one for three passengers. Her petticoats fluttered across his boots, and his hand brushed her arm as he reached for the reins. She was almost painfully aware of how his thigh was pressed into her skirts, and the blanket her mother tucked over their legs only bound them closer together. Three hours, she thought with growing dread; three minutes, and already her pulse was racing in her breast and her palms were damp inside her mittens.

"You be careful with my girls, Mr. Howland," said Mariah, stepping back with her hands tucked beneath her arms against the cold. "Rachel, keep under the blanket so that cough grows no worse, and mind you use your handkerchief if you need to."

Rachel waved gaily as Robin flicked the reins across the horses' backs. But Bethany stared steadfastly ahead, concentrating on the other horses and carts and wagons in the streets, the women walking slowly home from the Market House and the sailors ambling past on errands for their masters or merely bound for a rumshop, the stray dogs and cats and the sea gulls wheeling overhead, anything and everything but the man beside her.

She was only half listening to Rachel's chatter as the paved town streets gave way to dirt roads with stubbled fields on either side. The sky seemed darker here, a flat gunmetal gray. The wind that came from the water was colder, smelling of salt. With a shiver, she drew her cloak more tightly around her shoulders.

"Do you know the way to Crescent Hill?" she asked, her voice sounding stiff and forced.

"Oh, aye, who in Newport doesn't?" asked Robin easily. "When I was a boy, my father always called it 'the great house built from Spanish gold.' You can imagine how disappointed I was when he finally took me past it, and I saw it was only made of timber and bricks and mortar, same as any other house."

Bethany smiled in spite of herself. "I've never heard that," she admitted. "But you're right, it was the gold my father captured in the Spanish Wars that paid for Crescent Hill, just as the French War bought the house in town. I look at my father now and I can't believe he was such a great roaring privateer when he was younger, as wicked as any pirate."

Robin had no trouble at all imagining the older Captain Sparhawk as another Blackbeard, but he was wise enough to keep it to himself. "And what of my father?" he said instead, striving to keep his manner light. "Can you imagine him as a young man?"

"Oh, yes," she said blithely. "First because he's not so very old himself, only forty-seven. And secondly because to see him younger, all I have to do is look at you."

Robin raised one brow a fraction to match his lopsided grin, and too late she realized she'd admitted far more than she intended. "And what you see pleases you?"

Despite the cold, her cheeks felt on fire. Had he guessed how often she'd watched him, telling herself it was mere study for his portrait, when in truth watching him, his movements confident and full of natural male grace, was pleasure itself?

"Your father is a handsome man," she said, hedging. "You resemble him, as well you know."

"Because Bethany paints, she thinks she's entitled to gawk at whomever she pleases," said Rachel, unwilling to be left out of the conversation. "She'll outright stare at people if she thinks they won't notice."

"Then she may look at me all she wants," said Robin, and from the way he said it, Bethany knew he was perfectly aware of how often she glanced his way. "For Father's sake, of course."

"Of course." Mortified, Bethany tried to draw herself straighter in the seat, and kept her gaze determinedly on the road before them. She'd have words with her sister later; "gawking," indeed!

She pointed ahead with her mitten. "You'll want to take the turning there, beyond that hill. Then, at the next rise, you'll see the roof and the chimneys of the house."

They'd be there in just a few minutes more. With the three of them, plus Mrs. Belton, the housekeeper who watched over the property while the Sparhawks were in town, they should be able to unload the wagon in a quarter hour, at most. Then would come the trip back to town, shorter with the wagon empty. Another ninety minutes in all, guessed Bethany. Now, if she could just manage to keep her mouth shut and her thoughts where they belonged until they were safely back home. For ninety minutes, anything was possible.

"Oh, look!" cried Rachel, her face turned up to the sky. "Look, Robin! It's snowing!"

# Chapter Eight

By the time they reached the house, the snow had changed from haphazard flurries to a steady fall, the thick, fat flakes swirling downward at a dizzying speed. The ground and the dry grass were already coated as Bethany and Rachel climbed stiffly down from the wagon, the hoods and shoulders of their cloaks iced white.

Gleefully Rachel danced through the falling snow with her arms outstretched. "Just look at it, Bethany! Lovely snow, beautiful snow!"

"And they say it never truly snows in Newport before Twelfth Night." Bethany sighed, tugging a basket full of fruitcakes free from the snow-covered tarpaulin. "Come help me, Rachel, or we'll never be done. I hope Mrs. Belton has the kettle on the fire for chocolate. I'm frozen clear through."

Robin glanced up at the sky as he brushed the wet snow from the backs of the steaming horses. "Let's hope she's put more on the fire than chocolate. If this doesn't stop soon, we'll be staying for supper."

"We can't stay," said Bethany, appalled at the very idea. "We must go back to town."

"Not in this snow, we won't," said Robin firmly. "Not in an open wagon with a tired team, across hills that are difficult enough on a clear day. I promised I'd take care of you and Rachel, and if that means we stay here until the snow stops, then we will."

"Stay here?" Rachel squealed with delight, still pirouetting across the yard, with her braid swinging around her. "At Crescent Hill, without Mama and Father?"

Her joy, and her spinning, were cut short by a sudden spasm of coughing, enough to make Bethany glare at Robin as she pulled her sister towards the house.

"You know, Robin, if we'd waited until tomorrow the way I wanted, we'd be warm and safe at home now," she said, her words turned to angry little clouds in the cold air. "But *you* had to insist, didn't you?"

Before he could reply, she turned on her heel, skidding a bit on the snow-covered grass, and marched toward the door. She braced the basket against the pilaster to free her hand to open the door, but though she jiggled and twisted the knob, then pounded and called for Mrs. Belton, the door stayed locked and the big house behind it silent.

"Where do you think she is, Bethany?" asked Rachel, coughing again. "I'm cold."

"We all are." Bethany set her basket down on the step with a muffled thump and circled around to the last window, near the west corner of the house. Tugging off her mitten, she slid her hand beneath the shutter until her fingers touched cold brass and she pulled free the spare key that hung there. "Mrs. Belton has a married daughter on a farm near Portsmouth. Maybe she went there. She didn't expect any of us until tomorrow night.''

With a squeak, the key turned in the lock, and Bethany pushed open the door. The kitchen was dark and cold, and from the clean-swept fireplace it was clear that Mrs. Belton had been gone all day at least, with no intention of returning soon.

''There's no hot chocolate,'' said Rachel, drooping with disappointment.

''Nor will there be, unless we make it ourselves.'' Bustling about the empty kitchen, Bethany set her basket on the table and searched for the striker to light first the candles in the hanging lantern overhead and then the tinder beneath the logs in the fireplace. She thrust a bucket into Rachel's hands. ''Please go to the well and draw us water. Go, Rachel, on with you!''

Robin set another load of her mother's bundles and baskets on the table. His brows rose as he saw Bethany struggling with the flint near the fireplace. Her muttered oath straight from her seafaring brothers.

''Can you manage that?'' he asked, coming to stand behind her.

''I can very well, thank you.'' To her infinite relief, at that same instant the shower of sparks took hold of the tinder and began to burn. She sat back on her heels, cupping her hands over the growing fire. ''It's only that this isn't exactly what I expected.''

''Life never is,'' agreed Robin. He held his hand out to help her up, and to his surprise, she took it. ''Though this could be far worse.''

With her hand still in his, she looked at him uncertainly, and decided to believe he meant the house, not her company. How had he managed to keep his hands so warm, when her fingers felt like icicles? "I suppose there are worse places to be stranded."

"Oh, aye," he said wryly, his glance taking in the whole expanse of the large, lavishly furnished house. "And we won't starve, not with all that fruitcake."

She smiled. It was impossible to stay angry when he looked at her like this, his dark eyes so merry beneath his snow-covered hat. Being here at Crescent Hill made things somehow different between them, as if being trapped by the snow had magically freed them from far more than just being back in Newport in time for supper.

As if standing here with soot on her face, snowflakes melting in her hair and her hand in Robin's, weren't perfectly acceptable, perfectly right...

"Must I do all the work?" wailed Rachel pitifully as the full bucket of water in her hands crashed into the side of the kitchen door.

Bethany flew apart from Robin and rushed to take the bucket from her sister before any more of the water could slosh onto her or the floor.

"Oh, look at you, Rachel!" she said, scolding to cover her own embarrassment at being caught holding Robin's hand. "You'd think you'd never drawn a bucket of water before in your life, and now your skirts are soaked as much as if you'd fallen in the well itself! Have you any clothes left in the chests upstairs?"

"Nothing that will fit," said Rachel with a dejected sniff.

"Then go pull a coverlet from one of the beds and wrap yourself in that until we can dry your petticoats by the fire," ordered Bethany. "Go on, I don't want Mama blaming me for your carelessness."

With an exasperated sigh, she watched her sister go, trailing water from her skirts. Even if the snow outside weren't keeping them from traveling back to Newport, Rachel's wet clothes now would.

"What a master drill sergeant!" said Robin teasingly. "I've never seen this side of you, Bethany Sparhawk."

Bethany whirled around to face him, her hands on her hips, unwittingly echoing her mother's favorite stance when she wanted things done. "Then I won't spare you, either, Robin Howland. Have you taken the horses to the barn, or left the poor creatures out there to freeze?"

"Nay, ma'am," he said as he tapped his knuckle to his forehead with a proper workingman's deference, "but I'll see t' it directly, ma'am, if ye please, after I've finished unloading th' cart."

She could still hear him laughing as he led the horses to the barn, and the sound was infectious. She knew she should be dreading spending the night here, but instead she felt oddly excited, like a child on some imaginary adventure. If none of this was as she'd expected, then none of it seemed quite real, either.

Poking through Mrs. Belton's cupboards, she found dried peas that she put to soak with onions, potatoes and carrots for soup, and ground corn and eggs that would do for improvised johnnycake. Only briefly did she consider cutting into the huge smoked ham they'd brought with them. Though a slice or two would add much to the soup, she knew her mother would only consider outright starvation sufficient grounds for cutting into the Christmas Day ham, and for all Robin's joking, the fruitcakes would be equally sacred.

By the time Rachel came back downstairs, grandly draped in a red-and-white patchwork quilt, and Robin returned from the barn with his cheeks still ruddy from the cold, Bethany could welcome them both with the promised pot of steaming chocolate. It was great fun to play at being the mistress of the house, she decided as the three of them sat around the battered trestle kitchen table. How strange to remember, with a fresh pang of uncertainty, that when she awakened in William's house as his wife on Friday the game would be for real.

"It's almost dark," she said, glancing out the window to where the fat white flakes still swirled and danced. "I wish there was some way to let them know at home that we're all right."

"Mama won't worry." Rachel fished out the last clumps of chocolate from the bottom of her cup. "She knows you'd never do anything wrong. Why, if the wagon had slid off the road into a drift, you'd likely figure out a way to get it back to rights by yourself, just so you wouldn't be a bother to anyone else. That's why Mama trusts you. She wouldn't let me cross the street with Jerusa."

"Don't be foolish, Rachel," murmured Bethany, wondering what her mother would say if she knew the truth. Loyalty and love, right and wrong: how had things that had always seemed so clear to her before become so muddled? "She's bound to be worried, and William, too."

"For you, perhaps, but I doubt Father's wasted much concern on me." Robin had intended to reassure Bethany, but the old bitterness had crept into his words anyway. No, that wasn't quite honest. He'd said it to reassure himself, not about his father, but about her. "Likely he hasn't even noticed I'm gone, or else he's picturing me carousing with the harlots in a tavern on Thames Street."

The compassion in Bethany's eyes reached to every corner of Robin's soul, smoothing away the bitterness, even though he knew he'd no right to the comfort only she could bring. He teased her, laughed with her, found pleasure in the graceful way she moved and how the candlelight shimmered on her honey gold hair, but it was for her understanding and her kindness that he loved her most.

*He loved her.* God help him for a fool, he loved her.

Rachel giggled and licked her spoon. "Fancy you and me Thames Street harlots, Bethany. Can you imagine what Father would say?"

"What Father would say, Rachel, is that you have entirely too free a mind for a maid your age." With a righteous clatter, Bethany cleared away the cups. Not that she had any claim to righteousness herself tonight, not with this strange, warm feeling that spread through every inch of her body whenever Robin looked at her. "I hope you'll find a subject more suitable for polite discourse. We've at least a good two hours until supper."

"Plenty of time for an appearance from Chloe, Daphnis, and the angel on high," said Robin heartily. "How fortuitous that they made the journey with us!"

For the next hours, the kitchen became their theater. From the attic and workroom upstairs came the final pieces of their improvised stage. The three puppets would perform on top of an old dining table, raised high enough that all the audience could see, while a backdrop curtain hung from a quilting frame would hide the puppeteers as they stood on chairs.

The cutout bits of scenery that Bethany had painted on board—a weeping willow, a peacock perched on an urn with his tail elegantly spread, the ruins of a pagan temple, all meant to look vaguely antique and picturesque—were stuck to the table with blobs of sealing wax. Branches of holly that had been intended for decorating the parlor mantelpiece were tucked cheerfully along the sides of the curtain; Bethany was sure her mother wouldn't miss it, unlike the ham. For footlights, she wedged candle stubs into the bottoms of tilted custard cups, and they each took turns stepping out front to see how vastly grand the effect would be.

For the last time, the wooden actor and actresses rehearsed their roles, from the opening scene, with Chloe calling her never-to-be-found sheep, to the grand finale, when the angel solemnly intoned her best wishes for Christmas and the New Year, and Daphnis and Chloe finally clattered into each other's arms.

Determined to have this last scene perfect, Rachel insisted on doing it again and again, even as her voice grew hoarse with repetition. Yet each time the girl tried to improve her puppet's speech, Robin in turn made Daphnis's final declaration sillier and more far-fetched, until Bethany, laughing too hard, accidentally let Chloe drop with a thump.

But this time, instead of laughing with them as she always had before, Rachel burst into tears.

"You—you don't care about anything!" she sobbed, clutching the countess-turned-angel in her arms as she climbed off her chair. "Ev-eryone will be here to watch, and you don't *care* if it's right or not!"

Quickly Bethany hopped off her own chair to put her arms around her sister's shaking shoulders. "I'm sorry, lamb, I didn't know this was so important to you. I promise you that on Christmas Eve Robin and I will do everything exactly right, and you'll be the best angel ever seen."

But Bethany frowned as she hugged Rachel. "You're feverish, aren't you?" Her frown deepened with concern as she laid her palm across her sister's forehead. "How long have you felt hot?"

Rachel hiccuped and coughed. "I don't know. I only wanted to do the puppets with you and Robin."

"Rehearsal's done," said Bethany. "You're going to bed."

But even with a fire in the bed chamber and a hot brick beneath the sheets and a pile of coverlets, Rachel still complained of being cold, though to the touch her skin was hot and dry. She refused her dinner, and as the evening wore on she grew rapidly more ill, with the cough she'd had all day turning to a wheezing rasp with every breath she struggled to take. Bethany did what she could, keeping her covered and putting a steaming kettle on the bedchamber's fire, but she felt helpless and frightened. Rachel was sick, very sick, and when she wept and tried to cry for their mother, Bethany longed to join her.

Her only comfort came from Robin. Like Bethany, he stayed at Rachel's bedside, amusing the girl with stories of London when she was awake and watching her in silence when she dozed fitfully.

"The snow's nearly stopped," he said to Bethany quietly as he brought more wood in from the shed outside. "There must be a good eight or nine inches on the ground. Our wagon's here to stay until that melts, but I'll wager a guinea your father or mine will be out here with a sleigh at dawn."

Bethany shook her head wearily. "Mama will come herself, if they don't." Her hands twisted in her apron as she listened to her sister's ragged breathing. "Oh, Robin, this is my fault!"

He reached out and covered her hands with his own to still them. "Now how could this possibly be any fault of yours?"

She glanced up at him unhappily, wishing she could confess that she'd been unwilling to trust herself alone with him. How selfish it seemed now! "I knew Rachel was sick, but I asked her to come with us anyway."

"You thought she would enjoy the ride. There's hardly blame in that," he said easily. Of course, he guessed the real reason, but there'd be nothing gained by saying so. "She'll be all right. As is pointed out to me over and over, you Sparhawks are a hardy lot."

Bethany smiled at that. "Hardy as in 'too thick-headed to come to harm'?"

"Nay, we Howlands have the claim to that particular quality." He laced his fingers into hers, marveling at both the strength and the delicacy of her hand and trying to ignore his father's ring on her finger. "You'll be relieved to know I've taken lodgings at Whitehorn's from the night of the wedding until I sail.

Somehow I doubted you newlyweds would want to be bothered with a guest under your roof.''

Bethany looked down at her lap and gently eased her fingers free of his. She wanted to tell him she would miss him, but that could be as easily misunderstood as their clasped hands, and so, again, she said nothing.

"Captain Haskins is planning to clear for Bristol next Tuesday,'' he continued. "I've booked my passage with him, and I'll take the coach from Bristol to London.''

"I'm sorry your plans to convince your father came to nothing,'' she said, choosing her words with care. "But he is certain there's no danger from the king or Parliament at present.''

Robin sighed. "Stuck in the middle of it, what else could Father say?''

"A thousand other things to ease the distance between you two, but he won't say them, either,'' she said sadly, remembering how William had spoken of his first wife. "Was it really so important that he come to London, to see for himself how you've prospered in spite of his banishment?''

"Was it that obvious?'' He looked away and tapped his fingertips together on his knee. "Doubtless he'd figured it all from the first.''

"No, I don't think he has even yet,'' she said softly. "But he does love you, Robin. Don't ever doubt that.''

"He's given me precious little proof so far. Not even you can change that, Bethany.''

She had never seen any man so despondent, except perhaps William himself, and again she longed to be able to make peace between father and son. How had the walls of pride and stubbornness grown so high between two men who so clearly cared for one another?

Troubled, she glanced back at her sister's flushed face, against the white pillow. "Somehow," she said softly, "somehow everything will be all right."

*It was night and it was snowing, and she was cold and lost. Her shoes were soaked through, her skirts weighed down by the ice that clung to them as she stumbled through the drifts. The swirling snow stung her cheeks and eyes until she lost any sense of direction, but still she trudged onward, struggling to keep her footing as the wind whipped at her hair and cloak.*

*"Bethany, lass, where are you?" called William from the uncertain distance. "Come to me, sweetheart, and you'll be safe!"*

*"William, I'm here!" she shouted back, but the wind tore her words from her lips. "I'm here!"*

*"I can't find you, Bethany," he called, his voice growing fainter and fainter. "You must come to me."*

*"I'm coming, William," she cried, her tears freezing on her cheeks. "I'm coming, if you'll only wait!"*

She woke with a gasp, her hand still outstretched to reach for William's and her cheeks wet from weeping.

"Hush, Bethany, it was only a dream." Robin took her hand and drew her, trembling still, into his arms. "Only a dream."

"But I was lost, Robin, lost in the storm, and I couldn't reach William!"

"You're not lost at all, sweetheart," he said gently, stroking the back of her head to calm her. "You're very much found, and as safe as you're ever likely to be.''

She liked the feel of his soft wool coat beneath her cheek and the sound of his heartbeat beneath her ear and the way his hand moved along the back of her neck. Still halfway between sleep and waking, she let herself relish the warm sensation of well-being his arms brought. Then she remembered, and with a shuddering sigh she pushed herself away.

''I fell asleep in the chair,'' she said, explaining to herself as much as to him. ''Is Rachel—''

''Stop worrying.'' Robin turned her so that she could see her sister, peacefully curled on her side. ''She's fine, I swear it. While you slept, her fever must have broken.''

Swiftly Bethany knelt to touch her sister's forehead for herself. ''Praise God, she'll be all right.''

''I told you the Sparhawks were hardy.'' Gently Robin raised her back to her feet. ''Come with me, Bethany. There's something I want you to see.''

He led her into the hallway, to the tall triple-arched window at the landing. The clouds that had brought the snow were gone, and the clear night sky was inky-black, scattered with stars and a bright quarter-moon. In the moonlight, the fresh snow sparkled like diamonds, the usually rough meadows and fields smoothed into uniform, undulating hills that stretched unbroken to the dark silver band of the river and the sea beyond.

Lightly Bethany rested her fingertips on the cool glass of the window, an unconscious smile on her lips as her artist's soul drank in all the loveliness of the scene spread before her.

"Oh, Robin, I've never seen anything like it," she murmured, tracing the frost on the window with her fingertips. "It's all so unbelievably beautiful."

"But none of it as beautiful as you."

Startled, she looked at him, scarcely daring to hope. "Oh, Robin, I—"

"Hush, sweetheart, don't spoil it." Gently he lifted her face to his.

Wide-eyed, she nodded as her gaze met his in the soft, cool light of the moon, and then, before she quite realized how, his lips found hers. She closed her eyes, both to reason and to better savor the sweetness of his kiss, and on their own her hands crept up to rest on his chest.

He kissed her slowly, gently, drawing her full lower lip between his until her mouth parted with the breath of a sigh and he coaxed her to open further for the velvet surety of pleasure. Shimmering waves of heat swept through her body as he deepened the kiss, and she swayed against him for support, her arms sliding beneath his coat and around his lean, narrow waist.

She felt his hand move along the front of her gown over her whalebone stays until he found the soft, waiting curve of her breast above the top of her bodice. Aching in innocent anticipation, she shivered as his fingers slipped into her gown to caress her breast. With an eagerness that was sliding into open desire, she hungrily sought his mouth, the only fulfillment within her reach. She had known nothing like his touch, felt nothing like his kiss, and as she moaned deep in her throat, it seemed that all her life had narrowed to this moment and this man.

But Robin knew more, and he knew better. He had meant to kiss her, that was all. A single kiss he could remember forever. But one kiss from Bethany wasn't enough. How could it be? He had never loved a woman as much as he loved Bethany, and because of it he'd never come close to this level of raw, physical need. Another moment and he would be beyond stopping, and with the last shred of his conscience he held her away.

"Bethany, sweetheart, I can't," he said hoarsely, fighting the temptation she offered. "We can't."

Bethany shook her head, uncomprehending and almost dazed, her eyes heavy-lidded with longing and her lips swollen from his kisses. He couldn't blame her. To understand would be to accept what they'd done, and too well he knew the price of that.

With his thumb he traced the curve of her cheek, and in the pale wash of moonlight he saw the pain that filled her eyes.

"William," she whispered, her voice breaking with anguish as she touched the place on her cheek that he'd just caressed. "God help us, Robin, what have we done?"

# Chapter Nine

With the two sticks that controlled Chloe's strings in her hands, Bethany stood poised on the chair behind the makeshift stage and looked out across the merry, well-fed faces before her. There were twenty-seven guests at Crescent Hill for Christmas Eve supper and dancing, all the Sparhawk relatives that the colony could boast, laughing and chatting and joking among themselves here in the hall. Tomorrow, for the wedding itself, friends and neighbors would gather with them, as well, and swell the number to nearly fifty.

Crescent Hill had never looked more festive, decided Bethany, with holly and fir branches tied to the balustrade and over paintings, sprigs of mistletoe and white ribbon strategically hung in the doorways and polished silver bowls filled with oranges on all the tables. The air was pungent with the fragrance of the pine boughs and the bayberry candles her mother used only for the Christmas holidays, and in the back parlor Bethany could hear the three Irish fiddlers, drawn from the crews of Sparhawk ships, tuning their instruments for the jigs and other country dances that would follow the puppets.

In the front row of chairs sat her parents, little Jeremiah on Jon's lap, her grandmother and great-aunt, and in the middle, in the best seat, William. He smiled happily when her gaze met his, nodding his encouragement, and she tried to smile back.

"Isn't this wonderful, Bethany?" whispered Rachel, standing on the chair beside hers as the angel puppet dangled from her hands. Tonight the girl's eyes were bright with excitement, not the fever that had so frightened Bethany earlier in the week. "This has to be the best Christmas ever!"

"Certainly it's the most crowded," murmured Bethany, painfully aware of how noncommittal an answer that was. Everything she'd said these last three days seemed to be like that.

"That's because of your wedding, silly." She grinned impishly. "Jerusa told me that next year we're sure to have one more at the table, because by then you'll have had a baby."

*"Rachel!"*

"Are you ready, ladies?" asked Robin as he climbed up onto the last chair in the row, nodding curtly as he swung Daphnis onto the stage. By the candlelight, his handsome face seemed drawn, and at supper he had remained nearly silent, the only gentleman in the company to leave her father's infamous Christmas punch—Newport rum, sherry, brandy, whipped eggs and cream—untouched.

Gone was Robin's characteristic playfulness, just as Bethany's own shy smiles and laughter had vanished behind the same formal facade of polite good breeding. They both knew why. Since that shameful, glorious kiss on the night of the storm, there had been no other choice for either of them. She would marry William and Robin would sail for England, and whatever had passed between them would be buried by time and distance as if it had never happened.

With a taper Jerusa began lighting the footlights in the custard cups, and the audience hushed with anticipation. Bethany stole one last look at William; he was smiling still, his happiness so obvious that it cut straight to her guilty heart. Lord, what she would give to have things again as they'd been when she promised to marry him!

"Christmastime," began Rachel grandly as her angel swept across the stage on linen strings and gilt-paper wings. "A time for rejoicing and merriment and love, even among God's most mortal creatures."

Daphnis ambled across the stage, singing to himself in the odd warbling voice that Robin had created for the shepherd, and the first wave of laughter swept through the audience. After the weeks of rehearsal, Bethany automatically sent Chloe racing to greet him with such a squeal of enthusiasm that one of Bethany's brothers shouted his approval with a bawdy invitation.

With the laughter and applause to spur on the puppeteers, Bethany forgot the tension that existed between her and Robin. In performance, their play became even more boisterous than when they'd practiced it, with Robin's Daphnis in particular growing so outrageously ardent that he toppled the painted temple, and Chloe with it.

Finally Rachel began the angel's closing Christmas speech, and Bethany danced Chloe next to Daphnis for their final lines. Daphnis raised his hand to his heart, but instead of the foolish, pompous declaration that Bethany expected came only three short words, spoken in Robin's own voice.

"I love you."

Stunned, Bethany jerked her gaze away from the puppets to stare at Robin. His face was oddly lit from beneath by the little footlights, all shadows and planes, but there was no mistaking the look in his eyes. He had told her she was wise, that she was clever, that she was beautiful, but he had never before said he loved her.

"I love you, too," she answered breathlessly, Chloe forgotten, limp in her hands. "Oh, how I love you!"

The shocked silence in the hall was louder than any of the laughter had been, a silence that only two-year-old Jeremiah dared break.

"All gone?" he asked, mystified, twisting on his father's lap. "Dollies all gone?"

Then William was rising to his feet, clapping his hands as loudly as he could. "Nay, lad, not gone, but done, and right handsomely, too! Who'd have thought that little shepherd couple would end so happy, eh? Rachel, Bethany, Robin! Show yourselves now, you three, come out here into the light, so we can have a proper look at you before King George himself commands a performance!"

With palpable relief, the others around him began to clap and cheer and stamp their feet. Rachel ran forward first, presenting her cheek to William for a kiss before she turned to her parents. Bethany followed more slowly, her smile wooden and her eyes fixed on the soft ruffles of William's neckcloth, instead of his face, as she stepped into the welcoming circle of his arms.

*God help her, what had she done?*

"Anny-Beth? Are you still awake?"

Bethany sighed. "Of course I am. Did you really think I'd sleep tonight?"

"The clock below just chimed twelve. Happy Christmas, Anny-Beth."

"Happy Christmas to you, too, Jerusa."

The pause that stretched between them was awkward, full of things neither dared say. Not Jerusa, too, thought Bethany miserably, not on the last night she'd spend in this bed.

"You shall be happy, won't you?" her sister asked at last. "I mean with William?"

"He's a good man, Rusa, and he cares for me."

"But what about you, Bethany?" asked her sister anxiously. "William might have been fooled tonight, but no one else was. Oh, Anny-Beth, how can you bear to marry William, if it's Robin you truly love?"

"Because William asked me, and I said yes." Her voice was steady from will alone, her heart so close to breaking that she wondered that it didn't shatter right now in her breast. "He wasn't any more fooled than the rest of you were tonight, but because he cares for me, he pretended he was. How could I ever do anything in turn to hurt him?"

"Even if you must suffer yourself? And, oh, what will become of poor Robin?"

"Robin will return to England, and I will marry William as I promised."

"Oh, Anny-Beth." Jerusa found Bethany's icy hand beneath the coverlet, linking their fingers together this last time. "Are you sure?"

"Of course I'm sure," said Bethany. "How could I dare not be happy with a man like William as my husband?"

Jerusa sighed. "I pray you're right, Anny-Beth. When I marry Tom in June, I mean to be happier than I've ever been in my life."

"Then you will be, Rusa." In the dark the tears were hot in Bethany's eyes. "How could you dare be otherwise?"

The next morning Bethany dressed in her parents' bedchamber, with only her mother to help her. Downstairs she could hear the laughter of her father and brothers and the guests who'd arrived in time to share a late breakfast. In a quarter of an hour, at eleven o'clock, she would go down the stairs on her father's arm, and by noon Bethany Sparhawk would be gone forever, replaced by someone named Mrs. William Howland.

She stared at her reflection in the tall looking glass as she hooked pearl-and-opal earbobs, another gift from William, into her ears. Her gown was cream-colored Spitalfields silk, woven overall with a damask pattern of small flower sprays, the most elegant fabric to be found in Newport on six weeks' notice, cut simply, with only a single scalloped flounce at the hem to flatter Bethany's short, rounded figure. Earlier Jerusa had rubbed a scrap of the same silk over Bethany's honey gold hair to make it shine, and then brushed it back for her into a loose knot, crowned with green ribbons and a tiny sprig of white-berried mistletoe. Could this pale, unsmiling young woman dressed like a bride really be *her?*

Her mother pursed her lips critically as she looked over Bethany's shoulder into the glass, plucking her skirts fuller until, pleased at last, she nodded and smiled with approval.

"You're a beautiful bride, Bethany," she said softly. "Your William will never forget how you look this morning."

She lifted Bethany's hand to slip a gold-and-pearl cuff around her wrist. "Here, lamb, for you, a remembrance to carry with you from your mother," she said with a fond pat. "You know the pair of them were given to me on my wedding day by your grandfather. It seems right that you should have one now, and the other shall go to Jerusa when she weds Tom."

Bethany stared down at the bracelet, overwhelmed by the love and generosity that came with such a gift. She didn't deserve the bracelet any more than she deserved the good man waiting to be her husband, and she pressed her hand over her mouth to fight back the tears.

"There now, child, I didn't mean to make you weep." Mariah slipped her arm around Bethany's shoulders. "Will it help if I tell you that nearly every bride finds a reason to shed some tears?"

Bethany only shook her head, determined not to let her tears fall. If they began, she knew, they'd never stop.

But, without a word spoken, her mother knew.

"It's not that simple, is it?" Mariah sighed deeply, her own smile forced now as she held Bethany's hands. "Bethany, you don't have to do this, at least not today. Your father can go speak to William and then send everyone away, and we'll just have Christmas here among ourselves."

"I can't, Mama!" Her voice broke with a dry, anguished sob. "I can't."

"No one's going to make you marry against your will, Bethany. The gown, the gifts, the guests, all of it comes to nothing against your happiness."

"I would never hurt William that way!"

" 'Tis far better to be a seven-day tattle than to ruin both your lives," said her mother firmly. "If you find in your heart that you do not love William as you should—"

"But I must! I wouldn't have accepted him if I couldn't, and now I mean to be the best wife in the world to him."

Unconvinced, Mariah searched Bethany's face for the truth. "There have been times these last weeks when I've wondered if perhaps Robin Howland had tried to take his father's place in your affections."

"Robin loves his father too much to do such a base, dishonorable thing," said Bethany, her voice quavering miserably. She had not seen him again after their performance with the puppets was done. No one had. He had vanished from the house, into the night. She told herself it was for the best, and better still if he disappeared as completely from Newport, too. Better, best, the right thing—but still it hurt. "Whatever else he seems, Mama, Robin is a gentleman."

"Sometimes even gentlemen can act like rogues," said Mariah sadly. "Sometimes their feelings don't give them a choice."

Bethany shook her head, her shoulders sagging beneath her despair. "Not Robin. He means to sail for

London on Tuesday, and I would be surprised if he ever returns to Newport. Nor would I dare place myself between father and son.''

"Oh, child," murmured Mariah. "You've set yourself a high, hard road to follow."

"How could I do otherwise, Mama?" She swallowed, her eyes pleading for understanding as she tried not to think of how she'd never see Robin again. "I can never knowingly hurt William. Haven't you and Father raised me that way, to be good and honorable?"

With tears in her own eyes, her mother began to speak, changed her mind, and instead hugged Bethany close. The familiar fragrance of her mother's scent and the security of her embrace brought fresh tears to Bethany's eyes. Already their relationship was changing. Now she would be William Howland's wife first, and Mariah Sparhawk's daughter second. Her allegiances, as well as her mother's confidences, would never be the same again.

"Along with you now, Bethany," said her father as he opened the door to the bedchamber, and behind him echoed the sound of the tall clock downstairs chiming the hour. "High time we went below. I won't have you late to your own wedding."

"You hush, Gabriel," said her mother as she separated from Bethany and stuffed a handkerchief into her hand. "Let the poor girl compose herself."

Bethany stepped back, dabbing at her eyes as she straightened her shoulders. No matter that her heart was breaking, she refused to have anyone see the proof on her face. She would try her best to be the joyful bride that William deserved, and try to forget that this was only the first day of a lifetime of pretending.

Forcing herself to smile, she linked her hand through Gabriel's arm. "I'm ready, Father."

He smiled down at her with open love and admiration. "You do me proud, Bethany. I hope that bridegroom of yours realizes what a prize I'm granting him."

"He will," said Mariah as she kissed Bethany's cheek one last time, "or he'll answer to me."

But as Bethany walked at her father's side, she knew too well that neither of her parents could help her now. Somehow she managed to place each foot before the other, the toes of her silk-covered shoes pointing determinedly ahead from beneath her hem.

She was only half-aware of moving through the guests, of their curious stares and their soft exclamations and excited whispers as she passed. Before her stood Dr. Carter, with his oversize prayer book, open to the ceremony, in his hands. Beside the minister, then, would be William, and deliberately she shifted her gaze to find him.

He was smiling, but not the eager, joyful smile she expected. This smile was bittersweet, almost melancholy, tinged with unmistakable sadness and a measure of regret, and she would have worried and wondered at his mood, if at that same moment she hadn't discovered Robin.

*God help her, why must he be here?* He stood to the right of William, impeccably dressed in royal blue, his hands clasped. His handsome face was rigid as he locked away any hint of expression from his features, but his eyes said more, to her alone, than she had any right to hear.

Stunned from the surprise of seeing him, she was trembling uncontrollably, and she knew that if her father hadn't been supporting her she might have fainted. Still she struggled to focus instead on Dr. Carter's prayer book and the words he had begun to read.

*Dearly beloved, we are gathered here in the sight of God and in the face of this company to join together this Man and this Woman in holy Matrimony...*

If she had not known herself in her mother's mirror, now she knew even less. This man, this woman, the same one whose heart thudded so loudly in her breast as her panic grew.

*...not by any to be entered into unadvisedly or lightly...*

She had told herself she was marrying William for all the right, noble, true reasons. Then why did she doubt herself, why was she suffering so?

*...if either of you know any impediment, why ye may not be lawfully joined together, ye do now confess it...*

She could not do this. She could never love William as she loved Robin now, and she could not, must not, do this. She had to stop before she made the worst mistake of her life, before she—

"Forgive me, Dr. Carter, but you'd best stop right now."

Bethany froze, the words so exactly matching her thoughts that she didn't at first realize they were spoken not in her own voice, but in William's.

She felt her father's fingers tighten on her arm as he wheeled around to challenge William. "What do you mean by this, sir?"

"I mean that I cannot marry your daughter, Captain," said William, with the same sadness Bethany had seen on his face. "When I asked for her, I believed we would suit one another. She's a charming lass, your daughter, and I've grown powerfully fond of her, and I still believe we could have had a good life together. But the truth is, I can't give her the kind of love a young creature like her deserves, and as I truly wish to see her happy, I won't be selfish enough to pretend otherwise."

The guests gasped and whispered among themselves, barely able to contain their excitement. This went beyond mere scandal; this was a legend in the making.

Stunned, Robin could only stare at his father as he scrambled to make sense of what he was hearing. His father was stopping the wedding. He was admitting to everyone in this room that he didn't love Bethany as he should, and that he couldn't marry her. Was this, then, the reason his father had insisted on Robin coming this morning, almost to the point of threatening him if he didn't?

Dr. Carter fingered the marker in his prayer book, glancing uncertainly from William to Gabriel and back again. "Am I then to believe, gentlemen, that there will be no ceremony this morning?"

"I didn't say that, did I?" said William, testily. "I said I couldn't make this young lady happy as her husband, but that doesn't mean there's not another here that might be able to please her."

He came to stand before Bethany. "Last night, before this company, you said you loved my son. Now, was that just those puppets talking, sweetheart, or was it you?"

Her mouth dry and her heart pounding, Bethany told the truth. "I said it," she confessed, barely above a whisper. "I'm sorry, William, I'm—"

"Nay, lass, no apologies." He swung around toward Robin, beckoning impatiently. "Now you, Robin. Last night you told Bethany you loved her. Would you say it again this morning?"

Robin looked at Bethany. She seemed small and fragile in her wedding finery, unbelievably lovely and impossibly dear. Of course he loved her; it was hard now to remember a time when he hadn't. "Aye, Father, I will. I love you, Bethany Sparhawk."

"Then what are you dawdling for, son?" demanded William. "There's a bride and a minister and witnesses, and enough fruitcake to feed a regiment."

Suddenly William's face softened, and for once he let the love he felt for his son show for all the world, and most of all for Robin, to see. "I'm handing you the best Christmas present there is, Robin," he said with gruff tenderness, "and all you have to do is make it your own."

Bethany forgot to breathe as Robin walked toward her and sank to one knee at her feet. "Bethany, my love," he said softly. "Will you do me the honor of becoming my wife?"

Too overcome with joy to think twice, she released her father's arm and reached out both hands to Robin. "Yes, Robin," she whispered as he rose to take her in his arms. "Yes, oh, yes!"

William made a deep sound of satisfaction in his throat and nodded to the minister. "There you are, sir. Read the words over the pair of them and make it right."

"This is hardly proper, Mr. Howland," sputtered Dr. Carter. "One cannot simply trade bridegrooms at will. Why, new banns must be published, and—"

"It's Christmas Day, Dr. Carter," said Gabriel in his most formidable captain's rumble, "and it's my house, and if my daughter Bethany wishes to wed this man today, then she shall."

And she did.

And when at last they were joined as husband and wife, the mistletoe in Bethany's hair trembled as Robin kissed her.

"Oh, Robin, I do love you!" she said as her heart overflowed with the joy she had thought she'd never find.

"Merry Christmas, love," he whispered for her ears alone. "Merry, merry Christmas."

\* \* \* \* \*

If you enjoyed *Bayberry and Mistletoe,*
be sure to look for Miranda Jarrett's
latest novel,


*The Sparhawk Bride*


On sale now
wherever Harlequin books are sold

Turn the page for a preview of
this passionate new historical romance...

*Newport
Colony of Rhode Island
and Providence Plantations
1771*

He hadn't meant to come here to the house, not on the night of the wedding. If anyone recognized him, he could be dancing at the end of a rope before he knew it, and then how would justice be served?

Another carriage stopped before the house, and Michel Géricault shrank back into the shadows of the tall hedge. More wedding guests—more red-faced, overdressed Englishmen and their blowsy ladies—braying to one another as they tried and failed to ape their betters in London.

Mon Dieu, *how foolish they all were, these An-*glais, *and how much he hated them!*

The front door to the house swung open, candle-light flooding into the streets. Instead of the servant Michel had expected, the unmistakable figure of Gabriel Sparhawk himself appeared, his broad shoulders silhouetted in the doorway as he welcomed the newcomers to his daughter's wedding. After a week of watching the man, following him like a shadow from his home to his counting house to his ships, Michel could look at Sparhawk now almost impassively, without the white-hot fury he'd felt at first. It was better that way, much better. He'd long ago learned that passion of any sort led to the kind of carelessness he could ill afford tonight.

Farther down the street he heard a woman's soft laugh and the footsteps of her companion on the brick sidewalk, and swiftly Michel eased deeper into the tall bushes that formed the hedge. He was in an empty, formal garden now, between a *panterre* of roses and an arbor of wisteria with a lady's teakwood bench. Beyond that the clipped lawns rolled clear to the very edge of the harbor itself. From inside the house came the laughter of the guests, mingled with the more distant sounds of hired musicians tuning their instruments. Somewhere upstairs a tall clock chimed the hour: eight bells.

*He should leave now, before it was too late. Only a fool would stay.*

But from here Michel could see through the open windows into the house and the parlor itself, and like the set of a play when the curtain first rises, the scene beckoned him to stay, to watch. On a laden supper table in the center of the room sat the wedding cake, raised high on a silver epergne festooned with white paper lace and chains, and on another table was arranged a display of wedding gifts, a king's ransom in silver, glittering in the candlelight. The score of candles that lit the empty room were the finest white

spermaceti, not tallow; that alone was an unimagin-
able extravagance.

*A coarse, vulgar display, a barbarous English show
of wealth without taste. They said Captain Sparhawk
had spared nothing to celebrate his favorite daughter's marriage. What price would he offer, then, when
the chit vanished without a trace?*

A flicker of white in the moonlight at the far end of
the house caught Michel's eye, a pale curtain blown
outward through an open window. But why only that
window, on a night as still as this one, unless the curtain was being pushed by someone within? Warily
Michel touched his belt with the pistols and knife, and
swore softly to himself, wishing the street were clear so
he could retreat through the hedge.

But to his surprise, a lady's leg came through the
window next, a long, slender leg in a silk stocking with
a green-fringed garter, followed by its mate as the
young woman swung herself over the window's sill
and dropped to the grass. Cynically Michel wondered
if it were her father or, more likely, her husband that
she'd escaped, and he glanced around the garden again
to see if he'd somehow overlooked her waiting lover.

The girl paused long enough to shake out her skirts,
her dark head bowed as she smoothed the cream-
colored sateen with both hands, then hurried across
the grass with a soft rustle of silk. As she came closer,
the moonlight caught her full in the face, and unconsciously Michel swore again.

She froze at the sound, one hand raised to the pearls
around her throat as her startled gaze swept the shadows until she found Michel.

Startled, but not afraid. "You've caught me, haven't you?" she asked wryly. "Fair and square. You must be one of my brothers' friends, for I don't believe I've met you, have I?"

"But I know you," he said softly, his voice deep and low, his accent barely discernible. It had been nearly twenty years, yet still he would have recognized her anywhere. "Miss Jerusa Sparhawk."

"True enough." She bobbed him a little curtsy. "Then you must be friends with Josh. He's the only one of my brothers I truly favor. As it should be, considering we're twins. But then I expect you knew that already."

Michel nodded in agreement. Oh, he knew a great many things about the Sparhawks, more than even she did herself.

"Miss Jerusa Sparhawk," she repeated, musing. "I'll wager you'll be the last to call me that. While you and all the others act as witnesses, in a quarter hour I'll become Mrs. Thomas Carberry."

Her smile was dazzling, enough to reduce a man to instant fealty. He'd heard much praise of her beauty, the perfection of her face, the flawlessness of her skin, the vivid contrast between her black hair and green eyes and red mouth, but none of that praise came close to capturing her charm, her radiance. Easy even for him to see why she was considered the reigning belle of the colony.

Not that any of it mattered.

She was still a Sparhawk.

Still his enemy.

"Is this really the great love match they say?" He didn't miss the irony that she'd mistaken him for a

guest, let alone a friend of her brother's, and that she
trusted him to the point of not even asking his name.

*Like a pigeon,* he thought with grim amusement, *a
pretty, plump pigeon that flew cooing into his hands*.

The girl tipped her head quizzically, the diamonds
in her earrings dancing little fragments of light across
her cheeks. "You dare to ask if I love my Tom?"

"Do you?" He was wasting time he didn't have, but
he wanted to know exactly how much suffering he'd
bring to her family this night.

"Do I love Tom? How could I not?" Her smile
outshone the moonlight as her words came out in a
tumbled, breathless rush. "He's amusing and kind
and, oh, so very handsome, and he dances more
gracefully than any other gentleman in Newport, and
he says clever things to make me laugh and pretty
things to make me love him even more. How could I
not love my darling Tom?"

"Doubtless it helped his suit that he's rich."

"Rich?" Her eyes were innocently blank. "Well, I
suppose his father is. So is mine, if you must put so
brass a face on it. But that's certainly not reason
enough to marry someone."

"Certainly not," agreed Michel dryly. She'd never
wanted for anything in her sweet, short life. How
could she guess the lengths she'd go to if she were cold
enough, hungry enough, desperate enough? "But if
you love him as you claim, then why have you run
from your own wedding?"

"Is that what you believed I was doing? Oh my!"
She wrinkled her elegant nose with amusement. "It's
Mama, you see. She says that because I'm the bride I
must stay in my bedchamber until the very minute that

I come down the stair with Father. If even one person lays eyes upon me before then, it's bad luck, and I'll turn straight into salt or some such.''

*Another time, another woman, and he might have laughed at the little shrug she gave her shoulders and the sigh that followed. Another time, another woman, and he might have let himself be charmed.*

She sighed dramatically. ''But I *would* want a rose from this garden—those bushes there, the pink ones—to put in my hair because Tom favors pink. Banished as I was, there was no one else but myself to fetch it, and so you found me here. Still, that's hardly running off. I've every intention of returning the same way I came, through the window into my father's office and up the back stairs.''

''Don't you fear that they'll miss you?''

''Not with the house full of guests that need tending, they won't.'' Restlessly she rubbed her thumb across the heavy pearl cuff around one wrist, and, to his surprise, Michel realized that much of her bravado was no more than ordinary nervousness. ''The ceremony proper won't begin until half past eight.''

No matter what she said, Michel knew time was fast slipping away. He'd dawdled here too long as it was. His mind raced ahead, changing his plans. Now that she'd seen him, he couldn't afford to let her go, but perhaps, in a way, this would be even better than what he'd originally intended. His fingers brushed against the little vial of chloroform in the pocket of his coat. Even *Maman* would appreciate the daring it would take to steal the bride from her own wedding.

The *Sparhawk* bride. *Mordieu*, it was almost too perfect.

"You're not superstitious, then?" he asked softly, easing the cork from the neck of the vial with his thumb. "You don't believe your mother's unhappy predictions will come true now that I've seen you?"

She turned her head, eyeing him with sidelong doubt. "You'll tell her?"

"Nay, what reason would I have to do that? You go pick your roses now, *ma chère,* and then back in the house before they come searching for you."

Hesitancy flickered through her eyes, and too late he realized he'd unthinkingly slipped into speaking French. But then her doubt vanished as quickly as it had appeared, replaced by the joyful smile he was coming to recognize. With a pang of regret that caught him by surprise, he knew it would be the last smile she'd ever grant him.

"Then thank you," she said simply. "I don't care which of my brothers is your friend, because now you're mine, as well."

She turned away toward the flowers before he could answer. Her cream-colored skirts rustled around her as she bent gracefully over the roses, and the sheer lawn cuffs of her gown fluttered back from her wrists in the breeze as she reached to pluck a single, pink rose.

So much grace, thought Michel as he drew the dampened handkerchief from his pocket, so much beauty to mask such poisoned blood. She struggled for only a moment as he pressed the cloth over her mouth and nose, then fell limp in his arms.

He glanced back at the house as he carried the unconscious girl into the shadow of the tall hedges. There he swiftly pulled off her jewelry, the pearl necklace and bracelet and ring, the diamonds from her ears, even the paste buckles from her shoes. Whatever else they called him, he wasn't a thief, and he had pride enough to leave her jewels behind. He yanked the pins from her hair and mussed the elaborate stiffened curls until they fell in an untidy tangle to her shoulders, shading her face. With his thumb he hurriedly smudged dirt across one of her cheeks and over her hands, trying hard not to think of how soft her skin was beneath his touch.

*She was a Sparhawk, not just a woman. Think of how she would revile him if she knew—when she learned—his father's name!*

He used his knife to cut away the bottom silk flounce of her gown, baring the plain linen of her underskirt, which he dragged through the dirt beneath the bushes. Finally he yanked off his own coat and buttoned it around her shoulders. As he'd hoped, the long coat covered what remained of her gown, and in the dark streets, with her grimy face and tousled hair, she'd pass for one more drunken strumpet from the docks, at least long enough for him to retrieve his horse from the stable.

Briefly he sat back on his heels and wiped his sleeve across his forehead as he glanced one last time at the candlelit house. The girl had been right. No alarms, no shouts of panic or pursuit came through the open windows, only the sounds of laughter and excited conversation. It took a moment longer for him to realize that the loud, rapid thumping was the beat of his own heart.

*One last task, that was all, and then he'd be done.*

Swiftly he retrieved the rose she'd picked from where it had fallen and laid it across the pile of her jewelry. He dug deep into the pocket of his waistcoat until he found the piece of paper. With fingers that shook only a little, he unfolded and stabbed the page onto the rose's thorns so that the smudged black *fleur de lis* would not be missed.

*The symbol of France, the mark of Christian Saint-Juste Deveaux.*

*A sign that Gabriel Sparhawk would read as easily as his own name.*

*And at last* Maman *would smile.*

\*   \*   \*   \*   \*

The Sparhawk Bride
*is now available wherever
Harlequin books are sold.*

## Miranda Jarrett

Before she turned her hand to writing historical
romance, Miranda Jarrett was an award-winning
designer and art director. Her first book, *Steal the Stars*,
was released by Harlequin Historicals in our 1992
March Madness New Writers Promotion and was
nominated for a Reviewer's Choice Award from
*Romantic Times*. Since then, she has been
concentrating her stories on the ongoing saga of a
seafaring family from Rhode Island, the Sparhawks,
and earned herself nominations for Best Up-and-
Coming Author and Best Historical Romance set in
North America from *Affaire de Coeur*.

If you enjoyed *Bayberry and Mistletoe*, be sure to
look for Miranda Jarrett's latest novel from
Harlequin Historicals,

*The Sparhawk Bride*

On sale now wherever Harlequin books are sold!

Turn the page for a preview of this passionate new
historical romance…

**Harlequin® Historical**

## WOMEN OF THE WEST

Don't miss these adventurous stories by
some of your favorite Western romance authors.

Coming from Harlequin Historical every month.

Don't miss any of our **Women of the West!**    WWEST-1

*"Whether you want him for business...or pleasure, for one month or for one night, we have the husband you've been looking for. When circumstances dictate the need for the appearance of a man in your life, call 1-800-HUSBAND for an uncomplicated, uncompromising solution. Call now.*
*Operators are standing by...."*

Pick up the phone—along with five desperate singles—and enter the Harrington Agency, where no one lacks a perfect mate. Only thing is, there's no guarantee this will stay a business arrangement....

For five fun-filled frolics with the mate of your dreams, catch all the 1-800-HUSBAND books:

Coming to you only from American Romance!

*Harlequin Romance* ®

# New from Harlequin Romance a very special six-book series by

MIDNIGHT SONS

# DEBBIE MACOMBER

The town of Hard Luck, Alaska, needs women!

The O'Halloran brothers, who run a bush-plane service called Midnight Sons, are heading a campaign to attract women to Hard Luck. *(Location: north of the Arctic Circle. Population: 150—mostly men!)*

"Debbie Macomber's *Midnight Sons* series is a delightful romantic saga. And each book is a powerful, engaging story in its own right. Unforgettable!"

—Linda Lael Miller

### TITLE IN THE MIDNIGHT SONS SERIES:

DMS-1

**FREE GIFT**
with purchase
see inside

Harlequin has a special gift for you this holiday season—absolutely FREE!

With the purchase of

# CHRISTMAS ROGUES

you can send in for a beautiful gold-tone necklace—absolutely FREE. The perfect complement for any outfit!

To receive your FREE necklace, simply send in your name, address and zip or postal code, along with ONE proof-of-purchase coupon from Harlequin's CHRISTMAS ROGUES, plus $1.25 U.S./$1.95 CAN. for postage and handling (check or money order—please do not send cash), payable to Christmas '95 Offer, to :

| In the U.S. | In Canada |
|---|---|
| 3010 Walden Ave. | P.O. Box 621 |
| P.O. Box 9056 | Fort Erie, Ontario |
| Buffalo, NY 14269-9056 | L2A 5X3 |

Please allow 4-6 weeks for delivery.

*Hurry!* Order your FREE necklace now; quantities are limited.
Offer good until February 29, 1996, or while quantities last.

# ONE PROOF-OF-PURCHASE

076-KCM

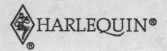

HARLEQUIN®

# HARLEQUIN SUPERROMANCE®

**WOMEN WHO DARE**
They take chances, make changes
and follow their hearts!

## *Christmas Star*
## by Roz Denny Fox
## Harlequin Superromance #672

Since her childhood, Starr Lederman has always wished on
what her mother called the Christmas star—the first star out
on those December nights just before Christmas. Now her
adopted daughter, SeLi, does the same thing.

But SeLi isn't wishing for toys or video games. She's
out for the serious stuff—a dad for herself. Which
means a husband for Starr. And SeLi's got a man all
picked out. Clay McLeod, rancher.

Clay's not looking for a wife, though. Especially not a woman
as independent and daring as Starr. A woman *he* believes is
having an affair with his brother. His married brother.

But at Christmastime, things have a way of sorting
themselves out....

Available in December, wherever
Harlequin books are sold.